D0190496

TAYLOR SMITH

# the night café

MIRA®

**MIRA**

ISBN-13: 978-0-7783-2522-2
ISBN-10:  0-7783-2522-9

THE NIGHT CAFÉ

www.MIRABooks.com

**Printed in U.S.A.**

This one goes out with love and thanks to The Plot Queen, Linda McFadden—ally, muse and coconspirator. Neither time nor distance can squelch a great friendship.

It's been a decade and a half (hard to believe) that I've been working with the wonderful people of MIRA Books, and I feel as lucky today as I did fifteen years ago when they offered to publish my first book. My deepest thanks to Miranda Stecyk, my editor, with whom it's a joy to work—and to hang out, on those happy occasions where we find ourselves in the same city.

My family, near and far, is unfailingly supportive. Love and thanks especially to my amazing husband, Richard, and our beautiful, brilliant and all-grown-up daughters (how is that possible?), Anna and Kate.

I am thinking of frankly accepting
my role as madman.
—Vincent van Gogh, in a letter to his brother,
Theo, March 24, 1889

Just because I am always bowed down under this difficulty of paying my landlord, I made up my mind to take it gaily. I swore at the said landlord, who after all isn't a bad fellow, and told him that to revenge myself for paying him so much money for nothing, I would paint the whole of his rotten shanty so as to repay myself.

—Vincent van Gogh
Letter to his brother Theo
Arles, 8 September, 1888

# Prologue

*Los Angeles*
*January 1*

"*People remember pain. They've done studies. You want to make a point with a person and make it stick, hurt 'em. Works every time.*"

Afterward, before she stopped talking altogether, volunteer museum guide Dorrie Schaeffer kept repeating over and over what one of the intruders had said. She was in shock, of course, what the shrinks call posttraumatic stress disorder. But there was disbelief in her quavering voice, too—incredulity at the monstrous callousness of the man.

It wasn't that Dorrie was naive about the potential for human cruelty. You don't get through seventy-six years without witnessing some real wickedness. But this brutality at the Arlen Hunter Museum came out of nowhere.

The sun had gone down after a showery New Year's Day, and Santa Monica Boulevard twinkled under holiday lights still strung on buildings and over the roadway. There'd been long, snaking queues outside the museum since opening, patrons anxious for one last chance to see the Madness & the Masterpiece exhibit, the high point of the Arlen Hunter's fall season.

When the trouble started, Dorrie should have been far away. The crowds had gone home, the doors were locked. For the next twelve hours, a skeleton security staff would have the treasure to themselves, enjoying the collected masterpieces for a few hours more before the group was split up and the borrowed art returned to its owners.

Dorrie was in the underground parking lot, hurrying to get home to *Wuthering Heights* on Masterpiece Theatre. But as she was unlocking her car door, she remembered the van Gogh print she'd bought for a niece who was coming by the next day. Her brother's daughter never failed to remember her birthday or to include her in family holiday celebrations. Knowing how much Renata loved van Gogh, Dorrie had bought her a beautiful lithographic reproduction of *The Night Café*, signature piece of the Madness & the Masterpiece show. Except, like a nitwit, she'd left it in her locker.

Bemoaning her absentmindedness, she reentered the building, backtracking toward the staff room located off the south gallery. She was in the hall just outside that gallery when she heard a shout. She froze at the sight of two men near the end of the gallery, their backs to her. Bert Fernandez, an old night guard, was on his knees facing her, although the intruders had his full attention. A brutal kick from one of them suddenly sent him sprawling, blood spurting from his mouth.

Luck found Dorrie standing next to an unlocked custodian's cupboard and fear drove her inside. Her entire body shaking, she watched through a crack between the frame and the door as a third man, black-hooded like the others, rounded the corner from the west hall, shoving another security guard ahead of him.

There was no doubt this last man was in charge. He looked young to Dorrie, his body lithe, yet he seemed to harbor a sense of his own intellectual superiority and to feel a mission to instruct his colleagues on the efficacy of torment to ensure compliance. There was no other explanation for the violence. From what Dorrie could see, neither security guard offered any real resistance.

"People remember pain," the leader said. "A bullet to the brain shuts 'em up, of course, but what if you need a pass code or something later? Bloody corpse on the floor's not gonna do you much good."

And so they used fists that flashed with metallic gleam—brass knuckles. Dorrie watched, stunned and terrified by the casual brutality. The younger guard, just a boy, really, tried to protest, but the leader swung a short wooden bat and the lad's knee shattered like a teacup. Dorrie clamped her hands over her mouth as he crumpled, screaming, to the floor. Bert tried to drag himself over to help him and was rewarded with an equally vicious clout with the stick.

The leader bent down next to Bert, murmuring in a voice too quiet for Dorrie to hear. The old guard raised a shaking hand and pointed around the corner.

"Wait here," the leader told one of the others. "If they move, shoot them." He cocked a thumb at the other intruder and the two disappeared into the east wing.

Dorrie's body shook like a thing possessed. The young security guards lay on the marble-tiled floor, crying and writhing with pain, his arms wrapped around his battered leg, while old Bert, face bloodied and swollen, glared at the thug standing guard over them.

Time seemed to stand still. Later, Dorrie couldn't say how long it took until the other two thieves returned carrying the one item they had obviously come for—the van Gogh.

As the guidebook for Madness & the Masterpiece reminded visitors, Plato had called creativity "divine madness, a gift from the gods." Psychobabble in the accompanying text discussed how great angst fed the vision needed to produce great art.

That "gift from the gods" was a mixed blessing, Dorrie had told her "goslings," the chattering patrons who pattered along behind on her guided tours of the galleries. The celebrated artists represented in the show—Jackson Pollock, William Blake, Edvard Munch, Georgia O'Keeffe and a dozen or so others—had all suffered from severe, debilitating depression or other psychological disabilities. And Vincent van Gogh, of course. No exhibit linking art, anguish and madness could possible ignore the gaunt, ear-slashed Dutchman. Most of these artists, Dorrie told the goslings, had been institutionalized at some point in their lives. Several, like Vincent, had committed suicide.

It was Vincent's *The Night Café* that was featured on posters and banners promoting the exhibit. The painting showed a nighttime scene in a harshly lit bar peopled by bereft-looking patrons who seemed to have nowhere else to go. Vincent had lived over the café during his time in the south of France, when his psyche finally began to unravel. Not long after creating this piece, he sliced off a piece of his ear and presented it to a prostitute.

The thieves' leader wrapped the painting in a sheet now, knotting the corners. Then he turned to his men.

"Okay, we're done here now. Finish them."

Dorrie watched, horrified, as one of the men fired into the head of the old security guard. The explosion echoed through the marble halls and Bert crumpled in a pool of blood. The other intruder hesitated long enough for the boy to start scrabbling away, dragging his bloody leg across the floor. The leader snapped a command. Then, eyes flashing contempt, he grabbed the gun, strode over to the boy and took him out with a quick tap of the trigger.

Tears coursing down her cheeks, Dorrie watched the intruders stroll out toward the lobby. A moment later she heard the opening and closing of the stairwell door leading down to the parking lot.

Then there was only silence.

*"People remember pain."*

Afterward, the police kept pressing Dorrie to remember more. Some tiny detail, they said, could be the key to bringing the security guards' killer to justice. Try, they insisted. But Dorrie didn't want to remember. She wanted to forget it, all of it.

Eventually she stopped answering their questions. Clammed up when the LAPD Robbery/Homicide detective in charge of the investigation pressed her for more details. Refused to speak to the gray-suited agents from the FBI's art theft division who showed up at her door. Even snapped at the kindhearted elderly neighbor who stopped by her home to ask how she was doing.

God, how Dorrie wanted them all to just go away. She became detached and unapproachable. Her sister in Minneapolis said she stopped returning phone calls. Her L.A.-based niece left reluctantly on a business trip, determined to call in professional help if her aunt didn't seem any better by the time she got back.

Except by then it was too late.

The manager at the local Vons supermarket down the road from the seniors complex where Dorrie lived said she started phoning in her meager food orders. The delivery boy said she left her payment in an envelope under the doormat and made him leave the bags on the threshold. The only time she scuttled outside was to snatch the mail when it started overflowing her curbside box. A neighbor who saw her out there one day reported that Dorrie's tidy brown helmet of curls had grown lank, frizzled and gray at the roots. Her normally pin-neat clothes hung rumpled and loose on a frame that seemed to have turned spindly and frail overnight.

One day the postal carrier found bills and junk mail spilling out of her box. When he knocked on her front door, he hoped she'd simply forgotten to arrange a vacation hold, but the dread in his gut told a different story. When no one answered, instinct made him call the police.

It was the cops' experienced noses that picked up the faint, sweet odor seeping from the cracks around the barred doors and windows. Hearts heavy, dreading what they knew they were going to find, they jimmied the locks, ripped the chain bolt from the wall and broke in.

Dorrie Schaeffer had been dead about a week. Sleeping pills, the medical examiner's report said. She'd swallowed enough to euthanize a horse.

*People remember pain…*

Dorrie Schaeffer had remembered. And like Vincent, when the agony became too much to bear, she had put an end to her suffering.

# One

*Hannah Nicks, loser. Black sheep. She whose bizarre line of work is not really suitable dinner-table conversation.*

The accusations ran on a loop through Hannah's brain during these family get-togethers. How could *anyone* not feel inadequate faced with the perfection that was her sister Nora?

Sliding onto a tall stool, Hannah tucked her unruly dark hair behind her ears and helped herself to a homemade scone from the linen-lined basket on the kitchen island.

The island was a granite oasis in a sea of domestic perfection. Nora's home in the upscale seafront community of Corona del Mar was right out of *Architectural*

*Digest.* Her kitchen was a Tuscan-inspired designer's vision of terra-cotta and honey tones, run through with a grapevine motif. Outside the mullioned French doors that covered the entire west side of the house, the view was of tented gazebo, patio and pool, the blue-gray Pacific Ocean beyond stretching to the horizon.

Selecting a jar from a carousel in front of her, Hannah spread preserves on the scone. She took a bite, then leaned back and sighed over the warm, flaky pastry. "Oh, Lord, these are bliss."

Nora, standing on the other side of the island, looked over and smiled. "Those are the last of the raspberries the kids and I picked at the cottage last summer." Her husband's family had a three-thousand-square-foot post-and-beam house in Ogunquit, Maine, where the California Quinns spent part of each summer. It was a "cottage" like the Hope Diamond was a bauble.

Hannah's travel destinations tended to be war zones, where accommodations were spartan, at best. Her own home, a condominium in the Silver Lake neighborhood of Los Angeles, was a replacement for the only house she'd ever owned—well, not owned, exactly, given the size of the mortgage, but it had been a real house, an old Craftsman bungalow in Los Feliz. Her ex had signed the property over to her in the divorce but sadly, before she got around to renovating the place, it had been blown up by Russian gangsters intent on her demise.

In addition to a condo and a broken marriage, Hannah was the proud possessor of a son she saw only intermittently and a bank balance that constantly hovered near the red zone. She, needless to say, was not the daughter their mom bragged about to the other white-haired ladies in her Tuesday-Thursday Aquasize classes. Nora, oldest child of immigrant parents, was the American Dream personified. For Hannah, a major achievement would be getting through a week without being shot at, maimed or killed.

She spooned another dollop of raspberry jam onto the scone. "Can I just say for the record that these are going to be the death of me?" She popped it into her mouth. "Want me to slather one for you?" she mumbled.

"No, I'm good. Thanks so much for that view, though."

Hannah opened wide. "Bwah-ha-ha."

Nora rolled her eyes. "Very mature."

Hannah grinned. She couldn't help it. Put her in a room with Nora and she was ten all over again.

On first encounter, Nora was often mistaken for Hannah's better-groomed twin. No one ever guessed that dark-eyed, glossy-haired Nora was a dozen years older than the misfit baby of the Demetrious clan. Of course, in affluent Orange County, the trickery of Botox and the surgeon's knife kept a lot of women looking preternaturally young. In Nora's case, though, the only magician at work was Mother Nature herself. At forty-two, she was an elegant beauty, grace personified. She knew the names of china patterns, the art of Japanese flower arranging and how to put together a gourmet dinner for twenty on a few hours' notice.

Hannah knew aliases and suspected hideouts for a dozen of the world's worst terrorists, the art of covert message drops, and how to dismantle and reassemble an M-16 assault rifle in sixty seconds flat. Nora invariably put others at ease. Hannah, who leapt into high alert at the snick of every opening door and scrutinized every stranger for signs of lethal intent, didn't even know how to put *herself* at ease.

As if grace, brains and beauty weren't enough, there was also Nora's gorgeous, castlelike home overlooking the Pacific Ocean, her doting, successful husband, Neal, and their two picture-perfect kids, Nolan and Natalie. (Nora, Neal, Nolan, Natalie—they were big on alliteration, the Quinns. Even the dogs, golden retrievers with sleek Lady Clairol coats, were called Nugget and Noodle.) Nora's entire, flawless life was a page out of frigging *Martha Stewart Living*.

Hannah, at thirty, was on her own but already on her second career, one she'd taken up after eight years as an L.A. cop. Switching from police work to the world of private security contractors was supposed to have been a lucrative career move, one she'd hoped would put her in a better financial position to regain custody of her son from her wealthy ex and his current squeeze. It hadn't worked out that way.

She finished her scone, then glanced down and froze. On her wrist, a red drop glistened under the glow of the pendant lights hanging over the island. Hannah could almost feel the pain of the gash, even though her rational mind said it was just a dollop of raspberry. Her memory flashed on gunfire in a dark desert night. On a young man's bleeding head cradled in her lap. On his life slipping away before her eyes.

"Here, use this." Nora reached across the island.

Startled by the sudden movement, Hannah shoved back, the legs of her bar stool screeching on the travertine floor.

"Hannah?" Nora's brow creased with the worried look she often took on when her baby sister was around. She indicated the blue gingham napkin in her hand. "It's okay. I was just trying to help."

Hannah gave her best Alfred E. Neuman dopey grin. Bringing her wrist to her lips, she licked away the sweet drop of jam, but when Nora sighed, she relented and took the napkin, dutifully blotting her wrist dry. She might have resented the fact that Nora still treated her like the awkward child she used to be, except she knew her sister couldn't help feeling the heavy responsibility of serving as maternal figure in Hannah's life.

They had an actual mother, mind you. Ida Demetrious—"Nana" to her three grandchildren—was snapping green beans over at Nora's antique pine trestle table this very minute. Nevertheless, Nora had been overheard on more than one occasion to say she'd "raised Hannah." Not altogether accurate. Not something you'd think she'd want to brag about, either, all things considered.

It was true that at seventeen, Hannah had been sent

from Chicago to live with the Quinns in Orange County. It was about the time that their father, Takis Demetrious, began showing signs of the Alzheimer's that would eventually strip him of his mind, his great physical strength and finally his life. Poor Nana. A sick husband and a rebellious teenage daughter were a tough hand to be dealt, especially when she was also trying to keep their import company afloat in those early days when Takis's intermittent confusion, intransigence and paranoia were threatening to run the family's once-thriving company into the ground. Something had to give and, in the end, that something was Hannah.

Nora's kids had been four and seven at the time. Hannah could give Nora a hand, the thinking went, and maybe if she escaped Takis's unpredictable rages, she might be less inclined to act out. But she arrived at Newport Beach High School carrying a lumber-sized chip on her shoulder. That, and shyness that came across as aloofness, pretty much guaranteed her the caption of "Most Inscrutable" in her senior yearbook photo. She hadn't set out to be antisocial, but even the Porsches and BMWs in the student parking lot seemed to be sneering at the hopelessly uncool Midwestern import with the wild hair and the uneasy dark eyes. She stayed with Neal and Nora for two years before moving into a dorm at UCLA. By February of her freshman year, she was pregnant. She dropped out of college and went to work as an L.A. Sheriff's Department dispatcher so that her hastily married hubby could finish law school.

Pathetic—which only made Hannah wonder why Nora would take the rap for raising her.

"Yee-haw!"

Home on spring break from Stanford, Nolan galloped into the sprawling kitchen, his surfboard-scaled flip-flops slapping the floor. Close behind came ten-year-old Gabe, grinning as he aped his big cousin's galumphing stride.

"Last one in is a horse's…um—" Nolan paused, glancing at his mom "—patootie!"

Hannah raised a hand, traffic-cop style. "Hold it! Gabriel Nicks, don't even think of going out there before I get sunscreen on you."

The boys' bodies were winter-pale but spring in Southern California meant the beginning of pool season, and this particular Sunday had turned out to be a scorcher. The thermometer on the blue-and-white striped cabana outside hovered in the mid-eighties. Neal was out there in shorts and T-shirt, stretched on one of the plush chaise longues, working the Sunday cross-word, while Natalie was at the beach with a friend. With the pool heated to a balmy eighty-eight degrees, even the adults might venture in, if only for a toe-dabble.

Gabe moaned. "Ah, Mom, it's only April. I'm not gonna burn. Besides, I'm tough like you. I can handle anything."

Hannah couldn't miss the exchange of another of

those "what are we going to do about Hannah?" looks between Nora and their mother. Hers wasn't the sort of family where fearlessness in dark alleys was considered a desirable trait.

"Ultraviolet rays don't read calendars," she said, restraining her wriggling son with one hand while she snagged the sunscreen off the kitchen counter with her other.

"Yeah, that's a fact, bro," Nolan said, turning back.

Gabe immediately stopped squirming. His mother might be a worrywart, but if Nolan, bless his heart, said something was so, then it was gospel.

"You slather up, too," Nora said over her shoulder.

The two boys exchanged eye-rolling grins, but Nolan took the plastic squeeze bottle from Hannah and went to work on himself.

At the granite island, Nora went back to spreading phyllo dough for the baklava she was preparing for dessert. Sunday dinners were a big deal at the Quinns'. Today, they would be eight—Nora and her gang; Hannah and Gabe; Nana Demetrious, who'd moved out to Orange County after Takis died; plus Nora's former college roommate. That wasn't many. Nora often fed what seemed like half the lonely hearts in Southern California, including single guys invited for the express purpose of meeting her unattached sister—and didn't Hannah just love being set up like that without her knowledge? Would there ever come a day when she would no longer be the official family fix-it project?

*Prague, the Czech Republic*

The straight razor gleamed in the morning sun as it passed it back and forth, back and forth over the brown leather strop hooked to a towel ring embedded in one of the blue-and-white ceramic wall tiles. Former Detective Superintendent William Teagarden of Scotland Yard always fell into a reverie as he went about his morning toilette. What he liked about the straight razor was that its handling couldn't be rushed. The slow rhythm of the archaic shaving routine—blade on strop, brush in bowl, steel on whiskers—forced him to slow his pace, order his mind and *think*.

He was deep in thought now. Setting the razor on the lip of the white porcelain hotel room sink, he took up the soap bowl and swirled his shaving brush round and round, each circuit of the bristles whispering the same refrain: *Where, where, where was the bloody van Gogh?*

The straight razor and boar bristle brush were old-fashioned things, but they were appropriate accessories for a man with such tall military bearing and a handlebar mustache straight out of the days of Empire. Teagarden had spent thirty years as an officer of London's Metropolitan Police, the last six and a half as head of the Yard's Arts and Antiquities Unit. He'd been raised in Manchester, the only child of a decent but rough-about-the-edges mill worker father and a beautiful, cultured mother whose family had withdrawn after she married down. She had been stoic about her reduced circumstances, living on a drab council estate, never an extra shilling for travel or pretty things, but she had engendered in her son a love of music and art, taking him to every free gallery, concert and museum she could, exposing him to library books that described the wonders of the world. Little surprise, then, that given the opportunity to help recover some of the multimillions of pounds' worth of art stolen annually, Teagarden had jumped at the chance.

As he soaped his cheeks, chin and neck, his memory skimmed the lists of stolen art documented in the British Art Loss Register and the New York–based IFAR, the International Foundation for Art Research. The number of masters alone sickened him—nearly three hundred Picassos, a couple of hundred Miros and Chagalls. Several Rembrandts. Manet, Munch, Vermeer, da Vinci, Goya—the list went on and on. And of course, there was the van Gogh.

Heading up the Arts Unit had not only capped his career at the Met, it had been his crowning achievement and the job of his dreams. He could happily have labored at it until his dying day, had he not been forced into retirement by bureaucrats. "Medically unfit for duty" after his second heart attack, they said, but that was bunk. The commander to whom he reported had been looking for a pretext to get rid of him. A diminutive micromanager with delusions of brilliance, the commander had transferred in from borough operations with a chip on his shoulder and lofty ambitions, and

God help anyone he perceived as a threat to his aspirations. It had been annoying enough that Teagarden was impervious to his bullying management style, but the last straw had been a splashy *Daily Mirror* spread on the work of the Arts Unit, complete with of full color photos of Teagarden and some of the works he'd recovered—da Vinci's priceless *Virgin of the Rocks*, a Brancusi sculpture, one of Degas's ballerinas. "Unseemly," the commander had sniffed. Of course, he never objected to any press piece that included a quote from *him* or a picture of his ugly mug, even in a rag like the *Mirror*.

Teagarden took up the razor and set to work on his face. He hadn't given a damn about the press, but every time one of those puff pieces appeared, hits on the unit's Web site had skyrocketed, as did tips from the public. No matter. Not long after the *Mirror* piece, the commander had ordered Teagarden to submit to a medical, then seized on the results to quote departmental policy at him and hustle him out the door. Within three months, the unit was downsized and swallowed whole by another section—a "redeployment of resources to higher priority tasks."

It was a travesty, sidelining a specialist at the peak of his operational effectiveness, but Teagarden's dismay had been short-lived. There were plenty of deep-pocketed private patrons who would pay extremely well, thank you very much, for the same investigative work that had netted him nothing more than a civil servant's meager pension and a flipping *here's your hat, what's your hurry* shove out the door from the Met. He'd solved hard-to-crack cases during his tenure there and that reputation had served him in good stead, oiling hinges and opening doors at Interpol, the FBI and other international police agencies. They even referred clients to him when their own investigative resources were constrained. That was how Yale University, owners of *The Night Café*, had made contact. Teagarden had been on the trail of the painting since forty-eight hours after its New Year's Day theft from the Arlen Hunter Museum.

These thefts were almost never carried out for the love of art. Faced with the possibility of discovery or arrest, thieves were more likely to destroy a painting than let it survive as evidence. With every day that passed, the risk grew exponentially that the fragile old canvas would be gravely damaged or lost forever.

The police in Los Angeles had been rather less welcoming, focused as they were on the murders that had accompanied the burglary. Teagarden, too, was appalled at the human tragedy, but as he tried to point out to the homicide detectives, the only way to find the killers was to learn who might have sought one masterpiece alone among the dozens that had been on view during the Madness & the Masterpiece exhibit.

Previous cases had taught him that the culprits often turned out to be petty thieves. *Occasio facit furem*—opportunity makes the thief, like a vagabond stealing laundry off a garden line. That was why so much stolen art was never recovered. As soon as the clothesliners felt the law breathing down their necks, they got rid of it. One thief's mother, hoping to keep her precious boy out of prison, had actually taken her kitchen shears to dozens of the priceless masterworks her little bastard had nicked, and chucked several others into a nearby canal. It turned his stomach to remember the torn, water-damaged, charred and vermin-gnawed master-works he'd seen.

The business of art theft had changed, however. In the past, a thief might hope to turn a quick profit through a ransom demand, but that was fraught with risk of capture. Finding a buyer these days was no easy matter, either. Recognizable works were impossible to sell to reputable collectors or dealers, even for pennies on the pound. In the old days, even if a buyer suspected a shaky provenance, he need only claim ignorance and wait out the clock. Once the legal statute of limitations had run out—five, seven, ten years, depending on the jurisdiction—thief and buyer alike were home free, and a lucrative payday might be worth the wait.

But these days, there was no pleading ignorance—not in an Internet age when the alarm was sounded far and wide for art gone walkabout. Many nations had also imposed stark penalties on trafficking in stolen work, and the publicity surrounding colonial plunder-ing of antiquities and theft from Holocaust victims put intense pressure on buyers to err on the side of caution. When a California Getty Museum director went on trial in Italy for purchasing stolen antiquities, her ordeal did more than anything else to put the fear of the gods into buyers around the world.

So, Teagarden mused, if not for resale to some reclusive billionaire aficionado or corrupt broker, who else would be in the market for a sixty-million-dollar van Gogh? There was only one other likely scenario— someone wanted to use it as collateral for another business transaction. The drug trade, gunrunning, human smuggling and fraud were all interrelated, and a painting like *The Night Café*, more compact than a comparable amount of cash, could serve as useful security until funds could actually change hands on a shipment. The masterpiece as currency.

He scrutinized his face in the mirror, looking for spots he might have missed, but his mind was on the security tapes he'd studied at the Arlen Hunter. There was nothing opportunistic about that burglary. It had taken just under twelve minutes from start to finish. A review of the museum's security setup had left no doubt in his mind that the theft had been carefully planned, possibly with inside help.

How could a world-class gallery have made so many blunders with hundreds of millions in borrowed art at risk? The curator of the exhibit had assured the paintings' owners that the security system was top-notch. Closed-circuit cameras. Multiple vibration sensors behind each painting. Saturation motion detection. Environmental sensors to pick up minute temperature changes, such as those that might accompany fire, smoke or the touch of a human hand.

The ugly truth was that some of the systems weren't yet fully functional on the night of the theft. Everything was supposed to have been in place before Madness & the Masterpiece opened, but what Teagarden learned was that the Arlen Hunter's budget for security was so bled dry by other demands that equipment orders constantly lagged. Delivery delays had meant that some crucial pieces of the system hadn't yet arrived. Overhead bubble covers should have concealed brand-new, 360-degree observation lenses, but the digital cameras and recording equipment were still on a dock in the port of Long Beach the night of the theft. There was an older existing closed-circuit camera system in use, connected via the Internet to the Los Angeles Sheriff's Department robbery unit, but that link proved to be a major vulnerability. The thieves had hacked the feed weeks earlier, downloading and recording the video. While the theft was going on, both the internal recording equipment and the external feed were being fed recycled footage. When it was analyzed later, it would be obvious that three of the four security guards seen patrolling on the tape were nowhere near the place on January first. Equally frustrating was that the thieves had managed to erase at least two other sections of the surveillance video, periods that would no doubt have shown them inside the museum, casing the security arrangements.

What a cock-up, Teagarden thought disgustedly, rinsing the razor under hot water and patting his face dry. He took up a small comb and smoothed down his dark mustache, then passed the comb over his thinning steel-gray hair. His eyes, coal-black under heavy eyebrows, flashed annoyance and energy; the former for the botched security that had allowed the painting to be taken, the latter for the thrill of the hunt.

He had little doubt that the theft was a professional operation carried out for strategic purposes that had little to do with art and everything to do with an illegal transaction that required collateral of the magnitude of a stolen van Gogh. There were only so many people involved in deals of this sort, and an even smaller number of subcontractors to whom they could turn to nail down the collateral. Teagarden, in fact, deemed only two or three people capable of the Arlen Hunter job.

Of those, one could be eliminated at once, since he was currently residing in Buckinghamshire, a guest of Her Majesty's Woodhill Prison, thanks to Teagarden's own efforts. Another was reported to be in Thailand, but when Teagarden tracked him down there, he learned he'd been knifed in a brothel two weeks before the heist in Los Angeles. Teagarden had visited the man in Phuket, where he was still recuperating. One look at his haggard appearance and the colostomy bag hanging from his belt convinced Teagarden that this fellow's thieving days were probably over.

It was on his way back to Bangkok airport that Teagarden had decided on a side trip to Prague to look in on another old nemesis.

Teagarden and Shawn Britten eyed each other over a round, zinc-topped café table as they waited for the espressos they'd ordered to be delivered. Britten's black hair was buzzed short as it had been in his time in the Royal Marines, but the look blended well among the close-cropped heads in the sidewalk cafés of Prague's Old Town. His three-day stubble was likewise par for the course in a coffee bar frequented by young Western tourists and the edgy shop and gallery crowd.

Britten was in his mid-thirties. He'd seen action in the first Gulf War, and that was where he'd developed his taste for art. Beautiful artifacts often fell into one's lap in the confusion of war and a smart man learned quickly what was valuable and what was dreck. There was little profit in fencing the latter, but for Britten, the arts became more than a means to earn some ready cash over and above his military stipend. It was, by now, something of a passion.

In addition to his on-the-job training in Middle Eastern artifacts, he soon became a self-taught expert on the Impressionist and Art Nouveau periods. After being demobbed from the Royal Marines, he'd gone independent, working his way up the food chain from estate silver robberies to consignment thefts of high-end art and jewelry. One day, Teagarden suspected, when

Britten had built his personal fortune, he might become a collector in his own right—*if* he lived that long. The kinds of clients who employed contractors with his skills tended to be a difficult lot.

In the meantime, he was one of a very small group of operatives to whom they could turn when rare and valuable objects needed liberating. Jobs like this took finesse. Hire a Philistine and your objet d'art could end up irreparably damaged or destroyed. Then where would you be? Neither history nor the gods smiled on those who despoiled priceless works of art. For that, at least, Teagarden appreciated the man's professionalism.

The two had crossed paths numerous times, but Britten was both clever and conservative in his style of operation, outwardly maintaining the fiction of working as a freelance appraiser and restorer of minor works. Although suspected of several heists, he had been able to dodge prosecution so far. That said, it was a couple of years since he'd dared set foot back in the United Kingdom. With Teagarden, at least, he no longer bothered with much pretense about the real craft that financed his relatively comfortable lifestyle.

A waiter deposited two demitasses on the table. "Can I get you something else, gentlemen?"

His English was accented but impeccable, Teagarden noted. Like most young Czechs, he would have no memory of his country's dreary days of membership in the old Soviet bloc. English was the language of commerce in the republic now, and the place was already flooded with young backpackers from western Europe, Australia and America. Group excursions were beginning to show up, too, more timid travelers who preferred to follow backward-walking guides holding neon flags aloft.

"I'd take one of those croissants I spotted in the case, mate, thanks much," Britten said, adding to Teagarden, "long as you're picking up the tab."

"Nothing for me," Teagarden told the waiter.

"So," Britten said, leaning back in his chair, "still working freelance, are you, Detective Superintendent?"

Teagarden nodded. He took a tentative sip of the steaming coffee, winced and set the demitasse down to cool.

"What can I do for you?" Britten asked.

"I'm looking for a missing van Gogh," Teagarden told him. "Naturally, I thought of you."

"I'm flattered, mate, but I prefer not to mess with the Yanks."

"So you know which van Gogh I'm talking about?"

"Oh, it sounds like your kind of case, Superintendent. Don't know what those sods were thinking, mind. They've got The Terminator for guv'nor over there in California. Old Arnold'll stick a needle in your arm soon as look at you."

"So you know about the murders at the Arlen Hunter, too."

"I heard something about it, yeah." Britten glanced up

at the waiter, who'd returned with his croissant. "Cheers."

"What did you hear?" Teagarden pressed.

Britten watched the waiter walk away, then shrugged as he bit into the pastry. "Heard about a security equipment fiasco—some of the equipment not installed, video feeds compromised. Bloody cock-up."

"That information about the video, that wasn't reported in the press. So how do you know about it?"

Britten shrugged. "Just because it's not my work doesn't mean I don't take a professional interest. Really makes you think, you know?"

"How so?"

"Well, it's harder to nick a shirt worth ten quid from Marks & Spencer than a painting worth millions. I mean, even Marks & Sparks have got their merchandise sensors, their plainclothes floorwalkers, their CCTV cameras. When it comes to shoplifting, they mean business—pardon the pun. But your average museum? Pitiful. Minimum wage rent-a-dicks, elderly docents. Scarcely a bit of high-tech equipment to be found."

Teagarden nodded. "That's true. But it's the high-profile exhibits that generate ticket sales, so that's where most of the money goes." Even world-class establishments like the Metropolitan Museum of Art or the Louvre were more vulnerable than they liked to admit.

"That's what I'm saying. Security's always the poor cousin to your revenue-generating bling." Britten shook his head ruefully, like he wasn't one of those very thieves who took advantage of those security weaknesses. "Mind you, doing the job on New Year's Day, that wasn't too daft. Always a good chance half the staff will have come down with cheap champagne flu. And them that are left—well, they're tired, aren't they? It's closing time and the last day of the exhibit, too, so everybody's guard is down. Prime time to act. You put a team together, get in and out fast, and Bob's yer uncle."

Teagarden raised a brow. "But you say it wasn't you."

"Give me some credit, mate. Just because Her Majesty trained me in the deadly arts doesn't mean I'm going to use them against civilians."

"So who do you reckon it was? One professional to another," Teagarden added.

"Oh, well, I don't like to rat out a colleague, even if he is the competition."

"Hardly a colleague, I would think. As you say, it was a very messily executed job—literally, given the body count. Not very flattering professional company to be keeping."

"That's very true. Gives everyone a bad name."

"On the other hand, who knows? Maybe that's what passes for professionalism these days."

"'Scuse me?"

"More efficient, I suppose. Eliminate all the witnesses."

"Nothing efficient about pulling down that much heat," Britten sniffed. "Only a rank amateur or a psycho uses that much brute force when he doesn't have to. And he didn't have to, did he, given that the museum practically sent out engraved invitations *asking* to be taken down, the way they mucked up security."

"Yeah, but this ringleader, whoever he was, showed some restraint, didn't he? After all, he only took the one painting."

"Self-restraint!" Britten snorted. "That wasn't *his* idea. That was a direct order from the client—take *The Night Café* and nothing more. You don't argue with orders like that, not when they come from that client."

"So you do know who did the job—and who gave the orders. Did the client come to you?"

Britten shrugged. "Might have."

"And? You couldn't handle it?"

"Couldn't handle it? Not bloody likely. A trained monkey could have done that job."

"Yet you turned it down."

Britten drummed his fingers on the table.

"Why?" Teagarden pressed.

"Look, mate, you and I have had our differences in the past, yeah? But we've got two things in common." Britten held up the first two fingers of his left hand, then pulled them down one after the other. "A, we both love beautiful paintings, and B, we've both done honorable service for Her Majesty's Government. Here's the deal—nicking that painting had precisely nothing to do with the client's love of art. And I spent the Gulf War dodging bullets from guns this bloke sold to Saddam

Hussein. So, thanks all the same, no, I did not care to take the man up on his offer."

"So who was the client? And who told him 'yes' after you said 'no'?"

Britten exhaled sharply. Then, signaling to the waiter for another espresso, he settled in resignedly for a long chat.

Teagarden, to be sociable, did the same. It would appear, he thought, that there was honor amongst thieves after all.

# *Two*

"Gabe, no more snacking. You'll spoil your dinner."

Hannah snatched the last of the nachos away from the poised hand of her son and carried them from the patio into the house. The western sun, low over the ocean, was making rainbows on the walls of Nora's kitchen. For the past couple of hours, the boys—one compact, the other tall and rangy—had climbed out of the water every twenty minutes or so, water streaming off their bodies. Splattering over to the patio table, they'd practically inhaled the fruits and crackers, cheeses and nachos that Nora had set out for them to snack on while Sunday's beef dinner roasted in the oven.

By now everyone was ravenous. The table was set, the salad made, the oven turned off and the veggies ready for steaming, but Rebecca Powell, Nora's college roommate, was late.

Hannah scraped the nachos into the garbage disposal, then rinsed the platter and slotted it into the dishwasher. Nora was at the long trestle table in the kitchen, folding starched linen napkins into swan shapes. Their mother, just down from napping upstairs, was putzing around the room, looking for something to clean or polish. Hannah watched her mother's slightly frenzied hunt. It was pathological. The woman would probably end up ironing the sheets on her own deathbed.

"Ma, come and sit down."

Instead, Nana picked up a dish towel and polished the taps and faucet at the sink until they gleamed.

Hannah sighed and turned back to her sister. "Could Rebecca have forgotten the invitation?"

Nora shook her head. "I was just talking to her last night. She won't have forgotten. She's probably stuck in traffic."

"She still living in Malibu?"

"No. The gallery's still there, but she moved into an apartment in Westwood."

"I thought she was getting the house in the divorce."

"Bill reneged. He got himself some shark of a lawyer and the lines suddenly shifted. I'm not sure exactly how he managed it, but poor Becs is fighting for her life here."

"You think the shark dug up something on her? Like, maybe she had an affair, too?"

Nora's shoulders lifted in a sad shrug. "I really don't

know. Becs hasn't volunteered and I don't like to ask. She's pretty wrung out these days."

"It's a blessing she and her husband didn't have children," Hannah's mother said. She'd moved on to wiping the brown speckled counter, even though it was already sparkling. If Rebecca didn't show up soon, she was going to wear a groove in the granite. Hannah could sympathize. She'd inherited her mother's restlessness, although in her case, it rarely manifested itself in an urge to clean.

"I suppose," Nora said.

Nana's head gave a sad shake. "Divorce is so hard on children."

Hannah's gaze dropped to her hands and she tried to ignore the stab in her solar plexus. Her mother wasn't trying to make her feel crummy about her own messy divorce and lost custody struggle, she knew, but the comment stung just the same.

"Anyway," Nora added, "I know she hasn't forgotten about today because she asked last night if you were going to be here."

Hannah glanced at their mother, then back at Nora. "Who, me? Why?"

"Something about a job."

"What would she need a security contractor for? Guarding overpriced seascapes?"

Hannah had gone with Nora one time to Rebecca Powell's Malibu art gallery. The place specialized in the kind of idealized, light-dappled images of coastal

California, conveniently sofa-sized, that tourists seemed to favor.

"I don't know why she needs your services, but here she comes." Sure enough, through the big, multipaned window next to her sister, Hannah saw a bright red BMW convertible roaring up the driveway. Nora set aside the last in her flock of linen swans and got to her feet. "You can ask her yourself."

It was courier work, it seemed.

Rebecca didn't broach the subject until well after dinner. Neal and the boys were in the den, watching a football game, and Nora and Nana were loading the dishwasher. When they brushed off all offers of help, Hannah and Rebecca escaped the warm kitchen and took their coffee out onto the softly lit, tented gazebo on the patio.

"It's for a client," Rebecca said, after explaining what she needed from Hannah.

She smoothed her cream linen slacks and crossed her dainty, espadrille-clad feet at the ankles before lifting her china cup to her lips. Rebecca was one of those L.A. women whose voluptuous breasts didn't seem to belong to her stick-thin body, like she'd ordered them from some mammary mail-order house—Boobs 'R Us. At least she'd avoided the clichéd long blond tresses, opting instead for short, ketchup-red spikes that made her look more arty than bimbo-esque.

"My client ordered a painting and he wants it delivered to his vacation home in Mexico."

"He never heard of FedEx or UPS?"

"It's a fairly expensive piece so he wants it hand-carried. A painting by August Koon."

Hannah shrugged. "Never heard of him."

Rebecca leaned forward to settle her coffee cup in its saucer on the patio table. As she did, her dangly silver earrings tinkled and a silver charm necklace swayed in the cleft of her ample breasts. Hannah's personal inclinations left her lusting after manly biceps, not bosoms, but it was hard not to be distracted by that much cleavage. At dinner, she'd caught Nolan's and even ten-year-old Gabe's eyes wandering repeatedly to the deep V of Rebecca's turquoise cashmere sweater although, she'd been happy to note, Neal had had eyes for no one but his wife. Bless his plodding, loyal heart.

"Koon's work is what they call *po-mo*. Postmodern," Rebecca said. "Not what I normally carry in my little gallery, but he's local and fairly trendy at the moment. His work gets pretty good reviews, although to be perfectly honest, I think he's overrated."

"And this client? He's a regular of yours?'

Rebecca hesitated. She might have been frowning, except her skin from the eyebrows up seemed frozen smooth. Damn Botox. It made reading faces really tough. Take now, for example. Instead of looking puzzled at the question, or cagey, or maybe just discreet, Rebecca only succeeded in looking dim. It was all but impossible to know what she was thinking.

"He hasn't bought from me before this, but he has a

home in Malibu—one of several, I gather, scattered all over the world. Anyway, he called a couple of weeks ago and said he'd been in my gallery a couple of times. I don't know that I can really place him, but when he asked me about purchasing this Koon on his behalf, I jumped at it."

"I didn't realize you did that. I guess I just assumed you sell what you're showing."

"I haven't really done much of this before. I mean, once or twice, I've acted as agent for a buyer who wanted something different from an artist I was showing, but never an artist in August Koon's price range. I'd love to do more of this, though. Much better than running a gallery." Rebecca shook her ketchup-red spikes. "All that financial overhead. Long hours. Trying to guess which way the market's going."

"Is being a buyer a full-time gig?"

"It can be. Most wealthy buyers prefer to work anonymously through a broker to keep the price down."

"So this Koon deal is a biggie?"

Rebecca's right hand seesawed. "Middling big. The purchase price is just over a quarter mil, plus my commission. Normally, the agent charges ten or fifteen percent, but when he called the other day, my buyer offered twenty percent before I'd even had a chance to name a rate."

Hannah did the math in her head, then whistled. "Fifty grand for a few hours' work. Nice little business you've got going there, Becs."

"I wish. Believe me, I don't usually get to play in this

big sandbox. That's why I'm not about to say no to this. Whatever this buyer needs, I'm happy to try to get it for him, even if I'm not crazy about his choices. Who am I to look a gift horse in the mouth?"

"I don't know," Hannah said. "Schlepping artwork… it's not really what I do."

Rebecca looked embarrassed—or that's what Hannah thought she was meant to look. Her face did seem to flush, but it didn't exactly register emotion. "No, I didn't think it was, really. Although," she added, "I guess I don't know exactly what it is you *do* do. I mean, I know you used to be a cop, and Nora mentioned that you're overseas a lot now, and that sometimes you do bodyguard work for celebrities. I saw the news after you rescued that kidnapped doctor, too, of course."

Hannah nodded. "It's kind of a mixed bag, what I do. Pays the bills, though." Most of the time, she thought. At the moment, she had a whopping tax bill that she was paying off in installments, the aftermath of the big reward she got for the doctor's rescue—a reward she didn't keep in the end, donating it instead to the widow of her partner in that caper. She'd forgotten about the tax angle. Dumb move, but when the IRS dropped the big bill on her, she chose not to pass it on to her partner's widow and negotiated a payment plan instead. No good deed goes unpunished.

"Would you be free to take a run down to Mexico this week?" Rebecca asked. "It's a quick in-and-out thing. And all your expenses would be covered, of course."

Hannah winced. She didn't like the idea of taking work from family or friends—or even friends of family. It was too hard to negotiate her usual steep fee, especially with someone whose messy divorce too closely echoed her own.

"You could do it in forty-eight hours," Rebecca added. "My buyer authorized up to ten thousand dollars for courier fees, plus expenses. That includes first-class airfare for you and the painting. He wants it hand-carried on board."

*Whoa. Ten grand. For two days' work.*

"Where in Mexico?"

"Puerto Vallarta. He's got a home down there. Like I said, one of several. I gather he's got places in New York and London, and…where else? Tel Aviv, I think. The man is not hurting for money, from the sounds of things."

"Tel Aviv? Who is this guy?"

"His name is Moises Gladding."

*Double whoa. Moises Gladding.* Not the first time Hannah had heard that name.

"Moises Gladding is a pretty shady character, Rebecca."

"You know him?"

"I know *of* him. He's an arms dealer. They say he supplies arms to some of the shadiest regimes and insurgency movements on three continents—and sometimes to both sides of the same conflict."

"Really?"

Hannah frowned. "And Gladding's been in your

gallery? Recently?" Last she'd heard, some Congressional oversight committee had been trying to subpoena him to testify about a reported illegal arms shipment to a right-wing paramilitary group in Venezuela that was trying to overthrow the regime of Hugo Chavez. One of Hannah's security buddies had told her that somebody, probably some spook out of Langley, was suspected of having given Gladding a heads-up and helped him slip out of the country ahead of the legal notice to appear—which would explain why Mr. Gladding couldn't carry his own damn painting to Mexico.

"I'm not sure when he was last in the gallery," Rebecca said. "Like I say, I can't really place him, and the request to make this purchase for him came by phone."

Hannah sat back on the patio chair, watching the light dance on the surface of the swimming pool, reflecting on the trees overhead, turning the yard into a magic fairyland. "You sure you want to be doing business with a guy like that, Becs?"

"It's just a painting. Somebody's going to get the business, so I don't see why it shouldn't be me. But I really need your help. I don't know who else to ask. I'd carry it down there myself, except I can't afford to leave the gallery for two days. Please, would you think about it?"

Hannah sighed. Ten grand was a nice little bite out of her tax bill. She really had no business walking away from easy money, especially since her dance card wasn't exactly full at the moment. At the same time, experience had taught her to trust her gut about certain people, and instinct told her that anything involving a character like Gladding could come back to bite her in the ass.

Still, as Rebecca said, it was just a stupid painting.

"I'll need to see this painting before I agree to carry it," Hannah said. "And to supervise the packing of it. No way am I getting on a plane carrying a sealed package I haven't thoroughly examined with my own eyes."

Rebecca actually giggled. "Oh, thank you, thank you! Hannah, this is *such* a huge help to me, you have no idea. You won't regret it, I promise."

*Lord,* Hannah thought. *Moises frigging Gladding. I sure hope not.*

It was well after nine when Hannah finally got home from her day at Nora's. She'd taken Gabe home to his father's first, enduring the weekly gut-wrench of saying goodbye and then watching him walk inside the house with the very pregnant woman who'd taken Hannah's place in her son's life.

Her ex, a high-profile criminal defense attorney, made his living helping celebrities avoid the consequences of their bad behavior. Cal was good at his job— very good. It had rewarded him with a gate-guarded mansion off Mulholland Drive, a gorgeous second wife, and the money to convince the courts that he and Christie offered a safer, more stable home environment for their son than Hannah could. The fact that the judge had probably made the right decision didn't make it any less painful. Or galling.

Pulling into the short driveway that fronted the row of garages next to her building, she hit the opener switch and watched the door rise. Her condo was on a quiet, tree-lined road that ran steeply uphill from Sunset Boulevard. The low brick building, constructed in the nineteen-twenties, had originally housed offices. Sometime during the real estate boom of the eighties, it had been converted to row town houses, but pleasingly so, retaining period details like deep crown moldings, gargoyled pediments and a few interior walls stripped back to showcase the red brick. It was a rare thing in L.A., real brick. Since the tightening of earthquake codes, nobody built with it anymore. The walls of Hannah's building had been reinforced with rebar during the conversion. Even so, she suspected it would crumble like a house of cards when The Big One hit, but like everyone else in the city, she lived in a state of perpetual denial.

The lights were on in the open garage bay next to hers. Hannah switched off the nearly silent motor of her Prius, grabbed her purse and wandered over to see what was going on at Travis and Ruben's. The intensely sweet smell of night-blooming jasmine wafted on the warm night air. Over the sound of traffic from nearby Sunset Boulevard, she heard the faint click of moths batting themselves stupid against the streetlight.

Travis Spielman was inside his garage, crouched next to his ten-speed touring bike. The bike, with a baby seat on the back, was leaning against a worktable that ran down the side wall.

"Hey, Trav. What's up?"

Her neighbor's curly blond head bobbed up and he smiled. He was dressed in faded jeans and a Grateful Dead T-shirt, washed so often that the black was now a tissue-thin gray. Jerry Garcia's hairy mug was barely visible on the faded cotton.

"Hey, girlfriend," he said. "Not much. Just tightening the bolts on Mellie's seat. We went for a ride today and it was feeling wobbly."

Mellie was his two-year-old daughter and she loved going for rides, whether on the back of Travis's bike or in the jogging stroller that Travis's partner Ruben pushed ahead of himself when he went for a run. The guys said the wind in her hair made her life. Child was obviously a born speed demon, although the cerebral palsy that threatened to lock up her little body left her unable to travel under her own steam.

There were only three units in the converted building. Travis and Ruben had the biggest space, with two large bedrooms and a massive open kitchen and entertaining space. On the other side of them lived a yuppie couple who seemed to work all the time. The couple had been in the building for over a year and neither Hannah nor the guys had seen either the husband or wife more than a couple of times. Their cars, matching black Mercedes sedans, were rarely in their driveway. Ruben said they were CIA assassins who spent all their time abroad carrying out nefarious plots. Ruben had an overactive imagination.

"Didn't you have Gabe today?" Travis asked.

Hannah nodded. "We went down to my sister's. My nephew was home for the weekend, so the boys spent the afternoon in the pool."

She stood in the open doorway watching Travis tighten the bolts that held the baby seat in position. He was a little guy, a couple of inches shorter than Hannah's five-seven, but what he lacked in height, he made up for in wiry fitness. The Grateful Dead T-shirt bulged around the sleeves as he worked the wrench.

"Great day for a pool," Travis said. "Don't ya just love how spring arrives with a bang in this place?"

Travis had grown up in North Dakota, so like Chicago-bred Hannah, he had a real appreciation for Southern California's nonexistent winters and early springs, even if they did they miss fall colors and the sparkle of snow at Christmas.

"For sure." Hannah pushed off the Jeep and sorted the keys on her chain, looking for her front door key. As she did, a thought occurred to her. "Hey, Trav, you ever hear of Moises Gladding?"

"The arms dealer?"

"Yeah. Wasn't he under indictment for something a while back?"

Travis paused, straightened and leaned against the

workbench. Ruben owned a reconditioned 1967 Mustang convertible that was parked to one side of the space. Neither bicycles, tools, nor anything else were allowed to approach with two feet of the Mustang for fear of scratching its lustrous red acrylic finish. Travis, on the other hand, owned an ancient and much-dinged Jeep 4x4 which he generally parked in the driveway or on the street. He had no qualms at all about clutter on his side of the garage.

Case in point: as he pondered Hannah's question about Moises Gladding, the bike suddenly took a tumble and crashed down against a small mahogany table that stood next to the workbench awaiting refinishing. Hannah winced as the carrier basket on the front of the bike scraped its way down the carved leg of the thrift-shop table, but Travis seemed more concerned about the cry that sounded from his daughter's open bedroom window.

"Shoot! We just got her to sleep," he murmured. The misfiring synapses in her brain always seemed to twitch her awake just as she was finally dozing off.

He paused to listen. Then, they heard Ruben in Mellie's room, crooning softly. After a moment, the toddler's crying snuffled out.

Travis picked up the bike, satisfied himself that the baby's seat had taken no damage in the fall, then quietly lifted it onto its hanging pins on the wall. Grabbing an old rag off the workbench, he wiped his hands.

"I don't know that Gladding's under indictment," he said quietly, "but there was that Venezuela business. I also seem to recall that there were questions about him supplying arms to anti-Castro activists in Miami a while back."

Hannah rolled her eyes. "Like that old fart isn't going to keel over and croak any day now. Jeez Louise, when are those people going to figure out that we're better off trading with Cuba and letting Big Macs and MTV corrupt the revolution?"

"No kidding. So why are you interested in Moises Gladding all of a sudden?" Travis gave her a stern look. "Hannah Nicks, tell me you're *not* going to work for him, because, girl, that really would be beyond the pale. He is one sleazy customer, from what I hear."

"No, not work for him. Not exactly, anyway."

"'Not exactly'? What does that mean?"

"Somebody wants me to make a delivery."

"Weapons?"

"No way. A painting."

Travis snorted. "Yeah, right."

"Really. My sister's old college roommate owns a gallery over in Malibu. She got a commission to buy a painting for Gladding and she asked me tonight if she could hire me to deliver it to his home in Mexico."

Travis looked skeptical. "I don't know, kiddo. You sure you want to get mixed up with something like that?"

"It's just a painting. Trust me, I will examine it *very* carefully before I agree to carry it, and I'll supervise the packing myself. Nobody's slipping contraband into anything that I'm schlepping. Still, it's a quick in-and-out job and the money's good."

"You want me to do some checking up on Gladding, see what he's been up to lately?" Travis was a data wonk in the Los Angeles office of the federal Homeland Security department. His job was to manage the computer systems intended to help the feds track and identify suspected terrorists.

There had been a time, Hannah mused, when a gay man like Travis, no matter how brilliant, hardworking or honest, would have been barred from any kind of government work requiring a security clearance. In recent years, however, the feds had finally figured out that a person couldn't be blackmailed into betraying secrets if he were out of the closet before the whole world, including his own blessed grandmother.

"If you get a minute," Hannah said. "Just see if anything jumps out at you. I only told Nora's friend that I'd think about taking the job. I can still back out, but if it's just a matter of carrying canvas down to Puerto Vallarta and coming right back, I'm not about to sneer at easy cash."

Travis nodded, but he looked unconvinced. "I'll see what I can find out first thing tomorrow. Don't leave town till you hear from me, promise?"

"Yeah, yeah." Hannah turned and headed up the walk to her condo. Just what she needed—one more bossy older sibling.

*Puerto Vallarta, Mexico*

Moises Gladding stood on the broad, red-tiled terrace of his seaside villa. The last indigo light of day was slipping down to the horizon. Out over the ocean, a gilded moon was hanging over the sea like some splendid god casting shimmering coins across the water. The night was hot and humid, but an onshore breeze had arisen, clacking the stiff fronds of the rows of palms that traced lazy lines in the sand. Gladding's prize blue peacock, roused from slumber, cried out to the moon, its plaintive, two-tone wail a counterpoint to the low, steady drone of Pacific waves breaking on the shore.

Cell phone snug to his ear, Gladding welcomed the acoustic cover of the night. Indoors, it was far too easy for planted listening devices to overhear a conversation. Years of habits learned in the military, in the secret services of two nations, and then as a private entrepreneur had taught him to sweep his homes and vehicles for surveillance, but technology changed rapidly, and Gladding knew that no countermeasures were foolproof. Low-tech eavesdropping of the human kind was even more problematic. However well he paid his household staff, any one of them might be tempted by an enemy's bribes— and Moises Gladding had enemies in abundance.

To minimize the risk of bugging, Gladding used a succession of cheap, throwaway cell phones that he ran through a private encryption network. When the stakes were high, the wise international businessman avoided unnecessary risks.

Tonight, the international businessman was not happy. "This is not acceptable. You were meant to deliver on Tuesday. Now you tell me you can't do it?"

"No, no, not at all," the voice on the other end said soothingly. "We will deliver as promised. It will just take a little longer. Three days, no more."

The pitch of Gladding's voice dropped low. "I don't like delays."

It was a simple enough statement, but the uncomfortable silence on the other end told him that, as usual, the soft-spoken threat had had the desired intent. Gladding had not worked with this particular supplier before, but he had vetted him thoroughly. He could only presume that the supplier had vetted him, as well. If so, he would know that Gladding was not a man to cross.

"The device will be delivered on Friday, complete, compact and ready to go, as promised."

"I expect nothing less," Gladding said.

A shadow passed across the light spilling onto the terrace. Gladding turned. Gauzy white curtains hung across the open doorway and they moved with the breeze like a sultry dance of veils. His mistress, whom he had left in the shower a short time earlier, had come into the lounge. She stood facing him, holding a stemmed glass and a bottle, her sleek body silhouetted against the glow of the lamps at either end of a rattan sofa. The light of the lamps outlined the shapely figure and long legs under the creamy, diaphanous robe she wore. Her dark hair, still wet from the shower, spilled around her shoulders. Backlit as she was, her face was indistinct, but the way she raised the bottle and glass to him telegraphed the question.

Gladding nodded and she poured him a glass of something bubbly. A celebration, then. She set his glass on the low table by the sofa and reached for another to fill for herself. She wouldn't come out onto the terrace while he was in the midst of a business conversation. Even mistresses knew better than to run the risk of suspected eavesdropping.

"And the package that you promised me?" the voice on the other end of the line wheedled. "It will also be ready for the exchange on Friday?"

Scowling, Gladding turned back toward the ocean. The moon was high over the water now, a huge orb. "Are you suggesting I would not keep my end of the bargain?"

"No, no, of course not. I would never—"

"Good. So, Friday then."

"Yes, yes, Friday. You have my word. And I hope—"

Gladding disconnected. The word of a villain, he thought. How reassuring.

# *Three*

Hannah threaded her way westward through Monday morning traffic on the snarled Santa Monica Freeway. When it slowed to a dead stop, she used one hand to open the car windows while the other rummaged in her shoulder bag for a covered elastic. Gathering her dark gypsy curls into a knot, she inhaled the bright spring morning. Despite the normal heavy commute, an onshore wind had swept away all visible traces of smog, leaving the sky a pristine, aquatic blue. Not even being stuck in an endless line of cars could get a person down on a morning this pretty, the kind that made her fall in love all over again with her adopted city.

She was on her way to Rebecca Powell's gallery in Malibu. From there, the two would head over to the

Hollywood Hills studio of the painter whose work Rebecca had been commissioned to buy on behalf of Moises Gladding. At the thought of the client, Hannah's head made a rueful shake.

*Moises Gladding. Girl, you need your head examined.*

When Rebecca had mentioned last night that she was picking up the painting today, Hannah had insisted on going along. For a job involving a character like Gladding, she intended to be involved in every step of the operation, starting with taking possession of the consignment. Not only would she examine the piece closely, she'd also handle the packing. She was damned if she was going to get on a plane carrying anything she hadn't perused from stem to stern. Listening to her gut was the only thing that had kept her alive this far and she had no intention of abandoning the policy now. Her gut was adamant that having anything to do with the arms dealer could be a can of worms. Travis Spielman's reaction only served to underscore her own uncertainty.

Before going to bed last night, Hannah had done an Internet search on both Gladding and August Koon to see what she could learn about them. Both the arms dealer and the artist had mixed press. One investigative piece on Moises Gladding mentioned off-the-record reports that the man sometimes served as go-between when Washington wanted contact with certain people it couldn't speak to officially—forces opposing the shaky Saudi royals, say, or a Colombian drug lord with useful information about a troublesome trade partner's bad habits. But if he served as a sometime cutout for the spooks, Gladding was nobody's creature but his own, capable of ruthless pragmatism when it came to supplying arms to global hot spots regardless of official Washington's position on a dispute.

In the art world, meantime, August Koon also had his supporters and detractors. After studying some of his paintings online, Hannah decided she was in the naysayers' camp. Like the man said, she might not know much about art but she knew what she liked. Koon's work looked like nothing so much as the time Gabe had accidentally kicked over a tray of finger paints. According to the articles she'd read, some of his larger pieces commanded high six figure prices. Go figure.

She would have been just as happy to give both characters wide berth, but there was no need to cut off her cash-strapped nose to spite her cautious face. It wasn't like she'd never crossed paths with a shady character before. Private security work rarely placed her in the company of saints. For ten grand plus expenses, she could stifle her aesthetics and drop off the painting. It wasn't like she was running guns for Gladding.

Approaching the end of the Santa Monica Freeway, the vista suddenly changed, the aqua-blue sky downshifting to gray. This early in the season, the ocean was still cold, so no matter how hot the Southern California land mass, when warm air met cool, it turned to dense fog. In the space of less than a mile, the temperature dropped about ten degrees. Hannah shivered in the sudden damp, rolling the car windows back up. By the time she turned onto Pacific Coast Highway, the air was so heavy that she could scarcely make out the crashing surf.

Rush hour always meant stop-and-start progress on the two-lane highway, which traced the line of Southern California's beach communities. Lighter northbound traffic allowed her to move a hair faster than the poor saps heading south into the heart of the city, but like most road trips in L.A., this one wouldn't set any land speed records. She'd been in traffic so long by now that the NPR morning broadcast was repeating stories she'd already heard. When her cell phone bleeped, she snapped off the radio, happy for the distraction, grabbed the phone from the center console and glanced at the caller ID on the screen.

"Hey, big sister! What's up? Gabe leave something at your house last night?"

"No, not that I noticed," Nora said. "I'm just on my way from the Amtrak station. I put Nolan on the train back to school and now I'm in standstill traffic heading home."

"Yeah, me too."

"Maybe I shouldn't have called."

"Oh, believe me," Hannah said, "if a monkey took the wheel, it couldn't possibly get into an accident going this slowly."

"It's not the driving. It's just that I don't want to interfere."

"Interfere?"

Nora hesitated. "Are you still going with Rebecca to pick up that painting this morning?"

"I'm en route to Malibu as we speak. Why?"

"It's just that…I don't know. I should probably mind my own business…"

If it were anyone else, Hannah would heartily agree that yes, she should, but saying so would only upset Nora, who was a sensitive soul and a worrier to boot. Maybe it was a sign of long-delayed maturity that Hannah was finally—mostly—learning to keep her smart-aleck mouth shut instead of bristling every time her big sister slipped into mama bear mode. "Spit it out, kid."

"Well… I don't mean to tell you what to do, Hannah, but I'm really hoping you'll do this favor for her. You will, won't you?"

Hannah said nothing.

"Oh, I knew it. I've made you mad."

Hannah sighed. "I'm not mad, but I'm feeling a little pressured here, to tell you the truth. I just can't commit to doing something because it's your old roommate and you say I should."

"You shouldn't *not* do it for those reasons either," Nora snapped. Then, she relented. "I know you always think I'm trying to tell you how to live your life—"

"It's not that." Although it was, a little. Would there ever come a day, Hannah wondered, when she'd stop feeling like the loser kid sister? "It's that this is my business—my profession, I mean—and I know what I'm doing. I need to assess the whole picture before I agree to take on a job. It's what I always do—although in this case, I'm even more inclined to tread carefully. You may not be aware of it, but this client of Rebecca's is a real piece of work. Aren't you the one who's always nagging me to be a little more careful about what I jump into?"

It was Nora's turn to fall silent. Hannah wondered whether it was the "nagging" line that did it. Old family fault lines always ran deep and Nora knew she had a rep for being cautious to a fault.

"You're right. But my God, Hannah, did you see her yesterday? She looks like she's lost about twenty pounds since I last saw her. She stayed on to talk for quite a while after you left last night. You wouldn't believe what that bastard ex-husband of hers is putting her through. She'll be lucky to get out of this without a bankruptcy. You know why she's not getting the house like he promised?"

"Why?"

"Because in addition to maxing out every credit card they had—and some she didn't know they had—he took out second and third mortgages on the house. With the drop in the real estate market, they went into negative equity, totally unbeknownst to her. Of course, California's a community property state, so she's on the hook for half the debt. Even after the house is sold—*if* it sells—she'll still be in it up to her eyeballs. And the gallery isn't exactly a moneymaker. They rarely are, Becs says. Having her own gallery was always her dream, but after what Bill's done, she may have to pack it in and get a regular job just to pay her bills. And don't even get me started on what happens if she gets sick, as she's bound to at this rate, because of course she doesn't have health insurance."

"Oh, man, and I thought Cal was a schmuck."

"At least he gave you the house."

"Yeah, for all the good it did me. Anyway, you're right, it sucks, big-time."

"When you see Becs, don't let on I told you about all this, okay? She's mortified by what's happened."

"Not a word, I promise."

"And Hannah? I'm sorry. As far as taking on this job for her, you do what you think is best. I know you know what you're doing."

*Now there's a first.*

"Just pretend I never called. I'm really sorry."

Hannah rolled her eyes. "Stop apologizing already. It's no big deal. And Nora?"

"What?"

"Don't worry about Rebecca. This situation she's in—it's lousy, for sure. But you know what they say, what doesn't kill you makes you stronger. She's going to be okay."

"I really hope so." But Nora's sigh said she didn't believe it for a minute.

The Sandpiper Gallery was across the road and just north of the Malibu pier. If Rebecca had owned the building or the Malibu waterfront on which it stood, her financial problems would be nonexistent, but Nora had said that the property was a rental and not a cheap one at that. It had been Rebecca's husband, Bill, a wheeler-dealer Realtor with delusions of grandeur, who'd insisted on this pricey location. Apparently he'd had visions of bringing in wealthy clients to buy art for the multimillion-dollar McMansions he was hoping to peddle—except Bill spent more time playing the ponies at Del Mar and Hollywood Park than in flogging real estate. Now Rebecca was stuck with a long-term lease that even Sotheby's might have thought twice about taking on. How many commissions would you need to cover prime real estate like this and still pay the grocery bill? If the gallery was just some rich woman's hobby, it might not have been a concern, but as a breadwinning proposition, it was iffy.

Hannah pulled into the gallery parking lot, empty except for Rebecca's fire-engine-red BMW. Climbing out of the Prius, she stretched muscles gone tight from the hour spent in traffic. Something moved in the corner of her eye and she swung in time to see three gray pelicans flying in low formation over the choppy waves, hunting for a fish dinner. Or maybe they weren't hunting at all, just having an exuberant game of follow-the-leader in the morning light.

Hannah smiled, then reached back into the car, grabbed her soft leather messenger bag, slung it over her shoulder and headed up the gallery's sand-blown front steps. A sign in the front window said the gallery was closed on Mondays, but there were lights on inside, and when she tried the handle, the door opened and a bell tinkled softly. Instinctively, she kicked the sand off her shoes before stepping onto the gleaming hardwood floors.

She'd been to the gallery with Nora once before, and a glance around told her that it looked much the same. Hannah was no expert, but something told her that this much kitschy sweetness wouldn't fly in the serious art world. Although the paintings hanging on the walls looked similar to what Hannah had seen on her last visit, Rebecca had added tables and pedestals on which were arranged lower-priced vases, lamps and other pieces of wheel-thrown pottery—a way to expand the customer base, perhaps, and boost the bottom line.

The office was nestled into a corner of the gallery behind a long walnut credenza that served as a room divider. Rebecca was at her desk, an antique rolltop number with rows of pigeonholes and a green baize pad. Her head turned as the door closed and Hannah saw that she was on the phone. Rebecca smiled and held up a finger. Hannah waved, then started a slow stroll around, studying the merchandise.

Three or four fabric-covered movable walls were scattered throughout the long room, providing extra hanging space. On one of these near the entrance were three colorful paintings, each seemingly illuminated from within. One was a view of the mission at San Juan

Capistrano, red-orange and fuchsia bougainvillea spilling over the adobe arches of the courtyard walls. In the next painting, gulls wheeled and dove across a sparkling seascape while children gamboled along a sandy shoreline. The third picture was of an old California hacienda peeping through thick foliage. The scenes were familiar and nostalgic at the same time, sucking a viewer in as only a Southern California landscape could.

"Stop you right in your tracks, don't they?"

Hannah turned, surprised. She hadn't heard Rebecca come up behind her. Nora's friend was dressed in a gauzy, flowing, peach-colored summer dress, and platform espadrilles whose laces crisscrossed up her legs. Hannah had actually ironed a white cotton blouse that morning and gone so far as to wear a skirt—denim, but a skirt nonetheless. What's more, the pedicure to which Nora had treated her a couple of weeks earlier still looked good in her brown Joseph Siebel sandals. She'd even put on a pair of dangly earrings, but she still felt woefully underdone next to Rebecca. No matter, she reminded herself, this wasn't a job interview. She already had the gig, if she wanted it. She just needed to decide if she did.

"I like this one of the kids on the beach," Hannah said, turning back to the middle painting. "That darkhaired little boy reminds me of Gabe."

"You might have been to that beach with him. It's just north of San Diego." Rebecca smiled. "I would consider adding the painting to the payment if you'll take the Koon to Mexico for me."

"Sounds like a bribe."

"Guilty as charged. Can I get you a coffee? Some sparkling water?"

"No, I'm good, thanks."

"Okay, well let me just shut everything down and we'll head over to August Koon's. That was him I was just talking to. I told him we were on our way."

# *Four*

Rebecca suggested they take her car to Koon's studio in the Hollywood Hills, but Hannah hesitated. As a matter of principle, she preferred to be behind the wheel—you never knew when the situation might call for evasive maneuvers—but it made little sense to drive two cars. Since Rebecca knew the way, Hannah resigned herself to riding shotgun.

There were compensations. They dropped the convertible's rag top once they got inland, away from the thick marine layer, and Hannah leaned back in the BMW's butter-soft leather seats. There was no easy way to get from Malibu to the Hollywood Hills, but the slow cruise up Sunset Boulevard gave her chance to enjoy the gorgeous spring weather and the view of the rolling estates and breathtaking mansions along the way.

It should have been a relaxing ride, but her ease didn't last. Maybe it was Rebecca's platform sandals that made for the herky-jerky ride, gas and brake pedals stomped with equal vigor. Her hands were also in constant motion. If she wasn't tucking flyaway tendrils into the silk scarf stylishly wrapped around her head or turning the rearview mirror to check her teeth for lipstick, she was dialing through her iPod for appropriate road music. After Rebecca cut off yet another driver, who peeled around them on a shriek of rubber, flipping the bird as he roared past, Hannah regretted not insisting on driving. Her little Prius wasn't glamorous, but she'd survived assassins in the desert and gangbangers on L.A.'s mean streets, so the prospect of death-by-bimbo seemed undignified.

"Tell me something," she said to Rebecca.

"What's that?"

"Why are we picking up this painting? Why didn't this artist bring it to your gallery?"

"The great August Koon? He wouldn't deign to come into a little gallery like mine. He made it abundantly clear when we first spoke that he'd never heard of it. He probably wouldn't even be dealing with me if I hadn't been representing a client like Mr. Gladding. Koon is represented by one of the biggest agents in New York."

"So why didn't Gladding go to Koon's agent to procure the piece?"

"He won't work with the man. He told me the agent burned him on another deal in the past. If Koon wanted to sell, it had to be through Mr. Gladding's own representative—me. I still can't believe my luck. I'm just glad he remembered my gallery when he needed someone to handle this for him."

They were approaching an intersection and the light facing them was yellow, but rather than brake, Rebecca stomped on the gas and they barreled through, narrowly missing a cyclist who'd had the temerity to venture a few inches beyond the bike lane. It earned them yet another middle finger. Rebecca adjusted her sunglasses and pretended not to notice.

"I really don't understand what Mr. Gladding sees in August Koon's work," she confessed. "It makes me sick, the prices his stuff draws when so many more deserving artists are selling their work for pennies to his dollar—if they sell at all."

"Like the artists whose work you carry?"

Rebecca nodded. "Case in point. Those impressionist pieces you were admiring, for example. That man's work has been shown in major shows and several local museums, but he lives like a pauper. It just isn't fair."

"Life rarely is, in my experience. And to be honest, I'm still a little leery about dealing with Moises Gladding. He's a pretty shady character, by all accounts."

"So you said last night. But in *my* experience, saints are rarely patrons of the arts. Most of the really big sales these days are to Wall Street millionaires or Hollywood sharks. If I limited myself to customers who could pass a decency test, I'd have gone bankrupt long ago. Although I may yet," Rebecca added grimly.

"I guess you're right. Anyway, I've got nothing to say

on the subject, since I've had some dubious clients myself. What about this painting? Gladding's paying a quarter mil for it, you said?"

"That's right."

"Is that a good price for a Koon?"

Rebecca frowned—sort of. The Botox mystery expression again. "I think the price is a little high for such a small piece, to be honest. I'm not complaining, mind you, since my commission is based on the selling price. Still, I think he could have gotten a better deal if I'd been allowed to negotiate a little."

"Koon's not in high demand?"

"Well, I'm sure he's very comfortable."

"Curious."

"How so?"

"Well, I don't know anything about art markets," Hannah said, "but I do know something about characters like Moises Gladding. And the thing about arms dealers is, sometimes they trade in valuables other than cash. It's an idiosyncrasy of the arms market that sometimes the people who want weapons don't have much money, so they barter, trading something else for guns and rocket launchers."

"Paintings?"

"More often drugs—cocaine or heroin, say—or conflict diamonds mined by slaves in Africa. But sometimes stolen art is used as collateral, too."

"But the Koon painting Mr. Gladding is buying isn't stolen. It's an original."

"I know. And actually, I'd expect one of Gladding's customers to be trading a painting, not him. The IRA, for example, was once suspected of stealing a Rembrandt which they gave to a middleman who then financed the purchase of guns the IRA wanted. Terrorists have also been known to buy rocket launchers with stolen Picassos."

Rebecca nodded. "We get Interpol and FBI lookout notices about stolen art all the time. I always thought it was shady billionaires or Arab sheikhs or something who were buying them."

"Ah yes, the *Doctor No* scenario—the recluse with a private vault of old masters that he keeps for his personal enjoyment," Hannah said. "Apparently that's not how it works. Art, like drugs and diamonds, is just another form of currency—a Rembrandt traded for AK47s, cocaine for rocket launchers. Your basic commercial marketplace at work."

"And that's the business Mr. Gladding is in?"

"That's exactly the business he's in."

Rebecca's sunglasses had slipped a little way down her nose and she peered over them now at Hannah. "My, my. Nora's little sister. You look so young, and then you open your mouth and the things that come out of it. No wonder Nora wasn't sure you'd be interested in my little delivery job. Pretty small potatoes next to your world of rocket launchers and Rembrandts."

"Oh, yeah, my life is nonstop glamour. Believe me, most of this is just theory to me, too. Just like the Koons of this world mostly deal with big-time New York art agents, the world of Moises Gladding is far removed from anything I usually get hired for. I'm just a girl with a gun who likes to travel and gets paid for it."

Sunset Boulevard was far behind them now. They were heading uphill into canyon country.

"Anyway, it doesn't sound like this August Koon's a big enough name to factor into that world either. Although," Hannah added, looking around, "these are pretty fancy digs up here. He must be fairly successful."

Rebecca shrugged. "He does all right. But the man's in his fifties, I'd guess, and his prices only started to climb in the past five years or so. As far as I know, this has always been his home base. Property around here would have been affordable when he was starting out."

"So he lucked out in the real estate lottery, too." Hannah consulted the Mapquest printout that Rebecca had given her. "It should be the next left, I think, and then the first place on the right."

Rebecca took the left at the intersection and then a quick right at a tree-shaded gateway with an elaborately painted wooden signboard announcing the studio of August Koon. The crunch of the BMW's tires on the gravel driveway startled a klatch of doves. They followed a winding lane through a grove of scrub oak.

"I should warn you, he's not exactly Mr. Personality," Rebecca said.

"I stand warned."

As they emerged from the tree-bowered driveway,

the roadway widened into a circular gravel parking area before a two-story white clapboard house. A rickety-looking garage stood next to the house, its double doors swung wide on loose hinges to reveal an aged yellow VW bus inside. *Shades of the sixties,* Hannah thought. The bus was only missing a paint job of psychedelic flowers.

Rebecca parked the car and they climbed out. Eucalyptus and pine trees intermingled with the scrub oak around the house, and the air smelled intoxicatingly fresh. The paint on the house was peeling and the perennials in the flower beds were fighting for survival against an onslaught of creeping kudzu vines and milkweed, but there was still something magical about the place, one of the many little woodland glades that existed practically in the heart of Los Angeles. Rebecca was probably right, that Koon had bought it back when properties like this were affordable. Nowadays, if you weren't a Hollywood studio honcho or a trust fund brat, there was no hope.

The weather-worn screen door at the front of the house opened and a man stepped out. His severely receded hair was lank and mostly gray, curling over his ears. He wore a brown and yellow plaid cotton shirt that strained over a considerable paunch. His chinos were paint stained, the frayed hems puddling over equally paint spattered Birkenstocks. His thick brows nearly met at the deep frown creases over his nose, and matching creases ran down either side of a fleshy, unhappy-looking mouth. *A portrait of the artist as a crotchety old man,* Hannah thought.

"Good morning, Mr. Koon," Rebecca chirped as he clumped down the front steps. She held out a hand. "I'm Rebecca Powell. It's so good to finally meet you."

Koon ignored her outstretched hand, glanced dismissively at Hannah, then back at Rebecca. "Come for the painting, I suppose?" His voice was a deep, pack-a-day rasp.

"That's right. This is Hannah Nicks. She's a security consultant and she's going to be delivering the piece to the buyer."

"Humph." Koon turned his narrow gaze back to Hannah. She couldn't help feeling that he was finding her sub-par as security for his treasure.

Rebecca went around to the trunk of her car, her platform soles a little precarious on the rock-lined driveway. She withdrew a rectangular, padded black case from the trunk. "I brought a portfolio to carry the painting."

"You're not crating it?" Koon asked.

"It's not really necessary. We'll wrap it, of course, although not too tightly, since it's going to have to pass through Security at LAX. Hannah will be hand-carrying it and the painting will be carefully stowed with her in the first-class cabin. It'll be just fine, I can assure you. Shall we see it now?"

Koon hesitated, then nodded toward a walkway between the house and the garage. "Studio's this way," he grunted, heading off the porch.

Rebecca followed his rapid stride, but her platform espadrilles were having so much difficulty negotiating the uneven tile pavers that Hannah jogged ahead and took the bulky portfolio case from her. Rebecca smiled gratefully and then put her full concentration into trying to keep up with Koon. Dropping back behind her once more, Hannah noticed a small unraveling of fabric at the collar of her gauzy peach dress where it had gone tissue thin from much wearing. Like the strain in her face, it was a sign of the stress she was under. Hannah could empathize.

Koon's studio was a freestanding structure at the back of the property, better maintained than either the house or the garage, with what looked like a brand-new air-conditioning unit humming away in one of the large windows. Koon opened the screen door and propped it with one of his paint-splattered Birkenstocks while he fished a set of keys from the pocket of his chinos. When the inner door was unlocked, he stepped in, then backtracked at the last moment in time to catch the swinging screen door before it slammed shut on Rebecca. He held it until only she reached it, then turned abruptly and headed inside, leaving her to scramble to catch the swinging door. What a gentleman.

The studio was long and narrow, a large open space with windows all along the front and on the western side wall. Overhead were three skylights, although they were on a side of the roof that sloped away from direct sunlight. It was all designed, Hannah realized, to allow maximum natural light into the room without harsh shadow or exposure to harmful UV rays that might damage delicate painted surfaces.

Along one window stood a banquet-sized table laden with rolls of canvas, T-squares, rulers and a yardstick, as well as bins of tiny nails, a staple gun, shears and a variety of sharp blades and knives. Stacked against the opposite wall were frames and mounted canvases of various sizes. It took a moment for Hannah to realize from the splotches of paint on their edges that the multiple canvases propped face to the wall were probably finished paintings. On the wall above them were displayed still more paintings, large expanses covered with wide swaths of color. Maybe they were drying, she thought, or maybe he liked these better than the ones hidden from view. Most of them still reminded her of Gabe's finger-paint accident.

At the far end of the studio stood three separate easels, two of which held large canvases that may or may not have been works in progress. It raised the question—how did an abstract artist know when a work was done? Koon walked over to a framed canvas that had been propped against the long worktable and placed it on the empty easel. It was about two-foot by three, smallish compared to some of the mega works lining the walls.

"Here it is."

Rebecca moved forward, smiling. "Yes, I recognize it from the photographs Mr. Gladding sent me. I can see why he liked it. It's very vibrant."

Vibrant? Well, maybe, Hannah thought, in a dog's breakfast kind of way. It was nothing like anything Rebecca herself carried in the gallery and her enthusiasm seemed a little forced. On the other hand, a twenty percent commission on the painting's quarter-million-dollar price tag might turn anyone into an ardent fan.

Koon seemed to buy it, however, and proceeded to pull out several other canvases to show, his raspy voice rambling on about influences and innovations. Nothing more was required of them than noises of appreciation and these Rebecca offered with a frequency that Koon apparently found gratifying.

As the two of them made the rounds of his studio, Hannah moved aside to examine the tools of his trade arrayed on the table. Anything was better than to risk being asked her opinion of the paintings. Among the brushes and blades were putty knives crusted with paint, suggesting he used these to apply color as often as he used the brushes. There was also a well-used whetstone, its surface worn to a concave groove. Next to the sharpening stone sat a curve-bladed knife, its ebony handle smooth from use.

Hannah picked it up. Now, knives she knew something about, and this one was a beauty—well balanced, lightweight, yet sturdy at the same time. She ran a finger gingerly along the honed inner curve of the blade. It was wickedly sharp. What would he use a blade like this for? She studied the rolls of canvas and the wooden stretchers waiting for mounting and imagined the knife slashing through the tough cloth. It would do the trick. *Like butter*.

"Put that down," Koon snapped.

Hannah turned, frowning at the man's tone. Taking the blade by the point, she flipped it high in the air and watched it complete three perfect end-over-end circles before she caught it neatly by the ebony handle. Rebecca gasped.

"Nice knife," Hannah said blandly, setting it back down on the table.

Koon glared, clearly unimpressed. Well, all right, she *was* showboating, but the man was such a pompous pill. Maybe she shouldn't have been playing with his toys, but was the attitude really necessary?

She went over and retrieved the leather portfolio from the corner where she'd left it and handed it to Rebecca. Time to get this show on the road. Rebecca seemed to agree, because she opened the portfolio, withdrew a length of soft cloth and carefully wrapped the small picture before sliding it into the case.

After she handed over a check for payment and had Koon sign a receipt, they said their hasty goodbyes and the two women were on their way, leaving Koon to his studio, his paintings and precious knives and brushes.

As much as Hannah might worry about taking on a job involving Moises Gladding, nothing about this painting said it was the kind of masterpiece usually associated with illegal arms deals. This was a simple transport for easy cash. If Gladding had more money than taste, who was she to quibble?

# *Five*

It was nearly five by the time Hannah got back to her condo. She and Rebecca had gone for lunch after the trip to Koon's studio, a meal that had dragged on uncomfortably as Rebecca offered chapter and verse of her husband's betrayal, their broken marriage and ruinous divorce. Hannah could sympathize, having been there herself—although Cal, to his credit, had not added insult to injury by trying to ruin her financially after stomping on her heart. If taking this courier job could help Rebecca in a small way, Hannah was glad of it, although she could have lived without all the sordid details.

One they'd gotten back to the gallery in Malibu, Hannah had turned around and fought her way through traffic to Silver Lake. By the time she arrived at home, the day was shot and she was beat. She loved Los Angeles. but getting anywhere in the city was a joke. It had turned into another spring scorcher, and she was hot, grimy and thirsty. Time to kick back and relax before her early-morning trip to the airport and the flight to Puerto Vallarta.

She opened the fridge, grabbed the water filter pitcher and took a glass from the cupboard. Her kitchen was tiny, just wide enough to open the doors on the double wall ovens, but it had been well equipped by the yuppie developers who'd converted the old building, making it both functional and attractive—especially given that her only regular visitor was Gabe and that her culinary activities generally revolved around the microwave, the rice cooker and her fridge's vegetable bin. She was no gourmet cook, but she ate healthy. It was the only way to survive—literally—in a profession where the ability to move fast was the number-one requirement for long-term success.

After downing an entire glass of cold water, Hannah refilled it, then set the pitcher on the granite-topped breakfast bar separating the kitchen from the large, open living area beyond. The living space was on the second floor, over the garage, with bright, airy windows front and back and a small balcony at the front overlooking the street. It was a nice place to live—at least, when she made an effort to control the clutter and dust. Touches of Nora were everywhere.

As much as she sometimes chafed under her sister's overprotective watch, Nora could always be counted on to come through in a crisis. When Hannah's marriage and then her home had collapsed in rapid succession, it was Nora who'd found the condo, then served as informal decorator after Hannah bought it. As a result, Hannah lived in a colorful refuge of teals, tans and corals, the wall colors warm and welcoming next to the unit's exposed brick. Her mother had also passed on a number of textiles and curios from the art and antique shop in Beirut where Hannah had spent many a summer with her Greek-born grandparents. Her sister had artfully hung some of the woven pieces on the walls and made others into pillows and runners, which added yet another shot of bright color. It was thanks to Nora that she had a place that felt good to come home to, even if the daily absence of Gabe remained an open wound.

Moving around the breakfast bar, she paused to pick out a leaf that had fallen from the big ficus tree that anchored one end of the island. Her plants, too, were a contribution from Nora, appearing out of the blue one day when Hannah returned from an overseas security job.

"I was buying new plants for my house and decided you could use some up here," Nora had said, refusing to take payment for them. "They soften things and help clean the air. You need that, living in this city."

The care and feeding of the greenery came down to Trevor's partner, Ruben. At first, he'd just come in to water the plants when Hannah was out of town on a job, but after nursing one too many spindly specimens back to health, only to see it wilt again under Hannah's negligent ministrations, Ruben had clucked despairingly and taken over the job full-time. Hannah repaid him by babysitting little Mellie from time to time and by taking the guys' dog along whenever she went running. Chucky—part border collie, part God-knows-what— could never get too much exercise, and Hannah liked the rescue mutt's goofy, slobbering company.

Spotting Rebecca's carrying case where she'd left it on her overstuffed sofa, Hannah went to take another look at August Koon's work. Her condo faced west and the late afternoon sun, filtered through the gauzy sheers over the open patio doors, set the space aglow. Warm as the day had been, nights in L.A. remained cool until late June or early July, when the ocean finally had a chance to warm up. The temperature now was dropping fast. A soft breeze wafted the sheers. The low, steady hum of traffic on Sunset Boulevard was underscored by the distant wail of a police siren.

Setting her glass on the coffee table, she zipped open the leather portfolio and pulled out the painting. She examined it front to back, inside and out. If it weren't for a wire hanger on the frame and the artist's signature at the bottom right, there'd be no telling right from left, up from down on this "masterpiece." The canvas was a thickly painted mass of blues, greens and violets.

Flipping the picture over, Hannah examined the reverse side. Heavy kraft paper was stapled to the wooden frame. She shook her head and went to the kitchen for a sharp knife. No way would she not check under the paper. Lifting out half of the staples, she rolled the paper back, taking care not to crease it. The back of the canvas was grimy, but the paint-splattered pine stretchers and staples holding the canvas in place seemed relatively new. Nothing remotely untoward here.

After stapling the paper back in place, she propped the painting on the sofa. Then, she had another thought. She pulled the portfolio toward her and examined it closely. Rebecca had provided it, so if the case concealed something illegal, then Nora's friend was implicated. Hard to believe, but who knew? She wouldn't be the first person driven to crime out of desperation.

The case was padded and reinforced to reduce the risk of crushing. And maybe conceal contraband? Hannah took her Swiss Army knife from her messenger bag and used it to make a small slit in the lining. All she found inside was high-density foam wrapped around sturdy cardboard.

Setting the case aside, she took up her water glass again and settled into her favorite rocker to study the painting. Why would anyone want to own a piece like this? And pay a quarter million dollars for it, plus commission and shipping? It wasn't so much that it was ugly. Compared to other "high concept" art pieces she'd seen in the past, hideous things that left her head shaking, this one was okay. The longer she looked at it, in fact, the more she found herself picking out images, reading emotions into the dusky, gladelike colors. Maybe that was the idea.

Since this was the first time she'd ever acted as an art courier, Hannah had raised with Rebecca the legal ramifications of importing and exporting paintings.

"It's not a problem with modern work like this, as long as the paperwork's in order," Rebecca had said. "August Koon's work is hardly a national treasure."

She'd handed over an envelope. When Hannah had opened it, she'd found the bill of sale and an authentication certificate signed by Koon, as well as an import permit from Mexican Customs and her Los Angeles/Puerto Vallarta return air ticket—Alaska Air, 10:10 a.m. Tuesday morning, first class as promised. Rebecca said the airline had been given a heads-up that Hannah would be hand-carrying a painting and had affixed an amendment to her file noting that the portfolio was to be safely stowed alongside her in the first-class cabin.

Hannah examined the Mexican import permit that had apparently been arranged by Moises Gladding. It all looked very official. She suspected money may have changed hands under a table somewhere but, although she studied the paperwork closely for irregularities, everything seemed in order. No matter how much she might fret about dealing with Gladding, sometimes a cigar was just a cigar and a courier job was just that. All she had to do was carry the painting to LAX, board the plane, tuck the portfolio into its closet, then sit back with a glass of champagne and enjoy the two-hour flight. She'd be met in Puerto Vallarta, she'd deliver the picture, and then her work would be done. Easy money.

She rewrapped the painting in the soft cloth Rebecca had provided and slipped it back into the leather port-folio. In her bedroom, she propped it behind her bureau, then kicked off her sandals and pulled her T-shirt over her head. She was just heading to the bathroom to turn on the shower when the bleep of her cell phone stopped her in her tracks. It was in her messenger bag in the living room. She ran back into the other room, plucked it up and glanced at the screen. Her stomach did a backflip. The number was familiar enough that she recognized it, but not such a habit that she'd assigned it a permanent place in her phone list. That would be too much like asking for trouble.

She opened the phone. "Hi, there."

"Hey, stranger." John Russo's voice reminded her of bittersweet chocolate—deep, dark, rich but never cloying. It was like everything else about him, a balance of weirdly Zen calm and edgy tension that made him intriguing, unpredictable and just a little bit scary. He was unremarkable in appearance, not overly large or menacing, but the bad guys he encountered in his line of work would underestimate him at their peril. Russo was one of the best homicide detectives in the city. It would be easy enough, she imagined, for a suspect to be lulled by his easygoing demeanor, only to be stung by that laser intelligence and pit bull tenacity.

Hannah counted herself among the good guys, but Russo kept her feeling a little off balance, too. She wasn't sure what she was going to do about that. The two of them had been tap-dancing around each other for a couple of months now. If the irregular hours they both kept made it tough for them to find time to see one another, Russo had made it clear he wasn't about to let a few scheduling problems get in his way. The guy was determined, she'd give him that. And a damn good kisser, Hannah had discovered. Her stomach cartwheeled as she recalled their one and only real date. It was about ten days ago, dinner followed by a walk on the beach. Yes, a cliché right out of the classifieds, maybe, but it had worked. Unfortunately, it had come to a breathless but abrupt end when he'd been called out to a murder scene in West Hollywood. He wasn't supposed to be on call that night, but as luck would have it, a gang war had erupted in Compton and all of Russo's colleagues had been out picking up the pieces of carnage there when the dead sheet call came in.

"You're a tough lady to get hold of," Russo said now.

"I wouldn't want to seem easy." Hannah winced. Damn, was she flirting? She hated flirting. "Anyway, I called your office. You have a new partner."

"Yeah, she's a newbie. She'll be riding with me for the next couple of months. I'm her T.O." Her training officer. "Name's Lindsay. She just transferred in from the Twin Towers."

The Los Angeles Sheriff's Department, in addition to policing vast swaths of Southern California, also ran the detention facilities that housed men and women arrested anywhere in the county. It was impossible to climb through LASD ranks without sooner or later doing a stint as a corrections officer in one of the jails. Hannah herself had worked in the Twin Towers correctional unit for a year after graduating from police academy, and she'd hated every minute of it. The relationship between jailed and jailer was made up of equal parts suspicion, contempt and gamesmanship, bored inmates having little else to occupy them besides looking for ways to end-run the guards. The day her transfer to a patrol beat had come through, Hannah had danced a jig right there in the control tower.

"I'll bet she's glad to be out of there. I assume she's been on the street already?" Hannah asked. You didn't make detective in the Sheriff's Department until you'd put in your time on patrol.

"Yeah, she worked the Valley and Compton. She only just told me you'd called. When exactly was that?"

"Thursday or Friday, I think." Actually, Hannah knew precisely when she'd called, but there was no mileage in looking too eager. "She said you were out of town."

"Yeah, I had to go up to San Francisco. I got back on Friday, but I didn't get your message until a few minutes ago. The kid's in big trouble." Russo sounded annoyed. That was gratifying. "She misses another message like that and she'll be back on a beat before she knows it."

"Don't be too hard on her. She doesn't know me from Adam. Probably thought I was one of your groupies."

Russo made a dismissive noise, but cops did tend to attract a fan base. It wasn't just the man-in-uniform phenomenon. Plainclothes detectives held just as much fascination for civilians. It was the illusion of invincibility, maybe, that knight-in-shining-armor thing. As a former cop herself, Hannah knew the badge was no guarantee of valor or integrity, much less infallibility. Russo had certainly suffered his own share of personal and professional problems, but he seemed to deserve his rep for decency.

"Believe me, Lindsay knows now she'd better tell me right away if you call," he growled. "When I didn't hear back from you, I was beginning to think you were avoiding me. I was thinking about taking up stalking. Anyway, why did you call the desk instead of my cell?"

Hannah hesitated. Why indeed? Because she'd been hoping to get a recording and put the ball back in his court? Because the thought of seeming desperate, or of putting herself out there and getting hurt again was scarier than anything she could imagine? She'd walked into booby-trapped buildings with less trepidation than she felt at the idea of letting this guy get close. She'd been on her own nearly five years now. There'd been a couple of so-called relationships in that time, but she'd had no problem keeping them compartmentalized, tucked away in a little offside place that came nowhere near threatening her peace of mind. But when John Russo had walked into her life, she'd realized fast that she was in big trouble.

"How come I didn't call your cell?" she repeated. "I

don't know. Because the office number was the one I called, I guess. How are you doing?"

"Okay. Working too much, as usual. You know that murder I caught in WeHo the night you and I went to the beach?"

"I remember." Boy, did she. Hannah's face went warm, thinking about them necking on the beach like a couple of teenagers. "The paper said you arrested some movie writer. The guy who did that NASCAR picture—what was it called?"

*"Speed Demons."*

"That's right. He crashed a race car while he was re-searching that, I read."

"Yeah, what a bozo. You've heard of method acting? Looks like this guy invented method writing. He nearly bought it when he flamed out that car. Told me he wanted to get a sense of what a race driver feels when he's going around a curve at a hundred and twenty miles an hour. Another time, apparently, he climbed Mount McKinley to learn about life and death at high altitudes and nearly got his guide killed."

Hannah rolled her eyes. "Not a rocket scientist, it would seem."

"No kidding. So, this time he's writing a murder mystery about working girls, and the next thing you know, there's one dead hooker in his bed and another one running screaming down La Cienega Boulevard wearing nothing but rope burns."

"Yikes."

"He'd gagged and hogtied both girls—ankles and wrists linked to nooses around their necks. Left them that way while he went to the liquor store, if you can believe it. First girl passes out, strangles herself. Second girl manages to get free just as she hears the writer's car pull up. She slips out the front door as he's coming in the back. When he realizes there's a dead girl in his bed and the other one's gotten away, he hightails it out of town. We finally tracked him down to an old girlfriend's place in the Bay Area."

"So that's what sent you up there."

"Yeah. San Francisco PD picked him up for us. I flew back with him last night and he was arraigned this afternoon. I was hoping the bastard would be remanded over until the trial, but he made bail."

"Well, way to go. Guess his next script will be *Jailbird City*."

"What are you up to?"

"Getting ready to head out on a job."

"Again? A real job this time?"

"What do you mean, *real?* I work."

"Yeah, sorry. I know that. I meant a permanent job, I guess. With regular hours."

"Like yours, you mean?"

"Point taken." He sighed. "We're a pair, aren't we?"

A pair? If only. In the three months since they'd met, they'd had exactly two lunches, several dinner dates that ended up canceled either because Hannah got last-minute calls for jobs she couldn't afford to turn down or he had to work overtime. At this rate, Hannah thought, she'd be on Social Security before they ever got to second base. And by then Russo, a decade older than she was, would be dead or too pathetic to do her frustrated libido much good.

On the other hand, he was still calling. Points to him for persistence.

"I was hoping we could go for dinner or catch a movie or something one night this week," Russo said. "How's your schedule looking."

"I'm going to be out of town for a couple of days."

"Oh, well…I just thought—"

"But you know what? We should celebrate you closing this crazy writer case." God forbid he should think she was making excuses.

"Yeah?"

"For sure. I'm flying out tomorrow but I'll be back the day after."

"What's the job?"

Hannah told him about Nora's old college roommate and Moises Gladding's sudden desire to own a painting by August Koon.

"Moises Gladding? I've heard of him, I think. Didn't he get called up on some terrorism beef?"

Hannah nodded. She'd done her research since talking to Rebecca at Nora's Sunday dinner. "He testified before Congress last year about arms sales to Al Qaeda, but he was on the side of the angels on that one, it seems. He's not always, mind you."

"You're sure it's a painting you're taking down there?"

"Yeah, I've examined it thoroughly, believe me. I don't even know why I'm doing it, except it's good money and a quick turnaround. Safeguarding a few square feet of canvas beats dodging insurgents in Iraq. Can I call you when I get back into town?"

"Absolutely. But call me on this number, okay? It's my cell. You need to write it down?"

Hannah smiled. "No, it'll be in my phone now. I'll store it and use it, I promise."

"I'm holding you to it."

Hannah allowed herself a pleasant mental picture. John Russo could hold her anytime he wanted.

# *Six*

After a shower, Hannah ran her fingers through her dark curls, leaving them to air dry, then pulled on the Garfield flannel pajamas Gabe had given her for Christmas. It was early yet, not quite seven o'clock, but it was always nice to nest the night before a job. After rummaging through her kitchen, however, she realized that she might have to change back into street clothes. Either that or change her name to Mother Hubbard, her cupboards were that bare. She had meant to go grocery shopping after picking up the painting but then postponed the trip, not willing to leave the Koon in her car while she ducked into Whole Foods. With a guilty sigh, she pulled a box out of the cupboard and put a pot of water on the stove to boil. Processed mac and cheese. Pathetic. Why did she even have this stuff in the house? Easy. Because Gabe liked it and his stepmother, to her credit, refused to buy it.

When he was little, Hannah had conscientiously

made his mac and cheese from scratch. Then, one day when he was around four, he'd come home from a playdate singing ecstatic praises for the orange noodles he'd had at his friend's house. On their next trip to the grocery store, he'd spotted the Kraft Dinner box on a shelf and nearly had a meltdown when Hannah resisted buying it. It was about the time his father had left to move in with his latest squeeze, soon to be the second Mrs. Calvin Nicks, and Hannah hadn't had the heart or strength to battle their little boy over a stupid box of noodles. That had been the end of butter roux and hand-shredded cheese, however. Now, although Gabe took infrequent meals at her house, she still found herself buying the boxed quick dinner because he inevitably asked for it.

After her meal was cooked, she ate it standing up at the kitchen sink. This was not the kind of meal that deserved to be eaten sitting down with a nice glass of wine. She watched the dew gather on a web outside her kitchen window, sparkling drops on the precise loops and gossamer lines woven by some sure-footed spider. Must be nice, Hannah thought, to be so certain of what your job in life was and how to go about doing it.

She downed a glass of milk, then cleaned up the kitchen and headed for her bedroom, selecting a backpack for the trip that would allow her to bypass the airline baggage check and get quickly out of the airport after landing in Puerto Vallarta and going through Customs. She packed just enough for an overnight stay, but then, on impulse, tossed a bathing suit into the pack as well. Remembering Rebecca in her gauzy dress that morning, Hannah also went to her closet and slid hangers until she found a flowing skirt. Fancy resort, why not? She could head to the hotel after the painting was delivered, lounge on the beach, and then have a nice dinner on Moises Gladding's tab.

Unhooking the skirt and a matching tank top, she spotted the safe in the back of her closet where she kept her Beretta locked away. She would feel naked going out on a job without it, but since she wasn't checking bags, there was no way to carry it through airport security. The nature of the assignment hardly warranted it anyway, no matter how much of a genius August Koon might be in his own mind.

Three hours later, she was curled up on her living room couch, flipping channels, when the doorbell rang. Her eyelids had been getting heavy and she'd been thinking about packing it in for the night, but at the thought that Russo might have decided to drop by, she perked right up. Glancing down, she briefly considered a dash for the bedroom to change, but then the bell rang again. No matter. If Russo was going to pursue her, he might as well know the ugly truth—she was a woman who wore Garfield pajamas.

She flipped on the front porch light and glanced through the peephole, then paused, taken aback. It wasn't Russo on the other side of the door. Two clean-cut men in almost identical dark gray suits stood on her front porch. It was a little late for Mormon missionaries or Jehovah's Witnesses, so her money was on cops. And not just any cops. Feds.

"Who is it?" she asked through the door.

"Federal agents, Mrs. Nicks," one of them said.

Bingo. Through the peephole's convex lens, Hannah saw both men raise black leather folders with gold-colored shields on the top half and ID badges boldly emblazoned with the letters FBI on the bottom.

She frowned and opened the door a few inches, keeping herself and her Garfield pajamas mostly hidden. "Can I help you?"

They lowered their badges in unison and put them away. One was Asian-American, the other Anglo, but they were otherwise so alike as to be almost indistinguishable, with haircuts that were neither long enough nor short enough to be fashionable.

"I'm Special Agent Bruce Ito, ma'am, and this is Special Agent Joseph Towle," the Asian-looking man said.

"We'd like to have a word, if that's all right," Towle added.

"What's this about?"

"Can we come in?"

"Depends. Can you tell me what this is about?" Hannah asked again.

Ito and Towle glanced at each other, then back at her. "It's about your trip to Mexico, Mrs. Nicks," Towle said.

"How do you know about that?"

"Maybe we should discuss this inside?"

Hannah sighed, then opened the door wide and stood back to let them in. They seemed a little taken aback when they saw what she was wearing, but came in. She closed the door behind them.

"We're sorry to come by so late," Ito said, "but we wanted to be sure to catch you before you left."

"I'll ask again, how do you know about that?"

"We understand you're doing some work for Moises Gladding," Towle said.

Hannah studied them for a minute, then extended her arm toward the sofa. "I guess you'd better sit down and tell me what exactly it is you want."

The two agents nodded. "After you," Towle said.

Hannah led the way into the living room, took the rocker and left them the couch. She grabbed the remote and flipped off the television as they settled in. Ito was carrying a briefcase and he set that on the floor beside his feet. The two agents leaned forward, elbows on knees, and looked at her expectantly.

"What?" Hannah asked.

"You were going to tell us about this work you're doing for Moises Gladding," Ito said.

"You were going to tell me how you know about that."

Towle shrugged. "Information came our way. So, about the work…?"

"I don't know what 'information' has come your way, but I'm not working for Gladding."

"We know you're transporting some merchandise for him. What's your relationship to Gladding?"

"Relationship? There is no relationship. I repeat, I am not working for him. What I'm transporting is a painting, if you must know. I was hired by a gallery owner who purchased the painting on Gladding's behalf. Gladding wants the painting at his vacation home in Mexico. End of story."

"This is the first we've heard of Gladding's international dealings having anything to do with art," Ito said. "And from what we know of you, Mrs. Nicks, art's not your usual line, either."

Hannah shifted back in her chair. "In the first place, please don't call me *Mrs.* Nicks. I'm nobody's missus. And in the second, if you know about my work, you know that I'm a freelance security specialist. I usually do personal security or private ops—"

Towle grimaced. "You've had some interesting press."

She waved a hand. "A couple of jobs ended up high-profile because of the players involved. Most of what I do is pretty routine. Getting a painting safely to its destination is not that different from getting a politician or movie star to theirs. The point is, if you've checked me out, you know I'm one of the good guys, so I'm not sure why I should suddenly be deemed suspicious."

"But since you do have international experience, Mrs.—excuse me—*Ms.* Nicks, then you must know the kind of client you're dealing with here."

"I do. I don't take on a job until I have a line on all the parties involved. I've never dealt with Gladding before, but I've checked him out and I know his rep for playing all sides of the street when it comes to his arms deals—including acting as a cutout for you guys," Hannah added. When Towle began to demur, she waved away his objection. "Or the CIA or whoever. The point is, our government has made use of him in the past, from what I gather. I also know that high-end art is sometimes used as collateral in Gladding's business, but the piece I'm transporting is hardly in that league. He's paying more for it than I would, even if I had his money, but it's not the kind of high-prestige art your criminal class usually goes for."

"Do you have the painting here?" Towle asked.

She nodded. "Do you want to see it?"

"If you don't mind."

She went into the bedroom, withdrew the portfolio from behind her bureau and took it back into the other room, trying not to think too much about the figure she cut in bare feet and cartoon PJs. So much for her professional reputation. She unzipped the case and pulled out the two-by-three painting. The agents seem taken aback.

"Looks like one of my dad's old ties—*after* he spilled chili on it," Towle said.

Ito nodded. "That is one butt-ugly painting."

The feds moved up a notch in Hannah's estimation. Towle made a cursory search of the painting and frame, much as she herself had done, while Ito examined the leather portfolio, not failing to miss the spot where she'd slit the lining to take a closer look at the padding.

"As you can see, just a painting," she said. "Since you

guys are obviously way ahead of me here, want to tell me what this is really about?"

They glanced at each other, then Towle answered. "We'd like you to do a small favor for us while you're down in Mexico."

"I didn't realize we were on such intimate terms."

"We're talking about performing a service for your country. A contribution to national security."

*Always the war-on-terror angle,* Hannah thought.

"We imagine you're going to find yourself inside Gladding's home in Puerto Vallarta," Ito said. "While you're there, we'd like you to see if you can leave a couple of calling cards behind."

"Calling cards?" And then it dawned on her. "Oh, man, you want me to plant bugs in his house?"

"Surveillance devices, yes," Ito said. He picked up the briefcase by his feet, set it on the coffee table and rolled the tumblers. He snapped the locks but left the lid shut, looking up expectantly.

"Why do you want his house bugged?" Hannah asked.

"No specific reason." From the way Towle's blue-gray eyes shifted, Hannah suspected there was a very specific reason. "Let's just say that whatever services Mr. Gladding may have performed for our side in the past, of late he's dealing with people to whom Washington would prefer not to be linked."

"We and some of our sister agencies have been looking for an opportunity to get close for a while," Ito added. "It's just serendipity that you happen to have timely access. You can get in without arousing suspicion and slide the devices in with no one the wiser."

Ito lifted the lid on the briefcase and withdrew a couple of electronic devices about the size of a dime. "Nothing here you haven't seen before, I'm sure. These two are voice activated with a transmission range of almost half a mile, so our people can park listening posts well outside his property in areas that won't arouse suspicion. Dormant unless activated, with power packs that last for months. These ones," he added, lifting out a couple of small tubes, "are motion-activated cameras. Same kind of range and power pack. If you can plant any of them unobtrusively in his office and anywhere else that looks promising, it would be a real boon to our efforts."

Hannah picked up one of the devices and turned it over in her hand. "This is the best you've got? I thought you guys were a little more advanced than this. Are these even shielded?"

"They'll resist some sensors. Not all, but that's the point. An operator like Gladding is programmed to assume that he's susceptible to bugging. We let him find some and he figures he's outsmarted us."

"Even assuming I have access or the time to plant anything, what makes you think he won't find them all?"

"He might," Towle said.

"So what's the point?"

Towle looked over at Ito. "Show her the clincher."

Ito pulled out a small case and opened it. Inside was a matte rectangle, maybe half-by-a-quarter-inch in size, tops. Ito peeled it out of the case. It was paper-thin and virtually transparent. "What we'd really love is for you to try to attach this to Gladding's laptop. We know he keeps it on his desk, so if you can get a minute alone—"

"What is it?" Hannah asked.

"A keystroke logger. Gladding communicates primarily via e-mail and he sends out all his business info over an encrypted network. This device will record not only the encryption key, but every strike on the keypad. Unlike those other toys, this one's almost impossible to detect with standard sweeping equipment. It attaches with an adhesive—just peel it like a bandage. In a pinch, you could stick it almost anywhere on the laptop and it probably wouldn't be noticed, but I'd suggest opening the CD drive and sticking it under the tray."

Ito reached into the case and pulled out yet another device, about the size of a stick of gum. Hannah recognized this one. She'd planted something similar on a vehicle just a few months ago. It was how she first met Russo, in fact. He'd caught her planting it on the car of a surveillance target, but he let her leave it in place when they realized they were tracking the same bad guy for different reasons. And that, as they say, had been the beginning of a beautiful friendship.

"This—" Ito began.

"I know what that is," Hannah said. "You want me to put a GPS tracker on Gladding's car?"

"If the opportunity arises," Towle said.

Hannah sat back in the rocker. "Jeez, guys, how much time do you think I'm going to have? I'm just dropping this painting off."

Towle smiled. "You're an attractive woman, Hannah, and Moises Gladding is very susceptible to attractive women. From what I've heard, you think fast on your feet, too. I'm sure you can figure out a way to seed at least a few of these in his garden."

"And why would I do this?"

"Patriotism?"

She snorted. "Yeah, right. Look, I'm as patriotic as the next guy, but I'm going to be on my own, unarmed and on foreign turf. How dumb do I look?"

Towle pulled a laminated card from his pocket and handed it over. One glance told her what it was—identification for a federal air marshal. Her name and picture were on the ID.

"You've arranged for me to take my gun on the flight?"

Towle handed her his business card. "We know you can handle yourself and we know you have a registered firearm. It just seemed prudent for you to have protection while you're down there. My number is there for you to call if you run into problems or have any questions. One of us will meet you at LAX tomorrow morning and walk you through security so that there are no questions about the electronics or your weapon. Oh, and one more thing." Towle reached into his breast pocket and pulled out another business card, definitely not his own. The card was garish blue and featured a cartoon drawing of a lizard in sunglasses lounging under a palm tree, drinking some concoction that came with a tiny umbrella. The card was for a bar in Puerto Vallarta, the proprietor's name printed on the bottom. "Local emergency contact, just in case."

"You guys think of everything."

He shrugged modestly. "We try."

# Seven

With a tall glass of iced coffee in hand, Kyle Liggett parked himself in a dockside café to watch the first passengers disembark from a Carnival Cruise ship that had glided into port sometime before dawn.

After taking care of loose ends in Los Angeles last night, he'd had to scramble to catch a late-night flight to Mazatlán. He'd rather have flown directly into Puerto Vallarta, but unexpected circumstances had delayed him, and Mazatlán had been the closest destination available that would get him down here in reasonable time.

Liggett hated last-minute changes, rushed situations where he had to improvise. They were a recipe for mistakes and he hated mistakes—his and others.

He'd been down here before. He liked the scenery

well enough, although after a while, the slow pace of things made him so antsy he had to get the hell out before he started shooting things up just to see people get a goddamn move on. Fancy resort destinations especially irritated him, with their persistent souvenir hawkers and fat tourists in gaudy clothes and stupid hats.

Passengers began to stream like ants from the luxury cruise ship, pouring down the gangplank and spreading out across the tropical town. He spotted a handful of Asians in the mix, a few Hispanic-looking types, but most of the crowd off the Long Beach-based liner were white Americans who looked they could have been his corn-fed relatives. Too bad they'd just arrived, because he could easily have blended in with this group. But he had to be in Puerto Vallarta by mid-afternoon, when this ship would just be starting to round up passengers for an evening castoff.

A second liner, the *Galaxy Star*, had dropped anchor the previous morning and was scheduled to depart at 7:30 a.m. It was smaller, cozy by cruise liner standards with only a thousand passengers, and that fit his needs better. Mammoth ships like the Carnival liner offered safety in numbers but they were less concerned about empty berths, whose costs they could swallow with relative ease. A smaller ship had to make every fare count and could usually be counted on to welcome a short-haul passenger with few questions asked.

Over the years, he'd learned that small liners offered an easy way to slip in and out of ports, staying well under the radar, allowing him to move money, goods and himself from place to place without official notice. Guns were occasionally a problem. These days, most ports had metal detectors, and even if one didn't, most ships had installed them. That wasn't a problem on this trip, however. Any weapons he needed would be available down there, while delivery of another package was already arranged. He needed only to get himself to Puerto Vallarta.

Liggett looked over the laminated, bilingual breakfast menu the waiter had left him, big color pictures showing what was on offer just in case English or Spanish descriptions weren't enough. As a steak-and-potatoes Midwesterner, he viewed with suspicion all that mishmash—burritos, shredded meat, vegetables, eggs, God only knows what else. When the waiter returned, Liggett pushed the menu aside. He'd eat on the boat. He liked simplicity. Liked order and structure. His work was messy enough.

When the small cruise line's office opened, he headed inside to arrange passage on the *Galaxy Star*. An hour later, just before it set sail, he joined a few stragglers who'd spent the night ashore—a couple of them doing a little more partying than could be healthy, by the smell of them. He carried a small duffel bag and, like a couple of others, sported two colorful bags that suggested he'd done some souvenir shopping in Mazatlán—a nice last-minute touch, he thought.

His quarters were located in the bowels of the ship and

near the bow, where people complained of seasickness. But tight quarters and motion never bothered him. Except to observe, he had never been much influenced by his environment or by people around him. He slipped through crowds unnoticed. In his line of work, it was an advantage to be common looking—neither tall nor short, dishwater hair, average in every respect. Nothing about Liggett was exceptional, aside from an utter lack of the stupid fears that made lesser folk dare to take risks—and it wasn't like there was any external mark of that.

*Los Angeles*

Hannah stood by her bedroom window, examining the ammo clip on her weapon, smacking it in place, double-checking the Beretta's safety. She slipped the gun into the holster at the small of her back, then pulled on a light-weight linen jacket over her tank top to conceal it.

She patted the jacket. Her passport was in an inner pocket, while her wallet and the import permit for the Koon painting were stowed in a couple of the many zippered pockets on her cargo pants. Handbags, even her handy-dandy messenger bag, were a no-go. On the job meant remaining hands-free. Of course, she'd be encumbered this morning by the leather case holding the painting, but keeping a secure grip on that was the whole point of the exercise.

As security jobs went, this one had to be one of her easiest gigs. Ferrying a painting to a gorgeous Mexican resort town involved nowhere near the pressure of dodging insurgent fire in Iraq or keeping screaming fans off overpaid celebrities. She might actually have been looking forward to the jaunt to Puerto Vallarta had it not been for that late-night visit from the feds.

Nobody was paying her to bug Moises Gladding's house, so why had she agreed carry in their gadgets? Patriotism? Maybe. A more compelling reason might be too many memories of innocent victims of Gladding's bloody trade. Of course, her own government was the world's biggest arms dealer, bar none. And just because Gladding was apparently playing for the opposition these days didn't mean Washington always teamed with angels. She had agreed to try to plant the listening devices, though, and it was too late to back out now.

She gave herself one last glance in the mirror. Then, reaching for her backpack, she spotted the framed school photo of Gabe that sat on her bedside table. She touched the image of his dark curls (hers) and gorgeous cobalt-blue eyes (his father's). The tunnel vision she got when working was a blessing. It was the only thing that distracted from the daily ache of his absence.

She killed the bedroom lights, then did a quick walk around the condo to make sure the stove was off and the exterior windows and patio doors barred. She was outside, just locking the front door, when her cell phone bleeped. She fished it out of a pants pocket and glanced at the caller ID. Her stomach dropped. It was her worst nightmare—odd-hours calls about Gabe.

She flipped open the phone. "What's wrong, Cal?"

"Good morning to you, too." Her ex-husband's voice was well modulated, the voice of a schemer sure of his entitlement to live at the top of the food chain.

"Is Gabe all right?"

"Why would you think he wasn't?"

Hannah grimaced. "Why else would you be calling me at this ungodly hour?"

"Did I wake you?"

"No, I'm on my way to the airport. What's up?"

"Sorry to bother you. I just thought you might want to know that the assistant headmaster has called us in for a meeting."

"A meeting? When?"

"This morning."

"Are you serious?"

"Utterly."

Hannah glanced at her watch. It was just past seven. Gabe didn't start school for another two hours and was probably still asleep. "What does he want to see us about?"

"She. Mrs. Jennings."

"Whatever. And while we're on the subject, how long have you known about this?"

"She called yesterday."

"And you're just getting around to telling me now? You couldn't have called sooner? I've got an international flight at nine forty-five. You know what that means—a two-hour advance check-in."

"Right. Well, if you're too busy to be involved in your son's life, that's fine. I'll go in and deal with this mess myself."

"What mess?"

"I'll give her your regrets."

"Calvin? What mess, dammit?"

But she was talking to dead air. Typical. When he wasn't being passive-aggressive, he was pulling hotshot legal tactics, looking for ways to further undercut her access to their son. What a schmuck. What had she ever seen in that man? And how the hell could his DNA have gone into making a kid as awesome as Gabe?

And what "mess" was the school calling about?

"Dammit to hell." She fumbled to get the key back in the door lock. Inside, she threw her pack on a chair, set the portfolio aside, then sat down at the kitchen table, pulling out her paperwork to start dialing. First, the airline. No problem. There was another flight to Puerto Vallarta at one, and exchanging her reservation was no problem. Nor was there any concern about the arrangements that had been made for her to stow the painting in the first-class cabin. Money talks, and a first-class fare gets first-class service all the way.

Now, what about her other unofficial mission at Gladding's estate? She rummaged in her wallet for the business card Agent Towle had given her the night before, but when she called his number, she got voice mail. Not surprising. He and Ito had looked like eager beavers, but arriving at the office by seven was probably above and beyond the call of duty. She left a message.

"This is Hannah Nicks. Something's come up and I have to take a later flight today. Unless I hear from you, I'm going to presume that our arrangement is off."

She left her cell number so he could call back and let her know if she could still expect a walk-through at airport security. No way she was she sneaking around Gladding's house unarmed while she played Johnny Appleseed with their electronics. People in his line of work tended to be both paranoid and ruthless, and the more successful the arms dealer, the more that was true. If Towle didn't call back, no skin off her nose. She'd be just as happy to leave their toys behind in L.A., along with her gun.

Her last call was to Rebecca Powell, but she was no more an early bird than Agent Towle. She left a message there, too, hoping that whoever was meant to meet her in Puerto Vallarta would find out about the later flight.

That done, she went to her bedroom to change into something more appropriate for meeting the assistant headmaster at Dahlby Hall. Cal would no doubt show up in one of his Armani suits. She wasn't about to arrive looking like Gabe's poor backwoods relation.

Dahlby Hall's student register listed some of the most famous names in Los Angeles. The private academy, an L.A. landmark, occupied a sprawling hundred-acre campus high on a hill overlooking Mul-

holland Drive. Its tiered glass-and-redwood buildings had been designed to blend harmoniously with
the wooded surroundings. The visual impression on
driving through the main gates was of a serene
Japanese Buddhist monastery, a notion only slightly
undercut by the childish laughter and playful shouts
of uniformed kids in the playground awaiting the first
bell.

The city's wealthiest families signed their children
up for Dahlby Hall almost from conception and the
academy's waiting list was said to be backlogged into
the next generation. Gabe had attended public school
kindergarten in Los Feliz when he lived with Hannah,
but after her house there was destroyed and he moved
in with his father, Cal and Christie were able to use their
media and business connections to leapfrog the wait list
and register Gabe for first grade. Christie was now on
the school's board of governors, and she and Cal apparently made substantial annual bequests over and above
the academy's $50,000 tuition. It was a safe bet that the
next little Nicks, due to arrive in a couple of months,
would also be a Dahlby scholar.

Walking from the parking lot to the main building,
she scanned the crowd of students, looking for her
son, but the playground closest to the offices seemed
to be occupied exclusively by lower-school young-
sters. She entered the building and reported to the reception desk.

"My son, Gabriel Nicks, is a student," she told the girl

behind the desk. "His dad and I have an eight-thirty appointment with the assistant headmaster. I'm a little early."

"Ah, yes, Mrs. Nicks. Or, Ms. Nicks, I guess?" the young woman amended.

No doubt she was remembering the *other* Mrs. Nicks. Not only was Christie on the board of governors, but she'd been a high-profile local television news anchor before marrying Cal. Her career had shifted into lower gear after she took on the raising of his son. Instead of the evening news, she anchored the early morning program now, though she'd recently left on maternity leave as her pregnancy entered its third trimester.

The receptionist pointed down the hall. "Actually, Mr. Nicks is already with Mrs. Jennings. You can go right on in. Her office is the third door on the left."

Hannah followed the direction indicated by the receptionist's red acrylic fingernail. As she approached the office door, she found it slightly ajar, and Cal's mellifluous voice drifted out into the hall.

"She's always been a bit of a maverick. My ex-wife likes to blaze her own trail." He chuckled. "A natural adventurer, I guess you might say. All well and good, I suppose, but maybe not the best influence on an impressionable little boy."

"Maybe not. Is there nothing—" The woman paused as Hannah pushed open the door. "Can I help you?"

"I'm Gabriel's mother." Hannah crossed the room and held out her hand. "I don't think we've met."

Whenever humanly possible, she made a point of attending parent activities and getting to know Gabe's teachers. She'd also spoken to the headmaster on a couple of occasions, but this Mrs. Jennings was a recent hire, lured away, apparently, from one of the big prep schools back East. The new assistant headmaster might have been in her late forties or early fifties, although her dark hair, scraped back into a severe bun, showed not a wisp of gray. The woman got to her feet and reached across her broad desk. She was painfully thin, dressed in a nubbly, hot-pink suit trimmed with black braid and jet buttons, the kind of ensemble supposedly favored by Coco Chanel and ladies who lunch.

"How do you do? I'm Enid Jennings. I'm glad you could make it. I'm sorry we started without you, but Mr. Nicks said you were unavailable."

Her shake was one of those limp-wristed, four-fingered affairs offered backside up that always left Hannah wondering if she was perhaps expected to kiss the extended hand.

"I am heading out of town on business today," Hannah said, settling into the chair the woman indicated. "Naturally, I rearranged my schedule as soon as I heard you needed to speak to us." She shot Cal a pointed look. If he hadn't hung up on her earlier, she might have told him that's what she'd do.

Mrs. Jennings reseated herself in her high-backed leather chair. Her desk was a broad Mission-style red oak table, tastefully laid with a collection of porcelain sculptures and blooming African violets. There was very little in the way of paper clutter, just a single manila file folder with a large red N on the tab—for "Nicks," Hannah presumed. Gabe's school file.

"You haven't missed anything important. I was just asking Mr. Nicks if there'd been any recent upsets in Gabriel's life."

"Is there a problem? He seems very happy to me," Hannah said.

It was true. No matter how frustrated she might be about her own limited time with her son, Hannah had every reason to think that he was a secure and well-adjusted little boy. There was a new baby on the way, of course, but his relationship with his stepmother seemed good. However much Hannah had initially resented the "other woman" in her divorce, Christie had turned out to be a basically decent human being. Nor could Hannah doubt that Cal genuinely loved their son, however much he might irritate her.

Enid Jennings tapped the file in front of her. "He's a bright little boy and, from what I can see, he's doing well academically. I should explain. Part of my duties here at Dahlby Hall involve discipline issues. The reason I called you both in today is that I'm concerned Gabriel may not have a very strong grip on reality. It's causing some behavior problems."

Cal slid forward in his seat. Hannah recognized the danger signs. He was shifting into attack mode. This was a man who had great success playing the adversarial role for his clients. Hannah would not want to be in Mrs. Jennings's shoes if she made an enemy of Calvin Nicks.

"No grip on reality?" he said. "Bull. He's the most grounded kid I know."

Hannah agreed, but she decided to try to take the high road. "What's happened to give you that impression?"

"Did you know that Gabriel's had detention twice in the last month for scuffling on the playground? Yesterday, he landed there for a third time."

"Scuffling?"

"Actually, it was a little more than that yesterday. This time he bloodied another boy's nose."

"What?" Hannah and Cal exclaimed simultaneously.

"I don't believe it," Cal snorted.

"This doesn't sound like him," Hannah agreed. "He gets along well with other kids. He has a lot of friends, and he's always been taught to use words, not his fists, to solve disagreements."

"This time he didn't. He got into a fight with one of the seventh-graders at lunch yesterday. The older boy teased him about lying and Gabriel lashed out. I'm not saying the other boy should have been teasing, but Gabriel *was* telling tall tales and refused to back down when he was called on it. And regardless of the reason, he can't go around smacking people in the face."

"I've never known Gabe to lie," Hannah said.

"How would *you* know?" Cal asked.

"Have you caught him lying?" Hannah shot back. Cal shook his head. She thought not. She turned back to Jennings. "Look, obviously we can't overlook hitting, but this really sounds out of character. What exactly was Gabe saying before things escalated?"

Mrs. Jennings leaned forward, crossing her arms on her desk. "Actually, Mrs. Nicks, he was talking about you. He's been saying his mom's some sort of action heroine—Lara Croft meets Wonder Woman, I gather."

Cal leaned back, exhaling heavily. "Bingo. There's your problem."

Hannah shot him an irritated look. "Excuse me?"

"Well, what did you think would happen? You tell him these wild stories and then, of course, he repeats them and gets into trouble." He turned back to Mrs. Jennings with a grimace. "Not a good influence, I think you'll agree."

"I do not tell him wild stories. What exactly did Gabe say about me?"

"That you used to be some sort of super-cop. That your house was blown up by gangsters. That you have a black belt in karate and you fought in Iraq. That kind of thing."

Hannah nodded to Cal, vindicated. "All true," she told the assistant headmaster. "Well, except the 'super-cop' business, maybe. I was a police officer, though, and my house was actually destroyed by a gangster five years ago. He was a drugrunner. I'd worked an under-cover sting against him and was set to testify in court, so he tried to have me killed. And I do have a black belt—third level, as a matter of fact."

"And Iraq?"

"I was there a few months ago."

"Really?"

"Yes. Tell her." Hannah turned to Cal, but he only rolled his eyes. "Look, Mrs. Jennings, these are not lies. Get online and do an Internet search on my name if you want. The Iraq thing was reported in the press. I used to be a cop, and now I do private security work."

"Just because those things are true doesn't make her a good influence," Cal said.

Mrs. Jennings ignored the cheap shot. "Well, I'm relieved to hear that Gabriel's not fantasizing. Nevertheless, I'm still concerned about this rage of his."

"This older kid called him a liar. And it's happened repeatedly, by the sound of it," Hannah said.

"I take it you travel a great deal?"

"A fair amount."

"And you and his father don't share custody?"

"I have him weekends and alternate holidays," Hannah said defensively.

Mrs. Jennings frowned. "That's an unusual arrangement, isn't it? I understand that California family courts usually recommend shared custody."

"The court ruled that my wife and I provide a more stable home environment for Gabriel," Cal said. "His mother's lifestyle obviously doesn't."

"You have more resources to offer, not more love. And I concurred at the time of our divorce," Hannah added to Mrs. Jennings, cutting off his protest, "because my job had placed me in personal danger and I was afraid my son would get hurt. But he's very close to me and my extended family and spends a lot of time with us."

Mrs. Jennings nodded. "Good. But this does explain a lot."

"What do you mean?"

"I've seen it before in children of divorce. Usually it's an absentee father with whom the child overidentifies."

Cal nodded. "But Gabe, of course, has an absentee mother."

Hannah opened her mouth to protest, but Mrs. Jennings beat her to the punch. "Actually, I was thinking that it might be the animosity between his parents that's causing this anger in your son."

Hannah glanced at Cal. For the first time in memory, he seemed dumbstruck. She had newfound respect for Enid Jennings. Limp handshake notwithstanding, the woman was a tough cookie. Nobody got Calvin Nicks to shut up. Ever. For that alone, Hannah decided, she was all right.

"I've talked to Gabriel and he understands that fighting won't be tolerated," Mrs. Jennings said. "As for his anger issues, I could refer this to our school psychologist or I can leave it to you two. You need to work out a better way to share your son without infecting him with your issues. It's up to you. If you don't deal with this, no one will pay the price but Gabriel." She glanced at her watch. "And now, you'll have to excuse me. I'm late for another meeting."

# *Eight*

Travis Spielman had a headache and the day had barely begun. He'd left home early, hoping to get a jump on morning traffic and the usual gridlock around the twenty-eight-acre federal campus on Wilshire Boulevard, but he'd gotten trapped behind a fender-bender and ended up at a standstill just yards from his freeway off-ramp, unable to move, breathing exhaust for nearly forty minutes while his office building stood in sight but frustratingly unreachable.

At this rate, he thought irritably, he might as well have stayed home a few minutes longer, given Melanie her breakfast and had coffee with Ruben. He'd been in Seattle the day before and had gotten home well after they were both in bed. There'd been a lot of that lately, travel and long hours of overtime, and it wasn't going to let up anytime soon. Couldn't be helped.

He glanced at his watch. He had a series of conference calls and online meetings scheduled to start at nine and it was pushing that already. Damn. He'd hoped to do some quick info mining, see if there were any red flags on that arms dealer Hannah had asked him about the other night. He would have done it yesterday if he hadn't had to fly up for an emergency meeting with the Microsoft team helping develop Daxo, the new software system he'd been working on for the past eighteen months. He might have had time to run a check on Gladding before his teleconference this morning but now, thanks to the BlackBerry-reading idiot ahead of him rear-ending a Subaru, he was probably out of luck.

He only hoped Hannah wasn't out of luck, too. Spielman didn't like the idea of her dealing with a character like Gladding, no matter how innocuous the job. It wasn't like there'd be anyone watching her back out there. It was a bit irregular, of course, tapping into federal databases for private purposes, but his neighbor was good people and he didn't like to see her step into a snake pit. He would just check for recent activity concerning Moises Gladding on the federal intelligence files. If anything major jumped out at him, he could sound a warning without giving away the family jewels.

Most intelligence was severely compartmentalized, accessible on a strict need-to-know basis, but Spielman was one of a handful of data wonks in the federal system able to cut across departmental and operational lines. Traditionally, the various components of the intelligence community—CIA, FBI, Homeland Security and others—maintained high walls around their fiefdoms, jealously guarding their little pieces of the puzzle. 9/11, though, had shown how critical it was to share information.

Somebody had to be trusted to create the systems to do that. After fifteen years in government, during which he'd been investigated six ways to Sunday, Spielman's security clearance was now well beyond top-secret. His domestic arrangements might seem unconventional to some, but he'd never tried to hide who he was, and everything else about him was boringly straight-arrow, from the three-star general father, the computer systems doctorate from MIT, and a solid track record at the National Security Agency and then the FBI and Homeland Security. He was a nerd, right down to his plastic pocket protector.

When he finally arrived at the federal office tower where he worked these days, the elevator ride turned out to be as slow as everything else that morning, a milk run that stopped at nearly every floor on the way up to fourteen. There, the elevator door opened onto the lobby of the western regional office of the Department of Homeland Security. Framed headshots of the president and the director hung to either side of the large departmental crest on the wood-paneled wall. The seating area featured half a dozen comfortably upholstered armchairs and a couple of potted trees. Copies of *National Geographic* and the *Congressional Record* were neatly fanned on low glass-and-steel tables, and the mottled red carpet was plush. The place looked like a doctor's waiting room, except for the thick bulletproof glass surrounding the reception desk.

The woman behind the desk glanced up and returned Spielman's wave as he headed left toward the solid steel door guarding the Information Services unit. Briefcase in one hand, he was fumbling in his pocket for his photo ID magnetic key swipe when the door opened and the unit's office manager came flying out. A rotund, steel-haired grandmother in her fifties, Margie nearly bowled him over.

"Oh, Travis! I'm sorry!"

He recovered his footing and grabbed the door before it could swing shut. "No problem. I couldn't put my hands on my stupid key card. One of those mornings." His hand closed on the card. He took it out and clipped it to his shirt pocket.

"I'm just running down to grab a coffee," she said. "You want one?"

He grimaced. "Cafeteria swill? Oh, Lord, Margie, I need a coffee so bad, but that stuff is undrinkable. I couldn't persuade you to go across the road to Starbucks, could I? I'll buy—anything you want."

She frowned, then gave him an indulgent nod. "All right, I suppose I could. Things are pretty quiet this morning."

"Bless you. You're a lifesaver. I'm running really late." He pulled a wad of crumpled bills out of his pants pocket and dropped it in her hand. "Here. I'll take the biggest nonfat latte you can get—and an intravenous drip, if they have one."

"You've got it bad, my child."

"You have no idea."

"You want anything else? Muffin? Scone?"

He was sorely tempted, but he shook his head. "Better not. Ruben says I'm getting love handles."

She checked out his wiry frame and snorted. "Oh, please. You need meat on those bones."

He grinned. "Okay, mom. Surprise me, then. Thanks." He ducked through the door as she headed for the elevators.

The landscape changed to utilitarian-gray as he entered the unit, a huge room of shoulder-height dividers separating dozens of cubicles furnished with basic-issue desks, bookcases and file cabinets. Simple white Venetian blinds covered windows that overlooked Wilshire Boulevard, Westwood, and the nearby campus of UCLA. There were no carpets here to muffle the ringing of phones, the tap of keyboards and the muttering of voices, only speckled beige linoleum to minimize static buildup, which could play havoc with the section's sensitive electronics. On the far side of the unit in a glassed-in room, an array of mainframe computers hummed like a cyborg beehive.

Spielman waved and nodded to coworkers as he made his way toward his cubicle outside the computer room door. Created in 2003, the Department of Homeland Security had been charged with the daunting task of coordinating the domestic defense and emergency management efforts of some eighty thousand federal, state and local agencies. He had been one of the first systems designers pulled in to create the new HSIN-CI—the Homeland Security Information Network-Critical Infrastructure, a mouthful of a name for a program charged with disseminating threat warnings to all these agencies.

Tossing his briefcase onto a spare chair in his cubicle, he shrugged out of his sport coat, hung it on the back of the chair, then sat down. His desk was clear except for the small framed photo of their daughter that Ruben had given him for his birthday. Most of his co-workers' spaces were cluttered with pictures of kids, grandkids, spouses, dogs and cats, as well as trinkets and plants, but not his. Some might think his spartan surroundings were an effort to be discreet about his personal life, but Spielman wasn't trying to hide anything. He just liked things streamlined. It helped him think.

Anyway, his home was cluttered enough, given the toys and paraphernalia that came with having a toddler, plus Ruben's flair for decorating with bright colors, tchotchkes and fabrics. His partner had once had a tendency to bedeck himself exotically as well, but he toned it down now in deference to the conservative environment in which Travis worked. Poor Ruben.

Spielman yawned as he flicked on his computer terminal. This morning, he and the implementation team scattered in regional offices across the country would start downloading Daxo, the new software he'd been developing over the past eighteen months.

As his terminal warmed up, he slipped on his telephone headset and dialed into the conference bridge linking his IT colleagues across the country. The automated voice on the system told him that the conference call was already underway. Spielman settled in for a long morning of coordinating the minutiae of the Daxo download.

Only it didn't happen. The disembodied voices of his colleagues came on the phone line as he was entering his password to log into the internal IT managers' network. By the curses he heard through his headset, everyone else was getting the same message on their computer screens that now appeared on his: Access Denied.

"What the hell…? Okay, who did this?" Spielman demanded. "Who's been messing with the security protocols?"

They all insisted they had no idea how or why the system had locked them out.

"All right, stand down, guys," Spielman said wearily. "I'll try to track the source of the problem and get back to you."

As the rest of his team signed off, Spielman disconnected the phone, threw his headset aside and went to work, fingers flying over the keyboard as he tried several back doors to get back into the data stream. No luck. The only thing he could determine was that the problem had begun in the San Diego field office and that the system had been deliberately frozen by someone with an even higher access clearance than his own. Spielman got on the phone to his director in Washington.

"What took you so long?" were the first words out of Alison Walker's mouth when she answered.

"So you knew about this?"

"I only found out about an hour ago. All I know is that the block was ordered by the FBI."

"What's up and how long will it take?" The only reason for his team to be locked out of the system was that some sort of highly sensitive operation was underfoot and the system needed to be maintained in a stable state until it was done. That meant no messing around by the IT guys, lest the system crash at some inopportune moment.

"I don't know," Walker said. "I'm out of the loop on this one, too."

"I'm trying to think if there's been any increased chatter about an impending border op, but nothing comes to mind." The San Diego-Tijuana corridor was the focus of various initiatives to counteract the cross-border flow of people, drugs and other contraband.

"Best not to ask too many questions, Trav. If we were supposed to know, we'd know. All we can do is wait until the cowboys have finished doing whatever it is they're doing."

"We were right in the middle of uploading Daxo."

"Stand by. As soon as I know anything, you'll know."

Spielman sighed. Murphy's Law. He hung up and turned back to his computer terminal. Maybe there was a small upside here. If he couldn't get his work done, at least he could finally take a look at what there was on Moises Gladding for Hannah.

He put Daxo in sleep mode and logged on to one of the interdepartmental intelligence data files. When he entered the name of the arms dealer, however, the Access Denied message appeared again. He tried accessing Gladding's name on a couple of other lower priority file systems, and got the same message. His gut contracted a little tighter with every denial of access.

A person didn't work for a decade and half in this community without developing a little paranoia. This had never happened to him before, so what did it mean that it was suddenly happening now? Was the network really having problems, or was he personally being shut out of the system? Why? Did the FBI suspect him of disloyalty? The Bureau was responsible for the security vetting of government employees. He knew he was utterly trustworthy, so what might have happened in the past couple of days to change how he was perceived?

He could think of only one thing—his neighbor had gotten mixed up with Moises Gladding, and Spielman had offered to tap into the system on her behalf. He and Hannah had had the conversation in his open garage. Was he under surveillance? Was she? Why? He was as certain about Hannah's loyalty as he was his own, but

Gladding was another matter. Had they both stepped blindly into a hornet's nest?

He was about to call her when he thought better of it. If they were under surveillance, either one of them, the phones would be tapped. He drummed his fingers on his desk. Walk away from this, his gut told him. But could he? If there was any chance Hannah would be in danger down in Mexico, shouldn't he at least try to warn her?

The office manager appeared at his cubicle with his latte. "Here you go, ducks. And I bought a cheese Danish and a blueberry muffin. You can have whichever you want."

Spielman got to his feet, shrugged back into his jacket and took the coffee from her. "You know what, Margie? The system's down at the moment, so I'm going to run a few errands while I'm waiting for it to come back online. I'll pass on the goodies for now."

"You sure?"

But he was already on his way toward the door. He took the stairs down the fourteen flights to the ground floor and hurried to the parking lot. His sensitive job and his neighbor's penchant for misadventure fed his paranoia, but if there'd been no one else to worry about, he could have handled it. But he was a father now. He couldn't risk his job or Mellie's and Ruben's security. On the other hand, he couldn't leave his friend dangling in the wind, either.

Dodging in and out of side streets and heavy traffic,

he made good time driving home. He parked in the street so that Ruben could get his car out of the garage. As he ran to the front door, he glanced around nervously, checking for watchers. He had no clue what the signs might be. He was a computer nerd, not a trained spy. He wouldn't know a surveillance vehicle if it ran over him.

Just in case, he turned on music when he got inside and told Ruben what was going on. "It's probably nothing," he said.

Ruben squeezed his shoulder. "If it was, you wouldn't look so worried." He frowned and tapped a finger against his lip, thinking. Then, "I know. You stay here and watch Mellie. I'm going to run to the market."

"The market? Ruben—"

"Trust me. Is the earthquake kit still by the garage door?"

"The earthquake…?" And then Spielman realized what he had in mind. "But they might be listening to her phone."

Ruben pulled on a denim jacket, grinning, his eyebrows dancing mischievously. "Don't worry. I'll be back soon."

Ruben grabbed what he needed from the earthquake kit and jumped into his vintage Mustang, fired it up and headed for a market out of his immediate neighborhood. There was one where Hollywood and Sunset converged, and when he got there, he parked the glistening scarlet muscle car well away from others in the lot. He was always careful about dings but at the moment, what he was more concerned about was ensuring privacy for his call.

He felt proud that he could do this to help Travis, who did everything to provide for their little family. It was Travis who had insisted after 9/11 that they purchase a couple of throwaway cell phones, and Travis who had programmed the phone they kept in the earthquake emergency kit to play a blaring rendition of "When the Saints Go Marching In" that could be heard from anywhere in the house. After they adopted Melanie, Travis began to insist that if Ruben went out during the day, he check the phone for messages the minute he returned. The plan was that if Travis got wind of an impending terrorist attack on Los Angeles, he would call the earthquake phone and leave a coded message, Ruben's cue to grab Mellie and head to his family's cabin outside Cedar City, Iowa. If the worst happened, Travis wanted his family to survive.

Sitting in the market parking lot, Ruben dialed Hannah's cell phone and hoped it went to voice mail. He wasn't sure he could pull this off if she answered. He was in luck. As he listened to her away message, he ran a finger along the bright chrome console between the Mustang's black leather seats. It was a little crazy, keeping this car. It barely accommodated a child seat in back, and getting a handicapped child in and out of a two-door sport car would only get more difficult as she grew bigger. One day he might have to break down and sell it, but it would feel like abandoning an old friend.

When the beep of Hannah's voice mail sounded in his ear, he shifted his voice into a falsetto impression of his sister so dead-on that it could fool their mother. "Hello, sweetie, it's Monica." He pronounced the name with the Spanish long *o*. "My kittens are ready to leave their mama. They're going fast, so if you want one, you gotta call me *before* you go out of town. Okay, sweetie? You be sure and call me before you leave town, please."

Ruben disconnected, and then got out of the car and walked into the market, grinning. Finally, this talent of his might be coming in useful. He was a big man, built like a football player, but the female impersonations he'd been doing since his teens could bring down the house. He'd led a colorful life before Travis, but he'd toned down things in recent years. He didn't march in Gay Pride parades anymore, didn't wear such bright clothes, and didn't do the impersonation thing except with family and very close friends. But Hannah had been at a party at their house one night when Ruben had grabbed his sister's shawl and burst into full-on Monica Hernandez before segueing into Peggy Lee. His finale had been an imitation of Hannah herself. Their neighbor had laughed until she cried. He felt sure she'd recognize the name of the sister she'd met that night and put it together with Ruben, who called everyone "sweetie" when he did the act.

Hannah would understand that Ruben and Travis were trying to warn her, he told himself. She'd call back on this number to let "Monica" know. After she did,

Ruben would ditch the phone and buy a new one for the earthquake kit.

Hannah *would* get the message. She had to.

# *Nine*

Hannah's day had gotten off to bad start with the call from her ex-husband and the hasty detour to Dahlby Hall to meet with the assistant headmaster, but when she got to LAX, things began to look up. As she approached the e-ticket check-in kiosk, a woman on a nearby bench folded her newspaper, stood up and headed toward her.

"Hannah Nicks?"

"Guilty as charged."

"Joe Towle had another commitment this afternoon, but he got your message. I'm here to walk you through security, just in case anyone challenges your air marshal's identification."

"That's great, except since I didn't hear back from him, I left my weapon and his toys locked in the trunk of my car."

"No problem. I'll wait here while you go and get them." The woman shook out her newspaper and turned back to the bench. As she did, a sheet of white copy paper slipped out. She caught it deftly as it wafted down, but not before Hannah caught sight of the digital image of a woman who looked remarkably like herself.

Sprinting back to the parking lot was a minor inconvenience that proved well worth the effort when the agent walked her past hellishly long security lines that snaked from the departures area back to the check-in counters and out the door onto the sidewalks. Spring break travelers probably accounted for most of the congestion, but Hannah also recalled hearing something on the radio about a change in the feds' rainbow threat system—to orange? Crimson? Chartreuse? She couldn't remember and didn't really care. Like most people, she was beginning to tune out the hysteria. The American public wasn't as stupid as its government liked to think, and they got it that fearmongering these days had less to do with new terrorist threats than with politicians trying to knock their own shenanigans off the front page. But security at LAX was never less than a snarl, so getting a walk-through anytime was a gift.

When the pre-boarding for her flight was announced, the attendants fell over themselves to help her stow the padded art portfolio safely in the same closet where they kept their personal items, and her roomy leather seat at the front of the plane allowed her to keep a watchful eye on it. Working for the rich and powerful had its advantages, Hannah thought, taking a regretful pass on the champagne in first class while the rabble tried to shoehorn themselves into coach. She could have used a drink after the morning she'd had, but there'd be time for margaritas on the beach after the painting was delivered. In the meantime, it was better she kept a clear head.

The two-hour flight down the West Coast passed quickly. On its final approach into Puerto Vallarta, the plane circled out over the Pacific, then banked inland again, allowing a view of miles of pristine beaches, a yacht- and cruise ship-studded harbor and dozens of lush, sprawling resorts. This was her second visit to the city. She'd come down for a weekend getaway a couple of years back with a guy she was dating at the time. The resort had been great, the guy not so much when she realized his insatiable tequila thirst brought out a loud redneck disdain for any culture not his own.

At Mexican Customs, a cagey agent examined her documents, glanced around to make sure his supervisor was well down the line, then leaned over and murmured that the goods she was carrying might have to be impounded for further examination. He changed his tune when Hannah held up her import permit and inquired in flawless and very audible Spanish whether his superiors approved of him soliciting bribes from visitors upon whom the local economy depended. Apparently not, judging by the speed at which he stamped her passport and waved her through.

Outside the secure arrivals area, she spotted her name

scrawled on a piece of cardboard. Actually, it said "Ana Nix," but close enough. The man holding the placard was an inch or two shorter than she was but built like a Humvee, with blunt, powerful hands and a broad barrel chest. His leathery features were broad and flat, his nose displaying evidence of having been broken more than once.

"I'm Hannah Nicks," she said. "You're expecting me, I think?"

"You are late, *señora*."

She nodded. "Sorry. Family emergency. I had to take a later flight."

He grunted and reached for the portfolio, but she handed him her backpack instead. "Please, this is so much heavier." Better to play the helpless female than to let the painting out of her hands.

The driver hesitated, then took her bag and turned on his heel.

Outside the air-conditioned terminal building, a wall of hot, humid tropical air slammed into her. The sun was brilliant, turning the low stucco buildings of the airport and surrounding neighborhood into a world of bleached bones—a pleasantly ocean scented world, though, tinged with the spice and charcoal smells of a nearby taqueria. In the blistering heat, she was tempted to slip out of her lightweight jacket, but the gun holstered at her back made that inadvisable.

The driver led her to a late-model black Cadillac. At the chirp of his key fob, the trunk lid rose. He dropped in her backpack, but by the time he turned to reach for the portfolio, Hannah had already slipped it into the backseat and climbed in behind. Frowning, he closed her door and moved around to the driver's side. The car's interior was stifling. Why drive a black car with black leather seats when you lived in a tropical climate?

The car dipped as the stocky driver got into the front.

"Excuse me, what's your name?" Hannah asked.

He started the motor, then glanced in the mirror. "Sergio."

"Would you mind turning on the air-conditioning, Sergio?"

"Broken," he muttered. Shifting into gear, he peeled away from the terminal building, narrowly missing a hotel bus taking on passengers.

The window buttons on the door handle didn't work any better than the AC, she discovered. Child locks, maybe? "I can't get this window to go down."

"Broken."

*Great.* She slid across the seat, but the window on the other side was also on the fritz, it seemed. She leaned back on the headrest and closed her eyes. If Moises Gladding was such a rip-roaring success in the arms trade, you'd think he could spring for better wheels—or at least a good mechanic. The driver's window did work, however, and Sergio opened it now, letting in a little breeze. It mightn't have been so bad if she'd arrived earlier in the day as planned, but this was the hour when sensible people took siestas. Might explain Sergio's crankiness.

He turned north up the coast highway, but after a mile or so, they veered east. If the coastal area was a tourist playground, then inland, Hannah recalled, was the domain of the working and farming population that supported the booming vacation industry in what was called the Mexican Riviera. Palm trees gave way to market gardens, cattle rancheros and chicken farms, the terrain dotted with yucca trees and prickly cactus. After about thirty minutes of ever-increasing speeds and ever-diminishing signs of population, paved highway gave way to potholed macadam. A few miles after that, they were on dusty washboard gravel.

Hadn't Rebecca Powell said Gladding had a vacation home down here? Was it obsession with security, Hannah wondered, that would lead the arms dealer to build so far from the coast?

A flock of chickens flapped irritably as the Cadillac roared around a curve in the road and past a small red adobe farmhouse. A boy herding goats shaded his eyes to watch them pass. Soon, even farms seemed to peter out, leaving nothing but rock-strewn, sandy soil and the occasional spindly eucalyptus or cactus as far as the eye could see.

Warning bells began pinging in her brain. Unless the scenery changed fast, this was no place for a vacation villa. She glanced at the driver in the rearview mirror. His sunglasses obscured his eyes, but he seemed intent on the road ahead. Her hand reached out for the door handle and she did a test pull. No give. She tugged harder, but it was undeniably locked. Also "broken"? Or designed like the back of a police cruiser, keeping the occupant in until someone decided to let him out.

With a watchful eye on Sergio, she slid her hand behind her back and unsnapped her holster, taking comfort in the hard steel of her Beretta. Slipping it from the holster, she tucked it under her right thigh, her thumb on the safety, ready to flick it off at the first sign of trouble.

*Damn.*

She was tired. The day had started badly, and pleasant flight notwithstanding, she was now tense and primed for trouble. Maybe she was wrong about the way things were going here, but she hadn't kept herself alive this long by ignoring her gut. If old Sergio there tried to pull anything while she was locked in, she'd shoot the little schmuck. If he pulled over and hauled her out of the car for whatever reason, she was pretty sure she could take him down, despite his blocky build. A win-win scenario, she decided, although her bravado did little to soothe the unease in her gut or the tension building in her shoulders.

She was ready, however, when Sergio suddenly yanked the wheel to the right and careened off the road and into a sandy clearing. He climbed out with scarcely a glance back, but by the time he opened her door, he had a pistol in his hand and a nervous stance that told her he hadn't necessarily done this before. Not good. Amateurs were often the most dangerous adversaries because anything could set them off and their aim was pretty random.

Hannah tried to come across as fearful and unthreat-
ening. "What's going on here? What are you doing?"

"Get out."

She calculated the odds of getting the drop on him
now, but her range of motion was limited, as was her
line of fire. He had the tactical advantage for the
moment, but that could change quickly, especially if he
underestimated the *gringa* in the backseat. She decided
to play to that scenario.

"Please, why are you doing this?" The tremble in her
voice was a nice touch, she thought. "What do you want?"

"I want you to get out of the car, *señora*. Now."

"Are you going to hurt me?"

"Not if you do as you are told."

"All right. Just don't hurt me, please."

Sergio waved the gun barrel. "Get out. Now, if you
please."

She kept her body between him and the Beretta as
she climbed out. Her brain was racing. This made no
sense. If this guy really worked for Gladding, it had to
be a double cross. Gladding had already paid for the
Koon, so he had no reason to steal it. But if Sergio
wasn't working for Moises Gladding, then how had he
known she was coming and what she'd be carrying? Or,
she suddenly thought, was it about the painting at all?
Could it be the guy was just your garden variety rapist?

Sergio scowled, keeping the gun trained on her. But
then, she caught a break. He turned the weapon sideways, the way he'd probably seen street thugs do in

movies. She resisted the impulse to roll her eyes. No professional ever held a gun like that. You shoot a semi-automatic in that position, you get peppered with red-hot casings as they eject skyward from the side of the gun—assuming they eject at all. Gravity works, so more often than not, the slide jams as the bullet casings try to clear and the weapon becomes useless.

Playing gangbanger was Sergio's first mistake. His second was taking a step back without looking where he was going, narrowly missing a snake that was coiled around a rock near his feet. The snake moved just enough in his peripheral vision to draw his glance away for a split second.

It was all the time she needed. Her boot connected with his gun arm, sending the weapon flying into a clump of dusty sagebrush. As he wheeled to grab for it, her left hand chopped the side of his neck. Sergio crumpled to his knees, his face filled with pain and bewilderment. She kicked the fallen gun further out of his reach, then raised her own weapon where he could see it.

"Get up."

He stumbled to his feet.

"Turn around and face the car." She slammed him down on the hood, securing his arm in a hammerlock. "Who are you working for?"

No answer.

She wrenched his arm until he whimpered. She leaned forward and murmured in his ear. "Do not make me ask again, Sergio."

"No one."

Hannah elicited a little elaboration.

"Ow, ow! Please, *señora!* Señor Gladding sent me. He told me a courier was arriving with a painting that he had bought."

"So then what are we doing here? I don't see Mr. Gladding anywhere, do you?"

"A man," the driver panted. "My cousin knows a man in Mazatlán who will buy this painting."

"A fence? Someone who buys stolen art?"

He nodded. Made sense, she thought. Assuming the fence paid ten cents on the dollar, Sergio could still expect a $25,000 payday on a quarter-million-dollar painting. Even splitting it with his cousin made for a decent return in a country where most people earned a few thousand dollars a year.

But was it worth crossing a character like Gladding?

"Please, *señora,* I have a family."

"You should have thought of that before, my friend." Did he even know how his erstwhile boss earned his money, or the reach of the man's tentacles? No way. Nobody could be that stupid.

She glanced around. A eucalyptus tree stood a little way off, its bark peeling and rough. She used her jacket sleeve to wipe her forehead. The day was excruciatingly hot and the back of her T-shirt was plastered to her skin.

"Lift your foot onto the hood of the car," she told him. When he did, she pressed the muzzle of her gun into his neck, then used her free hand to work the laces out of his well-worn Puma sneakers. "Now the other one." She took the lace out of that one, too, then used one hand and her teeth to knot the laces together. She gave him a shove toward the tree.

"No, please," he said, as she had him lean against the tree and bring his wrists together around the back. "No one comes down this road. I will die if you leave me out here."

"Yeah, like that wasn't just what you had planned for me."

She looped the laces around his wrists, then yanked tight. The slipknot she tied would take him at least an hour to work free, but it wasn't impossible. As she lifted the car keys from his pants pocket, she remembered the bottle of water she'd carried off the plane. Retrieving it from her backpack, she brought it back to him and held it to his lips. After he'd taken couple of swigs, she set the bottle at his feet.

"Just so you know I have a heart," she said. "Good thing you wore comfy shoes, my friend. You've got a long walk ahead of you—if you manage to get free, that is."

"Please, *señora,* I am sorry. Do not leave me here."

She picked up his gun and stuck it in her waistband. "Let this be a lesson, Sergio. It's very rude to hijack guests." She waggled her fingers over her shoulder. *"Adios, amigo."*

*Amateurs,* she thought disgustedly, slipping into the Cadillac. She gunned the motor and headed back to town.

# *Ten*

His other sins notwithstanding, Sergio had told the truth about the car's air-conditioning. It was as dead as roadkill. With the Cadillac rocking down the washboard road, Hannah dropped both front windows and wriggled out of her jacket. Open windows meant breathing dust, but better that than passing out from heat exhaustion. April was the middle of the dry season down here anyway, and the Mexican Riviera was also suffering through an extended drought that hadn't brought rain in over a year. Global warming would not be kind to Central America.

She picked at her damp T-shirt, pulling it away from her skin. This trip was suddenly looking less and less like the quick turnaround she'd anticipated. She still had to find her way to Moises Gladding, who must be wondering by now where his painting had gotten to. As for planting the bugs that Special Agents Towle and Ito had given her…well, she'd cross that bridge when she came to it.

"Try to get these laid in, no matter what else happens down there," Towle had said. "Any problem, just give me a call."

Right. She pulled out her cell phone and glanced at the screen. She'd turned it on after her plane had landed, half-dreading more messages from Cal about problems with Gabe and what a lousy mother she was. She'd had a roaming signal at the airport, but her only message was a very bizarre one about kittens from someone named Monica who had a heavy Hispanic accent. Obviously a wrong number. Out here, she had bupkis—no messages and no signal. Sergio seemed to have taken her beyond the satellite footprint for her phone service. Murphy's Law.

She could try to reach Agent Towle from town, but there was no guarantee he'd be any more available now than he had been when she'd tried to call him that morning to let him know about her delayed departure. Then another thought struck her. She dragged her backpack across the front seat and rummaged in the side pockets, looking for the second business card Towle had given her the night before.

"An emergency contact, in case you run into any problems down there."

At the time, she'd been a little miffed that he thought she might need help on such a routine job. On the other hand, she *had* been wearing Garfield flannel pajamas when they showed up at her door, so maybe they could be pardoned for doubting her competence. Now, she wondered if Towle had known more than he was letting on about what she might face down here.

But with Gladding's driver out of the picture, she had no idea where to find his villa. While she could have grilled Sergio for the location, he was just as likely to send her into the clutches of his sleazy cousin or the art fence. Better to rely on her own devices—or Agent Towle's.

It was a simple enough matter to backtrack along the path Gladding's driver had taken from the airport, heading westward to the coastal road, then south again toward town. According to Towle, the local contact's bar was on the boardwalk, not far from Puerto Vallarta's main cathedral. She would head for the cathedral, then ask around for directions to The Blue Gecko.

Finding the Cathedral of Our Lady of Guadalupe would be no problem. She remembered it from her last visit, a redbrick church at the heart of the old town with a crownlike tower that was said to be modeled after a tiara worn by the mad wife of Emperor Maximilian. The Austrian Hapsburg prince had ruled Mexico for a couple of years in the 1860s after he was drafted by conservative landowners hoping to spawn some local royalty and hold back the rising tide of democracy. Turned out most Mexicans didn't want an imported emperor. They shot Maximilian, but the crazy Empress's sparkly tiara must have passed muster, since they topped a landmark church with a facsimile.

Hannah easily spotted the crown over the tiled

rooftops and sparkling white adobe buildings of the old town. The Malecón, a brick-lined seafront strollway near the cathedral, was packed with tourists, but eventually she found a parking spot. She tucked Sergio's gun into her backpack and locked it in the trunk of the Caddy, then shrugged back into her light linen jacket, checking her reflection in the car window to make sure it concealed the holster at the small of her back. The way her day was going, she was disinclined to venture out unarmed. Grabbing the leather portfolio from the backseat, she locked the car and headed toward the Malecón.

She was about to ask a boardwalk street vendor hawking silver chains for directions to The Blue Gecko when she spotted a hand-painted sign with an indigo lizard cavorting in a sombrero. A striped blue-and-white awning shaded a broad patio packed with tourists nursing umbrella drinks while they ogled the colorful parade of strolling sightseers and the bikini-clad girls on the beach beyond.

Inside the bar was another story. It was dimly lit and smelled of beer and whiskey that had probably been marinating the scuffed plank floors for decades. A few tables along the outer walls were occupied by middle-aged men with watery, bloodshot eyes, ropy bodies and weathered, leathered skin. No sweet mixed umbrella drinks in here. Every heavy Mexican glass tumbler held amber-colored liquid, straight up. The snatches of conversation she caught were all in English, but no one gave her a second glance. Not for this bunch the eager people-watching of the fanny-pack-wearing tourists.

The Blue Gecko, she guessed, was the watering hole of choice for a certain class of American expatriate. If she had to guess, she'd say they were ex-military or special-forces types looking to stretch their pension dollars by retiring to Puerto Vallarta's well-established "Gringo Gulch."

Under a faux Tiffany pendant lamp on the far side of the room, a lethargic game of pool was being played on a table that showed a couple of visible ripples in the green felt. Would make for some interesting bank shots, Hannah thought. A neon-rimmed clock advertising Dos Equis beer hung on the wall behind the table, its hands both dropped like those of a shy man caught naked in the shower. Hannah glanced at her watch. Just past five. Clearly, the clock was busted.

High over one end of the dark wood bar stained by countless glass rims, a basketball game played out on a wall-mounted flat-screen TV. The bartender, middle-aged and obviously American, stood polishing a bubbled glass as he and a young blond guy on a bar-end stool ran a desultory commentary on the game. The blonde had a fat lip under a bruised and swollen right eye. Aside from the action on the ESPN satellite feed, the only real energy in the room came from the Mexican waiters running drink and food orders to the tourists out on the patio.

Hannah settled herself on a stool at the opposite end

of the bar from the guy with the fat lip, tucking the leather art portfolio into the space in front of her knees. The game on the television was Los Angeles vs. Dallas. A basket of corn chips and a small dish of salsa materialized in front of her.

"Get you something?"

The bartender was in his fifties, she guessed, broad shouldered and ruddy complexioned. Graying hair curled over the collar of his plaid shirt. The head of a tattooed snake peeked out from one of his rolled-back sleeves, while the other forearm sported the crossed swords and dagger logo of the Green Berets. Yup, just as she'd thought. A special forces kind of joint.

"Can I get an iced coffee and some bottled water?"

"You bet." He went away and came back a couple of minutes later with her drinks. Setting them down, he followed her gaze up to the TV. "You like basketball?"

"I like it okay. This is last night's game, no?"

He nodded and cocked his thumb at the guy who looked like something out of a hamburger grinder. "Kevvie down there is a big Lakers fan. Doesn't have a TV at his place so he comes in to catch the games. Got into a little altercation last night, though, and missed the last half of the Dallas matchup."

"Missed the game, and now maybe he's missing a couple of teeth, too?"

"Yeah, well, only goes to show he should watch his mouth when there's Texans in the place. Lucky for him ESPN was rebroadcasting today."

Hannah lowered her voice to a murmur. "So I guess I shouldn't tell him the Lakers lost?"

"Ah, no. Guy's already hurtin'. That would be too cruel." He watched her down the entire bottle of water, then turn to the iced coffee. "You sure I can't get you anything else?"

"This'll do for now. Except you could tell me something."

"What's that?"

"Your name Donald Ackerman?"

He seemed taken aback. "Yeah, could be. Who's asking?"

Hannah slid Agent Towle's card across the bar. Ackerman lifted it up, read the engraved side, then checked the other side. "You're Special Agent Joseph Towle?"

She rolled her eyes. "Yeah, right. He gave me your name, wise guy."

"I don't know the man."

"Funny, since he seems to know something about you." She slid his own business card to him, the one featuring the same sombrero-wearing gecko pictured on the sign over the patio outside.

A low roar went up from the arena crowd on the television, followed by a groan from the guy down the bar. Hannah glanced up. The Lakers were about to get their wiry little butts kicked. Poor Kevvie.

Ackerman glanced around the room, then picked up her iced coffee. "Follow me."

Hannah grabbed the portfolio. He led her through a beaded curtain to the right of the bar. A short-order cook was in the kitchen grilling onions, peppers and chicken and folding them into tortillas as a waiter stood by with salad-loaded plates, waiting to carry the food out. What was it about the smell of fried onions? Hannah wondered, mouth watering. She hadn't eaten since lunch on the plane (thank God for first-class service), and it was getting on to dinnertime. First things first, though.

Ackerman continued on to a tiny office at the back of the kitchen. He dropped heavily into a rolling chair and shifted a stack of papers to make room on the desk for her iced coffee. Then he indicated a plastic chair for her.

"So," he said, "this Agent Towle said you should see me. I got no heads-up you were coming. What do you want?"

"First of all, who are you?"

"I'm a guy owns a bar. Who are you?"

"My name's Hannah Nicks. Who do you work for?"

There was something unmistakable about your average former covert ops guy, she thought, a combination of world-weary cynicism and a body not quite gone soft. They had the look of characters who never entirely let down their guard. If she had to guess, she'd say Ackerman here had gone from the Green Berets right into the CIA.

"I work for myself," he answered. "Like I said, I'm just a barkeep."

"These days."

He shrugged. "These days. And you? Working for who?"

"Also myself. Freelance security, usually. Courier work, at the moment. I've got a delivery for Moises Gladding but somebody tried to hijack the shipment. I need to get back on track."

"You making this delivery to Moises's house?"

"'Moises'? He a friend of yours?"

"I know lots of people down here. It's a small community. Who did the hijacking?"

"A driver named Sergio. Claimed to be working for Gladding but he tried to do an end run and steal the shipment I was bringing in."

Ackerman frowned. "Yeah, I know the guy. Sergio Chavez. Huh. Pretty dumb, trying to rip off Moises Gladding. But it makes sense, I guess."

"How so?"

"Oh, his wife used to be the cook out at Moises's place. Apparently she and Gladding's mistress had a set-to, though. The mistress got her fired, I heard. Guess Sergio figured it was payback time. Still, only a moron tries to steal from Moises."

"Yeah, not to mention trying to mug me in the middle of nowhere. Thanks for your concern, though."

"Oh, yeah, well, that too, goes without saying. Sorry. You're obviously okay, though."

She grimaced.

"So what happened to Sergio?" Ackerman asked.

"I left him tied up ten, fifteen miles outside of town. He may have worked himself free by now. He's got a long walk ahead of him. Meantime, I need to know how to find Gladding's place."

"He's got a beachfront villa about five miles south of the city. I'll take you there."

"No, I'd better go alone. He's expecting me. Just draw me a map."

Ackerman still had Agent Towle's card, and he tapped it on the table now. "You're making this delivery for the feds?"

She took back the card. The first rule of the spook business was "need to know," as this guy well knew. Ackerman had no operational need to know what she was and wasn't doing for the feds.

"How about you just draw me that map? Much obliged."

"You should really think about backup, especially the way your day's going."

"Yeah, thanks for the offer, but I can handle myself."

He shrugged and pulled a pencil out of a tin can and rummaged around on his desk until he found an old envelope. "Your funeral."

He spent the next few minutes scratching on the envelope and pointing out landmarks she should watch for. Then she followed Ackerman back to the front of the place. He returned to the bar, where Kevvie was complaining loudly about how much the Lakers sucked. Hannah headed out the door, but when she paused to hold it for a waiter going back in with a tray of dirty dishes, she happened to glance back.

Ackerman was paying no attention to Kevvie's critique of the Lakers. He was too busy dialing his cell phone.

# *Eleven*

A wave broke on the rocks beneath the cliff, sending spray high into the air. Blinded by the mist on the windshield, Hannah scrambled to find the Caddy's wiper switch without taking her eyes off the twisting road.

If the inland terrain north of Puerto Vallarta was made up of dry, rolling plains dotted with small villages and rancheros, the southern terrain was more rugged. The Sierra Madre mountain range ran close to shore here, squeezing the highway between dense hillside jungle and jagged coastline.

She could rappel up tall buildings or parachute out of an aircraft without hesitation, but careening around switchbacks that overlooked steep, rocky precipices was the stuff of her nightmares. Had Gladding's driver not turned out to be a thief, she fumed, she would have spent the drive up the coast dozing in the backseat, thinking pleasant thoughts about ten-thousand-dollar paydays and canoodling with John Russo. Instead, she was white-knuckle hurtling along a narrow, roller-coaster road in a boat of a car, hoping the damn brakes had been serviced more recently than the nonexistent air conditioner.

Nor could she take her time. The sun was beginning to sink and the transfer of the painting to its new owner was hours overdue. When she'd finally gotten a cell phone signal in town, she'd found a panicky message from Rebecca Powell, wanting to know where she was and, more to the point, why the painting hadn't been delivered. No doubt Gladding had been in touch with his buyer, demanding to know the same thing. Hannah had tried calling back to relate what had happened, but she'd gotten the gallery's voice mail. All she could do was leave a message, then bust her hump to hand over the canvas ASAP.

She wondered about the return trip to Puerto Vallarta. Although she was bringing back his Cadillac sans chauffeur, Moises Gladding would surely feel obliged to arrange for her transport back to town, even if he had to drive her himself. Not her fault the household help was rebelling. This was an object lesson in trusting her gut, she decided. She hadn't wanted to take this job, but she'd let herself be wheedled by her sister, by Rebecca's hard-luck divorce story, and by her own anemic finances.

*An easy gig, my foot. First-class travel, resort on the beach, fat paycheck. Yeah, right.*

No way she'd get in any serious beach time now. She

was scheduled to fly back tomorrow at noon. If she got up early enough, there might be time for a fast swim and maybe picking up a souvenir for Gabe. At the very least, she vowed, she'd have a decent dinner tonight on Gladding's tab. This resort where she was supposed to be checked in, would it have a spa? Open late, maybe, so she could get a massage to work out the insanity of this day? If not, she'd settle for margaritas and a Jacuzzi.

When the road straightened a little, she chanced another glance at Ackerman's map. The barkeep had said that Gladding's villa was just past the turnoff to a place called Santa Rosa.

"Slow down as soon as you see the sign for the village. His place is just beyond, right on the oceanfront. There's a gate and a guardhouse, so you'll have to be buzzed in. The man's a little tetchy about security."

*Well, duh…*

When she finally spotted the blue road sign announcing the inland turn toward Santa Rosa, she slowed. About an eighth of a mile later, a wide, paved driveway veered off toward an oceanfront property surrounded by tall trees and a very high stone wall topped with broken glass. The guard hut next to the wide, black wrought-iron gate had been designed to look like a tiny adobe house. It stood amidst heavy greenery—banana trees and pink and yellow blooming hibiscus. The gate looked impregnable, the kind of gate that screams rich and paranoid.

She pulled the Caddy up to the hut. The guard was bound to recognize the car as belonging to his boss, she imagined, so she'd have to do some quick-stepping around the awkward subject of how a *gringa* had ended up alone behind the wheel.

No guard showed himself, however. She waited, fingers thrumming the steering wheel. She was tempted to lean on the horn, but in light of Rebecca's panicky message, it didn't seem wise to annoy the client any more than she already had. Maybe the guard was on a bathroom break.

After another minute, she climbed out of the car. She glanced at the roadway, but she hadn't seen more than two or three cars since leaving town, and there wasn't a soul in sight now. She peered up the driveway beyond the gate. The roadway curved off to the right, making it impossible to see the house. Except for the distant crashing of surf, the place was shrouded in silence. No birdsong, no voices. No dogs barking to announce the arrival of a stranger.

Well, maybe Gladding didn't own a dog. Still, the unnatural quiet set off alarm bells. She reached behind her back and cautiously unsnapped her holster, keeping a hand on the butt of her weapon, just in case.

Inching forward, she peered into the window of the guard kiosk. No one there and no one in sight. She opened the door at the side, but the hut was deserted. There was a low counter and a desk chair, and the remains of someone's lunch. A rotary dial phone was mounted on the wall, the receiver out of the cradle and dangling by its cord. It looked to have been dropped in a hurry, but not very recently, judging by its stillness.

She drew her gun and backtracked out the door, holding the weapon down as she peered around both sides of the guard hut. Zip. Keeping one eye on the car, she sidled up to the wrought-iron gate. When she gave it a tentative shove, it swung silently inward on well-oiled hinges. Bad sign.

She debated what to do. Ideally, she would have preferred to proceed on foot rather than have a car engine announce her arrival, but the way her day was going, she'd rather not leave the painting behind in the road. Bad enough she was late. She wasn't going to lose the thing now. Nor would she have either agility or much surprise factor if she schlepped it up the driveway. She paused to listen again, but still perceived nothing but eerie silence. Experience said that whatever had happened here was already finished.

She pushed the gate all the way open, then returned to the Caddy and eased it up the wide driveway. The rust-colored pavers drew an undulating curve through lush greenery that met overhead, casting the waning light of day into even deeper relief. It felt like moving through a bad fairy tale with a wolf or wicked witch ready to spring from the shadows.

A few hundred yards up, the way cleared and the driveway divided, wrapping itself around a stone dolphin leaping from a circular fountain tiled in bright blue and white ceramic squares. A broad bed of red, white and purple flowers surrounded the fountain. On the far side of the fountain stood a sprawling tan brick hacienda fronted with graceful arches that opened onto a deep veranda. Bloodred bougainvillea spilled down the pillars holding up the arches.

A lush lawn rolled away from either side of the circular driveway. An old and dented truck was parked off to one side, the red pickup so battered that it was hard to know exactly where paint left off and rust began. The truck's bed gate was down. A gas lawnmower stood abandoned on the lawn nearby, but the gardener was as MIA as everyone else in this idyllic coastal ghost scene.

Hannah parked the Cadillac and slipped out, her weapon close to her side. Keeping herself low, she approached the front of the house. Up a couple of broad steps and across the broad, blue-tiled veranda, a double set of heavily carved wooden doors stood slightly ajar. A man lay sprawled on his back across the open doorway, boots toward her. He was dressed in crumpled khaki, a straw hat and pair of grass clippers fallen on the tiles beside him.

The gardener, then. By the stillness of those boots and the heavy spray of blood on the threshold and on the front of his shirt, she had little doubt that he was dead.

Flicking the safety off her weapon, she backed away and pivoted, flinching as she caught sight of another man sitting on the floor of the veranda, his back against one of the pillars. He was staring at her with dead black eyes. A third eye had sprouted in the middle of his forehead, but this one had dripped red. The missing guard from the gate, she guessed by his blue uniform.

She turned, taking a full scan of the area. There were no obvious threat indicators in her line of sight, but that didn't mean the danger wasn't there. She was a sitting duck out in the open like this.

Mounting the front steps in a couple of strides, she backed up against one of the arches of the veranda. Something sharp stabbed her in the shoulder. She cursed under her breath. Damn bougainvillea—gorgeous color, killer thorns. She pulled free of the wicked barb and felt a trickle of blood run down her arm.

She inched toward the inside wall of the veranda, regretting now that she hadn't accepted Ackerman's offer of backup. On the other hand, the way this day was going, who was to say the former spook hadn't known what she'd walk into here? Was that hasty phone call to let his buddy Moises know she was on her way?

Keeping the mass of her body low, gun doublegripped at the ready, she headed left along the front of the house, stealing quick glances around each of the veranda arches as she passed. When she reached a large window covered with a decorative grille, the glass spider-cracked with two bullet holes, she took a look inside.

The expansive interior had polished wood floors scattered with bright Mexican rugs, gracious white adobe walls broken by gentle archways, and several large, vibrant canvases displayed in the spaces between the arches. Three or four conversation groupings of heavy, carved chairs and tables were arranged around the room.

A rosewood grand piano, its lid propped open, angled across the far corner of the room. The polished body of the instrument bore angry-looking wounds that looked to have been made by the overspray of large-caliber bullets.

The wall behind the piano was splattered with a florid bloom of red. A bloody trail led from there to a nearby doorway but Hannah saw no sign of a body. Someone had lived long enough to crawl away.

Gladding? Armed and waiting for the return of whoever had launched this assault? Wonderful, Hannah thought, just freakin' wonderful. Some days it didn't pay to get out of bed.

She took a deep breath and continued her circuit of the exterior of the house. At every door, every window, she stopped and checked inside without entering. Old police habits die hard—first clear the perimeter, only then venture inside.

At the back of the villa she found two more bodies. An Asian-looking man was crumpled on the grass, shot twice, once in the leg, once up close, just over the bridge of his nose. She crouched and gingerly touched the still body. Still warm, with no sign of rigor.

In a cool climate, a body lost a couple of degrees of heat an hour, while rigor began to show in the small muscles of the face and digits after a couple of hours. Given the warm ambient temperature down here, however, all bets were off. She reached out and touched her forefinger to a drop of blood on a rock. A skin was beginning to form on the surface, suggesting it was probably less than an hour since this massacre had gone down. She wiped her finger clean in the grass.

The second body at the back of the house was that of a young woman. She was floating facedown in a kidney-shaped swimming pool, her dark hair streaming around her head. It almost looked like the dye in her red bikini had run, staining the water around her, but Hannah knew that wasn't fabric dye scumming up the blue coping tiles at the pool's edge. She couldn't see where the woman had been shot.

A quick check around and in the pool cabana turned up nothing. When she had completed her circuit of the house, she stopped once more at the body on the threshold. Everything she'd seen here said her first intuition had been correct—whatever had happened here was over.

Unless, of course, the assassin was holed up inside the house.

She studied the body of the gardener lying on the threshold. Poor guy. In the wrong place at the wrong time. Like the security guard and the Asian man at the back of the house, he'd taken two bullets, one in the chest and one in the head to finish him off. The killings were thorough, deliberate, methodical, carried out with a large-caliber weapon. Whoever had done this was determined to leave no witnesses. It was the work of a professional.

She looked at the gardener's scuffed boots. Their worn heels matched the impression of some of the footprints she'd spotted in the cleanly raked flower beds as she'd circled the house, but there'd been others there, too—three different sets. Athletic shoes, she surmised. Three different sizes and brands. One set was Nike, but she didn't recognize the other print patterns. All of the shoe prints were large. She was no expert at estimating size, but one of them had to be a thirteen or fourteen, she calculated, remembering her ex-husband's big ol' size elevens.

Donald Ackerman's hefty size popped into her mind, but it couldn't have been him. These victims hadn't been dead long enough for him to have participated in this massacre, then made it back to The Blue Gecko in time for her to find him there.

She stepped over the gardener and into the house. Moving quietly from room to room, she kept her body low, gun at the ready. It was the stance she'd learned in police academy and it had stood her in good stead over the years. Most perps expected to see a person come around the corner at shoulder height. The split second it took for them to spot the lower stance was all the tactical advance she needed to get the drop.

She went into the sitting room. The blood trail from the piano led out a door on the other side of the room and down a hallway, ending at an atrium in the center of the house. There, Hannah found a housekeeper in black uniform and white apron lying facedown, half underneath a glass table where she'd stopped crawling and taken cover. Hannah reached down with her free hand to feel for a pulse at the carotid artery. Nothing.

Then she saw the blood matted in the woman's black hair. Like the others, the maid had received a coup de grâce where she lay. Definitely a professional job.

Disgusted, she turned and followed her nose, which was picking up a smell of burned toast. In the kitchen, black smoke was leaking from around the edges of the oven door. The light inside the oven showed two charred loaves on a flat baking sheet. Across the room, the cook had fallen in front of the open refrigerator.

Using the hem of her T-shirt so as not to leave any fingerprints, Hannah turned off the oven but left the loaves inside. She was off her turf here. She needed to beat it before the *federales* arrived.

The words of Agent Towle came back to her. "Let's just say that Gladding is reported to be associated with people to whom Washington would prefer not to be linked, so no matter what you find when you get down there, try to plant these bugs."

No matter what she found? Did he have some forewarning of the mess she was blundering into?

No time to think about that now, but she'd be sure to ask him when she got back. Meantime…to plant or not to plant?

"What the hell…"

She dashed out to the Cadillac and returned with the listening devices, wiping each carefully before concealing them in the dining room, front parlor, the master bedroom.

In an office at the far end of the house, she located

a laptop computer. It was already turned on. Somebody had been logged on to the Internet, surfing porn sites. Lovely. Taking care not to leave any prints, she opened the CD tray and planted the keystroke logger.

If anyone found the bugs, it was no skin off her nose. On the other hand, if they didn't—and she was good at planting toys like this in locations where they were rarely found without the assistance of advanced detection equipment—they might yield useful information on who was after the arms dealer and why.

A competitor? A dissatisfied customer? A satisfied customer looking to cancel a debt? Whatever the case, it might reveal something about fault lines in the fractious international forces that Gladding serviced.

She had just finished placing the last bug inside an electrical outlet and was replacing the cover plate when she heard the sound of sirens in the distance. That was fast, she thought. But who would have called the police?

Hannah Nicks, independent cop for hire, mother of one, was not about to stick around to find out, much less try to explain her own presence there. Urban legends of Americans disappearing into Latin American jails, never to be seen again, looped through her mind.

She hustled back out to the Cadillac, but stopped in her tracks next to its big chrome grille. Not a good plan. Who knew where Moises Gladding was, or who might recognize his black Caddy?

She fished her backpack and the art portfolio out of the car, then used her jacket to hastily rub down anything she might have touched. She ran for the gardener's truck and tossed her stuff in the front seat. Jumping in, she reached for the ignition.

*Damn.* No keys.

Sprinting to the front door, she fished in the gardener's pockets until she found his keys. At the last second, she grabbed his straw hat and raced back to the truck. The sirens were sounding louder as she turned the key in the ignition.

The old pickup balked.

It coughed, then whined.

She stomped on the accelerator and tried again, praying that she wouldn't flood the thing. On the fourth try, the truck sputtered to life. Tucking her hair up inside the oversize hat, she pulled it low on her head, then roared down the driveway and past the guardhouse, careening on two wheels back onto the road toward Puerto Vallarta.

After about a hundred yards, she slowed the pickup to a sedate pace, an old beater huffing toward town, just as three police cruisers sped by in the opposite direction, sirens blasting.

Former Detective Superintendent William Teagarden was in the front passenger seat of the second of the three police cruisers. As they wheeled around a hairpin turn, Teagarden grabbed onto the safety grip above the door—what one of his former Scotland Yard colleagues used to call the "oh, Jesus! bar." He braced himself as the car ahead swerved into the oncoming lane, certain it was about to plow into a battered pickup truck approaching in the opposite direction. He only breathed again when the cruiser slid back into its lane at the last second, narrowly avoiding disaster.

"Lucky he wasn't speeding," he said of the pickup driver wearing a big straw hat.

Captain Luis Peña of the Puerto Vallarta Police shrugged. "Local peoples don't drive so fast here," he replied, shouting to be heard over the sirens. "Only the kids and *turistas*."

Teagarden nodded but kept his eyes fixed on the road ahead, convinced that only his rapt attention would forestall disaster.

He couldn't believe his timing. He'd dropped into local police headquarters to discuss stolen art and a possible lead on one case in particular, the van Gogh, the lead he'd picked up during his café breakfast in Prague with Shawn Britten, international art thief.

Captain Peña had turned out to be very interested in the subject, regaling Teagarden with a tale of recovering an ancient Mayan calendar stolen from a local museum.

"Well done," Teagarden had said. "Ninety percent of stolen art and artifacts are never recovered."

Peña's eyebrow shot up. "Is that so? Then it was very good work we did, was it not?"

"It certainly was."

Teagarden had guided the conversation around to foreigners who kept villas in the area, remembering the one Britten had said was working out of Mexico these days. Certain classes of wealthy individuals, Teagarden told Peña, were often the recipients of stolen masterworks. "We try to publicize every theft in order to have more eyes and ears on the ground, watching for them, but sometimes there's a downside to that."

"A downside?" Peña said.

"I'm afraid so. Every time the media refers to a stolen painting or sculpture as priceless, it raises the value of the illicit currency, making it that much easier for these thieves to use it in trade for other commodities."

Peña nodded. "A very big problem, naturally. So tell me, Señor Teagarden, what brings you to Puerto Vallarta? You have knowledge of a stolen item here? Perhaps purchased by one of our foreign residents?"

"Perhaps. There are only a few people who deal in the most valuable artifacts."

"And such a person lives here?"

"I have a report that a subject of interest may be here at the moment, yes. A man named Moises Gladding."

Peña nodded. "Ah, *sí.* Señor Gladding has a villa a few kilometers south of the town. I was not aware that this was his line of business, however."

"Not normally perhaps, but I'm following up on intelligence that suggests—"

Teagarden was interrupted by the banging open of Peña's office door. A young policeman had rushed in, yammering in Spanish too rapid for Teagarden to follow. He did, however, clearly hear the name Gladding.

Captain Peña got to his feet and reached for his hat. "Señor Teagarden, your timing is good. It seems we have had a report of an incident at the villa of Señor Gladding."

"An incident?"

"Someone has reported hearing gunshots. Come. We will go and investigate."

It had seemed fortuitous to Teagarden at the time, his being with the good captain at that precise moment. Now, however, facing imminent and certain demise on this wild ride along a dangerous road, he could only regret his lucky timing.

# *Twelve*

It seemed like a good time to lie low. Hannah parked the gardener's battered pickup on a side street in old town Puerto Vallarta, then made her way with her backpack and the portfolio to the Malecón, losing the gardener's battered straw hat along the way.

A couple of blocks from The Blue Gecko, she came upon a down-at-heels hotel, the kind of place frequented by shoestring tourists and couples on one-hour dates. The lobby of the Hotel Tropical was about as appealing as its mildewed pink exterior. The floor might have been pretty once, covered in an Aztec-inspired pattern of bright tiles, but the grout was black and dozens of tiles were chipped or missing. The potted trees were all on life support. Rattan chairs and a couple of settees covered in threadbare chintz had also seen better days.

The clerk at reception was engrossed in a *telenovela* playing out loudly on a small television perched on the desk. His pressed white shirt was embroidered with the name of the hotel, and he wore a name tag that identified him as Miguel. He didn't look up from his soap opera until Hannah finally brought her hand down on the bell by his ear, and then he jumped.

*"Ah, señora, bienvenidos."*

"I'd like a room, please."

"Certainly." He pulled an old leather-bound register from under the desk. "How many nights?"

"Just one."

He opened the register and turned it around to face her. "Please sign here."

While he examined the pegboard key holder behind him, Hannah studied the register, amused by the number of Smiths and Garcias who'd checked into the place. There was even a Homer Simpson. Clearly, they weren't sticky about pesky things like identification.

"Maria Lopez," she wrote. Why not? The Mediterranean dark eyes and hair of her Greek heritage were a kind of ethnic pass key, marking her as a probable native in any number of milieus. It was a useful thing, allowing her to fly under the radar in places where blond women traveling alone became easy targets for obnoxious attention.

Up the stairs and down a short hall, the door to Room 9 creaked open when she turned the key. The place seemed clean enough, but musty, with a faint smell of mildew and stale cigarette smoke. The wallpaper, curling in places, was a decidedly uncheery brindle-brown imprinted with dark ivy—no doubt very fashionable in its day, but a dumb decor idea in a seafront town. They should have stuck with paint. The room was narrow, with a scarred pine dresser against one wall and a single bed opposite. The bed was covered with a multicolored striped blanket tucked in neatly beneath the mattress and smoothed over a flat-looking pillow. The red curtains had seen better days, but at least they covered the long windows that overlooked the busy street below.

She peered out at the tourists strolling along the boardwalk. In the near dark of early evening, cheerful lights were illuminated, strung like festive garland across shops, restaurants and pretty courtyards. She opened the window. If she angled just right, she could see the dead gardener's pickup where she'd left it parked in the street. On the outdoor patio of a café across the way, a mariachi band was serenading a young American family, whose two little children clapped their hands gleefully. Smoke rose from a brazier in back of the restaurant and something smelled delicious.

Hannah leaned her forehead against the glass and sighed as she watched the laughing kids. What a day. She was tired, she was hungry, and she wanted to hug her son. She yawned, then yawned again.

*A fugitive in Mexico. Great. Just freakin' great.*

She stretched out on the bed and was asleep in a nanosecond.

It had been a long time since William Teagarden had worked a murder scene. He'd begun his police career as a London constable, encountering plenty of street crime, a few murders and plenty of death by mishap. But it was only when he'd transferred to Scotland Yard that he'd really learned to discern the subtleties of a homicide scene. If he'd left death behind when he'd joined the Art and Antiquities Unit, his eye for detail had been honed to an even sharper degree by fine details of the stolen masterpieces he tracked.

He followed Captain Peña around the blood-spattered villa, every turn seeming to uncover yet another horror. The soft soil in the garden showed the imprints of several pairs of shoes—trainers, Teagarden decided, in various large sizes that didn't match up with the feet of any of the victims. There was one smaller set of boot prints, too. Nowhere did the boot prints overlap those of the athletic shoes, nor vice versa, making it impossible to know if this person had been on the scene before, during, or after the time those larger prints had been left. Could that possibly be a coincidence? Or had the fellow in the small-sized boots wanted to confuse the appearance of things?

Teagarden followed Peña into the kitchen, where the captain crouched on the ground to examine the murdered cook. Teagarden, however, was distracted by the oven.

"Do you have an extra pair of those latex gloves?" he asked.

The captain dug in his pocket and fished out a pair, tossing them across the room. Teagarden slipped them on and opened the oven door. The interior was still quite hot, the two loaves of bread on the rack burned to a crisp.

Why would the cook turn off the oven and then leave the bread inside to dry out and then burn? She'd fallen at the open refrigerator. It made no sense to Teagarden that she would have shut off the oven and then walked away. She would get the bread out first. No cook would take the time and effort to bake homemade bread and then just abandon it to burn. Even if she'd somehow forgotten and it had burned by accident, why not remove it as soon as she realized her mistake?

No, the timeline was wrong. Peña said the anonymous caller had reported hearing a series of shots fired around five o'clock. And the woman had been dead for about an hour, by the sedimentation rate evident in the bloodstains. The bread had still been baking when she was killed.

So the killer—killers, Teagarden amended, remembering the multiple sets of shoe prints—shot the cook and walked away, leaving the bread in the oven to burn to charcoal. But then, maybe in the last ten minutes or so, someone had turned off the oven.

"Did any of your officers come into the kitchen before us?" Teagarden asked.

Peña cocked a thumb at a young patrolman standing by the kitchen door. "Only Sanchez. Why?"

"We were right behind him. I didn't see him turn off this oven, did you?"

Peña shook his head, then asked Sanchez the same question in Spanish. Sanchez said no.

So who? Teagarden wondered.

Peña grunted as he got to his feet. He and Teagarden went out the back door and across the patio to the pool area, where two more bodies had been found. The woman floating facedown had, like the others, been shot twice. The Asian male—now who was *he?* Teagarden puzzled—had taken a shot in the back. That first shot hadn't killed him. A trail of blood on the ground and grass stains on the knees of his pants suggested he'd tried to crawl away, then turned to defend himself, only to be executed by a bullet between the eyes. His body lay faceup on the lawn, a nine-millimeter semiautomatic next to him on the grass. His own weapon, presumably, still fully loaded. He hadn't gotten off a shot. Very thorough, this killer or killers. Thorough and fast.

Teagarden walked back inside the house to the atrium, where a uniformed maid lay under a glass table. A potted plant had fallen off the table, spilling dirt on the floor. Someone had kicked a clod of dirt across the atrium, and it had come to rest against a baseboard on the far wall. Once again, the officers on the scene denied having done it. So, the killer/killers, then? Or the boot wearer? Or had one of the inexperienced young policemen simply not taken enough care where he was stepping, covering for his clumsiness when the visitor from Britain pointed it out?

At the front door, the gardener's and gate guard's bodies appeared to be in the position in which they had fallen. Teagarden stepped over the gardener and walked past the guard to the veranda steps. He scanned the front yard. A lawn mower sat abandoned on the lawn, the tracks of its four rubber tires leading back to the graveled circular driveway, where they stopped abruptly halfway across.

Teagarden frowned. He hadn't noticed a garden shed anywhere on the grounds. If the gardener was a full-time employee, where did he store his tools? Or was it more likely that he worked for a garden service? It would explain the lawn-mower tracks on the driveway, starting where the gardener had set the machine down— lifted off the bed of a truck, presumably. But if that was the case, where was the truck? The only vehicle on the premises when they'd arrived was a black Cadillac sedan whose license plate indicated it was registered to Moises Gladding, according to the police.

*"Señor?"* One of Peña's officers shattered Teagarden's concentration. "The *capitán* wishes to see you."

Teagarden followed the officer through to what appeared to be Moises Gladding's office. The captain and another of his officers were kneeling in front of a bookcase, one corner of a colorful carpet pulled back. A trapdoor in the floor stood open.

"Look here," Peña said, "I think I have found where Señor Gladding may have gone."

Teagarden watched as the Mexican scrabbled onto a ladder and disappeared down the hatch, calling for them to follow. Inwardly, Teagarden groaned. He hated tunnels, hated cramped spaces of all kinds, but Peña's men were watching. Reluctantly, he forced himself down the ladder. One of the young officers followed him.

The tunnel had not been built for a tall man. Stooping, he followed the beam of Peña's flashlight. Beads of sweat formed on his brow and his breathing turned shallow as he put one foot in front of the other, making his way cautiously along the dank passageway.

Suddenly, Peña let out a sharp hiss and came to an abrupt halt. Teagarden, hunched over to avoid hitting his head on the rough ceiling, managed to stop himself just in time, but the man behind plowed into him, cursed, then apologized. Peña drew his weapon and shone his light on a ladder leading to another trapdoor overhead.

"You have a *pistola?*" the captain whispered.

"No," Teagarden said. He almost never carried a gun. Didn't much care for them.

The officer behind him squeezed past, weapon drawn. Peña climbed the ladder and pushed the door open an few centimeters, pivoting his flashlight to examine the surrounding area. Apparently satisfied, he flung the hatch wide and climbed out, gun at the ready.

"*Nada.*" He signaled the other two to come up.

The young cop stood by while Teagarden climbed out. Once back in the fresh air, he struggled to regain his dignity, sweeping cobwebs from his hair and the stink of claustrophobic fear from his psyche. Teagarden heard waves crashing nearby, but there was almost no light left in the sky, and it was impossible to see a thing. Peña's flashlight picked out two sets of prints leading from the exit—not the same shoe prints Teagarden had seen in the garden. These two had been running—heel prints deep, toes digging in for traction. They followed the trail as it weaved through weeds and tall shrubbery, ending at a sandy clearing on a high cliff that over-looked the crashing surf. In the muted light of a quarter moon, the white of the surf glowed dimly.

The clearing was completely encircled by brush, but tire prints in the sand suggested that a car had been parked there. Impossibly, it seemed to have been driven straight out through dense, unbroken brush. A closer look with the flashlight revealed one set of footprints and some scrape marks in the sand next to the bush. Tea-garden took hold of a couple of branches and tugged at the shrubbery. The camouflage greenery moved easily, revealing a rutted roadway that led away from the villa. Straight back to the highway, he guessed.

"Clever bugger," he muttered.

The room was dark when Hannah awoke. The mariachi band across the street was belting out a tune, and by the volume of the chatter and laughter rising from the sidewalks, the holiday town's nighttime revel-ries were well underway. She lay sprawled on her back, watching the dance of shadow on the ceiling cast by the lights outside. The curtains wafted lazily in the open window, the breeze carrying the smell of something wonderful. She raised her wrist to check her watch, then realized she hadn't worn one.

Rolling over with a groan, she switched on a bedside lamp and fumbled in her pack for her cell phone. She flipped it open to check the time. Nearly eight.

She'd had the phone on vibrate and she'd missed two calls while she was sleeping. When she checked to see who from, John Russo's number came up twice. She smiled. She'd told him she wouldn't be home until Wednesday night, but apparently, the guy missed her. Sweet.

She debated calling him now, but then images of the carnage at Gladding's villa came back to her, churning her insides. As much as she wanted to hear his voice, she had more pressing problems.

She thought about Donald Ackerman at The Blue Gecko, and how he'd tried to dissuade her from going out there. Had he known? The federal agents who'd come to her door had said the arms dealer was dealing with people to whom Washington didn't want to be linked. Those FBI guys had wanted his place bugged, but D.C.'s myriad intelligence agencies were notorious for running compartmentalized operations with no thought of keeping their sister organizations in the loop. Had the CIA, the Drug Enforcement Administration, the Defense Intelligence Agency or someone else pulled a wet job down here in an effort to eliminate a potential source of embarrassment or scandal to the Administration? Was someone looking to bury dirty secrets before they leaked?

If so, they'd done a piss-poor job of it, Hannah thought angrily. Gladding might have been the target, but the killers seemed to have missed him altogether and taken out a raft of innocent bystanders instead.

It didn't seem possible that someone in Washington could order such a massacre. She wasn't naive about her own government's involvement in black ops, no matter how many laws Congress passed to rein in the worst of the cowboys. Foreign policy, after all, had always been the art of the possible, and when you had vast resources, minimal accountability and the catch-all cloak of national security to hide behind, an awful lot was possible—including assassination, direct or by proxy.

On the other hand, Moises Gladding swam in a veritable cesspool of international bad actors. He had to have any number of lethal enemies. Who knew who the guy might have shortchanged or double-crossed over the years?

She sat up and stretched her arms and spine, trying to work out the tension of the day and other kinks added by the lumpy mattress. Arching her neck, head tilting to one side then the other, her gaze fell on the leather portfolio she'd left propped against the bureau. She froze.

What if she had this all wrong? What if the killers had been after the painting? It would have been delivered hours before they showed up if she hadn't been taken a later flight that morning. In fact, if she hadn't been sidetracked by Sergio's attempt to steal the painting and then by her visit to Donald Ackerman's bar, she might have still been at the villa herself when the killers showed up.

She grabbed the case and put it on the bed, unzipped it and removed the painting. Turning the artwork on its face, she ripped the protective paper from the back of the frame. Wishing she knew more about art, she examined the exposed back of the canvas once more, just as she'd done the night before she'd left home. Last night, she realized. Good God, would this day never end?

When she and Rebecca had gone out to his studio, August Koon had mentioned that he'd reworked this painting several times before it was completed to his satisfaction. He was too easily satisfied, she thought ruefully, leaning the frame against the wall. He should have gone it over again with a house-painting roller. A blank canvas couldn't have been less appealing.

Why would Moises Gladding pay a quarter of a million dollars for something that Gabe might have done while still in diapers?

She thought about the paintings she'd seen hanging on the walls of his villa, bright, colorful pieces, some realistic, some abstract. What did she know? Maybe this piece was a worthy addition to that collection. But two-hundred-and-fifty-thousand-dollars' worthy? Even Rebecca had thought it was overpriced, with August Koon riding a short wave of popularity in the current market.

Hannah shook her head. She didn't know art, but she knew for sure that this splotchy mess wasn't worth the lives of an entire household of innocent people.

Another thought struck her. Maybe it wasn't the canvas at all. Maybe the painting was just an excuse to

transport the frame. After all, people who wanted arma-
ments traded what they had, sometimes in elaborate,
multilevel deals involving many other commodities as
currency. The inventiveness of thieves and smugglers
was legendary, with items like cocaine or heroin resin
often reconstituted, shaped and camouflaged to look
like something else.

She hefted the frame in her hands, trying to gauge
the weight of it. Not wood, she thought. Some kind of
molded synthetic? She scratched at the paint with her
fingernail, then sniffed and tasted the flake that came
away. Nothing obvious. She ran her fingers along all the
surfaces, then set the picture down on the floor once
more and crouched in front of it, frowning.

Her stomach rumbled. She needed to eat, and she
needed a knife. The café across the way would do for
both purposes. She tucked the painting under the bed
and, after double-checking the lock on the door behind
her, made her way downstairs. There, she found Miguel,
the clerk, dozing behind the desk as yet another overheated *telenovela* played itself out on the TV screen.

At the café across the road, the tables were mostly
occupied by couples and groups, but a four-seater bar
was wide open. She took a stool there, ordering up
*carnitas* and a coffee. Only about half the people in the
place seemed to be foreigners, while the rest looked like
locals. That was always a good sign.

When the roasted pork came, she asked for a knife
to go along with the fork the barman had left on a paper

napkin. She laid strips of the spicy meat on a fresh corn tortilla, added rice and beans drenched in hot salsa, then wrapped the thing up. She devoured it in about five bites and set about rolling up seconds. The food was awesome, and not just because she was starving. The old barman smiled at her healthy appetite as he poured her another cup of coffee.

By the time she was done her meal, he was off mixing margaritas in a blender further down the bar. Pulling some wadded bills from her pocket, she smoothed them out next to her empty plate. She glanced around to make sure no one was watching, then slipped the knife up her sleeve and headed out the door. The money she had left on the bar was more than enough to cover the meal, a good tip and the knife.

Back in her room, she pulled the painting back out from under the bed and used the steak knife to raise the pins that held the canvas in place. Setting the canvas aside, she went to work on the frame. The tip of the knife broke off as she pried apart the four sides of it, but it did the job. Taking one of the long sides in her hands, she cracked it over her knee. Ten minutes later, the molded frame lay in a dozen pieces and she had a cut on her thumb and the beginnings of a bruise on her knee. If the frame was made of anything other than a high-end synthetic resin, it wasn't obvious, and she was still none the wiser as to whether there was a link between this and the murders at Gladding's villa.

Frustrated to the max, Hannah turned to the portfolio, tearing out the lining, cutting open the pockets and padded handles, looking for anything—drugs, papers… hell, even a microchip. Zip.

Next, she reexamined the canvas yet again. She was tempted to take it off the stretchers to examine those wooden pieces, but sanity prevailed. She had taken this job because she'd empathized with Rebecca over the financial and emotional mess she was in due to her schmuck of an ex-husband and messy divorce. Damaging the painting by ripping the canvas or chipping paint was doing no one any favors.

As it was, she thought, ruefully examining the mess she'd made of the frame and portfolio, it might be a problem carrying the picture back into the States. She had no documents for a northbound entry. It wasn't so much border guards she was worried about. U.S. Customs rarely gave much attention to the souvenirs carried by returning tourists from Mexico. If she did run into problems, she could always contact FBI Special Agent Towle and have him vouch for her.

But if American officialdom wasn't really a concern, she continued to be vexed by the notion that the villa murders might be linked to the painting. Neither Moises Gladding nor his would-be assassins were characters to be trifled with. What if someone was watching the airport, waiting for a courier carrying a painting to show up for a scheduled return flight? After seeing what had gone down at the villa, did she dare risk being caught with the thing?

Why hadn't she just left it at the villa?

Right. Toss a quarter of a million dollars on the bed in the middle of a bloodbath and hope for the best. Between the killers, Gladding and the police she'd passed on her flight from the villa—who were probably even now looking for clues to what had gone down out there—all she needed was to broadcast her own presence. She'd been careful to watch where she stepped at the villa so as not to pick up blood on her boots or blend her footprints with those of the intruders.

She gathered up the broken pieces of the frame and stuffed them into the bottom of the portfolio. She rewrapped the painting in the cloth Rebecca had provided, then packed the canvas back into the ruined portfolio as best she could. After that, she sat on the edge of the bed, thinking.

She checked the time on her cell phone once more—nearly ten. Towle had told her to contact Donald Ackerman if she ran into any problems down here. Well, if the adventure with Sergio the thieving chauffeur was a slight contretemps, it was nothing compared to the mess she found herself in now.

She thought about the ex-spook who'd kept insisting he was just a barkeep these days. Protesting a little too much, perhaps?

On her way out of his bar, when Hannah had spotted him dialing his cell phone, she'd thought he might be calling whoever he dealt with in the government these days, checking out the story of the *gringa* who'd shown up unannounced. Now, she wondered whether Acker-man might be playing both sides of the street.

How was she supposed to know who to trust?

One way or another, she had to figure out how to get out of here in one piece. Since she was short on other options, her best bet might be to pay Ackerman another visit, ideally when he wouldn't be expecting her. That meant catching him alone after the bar closed.

And August Koon's picture?

As she looked around for a secure place to hide it, her gaze rose to the ceiling. It was composed of acoustic tiles suspended on one of those cheap aluminum frame systems. She could stick the picture up there, maybe, but as a hiding spot, it felt a little too exposed.

On the other hand…

She went to the closet. The tiles extended in there, and there was a wide shelf over the hanging rod. That might do. Pulling over a chair, she climbed up, lifted a couple of tiles and set them aside, then slipped the port-folio into the space overhead. After resetting the tiles, she returned the chair to its place next to the bed and double-checked that there was no sign that she had dis-turbed things. But the linoleum floor, if worn, was clean, in the closet and in the room itself, so there was no dust in which to leave a trail. She wouldn't leave the crown jewels in a place like this, but as a temporary hiding place for Koon's painting until she could figure out her next move, it would do.

Setting the alarm on her phone, she stretched out on the bed once more to grab a couple more hours of sleep. She might have a long night ahead.

# *Thirteen*

The sun had long set by the time Travis Spielman made his way home to Silver Lake, exhausted yet wired. The half-dozen cups of coffee he'd drunk during the day probably contributed to the buzz, but it was more than that. There was utter confusion—and a little fear—about the way the day had unfolded.

After Ruben had gotten back from the market, where he'd hung around for a while, hoping in vain that Hannah would get back to his cryptic message from *Monica*, Spielman had headed back into the office. He'd spent a couple of hours twiddling his thumbs before being startled by the beep of his computer terminal telling him the system was up again. He was none the wiser as to why the network had gone down in the first place.

It was probably paranoid to think he'd been targeted

because of Hannah's mission for Moises Gladding, or because he'd offered to check for recent intel updates. After all, if he were suddenly under a cloud of suspicion, he would have been frog-marched out the door by internal security goons. That was how it worked, right? Instead, as the screen in front of him showed, he once again had full access to the network.

Or did he? Now he was afraid to try to navigate beyond the implementation protocols for the new Daxo software, fearing he'd find himself as blocked as when he'd attempted to access information on Moises Gladding.

If he had suddenly become the subject of a security investigation, what would that say about what was up on his terminal now? Was it a fake access port to Daxo, some elaborate Potemkin cybervillage created to lull him into thinking he was above suspicion? Isn't that what they'd done to the FBI spy Robert Hanson, keeping him busy with make-work projects, isolated from critical files, completely unaware and unsuspecting while they built an airtight legal case against him?

Spielman pulled into his garage. But he wasn't a spy, dammit!

"Argh!" He pressed his forehead into the steering wheel, tugging his hair. His entire day had been nothing but crazy-think. Working in this business could make a person nuts.

Sighing, he climbed out of the Jeep and reached for the door button on the garage—then froze at the sight of a white utility van across the road. Surveillance? On him? On Hannah?

He stood there in the dark garage, hand still poised over the door button, afraid to move. Only when a man in overalls came out the front door of the house opposite, carrying a toolbox and plumber's snake, did he realize he'd scarcely been breathing. Idiot! He pressed the door button and headed for the house.

That was it. He had to mend his ways. He really liked Hannah and wanted to help her out, but he couldn't be cutting corners on security anymore. No more snooping, putting his family at risk.

The tantalizing smell of Ruben's marinara sauce greeted him when he opened the door to his condo. Melanie was on the floor of the family room, tucking her stuffed Snoopy into his bed. Ruben was in the nearby kitchen area, dancing a samba to an MTV video of Ricky Martin.

*"Hola,"* Ruben called. "Mellie, look! Daddy's home."

Mellie held up her arms and Travis picked her up, kissing her. He carried her into the kitchen, where he leaned over and gave the spaghetti sauce an apprecia-tive sniff, then planted a kiss on Ruben's cheek.

"Did Hannah call back?" he murmured, thankful for the loud music, conscious still of the fear that had plagued him all day.

"No," Ruben whispered, obviously enjoying what he thought was a great game. "I didn't see her around, either. Maybe she took the job after all?"

Travis leaned wearily against the counter, head shaking.

Ruben obviously saw the change in him. His playful expression evaporated. He went to the fridge and got an open bottle of red wine, poured out two glasses and handed one to Travis. "She'll be okay, *mi amore*."

"God, I hope so. I shouldn't have told her I'd check things out. Now I feel like I let her down, and for what?"

"Oh, come on. I can see you've spent the whole day fretting. Hannah's a smart cookie. She wouldn't have taken the job if she had any real concerns about it. Who knows? Maybe she didn't even go. Don't worry. Let's have dinner and relax." Ruben tickled their daughter and she laughed. "Right, Mellie? Daddy's worrying for nothing."

The toddler must have agreed, because she laughed and patted Travis's cheek.

You had to hand it to the Germans, Moises Gladding thought. They were masters at engineering comfort.

He knew people who had refused to buy anything German-made ever since the Holocaust, but he himself was a pragmatic man. He traded wherever it suited him. Not to do so smacked of fearfulness, and he feared no one and nothing.

His personal silver Mercedes SLE had rich leather seats and dark-tinted windows, the better to go about his business discreetly. Although he kept a Cadillac and driver for the use of his mistress and other household business, his own car was always kept at a distance from the villa. It was the same at all of his homes no matter where in the world they were located. His father had escaped the Nazis a week after Kristallnacht in a boat secretly purchased in 1937, and had impressed upon young Moises the need to plan and be prepared for the unexpected. Gladding felt sure the old man would be pleased to know his lesson had been taken to heart.

He would not have approved of his son's present action, but that couldn't be helped. Gladding moved in dangerous, ruthless circles. If word leaked that he could be defied with impunity, he was finished.

His bodyguard parked the Mercedes at the end of Via Allende, a narrow street north of the cathedral. The small houses of the working-class neighborhood were peopled by the maids, waiters, bellhops and taxi drivers who underpinned Puerto Vallarta's busy tourist economy.

When Gladding had bought his oceanfront villa, he had asked another expatriate, a sometime professional colleague, to recommend reliable household staff. Among the locals Donald Ackerman had suggested was a couple who lived on this street.

Gladding had taken on Clara and Sergio Chavez as cook and driver/handyman respectively, but now he regretted taking Ackerman's advice. After he'd fired Clara for insubordination, had Sergio stupidly attempted payback? Gladding had sent the man to watch for the courier coming in from Los Angeles with his painting. Sergio had called at midmorning to say she'd apparently rescheduled her arrival, so Gladding had had him remain in town to wait for her. When they still hadn't shown up by late afternoon, however, he'd become suspicious. It would be just like one of these Mexicans to try to avenge himself out of misplaced machismo over a perceived an insult to his woman.

If he wasn't up to no good, where was the man? Sergio hadn't shown up before the attack on the villa, but perhaps Gladding had simply missed seeing him in his own rush to get out of the place.

His visiting associate had charged into his office just as the first shots sounded from the veranda. Outgunned and outnumbered, the two of them had made it out alive by the skin of their teeth, and even then, only because Gladding had had the foresight to install the escape tunnel. Now, the man was inside the Chavez house to find out if Sergio had ever come home. If he had, Gladding had told him to find out what, if anything, he knew about the assault on the villa and, most important, what had happened to the courier and his painting.

While he waited for his man to return, he studied the drab houses up and down the street. The smells of dozens of family dinners drifted on the night air. The light from TV screens flickered in every window, banal entertainment for people with dreary lives. Mixed with the sound of canned laughter came the shouts of scolding mothers, the cry of fretting babies and loud music with a Latin beat. It was a ramshackle, crowded and noisy neighborhood.

Good, Gladding thought, turning back to the door where his man had entered. The residents of Via Allende were too preoccupied with their *telenovelas* and their miserable little lives to notice the real-life drama now unfolding at the home of Clara and Sergio Chavez. Only Gladding, watching from the backseat of the Mercedes, saw when an exhausted-looking Sergio suddenly appeared at the corner and stumbled through his front door. Where on earth had he been? Gladding wondered.

He heard the cry of surprise as Sergio no doubt caught sight of his man inside, and he heard Clara whimper as the door slammed behind her husband. There was a crash—something falling perhaps. A child began to wail inside the Chavez house, but its cries were quickly muffled, perhaps by Clara's frightened clasp.

Gladding heard nothing more for several minutes. Suddenly, there came a sharp cry—only one—then a rapid series of strobelike flashes at the windows. The gun his man carried in had been fitted with a noise suppressor.

Life went on in all the other houses on Via Allende, and none of the Chavezes' neighbors seemed to notice anything out of the ordinary.

An ugly business, Gladding thought, but unavoidable. He sighed as his man opened the front door of the house, glanced around, then closed it behind himself and hurried back to the Mercedes.

Empty-handed, Gladding noted with irritation. Where was his damn painting?

The alarm on her cell phone jarred Hannah awake from the sleep of the dead. For a fleabag hotel, the room was reasonably comfortable. Or maybe it was just that she was unreasonably exhausted.

She roused herself with regret and checked the time on her cell phone. Nearly one in the morning.

She flicked on the bedside lamp and walked to the closet to double-check her hiding job, but no telltale signs gave it away. The painting was safe there for the moment. The more she thought about it, the more she couldn't see why it shouldn't just stay there until she knew for certain what was going on.

If Gladding had been killed at the attack on his villa and she had simply not found his body, then he wouldn't miss his painting. If he was on the run from his attackers, then he had bigger problems than August Koon's lost scribbles.

And if somehow the attack had something to do with the painting?

Well, she doubted it, but on the other hand, it might be just too much of a coincidence that Gladding had been hit the same day she was meant to arrive with it. Given the professionalism of the three hit men whose shoe prints she'd seen in the dirt, she sure as hell didn't want to face them down over a splotched canvas.

No, the painting could stay where it was. All she

could do was hope this crummy hotel didn't burn down before she could figure out what was going on and find out what to do with it.

Not for the first time, she kicked herself for taking a job that her gut had said was not a good idea. Moises Gladding? Please. Who knew what he was up to these days?

*Who knew?* Hannah sank back onto on the bed. "Oh, my God!"

Travis Spielman! When he hadn't called her, she'd presumed it meant there was no recent chatter about the arms dealer. Except there *had* been a phone message— that bizarre call from somebody named Monica, calling from a number she hadn't recognized.

That was *Ruben,* goddammit! Telling her in code not to leave town before getting in touch. Why the hell were those guys playing stupid games?

Unless Travis did have something to tell her— something serious enough that he was worried about tapped phones?

"Oh, man, I'm an idiot."

She pulled her unruly hair up into a ponytail, grabbed her backpack and the knife she'd liberated from the cantina, and made her way down the stairs, careful not to wake the dozing night clerk as she slipped out a side door onto an alleyway.

She passed the gardener's rusted pickup still parked where she left it. She didn't dare drive it. The cops would have found the gardener along with the others at the villa, and by now, might have an APB out for the truck. She fingered its keys in her pocket. She'd have to wipe them and ditch them.

She made her way to the Malecón, blending in with the drunks and college kids on spring break who were milling on the boardwalk. A couple of bars were still going strong, but most of the cafés and restaurants were closed or winding down for the night. When she got to The Blue Gecko, the patio was deserted except for a lone waiter sweeping beneath the tables and upturned chairs, a towel tucked into the waistband of his pants. A man and woman walked out of the place arm in arm, waving drunkenly to the waiter before they staggered off down the boardwalk. Inside, she spotted just one customer, the hapless Kevvie of the black eye and fat lip, head down on his arm, probably passed out.

She waited in the shadows for signs that the place was definitely closing up for the night. Several passing guys eyed her with interest but the expression on her face must have been sufficiently fierce that all but a couple of those walked on. The others she chased on with a hissed ,"Get lost, creep."

A pair of lovers were on the beach, necking outrageously. *Get a room, will you?* A few other people, couples or small knots of friends, laughed and chatted as they headed to wherever they were going. She felt the kind of hollow, aching emptiness that comes at two in the morning to those who are utterly alone. What was she doing? She was thirty years old, running around

Mexico in the middle of the night, no one needing her, no one missing her. Pathetic.

The waiter at The Blue Gecko made his way back inside, his outside sweeping done and the last umbrella folded. He propped the broom in a corner, pulled off his apron, then walked over to rouse the drunken Kevvie. The waiter pointed to the clock. Its hands still pointed shyly to half past six, but Kevvie got the message anyway. He staggered to the door, then bumbled off into the night.

She couldn't see Ackerman, and it worried her. She hadn't allowed for the possibility that the ex-spook might not be there. If he wasn't locking his own place up for the night, then she'd have to find out from the waiter where he lived. She'd ask nicely. Or not.

Just then, the waiter turned toward the back of the bar. He spread his hands, gesturing to someone out of sight. Ackerman. It had to be. The waiter nodded and locked the front doors. A moment later, the lights went out, leaving only the glow of the Dos Equis neon sign on the wall and a thread of light leaking from the kitchen and office area at the back.

She hurried down an alley and came up near the back door, where she clearly heard two voices, the waiter's and Ackerman's. A shadow fell across the screen as the waiter appeared.

"Lock it behind you," she heard Ackerman call.

*"Hasta mañana,"* the waiter called back, pulling the door shut. He jangled a set of keys, apparently looking for the right one.

Hannah yanked the ponytail elastic out of her hair, mussed her curls around her face and hurried over, shifting into her best rendition of a drunken woman on the prowl. The waiter looked up, surprised.

She pressed a finger to her lips, giggled softly, and slurred, "Shh! It's a surprise. I'm surprising Donny. Don't tell."

The waiter flashed a lascivious grin but didn't move. She swayed a little for effect and peered over his shoulder. Surely she wasn't the first woman to pay the man's boss an after-hours visit?

On the other hand, if Ackerman batted for the other team, this ploy was a really dumb idea.

But then, the waiter shrugged, opened the door for her and stepped aside. He leered as she cut him a sideways glance, and then he pulled the door shut once more. She heard the key turn in the lock. She waited until she heard his footsteps retreating down the alleyway.

Laying her pack down quietly, she drew her gun and headed for the lighted office at the back.

# *Fourteen*

Donald Ackerman was at his desk in the back office, a wad of cash in each hand. He froze as she came through the door, gun drawn, and shock flickered over his face. Surprised to see her at that late hour? Or surprised to see her alive? Whichever it was, his features settled right back into the usual world-weary boredom. What a pro.

"Be right with you," he said, going back to his counting.

Keeping the gun steady, Hannah pulled the spare chair over with the toe of her boot. She settled where she could watch both him and the door.

Finishing his count of the day's take, Ackerman folded a half-inch pile of dollars and pesos and tucked them into a pocket, then slipped the rest into a cash box. He closed the lid, locked it and put in a desk drawer.

"That's your security system?" Hannah asked.

"All I need. People know better than to mess with me."

"Tough guy."

"Nah, I'm a pussycat." He nodded at her gun. "Nice Beretta. You know how to use it? 'Cause if you do, that's okay, but if you don't, I'd just as soon you didn't point it at me."

"I can use it just fine, and I will if you don't hand over your piece right now."

He held up his hands, palms out. "Nothing up my sleeve."

"Hand it over, Ackerman. There's one at the small of your back. I spotted it when I was in earlier."

"Jeez, and she calls me the tough guy." Ackerman reached behind his back.

"Take it out easy, two fingers only, put it on the desk and slide it toward me." He did as he was told and she tucked his Glock in the waistband of her pants.

"Now, open the desk drawers, one by one, all the way out."

"There's no gun in there."

"Just the same…"

There were only two drawers, one per side. He pulled them wide, then pushed his chair back against the wall. It creaked as he leaned back and interlaced his fingers over his stomach. Hannah shuffled the contents of one of the drawers. Nothing but paperwork. The other held office supplies, including a ten-yard roll of Velcro tape. She pulled it out of the drawer and set it aside along with a pair of scissors. Very useful stuff, Velcro. Then, she ducked her head to glance at the underside of the desk. Sure enough…

She backed away. "Now, give me the other piece you've stuck under there. With your right hand," she added. She'd already noticed that he was a southpaw. She just hoped to hell he wasn't ambidextrous.

Ackerman rolled his eyes and slid back to the desk. She heard the crackle of the hook-and-loop tape ripping as he pulled another semiautomatic off the underside, his right forefinger hooked in the trigger guard. He slid that one across the desk, too, then leaned back once more, hands up. "Okay. *No mas,* boss, I swear."

"Terrific. Now we can talk in peace."

"Oh, goody, a social call."

"Not hardly. You want to tell me what went down at your buddy Moises's place today?"

"I don't know. You talk to him?"

"Nope. Did you set me up?"

"Why would I do that? I didn't even know you were coming, remember?"

"And yet you jumped on the phone the second I walked out the door."

"Just checking you out."

"Did you set up Gladding?"

"I have no idea what you're talking about."

He'd clean up in Vegas, Hannah decided. He had the perfect poker face.

"You seem to be real plugged in here, Don, so I'm finding it hard to believe this is all coming as a complete surprise."

"I told you before, I'm just a barkeep. I—"

"Don't!" she snapped. "Don't give me that patronizing, good ol' boy crap. I'm tired and I'm pissed off. I nearly walked into a trap out there, and I really, really don't like traps. Tell me what's going on or I swear to God, I'm going to take out your kneecaps."

Startled by the outburst, he reached a finger into his breast pocket, but it came away empty—the habitual stall of the smoker. His momentary puzzlement told her he'd recently quit. He'd chosen a bad time to change his evil ways. "Jeez, lady, take a Valium, or something, would you? Remember me? I'm the guy the feds told you to turn to for help."

"Listen, one thing I've learned about the feds is that they do a lousy job of keeping tabs on the cowboys they run in the field. I wonder if they have any idea the half of what you're into down here."

"So, I take it your business with Moises didn't go well."

"What makes you think that?"

"The hour. The gun. That peevish look on your face."

"Why don't you tell *me* what happened today?"

He shrugged. "How the hell should I know? You're the one who was there."

She let out an exasperated sigh. They were getting nowhere. She told him briefly what she'd found at Gladding's villa. "So you can see I've got good reason to look a little peevish. Walking into a bloodbath is not my idea of a fun day in paradise."

"A bloodbath? That bad, huh? Did they get Gladding?"

"So he's not 'Moises' anymore?"

He sighed. "Look, I'm sorry you ran into trouble, but I really didn't have a clue. Whoever pulled off this op, I don't think it was our guys."

"Our guys? So much for being retired."

"Well, semiretired. You know what it's like. You keep your hand in."

"Maybe it *was* our side," she said. "They seemed pretty antsy about Gladding's activities. Maybe you're just out of the loop."

"I don't think so. That guy has so many irons in the fire, could've been any one of a dozen bad actors looking for payback for some past deal gone sour. Or maybe unhappy with the terms of payment on a current contract."

"What's he dealing in these days?"

"Last deal I heard about was with some rebel faction in Sierra Leone. Gladding was moving grenades, rifles, rocket launchers."

"In exchange for blood diamonds, I suppose, the usual currency in West Africa."

Ackerman nodded. "You said you were making a delivery to him. What were you delivering?"

"A painting."

"Aha, the plot thickens. Smart lady like you, you've gotta know that stolen art and jewels finance arms trades."

"The term *art* is a stretch where this piece is concerned. It's just a piece of modernist crap that even the dealer thought was overpriced."

"What's it worth?"

"Gladding paid a quarter mil, plus commissions and my fees."

Ackerman frowned. "A quarter mil doesn't buy much these days. Gladding's deals usually run into the tens of millions. You sure what you had there?"

"Yup. I was with the dealer when she picked it up. I even met the artist."

"And yet they hit Moises's place the same day you're supposed to show up with this piece of dreck. A little coincidental, wouldn't you say?"

"Yeah, it occurred to me, too. That's why I'd like to get out of Dodge. I'm scheduled to fly back to L.A. at noon tomorrow, but he made the flight arrangements. I'm worried that if it did have something to do with the painting, somebody might be watching for me."

"You taking it back with you?"

"Nope."

"You left it at the villa?"

"Nope."

"So where is it?"

"Somewhere safe."

"Pretty risky. If I know Moises, he's not going to be happy that property he's paid for isn't delivered. And on the off chance this painting isn't just a piece of junk but something he needed to do a deal, the man will be livid. Take my word for it, Hannah, if the guy's still alive, you don't want to get on the wrong side of him."

"Not the first bad apple I've run into."

Ackerman shook his head. "Not like Gladding. And

he's got a guy working for him these days who's a complete sociopath. *Torture* is too pleasant a word for what he's capable of. You should tell me where the painting is. If Moises isn't dead, I'll see that it gets to him."

"Aw, Donny, you're worried about me. That's so sweet."

"I'm really not kidding."

"We'll see. Meantime, you got an Internet hookup there?" She cocked a thumb toward the computer on his desk.

He nodded. Hannah picked up the roll of Velcro, got to her feet and pushed the plastic chair up against the filing cabinet. When she pulled on the drawers, they were locked. Perfect. She attached one of the chair arms to the drawer handle with a couple of pieces of the Velcro.

"Now, my friend, I'm afraid I'm going to have to ask you to sit here."

"Come on, don't do this. I'm one of the good guys, remember?"

"That remains to be seen. Meantime, I need my hands and eyes to see about changing my flight, and that means I can't be watching you." She got to her feet and pointed to the plastic chair.

With a long, aggrieved sigh, Ackerman switched chairs. She tossed him a couple of strips of Velcro and had him tape his feet to the legs, and then one wrist to an arm of the chair. Only then did she feel safe enough to approach him to fasten the other hand. If he tried to make a move now, he'd be hampered enough to ensure she kept the upper hand.

Once he was tied down, she logged on to the Alaska Air Web site. There was a 7:00 a.m. flight to Los Angeles and first class was wide open. She switched her reservation and prayed Gladding didn't have a source at the airline. She had no such confidence about the Mexican authorities at the airport, but she had the international air marshal's pass from Towle allowing her to bypass airport security. With no bags to check, if she timed a tight arrival at the airport, she might be able to whip in, board the flight and be gone before anyone was the wiser.

Maybe.

There was a cot on the far side of the office. Ignoring Ackerman's complaints, she went over, wedged the pillow into the corner and settled in to wait for morning.

Gladding spent the night at the apartment he kept in town for visitors he wouldn't have at his villa and preferred not be seen at hotels. Kyle Liggett had been staying there while they awaited the delivery of the painting. Gladding now wished that he had sent Liggett to meet the courier, but Liggett had been delayed getting down here. There had been no reason to think Sergio Chavez couldn't handle picking up a female courier sent by that second-rate gallery in Malibu. Gladding had felt confident about that—until Sergio had failed to return.

Fool. A fatal mistake, as it turned out, not only for Sergio, but also for his wife and child.

Gladding wasn't an animal. He had children and grandchildren of his own and he regretted unloosing a psychopath like Liggett on the Chavez family, but he wanted the goods he had paid for. Equally important, if word got out that he could be double-crossed with impunity—by a lowly driver and handyman, no less—then how long would he survive?

"You're absolutely sure he didn't have the painting?" he asked Liggett as they drove away from Via Allende. "You checked everywhere?"

"I ripped the place apart. There weren't too many places it could be. House was the size of a closet. And no way would the guy lie to me. He knew I meant business. And that courier woman had him softened up, too. He might have thought he was pretty macho before this afternoon, but after some broad gets the drop on him and leaves him tied to a tree, he was plenty humble."

"And he was planning to do what with the painting?"

"He said a guy in Mazatlán offered to buy it from him. I got the information on the buyer, but believe me, old Sergio was telling the truth. He had the blisters on his feet to back it up. I can take a run to Mazatlán if you want, but that contact of Sergio's hasn't got it. The courier does."

"She should've taken Sergio down when she had the chance instead of leaving it to me."

Liggett nodded. "Might've gone easier for him if she had, but it still wouldn't have saved his family. I had to make sure the wife wasn't in on it. As it was, seems she had no idea what he was up to."

"Stupid fool," Gladding muttered.

But where was the courier? Not at the resort where he'd reserved a room for her. Gladding had called, ostensibly to confirm that all was well with his guest, but his man at the hotel said she'd never checked in. He promised to call if she showed up, but there had been no news and by now, it was clear she was AWOL.

Another thought occurred to him. As Liggett drove back to the town apartment, Gladding pressed the autodial on his cell phone for an informant he kept on retainer inside the Puerto Vallarta Police. The man answered after several rings and Gladding identified himself.

"Oh, *señor,* I am very glad to learn that you are alive."

"Were you one of the ones who went out to my place earlier tonight?" Gladding himself had placed the anonymous "shots fired" call as he and Liggett had sped away from the bloodbath unfolding at the villa.

"Yes. We have a large force still out there. The investigation is continuing. Who did this terrible thing?"

"I don't know. I wasn't there." In fact, he had been, but he and Liggett had beat a hasty retreat as soon as they heard the opening shots and realized they were outgunned. "What did you find?"

The contact filled him in. Six bodies—the maid, the cook, the gardener, the security guard from the front gate, Gladding's companion and an unidentified Asian man. Gladding knew who the Asian was but he didn't tell the policeman. The man was one of the team working on his current deal, and he'd been caught out by the pool when the shooting started. Gladding and Liggett had had to leave him behind.

"That's all?" Gladding said.

The policeman seemed taken aback. "All? Six people are dead."

"I mean did you see an American woman about the place?"

"*Una gringa?* No. Why?"

"I was expecting the delivery of a package. A painting, actually, about one meter wide. A modern piece. Did you see it? Wrapped, or in a carrying case, perhaps?"

"No, we saw nothing like that. *Señor,* you must come into the station to tell what you know of these murders."

"Absolutely not."

"But—"

"Absolutely not," he repeated. "We have not had this conversation and you have no idea where I might be. Are we clear?"

He heard only static for a moment, and then, reluctantly, "Yes, I understand." The high-ranking policeman was only a couple of years away from what would be, thanks to Moises Gladding, a very comfortable retirement. After years of turning a blind eye to any number of Señor Gladding's questionable activities, he would never risk having his association with the arms dealer become public knowledge.

The Mexican cop was no threat, Gladding knew. His business colleagues were another matter. If he didn't keep his end of the bargain, he was a dead man. No corner of the world would be dark enough for him to hide.

He had to have the painting.

# *Fifteen*

At a minute or two before six in the morning, Hannah stood up and stretched her kinked muscles, catching the phone alarm she'd set before it could ring. Ackerman didn't stir. He'd given up trying to talk his way out of the chair to which he was Velcro-taped. Leaning his head against the filing cabinet, he'd dozed off a couple of hours ago—the best revenge, as it turned out, since his jackhammer snore thwarted any hope of rest for her. Lucky she'd caught some shut-eye at that fleabag hotel.

She'd spent the time thinking about possible explanations for events at Gladding's villa and trying to decide what to do about the painting. Taking it to dump back in Rebecca Powell's lap was one option. If asked, she could always explain to U.S. Customs about being unable to connect with the buyer, and she had both Rebecca and the feds to corroborate her story. Worst case scenario—Customs would seize the painting and hold it until Rebecca untangled things.

But did she want to carry it back with her? Not really. It could be years or never before anyone removed the closet ceiling tiles in that hotel and stumbled across the thing. The painting was safe where it was. When the time was right, she could come back and retrieve it or tell someone else where to find it.

In the meantime, the thing was burdensome, hampering her movements at a time when trouble might pop up anywhere. She had no idea who might be watching for a woman carrying a painting. It wasn't like she could stick it down her pants to hide it.

She felt a glimmer of guilt about Rebecca. The woman had problems aplenty without getting caught up in a business dispute with a character like Moises Gladding. Hannah would happily do what she could to straighten things out once she was back in L.A., but first, she had to get out in one piece.

A cardboard box stood open in a corner of Ackerman's office, a pile of new black baseball caps spilling out of plastic bags. The Blue Gecko's sombrero-clad lizard danced across the crown over letters spelling out the bar's name. She slipped the covered elastic off her wrist and bound her hair up with it, then grabbed one of the hats and put it on, pulling her ponytail through the hole. Not a brilliant disguise, but better than nothing.

She glanced over at Ackerman, but he was still snoring. She took the tank top and Indian cotton skirt out of her pack, turned her back on him, pulled off the T-shirt she'd been wearing for the past twenty-four hours and slipped on the tank. Slipping out of her boots and jeans, she pulled on the skirt, then put a clean loose linen shirt over everything, leaving it untucked to conceal the holster at the small of her back.

When she turned around again for the sandals in her pack, Ackerman was watching her. She frowned. "Enjoy the show?"

"Hey, you want privacy, get a room. So, what's the plan?"

"Where's your car?"

"Out back."

She thought about the cars she'd seen in the alley while she waited for the bar to close. "That old green Barracuda?"

"Vintage, not 'old,' if you don't mind. Yeah, that's mine."

Good, Hannah thought, stuffing her dirty clothes into the backpack. If he'd had a newer car, she might have had to rethink the plan, but this could work. "You're going to drive me to the airport."

"What about the painting?"

"What about it?"

"Where's it at?"

"Why do you care?"

"I don't give a rat's ass about it, but if you think Gladding's going to take kindly to being ripped off, you're dumber than you look, girl. I wouldn't cross Moises over a doughnut, you hear me? Not a damn toothpick."

"I really appreciate the concern for my welfare. Now, about those car keys…"

"Right there on the desk. Untie me, then take the car. Just leave it in the airport parking lot and I'll have my man Juan run me over to pick it up later."

"Juan? That's the guy who locked up last night, right? What time does he come in?"

"Not till four. Bar opens at noon but he works the evening shift."

"And your other employees, when do they come in?"

"First two clock in at eleven."

"Okay, good. You're going to come with me."

"I told you, untie me and you can take the car."

"Not gonna happen. I'm not leaving you free to call for reinforcements."

"What part of 'we're working for the same side here' don't you understand, lady?"

"Everyone has a price, Don. Not only don't I know who's on which side, I don't even know what the damn game is. I intend to get out of here in one piece, so that means keeping an eye on you for now. Where's your cell phone?"

"Um, I think it's on the desk there."

She moved papers until she found it, then paged through his contact list. If Gladding's name was there, he'd filed it under something else. "Your man Juan have a cell phone?"

"Yeah, I've got him on the same plan as me. He's there in the phone list under *Juan J.*"

Hannah found the name. "Okay, good." She shoved the phone in an outside pocket of her backpack, next to her passport and wallet. "Now, I'm going to free one of your arms and let you do the rest, but no games, all right? Then we're out of here."

"Fine," he grumbled. "I'll drive you to the damn airport. You're welcome, I'm sure."

Moises Gladding passed a similarly uneasy night on one of the sofas at his in-town apartment, also trying to come up with a plan of action. Suddenly, he leapt to his feet and smacked Liggett on the shoulder. "Get up. We're going."

Liggett had been dozing on the other living room sofa, but he was instantly awake. "Where to?"

"To see the man who recommended Sergio Chavez. He's a clever guy. Too clever. He could be the brains behind that stupid little man's idiotic plot to steal the painting."

Fifteen minutes later, Gladding and Liggett were at the door of a bougainvillea-covered cottage in the area nicknamed Gringo Gulch, home to many of the expatriate artists, writers and retirees who called Puerto

Vallarta home. Gladding had never been to Donald Ackerman's house before, but he'd long ago found out the address and filed it away for future reference. He liked to know who he was dealing with. Ackerman, he'd learned, was ex-CIA and still freelance for the Agency. That was fine when Gladding was doing business on their behalf, but not so convenient when he had his own private affairs to attend to.

He waited in the car while Liggett quietly broke into Ackerman's place. There were no other cars in the driveway, and Liggett's return was so quick that Gladding knew Ackerman wasn't home.

"We'll try his bar," he said.

It was hardly surprising that Ackerman had taken up running a bar in his old age. Gladding was reasonably certain the man was a closet alcoholic. The place had probably even been purchased with Agency cash to provide plausible cover for Ackerman's ongoing activities on their behalf. If taxpayers ever got the full story on the myriad ways the spies found to squander their money, Gladding mused, there would be another American revolution.

His wait outside The Blue Gecko was even shorter than the one at the cottage in Gringo Gulch. Ackerman's green muscle car was nowhere to be seen. Liggett broke a window, reached in to unlock the back door and let himself inside, but Gladding was convinced now that Ackerman was gone. Spending the night with one of his lady friends, perhaps? Maybe, but it was entirely too coincidental that the man was proving so elusive at this particular moment. Gladding didn't believe in coincidences.

Liggett returned and got behind the wheel once more. "What now, boss?"

"He'll be back sooner or later and then we will definitely have a little chat," Gladding said. He stared at The Blue Gecko's scuffed blue door. All he had were questions and no answers. He hated unknowns, and right now, the biggest unknown was, where was his damn painting?

And then, he realized that he'd overlooked the obvious. "Ah."

Liggett glanced over. "What?"

"The courier. She's booked to fly back to Los Angeles later today. We'll watch the airport in case she decides on an earlier flight. She'll show up there sooner or later. Let's go."

The northbound road out of town ran parallel to Banderas Bay, and the airport runways ran east-west, right to the water's edge. When Hannah spotted a 747 coming in for a landing, she told Ackerman to slow down. The terminal was tiny, with a parking lot outside to match, as she recalled. Too exposed for what she had in mind.

"What's up?" Ackerman muttered. He was grumpy. Not unreasonable, Hannah supposed, after passing the night in an uncomfortable plastic chair, but it couldn't be helped.

She waved the gun to her left. "Turn down this side road."

He did as directed. She had him pull into the weed-choked lot of an abandoned warehouse of some sort. The doors and main-floor windows of the building were boarded up, but most of the second-floor windows had been smashed by vandals. The corrugated roof was more rust than metal. There wasn't a soul in sight.

Ackerman parked the car, turned off the ignition, then sat waiting, sulking. Hannah pulled the keys from the ignition, then waved him out with the barrel of her gun. She directed him to the back of the Barracuda, where she popped the trunk.

"Oh, no. No way."

"Sorry, buddy, but it's the only option. Get in."

He sat on the rim of the trunk. "I can't get out of here without outside help."

She pulled his phone out of her pack. "I'll call Juan and tell him to come get you."

"He'll ruin the car, prying the trunk open."

She rolled her eyes. Just like a guy to worry about the paint job. She might have mentioned that if he'd sprung for a later model car instead of trying to relive his misspent youth in this old muscle job, there would have been an emergency release built into the inside of the trunk. Every American car built since 2002 had one by law. Reminding him of that seemed unkind.

"I'll tell Juan where he can find the keys," she said.

"What if he doesn't have his phone on?"

"You'd better hope he does."

"Do you have any idea how hot it gets in this place?"

"I'm running late. We can do this the easy way or the hard way, but one way or another, you're getting in there right now." She aimed the gun for his kneecap.

He scowled and rolled back, wedging himself into the cramped space.

"Would you be more comfortable without your shoes?" she asked.

"Oh, no, you don't. You're not taking my boots."

"Suit yourself." She closed the lid. "The keys are on the rear driver's-side tire, Don. I'll be sure to tell Juan."

She heard his muffled cry. "Screw you, Nicks."

"Don't be a poor sport, Donny. This could have gone a lot worse."

She left the keys on the tire and grabbed her pack out of the backseat. As she jogged toward the terminal, she hit the autodial on his cell phone and roused Juan, the waiter. The man was drowsy, so it took a few strong words before she could impress upon him the need to hustle his butt over to a warehouse near the airport lot to free his boss. After telling him where to find the car keys, she rang off and tossed the phone away into some bushes as she cut across a vacant lot to reach the terminal.

Approaching the building, she shifted into hyper-vigilant mode, scanning every face, looking for anyone who might be looking for her. The ball cap from Ackerman's office and the change of clothing was as poor a disguise as there was, but she'd planned her arrival so close to departure time for her flight that she could only hope that she'd be on the plane before anyone was the wiser.

Inside the terminal, she found an automated kiosk and printed her boarding card. Then, spotting a manager behind the Alaska Air counter, she flashed the air marshal security pass Agent Towle had given her. He was clearly irritated.

"The doors are about to close," he grumbled. "There is no time for you to check your bag."

"Not a problem. I'll stow it in the cabin."

He sniffed, then got on his radio to alert the gate crew. He grabbed her by the elbow and they started to sprint. At the security check, he pulled her past the long line of tourists and around the metal detector, pausing only long enough to point to her air marshal's pass. Faced with a long line of overheated passengers, several crying babies, and a group of college kids who smelled like a distillery after apparently partying all night, the low-paid security guards happily deferred to the manager's authority and waved her past.

Just before turning the corner for the gates, Hannah risked one last glance back at the crowd waiting outside the secure area. Her heart skipped. There. A man she recognized. Or did she?

He had nothing with him—no carry-on bag, no duty-free booze, Mexican blankets or contraband Cuban cigars. The tanned and sunburned tourists in the airport all wore skimpy vacation wear, the men in tees or cotton polos. Her guy looked young enough to be one of the college kids on spring break, but something about his stance said he was no holidaymaker. His jacket was loose fitting, not unlike the one she herself used to conceal the gun she was packing. His eyes behind pitch-black shades were impossible to see, but every fiber of her being said he was checking departing passengers—especially the American women. Ogling babes in general? Or hunting for one in particular?

"*Señora,* please!" the airline manager shouted. "We are delaying the flight. We must run."

Fine by her. They flew, dodging waiting passengers and the souvenir kiosks making a last-ditch bid for tourist dollars. The attendant at the gate ripped her boarding pass and threw the stub back at her. Hannah stormed down the jetway.

By the time she dropped into her seat, the doors were closed and the plane's engines were revving. She stuffed her backpack under the seat ahead of her, buckled herself in, and only allowed herself to breathe when the plane began to roll backward. Even then, she wasn't sure she'd made it until the engines roared and the plane lifted off, bound for Los Angeles. For home.

Kyle Liggett's face was a grim mask as he walked back to the car. On the runway beyond the terminal, Gladding saw an Alaska Air Boeing 737 lift off the ground, engines roaring. He knew what his man would say as he climbed behind the wheel.

"She made it onto the flight."

They'd been so close. Gladding's informant at the airline had called him back the instant her computer terminal told her the Nicks woman had shown up to claim her ticket for the early morning flight to L.A.—too late, the ticket agent said. Final call for the flight had come and gone, and the doors were closing. There was no way she'd get through the long line at security in time.

At that moment, the arms dealer and his associate had just been pulling up to the terminal. Liggett had leapt out of the vehicle and sprinted in, charged with waylaying her and getting her back to the car, one way or another.

"Why didn't you stop her?" Gladding demanded now.

"She pulled a supervisor off the line and convinced him to hold the flight."

"What about the security check? You should have been able to catch her there."

"He walked her around it. I don't know why they let her through, but they did. Short of shooting her, I didn't see what there was to be done about it."

"Did she have the canvas?"

"I don't think so. All she had was a small backpack. It wouldn't have fit inside. Although…" Liggett pondered.

"What?"

"Maybe she took it out of the frame and rolled it up?"

Gladding looked aghast. "If she did, I'll shoot her myself." He drummed his well-manicured fingers on his knees. "And Ackerman? Did you see him?"

"Nope."

Gladding slumped. Where was his damn painting? If she hadn't left it at the villa and she hadn't carried it back, then she must have left it with someone she trusted. It had to be Ackerman. Why else would he have chosen this particular moment to vanish?

"Let's go," he told Liggett curtly, a plan formulating in his mind.

# *Sixteen*

The sleek Mercedes purred along the coastal highway back toward Gladding's in-town apartment building. In the backseat, he sulked and plotted, his small hands drawn into tight fists. The days were sliding out of control, colliding with his well-laid plans.

This Nicks woman who'd been hired to carry down his painting had become a liability. It was bad enough that that fool Sergio had tried to hijack the painting, but when she'd gotten past that problem, why hadn't she tried to fulfill her contract and deliver the piece? And if she wasn't able to do that, wouldn't a responsible courier simply have returned the consignment to the sender? Yet Liggett was certain she hadn't had it with her.

She seemed remarkably resourceful, this courier. Was it possible that Gladding's erstwhile colleagues in the intelligence community had gotten to her? They were determined to distance themselves from him after shamelessly using him for years when it suited their purposes. Now, he was a liability. If they had their way, he would be imprisoned or, better still, dead. After all, he knew where the bodies were buried—literally, in a couple of cases. He possessed career-terminating information that influential people would not want revealed.

If she *had* been operating down here with the help of the intelligence boys, who would she have turned to when she ran into trouble? None other than his old friend Don Ackerman, Gladding realized.

Liggett pulled into a reserved space in the underground parking lot of the exclusive low-rise apartment building. When he reached to kill the ignition, Gladding stopped him with a word.

"No. I have something else I need you to do."

"What's that?"

"Find Ackerman. I don't care how you do it. Just find him. Call me when you have him."

Liggett glanced over his shoulder and nodded as Gladding climbed out of the car.

The bump of the landing startled her awake. Hannah's hand shot instinctively toward the weapon at her back, but then she glanced out the window and saw the landmark Jetson-style modern building at the center of Los Angeles International Airport. She was home. A warm wave of relief flooded her body.

Customs was a fast walk-through. Outside the

terminal, she inhaled deeply, the city's habitual smog a welcome perfume. She sprinted across the road to the parking structure where she'd left the Prius.

Forty minutes later, she entered her condo, shoes, shirts, skirt and undies marking a trail from door to bathroom. She stood under the showerhead until the hot water ran to cold, tree huggers be damned.

Then, a towel wrapped around her head, she dialed Rebecca's number. It went to voice mail.

"I'm back, Becs, and I have to tell you, I'm not a happy camper. We need to talk. Call me when you get this message."

She hung up, stripped off the towel and slid between the sheets, thinking that it would be better if she told Rebecca in person that she'd left August Koon's painting behind. She'd probably have to run back up to the gallery in Malibu.

It was the last thought she had for several hours.

William Teagarden was back at the Gladding villa with Peña, but the police captain seemed remarkably unfocused. He'd actually sat down at the bullet-ridden grand piano and begun serenading the last couple of crime scene technicians on-site with cabaret renditions of old Sinatra tunes. He was a pretty decent pianist, and his voice wasn't half-bad either, but it seemed to Teagarden like an odd time to fool around.

Peña's fascination with the piano, however, gave him free rein to comb through the villa, looking for clues—

although not to the identity of the murderers, whose victims were now in the Puerto Vallarta morgue. He was hunting for something that might tell him what had happened to *The Night Café*.

He rifled through every closet and drawer, then examined the laptop the cops had left on Gladding's desk. It was an oversight the boys from Scotland Yard wouldn't have made, but it didn't tell him much. Most of the document and e-mail files were password protected. Someone with better computer skills might have been able to break in, but he himself was a dinosaur. It was all he could do to manage his own e-mail account, and if it hadn't been for the fact that it had become the preferred way of communicating for many of his current clients, he wouldn't have bothered with that.

The fax machine was a little more helpful. As he scrolled through the list of recent faxes received, he found a number with a Los Angeles area code. The machine allowed him to print a duplicate of the message received from that number. It was from the owner of an art gallery in Malibu, confirming the shipment of a painting by August Koon. The delivery had been set for the previous day.

Teagarden frowned. He'd heard that artist's name somewhere. He went back to the laptop and logged into an Internet search engine. August Koon, it seemed, was a contemporary painter living in Los Angeles. Photographs of some of his work meant nothing to Teagarden, but something about the painter's name niggled.

He logged off the Internet, folded the fax and slipped it into his pocket. Then, he went to look for Peña. The music had stopped, and he had no idea how long ago. He found Peña basking in a padded chair out on the veranda. A blue peacock was strolling across the lawn. Peña waved his arms to startle the bird, and it opened its tail to a rainbow swirl of color.

The captain grinned. "He's very beautiful, no?"

"Aye, that he is," Teagarden agreed.

"So, Señor Teagarden. My men are finished here. Is there anything else you would like to see?"

"I'd like to see that missing van Gogh, but it doesn't seem to be here. Any word on Mr. Gladding's whereabouts?"

"*Nada.* But I am not surprised. Men like Gladding have places where they can lie low when trouble comes. I would imagine that he is very far away by now."

Teagarden nodded. "You're probably right, and I've taken up too much of your time. I think I should be on my way, too."

"Where will you go next?"

"The painting was stolen in Los Angeles, so I suppose I'll head back there." The fax in his pocket also suggested that L.A. was his best bet, but he declined to mention that to Peña. "There are a couple of flights this afternoon. I should be able to get a seat on one. Do you think someone could drop me at the airport?"

Peña got to his feet. "Most certainly. I will do it myself."

\* \* \*

Access Denied.

Travis Spielman glared at his computer screen. All San Diego–related files were down. He was still working on getting the new data network up and running, but the southern tier of the system continued to be frozen out. He'd called his director in Washington again this morning, but all she knew was that something was going down and they had to wait. She'd let him know when the access ban was lifted.

Spielman had no choice but to work around it. With Hannah still AWOL, he was dying to try to run a search of Moises Gladding once more, but after yesterday's scare, he didn't dare risk it for fear someone would want to know why he was so interested in a red-flagged file.

He picked up the phone and dialed home. Ruben answered on the third ring. Mellie was crying softly in the background.

"What's wrong with the baby?"

Ruben cooed to her. Spielman could picture his partner bobbing her on his hip. He'd have her laughing again in no time, he knew. "We were doing our physio, weren't we, sweetie?"

Daily physiotherapy was a critical part of Melanie's care. Otherwise, her cerebral palsy would lock up her muscles, risking serious deformity to her limbs. The more flexible they could keep her, the better her chances of leading a close-to-normal life, and maybe even learning to walk eventually. Ruben, an athlete himself, was a wizard at taking her through her daily physio routine.

"I was just wondering if you and Mellie have spotted that little rabbit today?"

"Rabbit?" Ruben puzzled. "Oh! The rabbit! No, we haven't been out yet. We got kind of a late start. But you know, we're going for a run in a few minutes. Maybe we'll look for the rabbit when we do."

"I'd be interested to know if you see it."

"No problem. We'll call and let you know, won't we, baby?"

Sure enough, Spielman heard Mellie giggle. Ruben was a wonder.

He hung up the phone and wandered over to the window, pressing his forehead against the glass, watching tiny pedestrians far below pass under the flowering arches of purple blossoms on the jacarandas lining Wilshire Boulevard.

Hannah was out there. Somewhere.

Kyle Liggett sat at a corner table in The Blue Gecko. He had his baseball cap pulled low, but there was little chance of being recognized here, among the tourists and hard drinkers who populated the place. He sipped his Dos Equis beer and flipped the pages of a local English language newspaper.

Ackerman had shown up a short while earlier looking unshaven and miserable, snapping at the waiters, answering the gibes of the regulars with bad-tempered grunts.

Somebody got out on the wrong side of the bed, Liggett thought. But which bed were you in, Donnyboy? Because it wasn't your own. We were there.

They would know soon enough. He'd parked in the alleyway out back, and he was just waiting for the right moment to get Ackerman alone. Then, the old spook would tell them everything they wanted to know. Liggett would make sure of that.

He might be a baby-face, but he knew something about interrogation. It was a skill set Moises Gladding appreciated in him. He'd worked for Gladding a few times before. Not long ago, Gladding had taken him along to West Africa to deal with a man who'd doublecrossed him. Gladding had sat by, impassive, while Liggett worked the man over, just to impress upon him the seriousness of the situation. He might have thought confession would earn him a reprieve, but of course, it hadn't. When Gladding gave the nod, Liggett had snapped the man's neck.

Ackerman told one of the waiters to take over the bar and he headed through a beaded curtain to a room out back. This was the moment Liggett had been waiting for. While the barman had his back turned, he sidled over to the curtain and slipped through. Ackerman was talking to the cook, berating him for failing to buy some ingredient. Pimentos? Peppers? Liggett couldn't catch the Spanish. But Ackerman threw a wad of bills at the man and pushed him out the back door.

"And you make sure you're back in five minutes, *comprende?*" he bellowed.

Perfect.

When Ackerman turned back around, he didn't see Liggett for a moment. But then, Liggett hissed. The other man looked startled. Liggett held his fingers to his lips. "Let's go for a walk," he murmured.

"Oh, for chrissake," Ackerman muttered. "Sure. Fine. Whatever. Anyone else want a piece of me?"

They left through the alley door. Liggett patted Ackerman down to make sure he wasn't carrying, then pushed him into the backseat of the Mercedes. He'd set the child locks so that once closed, the back doors couldn't be opened until he was ready to let him out.

On the way over to Gladding's place, Ackerman did his best to find out where they were going, but Liggett maintained stony silence. The best way to unnerve an opponent, he'd learned, was to remain inscrutable. He might be young, but his skills were definitely improving. He might work for Moises Gladding now, but one day soon, he would take that son of a bitch down and run his own show.

Ackerman came to again in a cavernous room with a concrete floor—a warehouse? A hangar of some sort? Hard to say. He had no idea where he was, or why he was there. Hell, he could hardly remember who he was.

His head was ringing and every inch of his body ached. He tried to itemize where the pain was localized, but it was so widespread that trying to pin it down just made his head hurt more. Instead, he tried to itemize what he could.

He squirmed but didn't manage to move much. He was bound to a chair with plastic ties. The restraints cut into his wrists, but they were the least of his problems. He turned his head and squinted through the one eye that wasn't swollen shut. Sure enough, there was Moises Gladding, leaning against his fancy Mercedes. Ackerman frowned. Was that his own green Barracuda parked a couple of stalls over from the Merc? How had it gotten here?

He continued down the checklist of what he knew.

The man who'd taken him from The Blue Gecko had made a phone call as he drove. When he pulled into an underground parking lot, Gladding had been waiting for them. The driver had opened the rear door of the Mercedes, but before Ackerman was halfway out, the little creep had brought his gun down hard on the back of his head. The last thing Ackerman remembered was his face hitting the concrete floor.

When he'd come to, he'd been bound to the chair. And then, the fun had begun.

The memory of the past few hours came back with sensations of pain in every quadrant of his body. Gladding's thug, the most cold-blooded little prick Ackerman had ever run into, had seemed to enjoy practicing the art of inflicting agony. Gladding, meantime, had stood by, impassive, posing the occasional question, then nodding at the kid when he didn't like the answer, unleashing another round of torture.

His feet were bare, he now noticed. Not tied to the chair, however. No need. Even if the restraints at his wrists were suddenly to vanish, he couldn't have run. His good eye peered down. They were hardly recognizable as feet anymore, swollen and purple as they were. It seemed he'd heard the bones break before he registered the baseball bat making contact with them. He could only be grateful that, swelled up as they were, there was little circulation. They could have been numb blocks of ice at the end of his legs, for all he could feel them.

The pain in his right shoulder was far worse. His shirt had been cut away and the kid had pierced him repeatedly with something long, sharp and red-hot, clotting his vision so thickly that he couldn't think. He took a deep breath and closed his good eye, forcing his inner mind to locate a muscle somewhere, anywhere, that wasn't in pain. He found one in his left thigh, focused on it, and repeated a mantra. *Relax, relax, relax…* It was a torture surviving technique taught at The Farm, the CIA's training facility at Camp Peary, Virginia.

"Don?" Gladding's voice pierced his hard-won calm. "Are you sleeping, my friend?"

"Not bloody likely," Ackerman growled. He opened his eye. Bloody was right. The concrete floor in front of him was spattered with red. His tongue made a tentative exploration of his mouth. That's right. Shy a few teeth now, as well.

"You were telling me about Hannah Nicks. Who is she working for?"

Ackerman shook his head, but as soon as he did, the bat came down on it. Not hard enough to do permanent damage, much less knock him unconscious again. Gladding's boy was pulling his punches now. The old man must have reamed him out during his last nap.

"You mentioned the FBI," Gladding reminded him.

"She had a card from some agent. I never heard of the guy, but apparently he'd told her to get in touch if she ran into problems down here."

"And so she came to the bar."

"S'right." Ackerman saw the kid's fancy Nikes in his peripheral vision. He turned his head and spit. A red clot landed square on the toe of the athletic shoe. He saw the kid wind up with the bat, but Gladding hissed and he swung wide of his mark. Ackerman felt the breeze as the wood passed a millimeter from his cheekbone.

"She came after she ran into trouble with Sergio," Gladding said.

Ackerman nodded. "She wanted to know how to get to your place. She said she had a delivery for you."

"And you told her how to get there?"

"Yup."

"But I never saw her."

Ackerman started to shrug, but that was a bad idea. *Relax, relax…* "Ships passing in the night, maybe? She said you'd had some other visitors already."

"I see. So she told you about the gunmen?"

"She did." He felt groggy, Ackerman realized, but he didn't think they'd drugged him. Probably had a concussion from all those whacks from the bat. Anyway, he had no problem telling Gladding what he knew. The truth was always easier to maintain than a lie, and if he had any hope at all of getting out of this, consistency would be critical. Fact was, he didn't really know anything critical anyway, and the Nicks woman was long gone, far as he knew.

"What did she tell you about the delivery?"

"She said it was a painting."

"Did you see it?"

"Nope?"

"Come on, Don! She left it with you."

"No, sh—" The bat landed on his spine and something crunched. Ackerman nearly passed out from the pain. "She didn't leave it and I didn't see it, dammit!" He peered over at the short, balding man who held his fate in his hands.

Gladding shook his head sadly. "I thought we were friends, Don."

"Moises, give me a break. We've known each other for how long? Eight, nine years? We play chess, we drink together, and I help you out from time to time."

"When your masters tell you to. They seem to have decided that I'm not worth helping anymore, however. Now, they would like to pretend they don't know me."

"I don't know anything about that, and I don't know anything about any goddamn painting."

Gladding studied him for a moment, and then he looked over at the young man. "Show it to him."

The cavernous space echoed with the sound of wood being dropped on concrete, and Ackerman saw the bat roll a little way from his chair. He winced involuntarily as the kid unrolled a poster and shoved it before his face. He squinted. He only had one good eye at the moment and even that wasn't working so hot. He saw a copy of a painting done in mostly reds and yellows. An old café, French by the look of it, lit by the garish light of gas lamps. A green billiard table stood in the center of the room, but nobody was playing. The few patrons in the place were slumped over small tables, half passed out. It looked like The Blue Gecko at closing time.

"What's this?" Ackerman asked.

"It's the painting that woman was supposed to deliver. Now do you recognize it?"

Ackerman shook his head. "I told you, I didn't see the painting she had. But this isn't it. She said it was an abstract piece. 'Like somebody kicked over finger paints,' was her exact description, I think."

Gladding nodded. "Yes, it was camouflaged. This is what was underneath. A restorer is standing by as we speak to remove the covering layer and reveal the masterpiece beneath. It's delicate business, but not all that difficult to do, as it turns out."

Ackerman turned back to the poster, leaning forward to read the title printed on the white mat surrounding the picture. *The Night Café by Vincent van*

*Gogh*. And in the corner of the painting itself, one tiny scrawled signature: Vincent.

"Oh, shit," Ackerman breathed. No wonder Gladding was so obsessed with getting the thing back. The van Gogh would be priceless, or near to, but Gladding wouldn't keep it. It was collateral for some big deal. The trade would be big—big and ugly.

"I don't know what she did with it, Moises. I told her she should leave it and I'd get it to you, but she didn't trust me. She just needed me to be her chauffeur so she could get back to the airport and beat it out of town. She left me stuffed in the trunk of my goddamn car, for Pete's sake!"

"I see. Well, I'm very sorry to hear that, Don. Clearly, you've had a difficult day."

No kidding, Ackerman thought. And something told him it was about to get much, much worse.

# *Seventeen*

*Los Angeles*
*Thursday, April 20*

Hannah awoke to the bright light of morning. She'd slept later than she meant to. Gee, could it be the stress of the last couple of days? Now she'd have to fight morning traffic to get up to Malibu.

She'd tried repeatedly to call Rebecca since getting in yesterday, but without success. She could have tried calling again this morning, but as she lay awake last night, wrestling with her hyper-stimulated brain, she realized that was the coward's way. News like hers deserved to be delivered in person.

In record time, she hit the shower, dressed and grabbed a banana on her way out the door. The Prius streaked from the garage and down the hill toward the freeway—where she came to an abrupt halt. Sighing, she flicked on the radio, peeled her banana and settled in for a slow drive.

She merged into westbound traffic on the Santa Monica Freeway while she ate the banana. Then, inching along, she pulled her cell phone out of her messenger bag and scanned the missed-call list. Cal had called, but his was the last voice she needed to hear right now. If there had been a problem with Gabe, he wouldn't have given up at one call. Maybe he was taking Mrs. Jennings's advice and calling to bury the hatchet, she thought. Yeah, right. That was about as likely as her taking up knitting. She'd call him back later.

Nora had called three times, and that was more worrying. Visions of her mother taking a fall flashed through her mind. Her mom would be seventy-three on her next birthday, prime time for broken hips, and from there, it could only be downhill. But when she tried to get Nora back, she got voice mail on both the house line and on her cell. She called her mother's line, but it just rang and rang. Nothing could convince their mother to get an answering machine.

"Why do I need that? I hate those things. Anyway, I'm always home, and if I'm not, I'm with one of you, so you don't need to phone to talk to me, right?"

You couldn't argue with the woman's logic.

A call from an unfamiliar number interested her. Could it be from Special Agent Towle, wondering if she'd planted their toys? Boy, did she have a story for him, but first, she would tell the person most affected by Moises Gladding's troubles.

Traffic sped up, but it was one of those cruel jokes L.A. freeways liked to play, because five hundred yards later, it slowed to a crawl once more. Another thought occurred to her about the unfamiliar number. Could it be Gladding calling, looking for his painting? It was a 310 area code, though, one of the dozen or so Southern California codes. In fact, she realized, Rebecca's gallery in Malibu had a 310 number. The traffic stalled completely and she peered at the number again, then pulled up her phone's number list. Nope, different number.

A horn blared behind her, and she looked up to see that the car in front of her was fifty yards gone and picking up speed. She waved in the rearview mirror. "Sorry." She tossed the phone aside. She refused to be one of those people who drove like idiots because they were too busy yammering on their cell phones. It was such a cliché.

She'd talk to Rebecca and see what she wanted to do about their little problem. After that, she'd go home, return all those calls, check in with Special Agent Towle and tell him she'd salted his electronic devices at Gladding's, for all the good it would do him. Then, she'd open a bottle of wine and settle in to watch HBO.

She allowed herself a smile. Or maybe invite Russo over to share that bottle of wine? Better idea.

She was turning onto Pacific Coast Highway, only

about a mile from the gallery, when the phone on the seat beside started to vibrate. She caught it just as it was about to skip itself off the seat and she glanced at the screen. Speak of the devil. But as much as she wanted to talk to Russo, she was steeling herself for Rebecca's inevitable dismay when she found out Hannah had blown the job that was supposed to save her butt. Russo would have to wait.

Ruben made himself a cup of coffee, knowing full well that Travis would stop at Starbucks on his way into work, probably giving in to the lure of one of those calorie-laden pastries while he was at it. The healthy breakfasts he tried to make were wasted on his partner during the week. He pulled a stool up to the breakfast bar and opened the *Los Angeles Times*. Mellie was still sleeping and Trav's shower had just shut off. Ruben glanced at his watch. In five minutes, Travis would race into the kitchen, plant a kiss on his cheek and fly out the door.

He had finished the front page and turned to the sports section when Travis came running through, briefcase in hand. As the garage door opened and the Jeep roared to life, Ruben glanced at his watch and smiled. Five minutes on the dot. The man was so wonderfully predictable.

He poured himself another cup of coffee and checked out the scores from last night's Dodgers game. With luck, he might have half an hour before Melanie woke up. Then, it was breakfast, physio, a little playtime, and then maybe a trip to the garden center to buy some flowers for the patio.

He was just finishing the paper when he heard the hum of Hannah's garage door opening. By the time he made it to the window, her blue Prius was already on its way down the hill. He reached for the phone to call Travis and let him know that the rabbit was back in her hole.

Los Angeles energized William Teagarden. He knew many people found the place crass and uninteresting, dozens of suburbs in search of a city, but he wasn't one of the naysayers. He liked the sunshine, the palm trees, the optimistic architecture, even the traffic, especially now that car rental companies offered the option of GPS devices to keep him on track. Remembering to keep to the right side of the road was nothing compared to the challenge of negotiating freeways and canyon roads. Now, with satellite navigation aids, he could drop the top on the convertible he always ordered and pretend he was Frankie Avalon on his way to a date with Annette Funicello.

When he'd arrived from Puerto Vallarta the previous afternoon, he'd gotten a red Sebring convertible at the car rental agency and a room at the Mondrian Hotel on the Sunset Strip. This morning, he was scheduled to meet with a local FBI contact referred by the Washington-based head of the Bureau's Art Theft unit. Teagarden and Special Agent Lou Eppley had worked dozens of cases together, sharing information, coordinating recovery efforts, arranging arrests and putting together prosecution evidence.

Eppley had also introduced him to the game of baseball, and Teagarden tried to attend at least one Major League game whenever he was in the States. The game was reminiscent of the cricket he'd played as a boy, but faster. He'd talked to the concierge at the hotel last night about the current schedule. There were three teams within easy driving distance, so he had high hopes of catching a game before he left town.

First, however, he needed to track down the gallery he strongly suspected had arranged the shipment of Yale University's van Gogh, and the courier who, knowingly or not, had been hired for the job. Eppley had done some digging and come up with some key information. A joint FBI-CIA task force had already been looking at Moises Gladding when they caught a break and found out about the transport of the painting. As a matter of courtesy, the Los Angeles field office would be happy to meet with the former Scotland Yard Detective Superintendent and brief him on what they knew about the shipment.

*"In one mile, turn right, then arrive at destination on right."*

"Thank you, Pamela," Teagarden said to the GPS. He liked to stay on the good side of his little traffic help-mates with their lovely, reassuring voices. That included christening each one with a pretty name.

By the time Travis Spielman got his partner's call about Hannah's return, his mind was already on the day ahead. Installation of the new software was running well over schedule because of the system lockouts of the last couple of days. Half a dozen sister agencies had already called in complaints about the delays.

This kind of problem only fed the parochialism rampant in the intelligence community, where each department jealously guarded its turf and resisted all efforts to coordinate and share information with the others. If Homeland Security couldn't prove that it was capable of providing efficient service, they would soon lose the cooperation that had been won only through the knocking together of heads, and the system would start to break apart into little fiefdoms once more.

Of course, if the spooks would give warning when an operation was in play and the system was going to be frozen, at least the Homeland data wonks could answer the complaints and tell their clients how long the problem would last. As it was, they just came off looking incompetent—and Travis Spielman hated to be thought of as incompetent.

So when Ruben called, he was pleased to know that Hannah was safely back home, and he felt a little foolish about the paranoia he'd been feeling, worrying whether he personally was in some kind of trouble. Right now, she was the least of his problems. He had angry bureaucrats to wrangle. Compared to those battles, Hannah's line of work sounded easy.

# *Eighteen*

The first sign of trouble was the black-and-white police cruiser at the side of the roadway, its rooftop lights spinning. A Sheriff's Department deputy was planted in the middle of the highway, his arm waving irritably to keep the looky-loos moving past the action on the side of the road. It must be a traffic accident, Hannah thought. Pacific Coast Highway was notorious for them, especially at this time of year, when the marine layer socked the road in fog for much of the day.

But as she drew closer to the strip mall where the Sandpiper Gallery was located, she saw another half-dozen patrol cars in the parking lot, as well as a couple of unmarked cars with police plates. Yellow crime-scene tape strung around the buildings flapped in the wind. She tried to turn into the parking lot, but the traffic cop screamed at her to keep going. By the line of huddled civilians and wet-suited surfers standing along the ocean side of the roadway, craning their necks to see over the passing cars, she could only imagine that others had tried to get into the plaza already. The cop was in no mood to listen to anybody's pressing excuses for being there.

She sighed and drove a few hundred yards farther north, pulling into the parking lot of one of the seafood restaurants that dotted the Malibu beach side. It was too early for the place to be open, but there were already several cars in the lot, probably belonging to the neck stretchers across from the gallery. Hustling back down the road, she was just getting ready to argue with the traffic deputy when she heard someone shout her name.

*Russo.* "Let her pass," he called to the cop in the road.

The deputy nodded, held up his hands to stop traffic in both directions, then waved Hannah across. Despite the bad feeling she had about the yellow crime-scene tape at the strip mall, the sight of Russo stirred a flutter in her middle—his dark hair a little mussed in the breeze, the silver at his temples catching the light, open shirt collar under sport coat. Guy was a babe, no doubt about it.

He took her elbow. "Where the hell have you been? I've been trying to track you down."

"Well, hello to you, too. What's going on?" She glanced beyond him to the huddle of deputies outside the gallery door.

"Trouble, that's what. Come on." He led her to the

tape and nodded to the duty officer with the crime-scene sign-in sheet. "She's with me. Hannah Nicks."

The deputy wrote down her name while Russo lifted the tape for her to pass under.

"Why is Homicide here, John?"

"Why are you here?"

"I have business with the owner of that gallery. I—" She stopped cold, remembering the scene at Moises Gladding's villa. "Oh, jeez, not Rebecca, too."

It was Russo's turn to freeze. "What do you mean, 'too.' Who else?"

She started to speak but couldn't begin to figure out where to start. "I'll tell you after. What happened to her?"

"Somebody broke into the place." He nodded toward a heavyset, gray-haired woman sitting in the back of one of the patrol cars. "The lady who owns the gift shop next door came in this morning and found a couple of FedEx packages outside the gallery door. The lights were on inside, so she knocked. The door was unlocked. That's when she found Ms. Powell. Medical examiner says she's been dead for more than twenty-four hours. Hard to be sure until the autopsy."

"How?"

He hesitated, but it was hardly her first taste of violent death and he knew it. "He snapped her neck."

"Oh, God." She thought about Rebecca at Nora's, remembered her painful thinness, her nervous manner. She wouldn't have put up any fight. She had to have been terrified.

At the gallery entrance, a blond woman came out the door and looked around, frowning. Then, spotting Russo, she skipped down the steps and walked over. Dressed in a crisp navy pantsuit and collared blouse, she was about Hannah's age, but blond where Hannah was dark, organized and efficient looking where Hannah was completely off-kilter, after her hellish week.

The blonde carried the blue notebook of the Sheriff's Department Homicide Bureau, a cartoon of a fierce-looking bulldog on the cover. She glanced at Hannah, then turned to Russo. Hannah had rarely felt so summarily dismissed.

"The M.E.'s done with the body for now. He wants to know if the coroner's people can remove it."

Russo nodded, but Hannah touched his arm. "Can I see her first? Please?"

She was thinking of Nora. Rebecca was her sister's best friend. Hannah had been to plenty of crime scenes, and she knew Nora would hate the impersonal manner of everyone working it. It wasn't the cops' fault. They had to develop a thick skin or the job would destroy them. It messed them up pretty bad anyway. Just the same, Nora would want to know that at least one person had been here to grieve for her friend.

The blonde raised an eyebrow as she waited for Russo's inevitable refusal of Hannah's request to go in. When he said "all right" instead, the eyebrow shot up even higher.

Russo couldn't help but notice. "Hannah, this is my new trainee. Lindsay, this is Hannah Nicks."

Lindsay Who-Didn't-Seem-to-Have-a-Surname nodded curtly, then stood aside to let them pass—although everything about her telegraphed, *You're in charge here, Detective, but what the hell are you doing letting a civilian into our crime scene?* It made Hannah really glad that Russo had introduced her as his trainee and not his partner.

She followed him up the steps and into the gallery, Lindsay close behind. The place was softly lit, much as it had been the morning—was it only three days ago?— that Hannah had come to pick up the Koon. But pictures were askew on the walls and a couple of the pedestals had been knocked over, sending pottery shards across the carpet.

The coroner's gurney stood just this side of the divider that separated the gallery space from Rebecca's office area. An M.E. Hannah remembered from her own days on the force was making notes on a clipboard. He glanced up and did a double take when he spotted her. Clearly, he remembered her, although her name seemed to be escaping him.

"Uh, hi. Long time, no see. How you been?"

"Good. You?"

"Okay. You know."

"Yeah." Not a conversation that would be remembered for sterling repartee, obviously. But then, there *was* a dead woman lying three feet away.

The M.E. turned to Russo. "I'm all done here. You got everything you need from the body? If so, the guys there will get out of your way. Let you get on with your work."

"Hold on a minute, would you?"

"Sure."

Hannah came around the divider. The first thing she saw were the dainty lace-up espadrilles, the same shoes Rebecca had worn to dinner at Nora's. She was lying on her back, head tilted sharply to one side. She had on another flowing skirt, much like the one she'd worn Sunday, but it was hiked up around her bikini briefs. If she'd been sexually assaulted, the panties would probably have been ripped off, but the M.E. would have been looking for preliminary signs of it anyway.

Hannah crouched next to her, then looked back up at Russo. "Can I?" she asked, her hand poised over the body.

When he nodded, she pulled down the hem of the skirt and smoothed it around the mottled calves, dark at the back where the blood had pooled after she died. She pulled down Rebecca's sweater, as well, to cover the incision mark where the medic would have inserted a thermometer to get a liver temp. Thankfully, Rebecca's eyes were closed and her face seemed peaceful, despite the dark marbling of her skin and awkward angle of her head. That, at least, was something she'd be able to offer Nora, Hannah thought.

She rested a hand on the skirt where she'd smoothed it over the leg. Rebecca felt so very cold. "Oh, Becs," she whispered, "I'm really sorry."

Russo's hand squeezed her shoulder gently and she got to her feet.

"Come on, let's sit over here and let the coroner's people do their thing," he said.

He led her to a padded bench set on one side of the gallery, positioned for viewing the maximum number of paintings—as well as the work of the crime-scene technicians, who were busy dusting, print-lifting and photographing every possible nook and cranny. When they sat down, Lindsay was there like white on rice, settling on the other side of Russo, her blue notebook open, pen poised.

"The victim's date book showed she met with you on Monday, Ms. Nicks. We also found your business card on the desk."

"I imagine you did."

"So what was your relationship to the vic."

Hannah bristled. "Look, her name wasn't 'vic,' Detective. It was Rebecca—or, better still, Ms. Powell."

"No need to get huffy. I understand you used to be a detective. You know how it goes here."

"Yes, but she was a close friend of my family. A little respect would be nice."

"It's not—"

"Lindsay." Russo's tone was weary. "Enough."

"I'm just—"

"Either sit quietly and take notes while I ask the questions, or go make sure the techs are getting everything we need."

Clearly, she didn't like either option, but she knew

better than to argue with her training officer. Under normal circumstances, Hannah might actually have liked her spunk. But these were not normal circumstances.

"So," Russo said, "this lady was the gallery owner you told me about. The one who asked you to make a delivery to Mexico."

Hannah nodded. Lindsay made notes. Was she wondering how her boss and Hannah knew each other? It wasn't like they had enough of a relationship that Hannah's portrait would be in a silver frame on his desk. But if she was curious, Lindsay didn't say anything—maybe because she didn't want to be sent away to dust doorknobs for fingerprints.

"You might have been the last person to see her alive," Russo said.

"Somebody must have seen her after that. I said I saw her three *days* ago."

He shrugged. "We're still canvassing, but you could be it. Her mail wasn't picked up from her box outside on Tuesday or yesterday."

"What about the gift shop owner who found her?"

"She noticed that the lights were on the last two days, just like she found them this morning, but these places do most of their business on the weekend. She didn't think anything of it when the place was so quiet. It was only when she tried the door to bring in the FedEx boxes that she realized it was unlocked. That's when she found her. All we can do is backtrack to what we do know, which is that you saw her—when, exactly?"

Hannah briefly described spending Monday morning and part of the afternoon with Rebecca.

"That was the day after you'd seen her at your sister's?"

"You know it was. I told you."

Russo cocked his thumb over his shoulder. "Tell it again for the detective here so she can get it in her notes."

So Hannah recounted the dinner at Nora's and Rebecca's job offer, then brought them back up to Monday afternoon. "She was alive and happy when I left her around two. Really happy. This commission was a big deal for her. She thought her bad luck was finally turning."

"Bad luck?" Lindsay asked.

"Messy divorce. Money troubles."

"And this guy in Mexico she was sending the painting to?" Russo asked.

"Moises Gladding." She couldn't fail to notice Lindsay's dramatic eye roll, although Russo, with his back to his trainee, missed it. "What?" Hannah demanded.

"Nothing."

Russo glanced back at her.

She put on her best "who, me?" expression. "Just taking notes, boss."

He turned back to Hannah. "He's a piece of work, this Gladding. There are about a dozen federal warrants out on him, did you know that?"

"You ran a background check?"

He nodded. "After I talked to you. Maybe your sister's friend made a deal with the devil."

"Yeah, I'm beginning to think she might have. I guess it's true what they say—if a deal looks too good to be true, it probably is."

There was a sudden bump and commotion over by the office area, and one of the coroner's people cursed. They had wrapped the body and were lifting it onto the gurney when one of the men lost his grip and dropped his end. The wrapping came open and a mottled arm flopped out.

Hannah closed her eyes, trying not to think of who it was they were manhandling. At the same time, the ex-cop in her registered the flaccidity of the body, the color of the skin, and the faint, sweetish odor that she'd been trying to block out from the moment she'd walked in the door. A body begins to enter a state of rigor about twelve hours after death as lactose acid locks up the muscles. By twenty-four hours, it's in the state that's the reason the term "stiff" was coined. Then, as decomp sets in, it loses rigidity at about the same rate over the next twelve or so hours. The state of Rebecca's body made it very clear that this couldn't have happened much later than Tuesday afternoon.

The men tucked the arm back in and managed to get the body on the low gurney with no further mishaps. They lifted and locked the stretcher in the up position, then rolled it to the door, which opened before them, held by a sheriff's deputy who looked like he'd just graduated from junior high.

On the deck behind the young deputy, Hannah was shocked to see her old buddies, Special Agents Towle and Ito, along with a third man she didn't recognize. As the men rolled the stretcher down the handicap ramp to the waiting coroner's van, the three men entered the gallery. Hannah, Russo and his partner all got to their feet.

The young cop quick-slipped around the new arrivals. "Excuse me, guys. Detectives, one of our guys is going on a coffee run," he said. "Get you guys some?"

Russo glanced at Hannah, who nodded gratefully. This was not the morning to have skipped her caffeine hit. Russo pulled out his wallet and handed over a couple of twenties. "I think we could use coffee all around right about now."

"Not for me, thanks," Lindsay said. Her rosy cheeks and trim build marked her as a runner. Hannah tried to remember the last time she'd gone for a run herself. Did dodging trouble in Mexico count?

Agent Towle turned to his partner, a thumb cocked at Russo's trainee. "She's always been like that. Total health nut."

Hannah and Russo exchanged puzzled looks.

"Excuse me?" Russo said. "Who are you?"

"Sorry. Special Agent Joe Towle, FBI." He held up the leather folder that showed his shield and ID. "And you, I imagine, are Detective Russo."

As Russo shook hands with him, he frowned back at his partner. "Towle? As in the brother?"

"That's him," Lindsay said.

"This is Special Agent Ito," Towle added, "and behind him is William Teagarden, formerly of Scotland Yard. Gentlemen, this is Detective John Russo and his partner, Lindsay Towle. My baby sister."

"Joe!" Lindsay snapped.

"Oops, sorry. *Detective* Towle, a brilliant and never less than thoroughly professional police officer who happens to have an annoying older brother." Towle turned to Hannah. "And this lady, speak of the devil, is Hannah Nicks. We were just saying on the way over here that we'd pay you a visit next. You've saved us a trip."

"Glad to help," Hannah said, even as her brain was making the connection. Russo's partner was Special Agent Towle's sister. Russo had called Hannah from work on Monday and she'd told him about making a delivery to Moises Gladding. A few hours later, FBI agents had shown up on her doorstep. Coincidence? She didn't think so.

Russo looked mystified, however. "How do you know Ms. Nicks?" he asked the agents.

"Agent Ito and I paid her a visit before she left for Mexico."

Russo said nothing for a moment, but Hannah saw his dark eyes flicker the second the penny dropped. He wheeled on his partner. "Detective, a word, if you please."

He marched to the other side of the room, Lindsay following behind like a defiant delinquent. They kept their voices low, but the body language left no doubt that Russo's trainee was getting a reaming out. She somehow managed to look chastened and unapologetic at the same time.

The older man who'd arrived with the feds turned to Hannah. "You've had quite an adventure, it seems, Ms. Nicks."

He had an accent you could cut with a knife. Somewhere in his sixties, he had grizzled, thinning hair, but a tall military bearing. His deep brown eyes twinkled and his smile could only be called mischievous. Under any other circumstances, Hannah would have been positively charmed. At the moment, however, she was only confused.

"I'm sorry, I didn't catch your name," she said.

"William Teagarden. Detective Superintendent, retired, at your service." As he took her hand, he flashed a disarmingly warm smile. "These days, I'm a private recovery consultant."

"And what does that mean?"

"I find lost works of art."

"Mr. Teagarden was referred to us by FBI headquarters," Agent Towle told her.

"That's right," Teagarden said. "I've done a great deal of work with the Bureau over the years, and the head of their Art Unit was kind enough to put me together with Special Agent Towle here. It seems we're running parallel investigations. I'm on the trail of a stolen van Gogh, you see. An irreplaceable work called *The Night Café.*"

"It was taken from the Arlen Hunter Museum in January," Towle said. "Two security guards were killed in the heist. Mr. Teagarden is of the view that the painting you carried to Mexico might have been the missing van Gogh."

"What?" Hannah exclaimed. Russo, who'd reappeared behind her, echoed her surprise.

Hannah turned to Towle and Ito. "You saw the painting when you came to my place on Monday night. That was no masterpiece."

"No, I wouldn't have said so," Towle agreed, "but Mr. Teagarden thinks the van Gogh might have been painted over to make it easier to spirit it out of the country."

"It wouldn't be the first time," Teagarden said.

"But wouldn't that destroy the van Gogh?" Russo asked.

"Not at all. Van Gogh painted in oils. If the overpainting was done in acrylics, then it would be removable with solvents that wouldn't damage the oils beneath. It's specialized work, but a man with Moises Gladding's resources would have no difficulty finding a restorer with the right set of skills, an anemic bank account and a broken moral compass. What was the size of the painting you carried to Mexico, Ms. Nicks?"

"Maybe two, two-and-a-half feet by three?"

Teagarden nodded. "Roughly seventy-two by ninety-two, a French size thirty canvas."

Agent Ito glanced around the gallery. "When Mr.

Teagarden told us this dealer was involved, we wondered how deep the art dealer was into the art fraud business."

"No way," Hannah said. "This was the first commission like this she'd ever taken."

"Are you sure? Did you see any other paintings when you were here the other day that aren't here now?"

Hannah glanced around the walls. She'd looked this stuff over while Rebecca was on the phone the other day, but she hadn't memorized what was here. Except...

She nodded at a hanger in the wall where a painting should have hung. "There was a piece over there, a beach scene. Rebecca said it was a California artist. I don't know who painted it. The same guy who did that one of the Mission at San Juan Capistrano, I think."

Teagarden nodded. "California Impressionism. It's an offshoot of the French Impressionist style. Not surprising, since the light here is the same as in the south of France. Excellent for painting outdoors, *plein air* style. Perhaps she sold the piece after Ms. Nicks saw it," he told Towle and Ito. "I doubt if there's a connection to any recent stolen art, but you never know. We can look into it."

"And the piece you carried to Mexico?" Towle asked. "What—"

Just then, the sheriff's deputy returned with a couple of cardboard trays of coffee and a greasy looking bag with a Krispy Kreme logo.

"Whoa! Hold it," Russo said. "I think we need to take this outside before we muck up the crime scene."

"Oh, right. Sorry, Detective," the young cop said.

"Not your fault. Come on, folks, out on the deck, please."

He herded them all outside like so many geese, the federal agents with ties firmly knotted, the tall older Brit a little rumpled in tweed, Detective Lindsay Towle all spit and polish, like the ambitious eager beaver she seemed to be. Well, fair enough, Hannah thought. Under other circumstances, that might have been her.

They regrouped around an area of benches and tables at one end of the wooden deck, and the deputy passed around coffee, milk and sugar. While everyone busied themselves with their cups and with eyeing the contents of the doughnut bag, Hannah's brain was racing, trying to think if Rebecca could have deliberately gotten mixed up with art theft. It didn't seem possible, but she was in pretty dire straits, and desperation can make a person do things they might otherwise never dream of.

"Mr. Teagarden, how did you connect Rebecca Powell to this missing van Gogh?" she asked.

"I worked backward from what I know about the market for stolen art. There are only so many thieves with the skills required to carry out a heist like the one at the Arlen Hunter, and only so many buyers for their ill-gotten gains. I've been tracking *The Night Café* since a few days after the theft, been halfway around the world and back. The information I was able to glean from my sources led me to Puerto Vallarta, where I learned that Moises Gladding had recently ordered a canvas through the owner of this gallery. That brought me to Los Angeles, and when I called on Agent Towle this morning, it turned out he was already aware of Miss Powell's dealings with Gladding."

"Our field office works closely with the LAPD and the Sheriff's Department," Towle said. "That's how we got word about her murder."

"Hannah, when you arrived and found us here," Russo said, "you said 'not Rebecca, too.' What did you mean, 'too.' Who else?"

Hannah sipped at her coffee, stalling while she tried to decide how much these guys needed to know.

"I expect she was referring to a spot of bother at Gladding's villa in Puerto Vallarta," Teagarden said.

Hannah looked up in surprise at Teagarden. Had he been there, too? All eyes were on her, and she sighed. It was going to be another really long day.

# *Nineteen*

*Airborne, 30,000 feet over Northern Mexico*

Moises Gladding traveled first class with just a carry-on garment bag. The Argentine passport in his inside pocket identified him as James Dunning. His pasted-on dark goatee and clean-shaven head matched the passport photo of the sixty-year-old banker from Buenos Aires, a member of one of those British families scattered around the world since the days of the Empire—people who can never see themselves going back to living in Her Majesty's damp old kingdom.

Gladding shifted in the wide leather seat and ordered up a double shot of Glenlivet single malt. His mind and gut were churning, although no one would ever guess it to look at him. He had spent decades refining his stoicism. Only Sylvia, his wife of nearly forty years, could read his moods and divine his secrets, and she was much too wise to ever take advantage of it. She was a good wife, a traditional woman who knew her place and knew that place was secure, however many mistresses he might take. She raised their children, kept his home—now outside Geneva, since he'd cut his ties to America—and she trusted him to do what was best. He was a lucky man.

At the moment, he took little comfort in his good fortune. Two developments in the past forty-eight hours had him troubled.

One was anger at having had to unleash Kyle Liggett on his old colleague, Donald Ackerman. He and the barkeep had had a longstanding relationship based on mutual respect and compatibility. A man in Gladding's business could not allow himself the luxury of many friends, but over the years, Ackerman had become the closest thing that he'd had in decades. Ackerman had shown courage and dignity to the last, and if his death couldn't be helped, Gladding had taken no pleasure in watching Liggett torture the man and then dispatch him in the trunk of his old car. But Ackerman had helped the courier escape Mexico before she could deliver his painting. He had pleaded that he was an innocent pawn. Well, perhaps, perhaps not.

His anger at Ackerman, Gladding knew, was also fueled by his disillusionment with the barkeep's masters at Langley. After using Gladding for years as a conduit for information and the delivery of weapons to their arm's-length friends around the world, the bureaucrats at Langley had suddenly decided he was expendable. Gladding had been instrumental in preventing several terrorist attacks on American soil. In return for his services, his friends in Washington had for years turned a blind eye to his private business dealings.

But one by one, as his old associates retired or died off, new people took their places and decided to make their mark by disavowing the practices of their predecessors. Suddenly, Gladding found he had no one in Washington to defend him when some ambitious young pup wanted to take him to task for business dealings with Cuba, Venezuela, a Colombian drug lord or whatever other villain of the week they decided to name.

Before he knew it, he was a wanted man. When his youngest daughter graduated from Yale, Gladding hadn't been able to attend the ceremony. Worse than that, federal agents had actually manhandled his wife and son. It was the last straw. Gladding had had enough of America. It might be the land of his birth, but he didn't belong there anymore. He couldn't stomach a country that used and then discarded its friends that way.

And so, Donald Ackerman had paid the price for Langley's sins. Too bad it had been necessary, Gladding thought, but there it was.

Ackerman had been a better man by far than the instrument of Gladding's revenge. Kyle Liggett was back in the economy section even now. The mere thought of him was distasteful. The boy called himself a patriot, but Gladding knew his type all too well. Patriotism had nothing to do with what really motivated men like that.

Liggett was ordinary looking, almost invisible—a not unhandsome, boyish fellow, clean-cut, outwardly charming. But he was a sociopath, pure and simple. A useful sociopath at the moment, admittedly, but his utility would soon come to an end. Gladding had always known that Liggett would have to die sooner or later. Working with him was like handling a rattlesnake. Sooner or later it was going to bite. It had to be stomped into the ground before it got the chance.

"Mr. Dunning? Are you all right?"

Gladding looking up at the pretty, redheaded flight attendant. "Yes, I'm fine. Why?"

She smiled and pointed to his fists, clenched on his tray table. "I thought you might be a nervous flyer."

He relaxed his hands and forced himself to chuckle. "Well, a little, maybe."

"Can I refresh your drink?"

"That would be nice, thank you. Just a single this time, I think. Got to keep a clear head, you know."

She nodded and took his glass, returning in a moment with another shot of the double malt. "There you go."

"Thank you, my dear."

She nodded and moved on down the cabin. Gladding took a sip of the Scotch. It wasn't the flying that had him tense. It was Liggett, and the unending cycle of questions about the attack on his villa.

He was wanted in the States on federal warrants in response to FBI, DEA and ATF charges over his various dealings. Even Homeland Security had been getting in on the act lately. But the CIA, no matter how much it had distanced itself from him, had no interest in having him come to trial. They would rather see him dead than stand up in open court and start talking about deals he had struck on the Agency's behalf over the years. Ackerman had insisted that the attack on his villa wasn't a CIA assassination effort. That kind of messy job wasn't their style, he'd argued, not when a sniper's bullet or a poison dart was so much quieter and more reliable.

Then who? Gladding wondered. The bomb-maker, trying to do an end run? Get his hands on the painting and then renege on his end of the deal? Had he been feeling heat coming down on him, too? If so, he had made an enemy of the wrong man. If Gladding found out he'd been double-crossed, the man would have far bigger things than the authorities to worry about.

He had already put his extensive information network to work to find some of the answers he sought. If the CIA's resources had been anywhere near as good as his own, Gladding mused, they would be unstoppable. As it was, they were forever playing catch-up these days, running behind adversaries who'd grown stronger, smarter, faster than they were. That was why the American Age was over, and why a once-great power was sliding inexorably into a state of permanent humiliation.

* * *

At the back of the plane, Kyle Liggett was jammed in a center seat. Overweight tourists crowded him from either side, and his legs were cramped by the duffel bag under his seat that he'd been too late to fit into the overhead bins.

He was working on his Zen calm, eyes closed, zoned out on the music blasting through his ear buds. Tanned and fit, his hair sun streaked, he looked like the Midwestern boy he was, coming home from a few days on the beach, passport worn and curved from riding in his rear hip pocket. He carried none of the tools of his trade. He could improvise when he reached his destination.

He thought about Donald Ackerman, acknowledging a grudging respect. If it ever came down to it, he hoped he could do as well in the hands of a skilled interrogator. After this operation, they'd all want a piece of him. He was about to enter the history books.

The road to here had been hard, but he'd earned his place. Kicked out of his last foster home the day he turned eighteen, he'd dropped out of high school and gone out to Colorado, where he got work in a mine. It was there that he'd come to appreciate the power and beauty of a well-handled explosion. He loved to blow things apart.

He'd joined the military, hoping to become a top munitions expert, but after only a couple of months, the army had released him. "Mentally unfit for duty," they said. Who the hell were those bureaucrats to tag him with crap like that? Weren't they scraping the bottom of the barrel these days, trying to make their recruitment targets? And then they turn *him* away, a man disciplined enough to study on his own time, train himself to do the most difficult jobs there were? Unfit? Him?

He'd studied everything he could get his hands on, learning what and how much explosive to use, where and how deep to place the charge, how to time the fuse to the split second. He'd never handled a nuke before, but this would be the biggest moment of his life. He was determined to get this right.

While in Los Angeles for the art heist, and again last week, he'd taken time out to run down to San Diego County to study the layout of the San Onofre power plant. The facility was located on eighty-four acres surrounded by San Onofre State Beach. As he scouted the oceanfront site, he wished he'd gone into the navy instead of the army. The Seals would have appreciated his talents and it would have been even better training for this operation.

His fingers drummed his knees, keeping time with the music in his ears.

It was pretty funny, when you thought about it, that the most grim institutions in California occupied some of the most scenic spots on its coastline. In the northern part of the state, the San Quentin maximum security prison sat on a magnificent point overlooking the Pacific. And south of Los Angeles, a glorious piece of beach property belonged to the U.S. Marine Corps' Camp Pendleton and the San Onofre Nuclear Generating Station—SONGS. (That abbreviation was pretty funny, too.) Camp Pendleton was the Marines' primary amphibious training facility. If most of the corps hadn't been over in Iraq, this op might have been harder to pull off. But thanks to the idiots in Washington wasting American money and lives in some foreign bog hole, the place was wide open. The San Onofre nuclear plant, meantime, provided power to fifteen million Southern California homes.

To reconnoiter the target, Liggett had picked up a young divorcée in San Clemente and taken her and her two kids to San Onofre State Beach, which ran practically right up to the door of the power plant. There they were, just another family out for a day on the beach. There was something really whack about all those little kids building sand castles under the shadow of the nuclear plant's twin domes, which looked like tits, Kyle thought, grinning, right down to their erect nipples. He'd taken plenty of pictures, pretending to capture every cute thing those kids did. Their mom had been so grateful, it was pathetic. The scouting trip had a good payoff—a home-cooked meal, a Disney movie on the DVR, then a romp in the sack with Mom after the kiddies went off to bed.

Of course, he'd used an alias and told the woman he'd call her. Wouldn't she be surprised when she saw his picture on the front pages of all the newspapers in a couple of days? He might even make the cover of *Time* and *Newsweek*. She'd probably call the authorities, but what the hell. It wasn't like he was trying to hide. Once this was over, he wanted all the publicity he could get— even, if it couldn't be avoided, a big show trial and the national audience it would give him to deliver his message. Lazy-minded couch potatoes might disapprove of what he'd done, but thousands would answer his call to arms, rising up to take back the country from the bureaucrats and U.N.-loving one-worlders who were dragging America through the muck, destroying everything that was noble and good about his country.

He ran through the plan again. From the outside, the nuclear plant didn't look all that well secured, but he wasn't kidding himself. The place had security up the wazoo, especially since 9/11. Not only that, but he'd studied enough about power plant construction to know there were layers of protection designed in. The Chernobyl disaster would never have happened if the Russians had been smart enough to use American engineering.

It didn't really matter that the dirty bomb Gladding was getting him probably wouldn't destroy the power plant. This was psy-ops, after all, a psychological operation designed to instill terror and uncertainty into the vast majority of people. That was the main reason it wasn't taking place in autumn, when Santa Ana winds would blow the radioactive fallout from the dirty bomb harmlessly out to the ocean. At this time of year, if the prevailing winds blowing in off the ocean were just right, the bomb would pollute the Marine base and much of San Diego County. If they were lucky, the wind might even carry radiation north into Orange and Los Angeles Counties. The whole country would be freaked out.

The Fasten Seat Belt sign came on and the plane began to bank. Kyle removed his earbuds and wrapped the cord around his iPod. The trick for him, he reflected, would be to make the old man believe he had died in the blast. With this in mind, he'd hidden money and fake ID in two locations, one in Dana Point, the other in Oceanside. Gladding had paid him one-third of his fee up front for this job, another third when they'd met up in Puerto Vallarta. He was scheduled to deliver the final third, plus a bonus, at their last planned meet-up in the Dominican Republic.

But Kyle had done his homework on Moises Gladding. The old man hadn't gotten where he was by being a nice guy. People who did wet work for him had a habit of turning up dead or disappearing altogether. If Kyle blew off their final rendezvous, it might be enough to convince Gladding he was dead.

Of course, there was always a chance that he might really be killed in the blast. In that case, he wouldn't miss the money. It had never been about that anyway. It was about making a point with the good old U.S. of A. Kyle wasn't looking forward to prison, but if he could survive long enough to be taken into custody by the feds, he could kick off his personal stage two of the plan—a wake-up call to his fellow Americans.

Yeah. He was about to make a mark and prove that he was a true patriot—one of the finest sons America had ever produced. Timothy McVeigh and the Oklahoma City bombing was amateur hour compared to what he was about to pull off. Soon, the whole damn world would know the name Kyle Liggett.

Sweet.

# *Twenty*

*Los Angeles*

By the time Hannah had given Russo, his partner, the FBI agents and William Teagarden an abbreviated account of her adventures in Mexico—leaving out the part about how she might have left a priceless van Gogh in the closet of a fleabag hotel—they were all champing at the bit to get their hooks into August Koon, the missing link between Rebecca Powell and Moises Gladding. Russo's partner wandered off to call Sheriff's Department headquarters and have them run a check on Koon.

Nobody was ruling out the possibility that Rebecca's murder might be unrelated to machinations of the arms dealer. But as the erudite Brit pointed out, "Ockham's razor still applies." When brows furrowed, Teagarden shrugged. "A fourteenth century countryman of mine,

William of Ockham. He said, 'all things being equal, the simplest answer is the best.'"

"Hang on, guys," Hannah said. "Simpler still would be to put your hands on Gladding. Rebecca told me he has a home in Malibu. Maybe he snuck back into the country after his place in Mexico was shot up."

Agent Towle shook his head. "We checked it out after we spoke to you the other night. There's no evidence of a property in Malibu or anywhere else in California."

"So he lied to Rebecca," Hannah said. "All he wanted was an intermediary between himself and August Koon."

Towle nodded. "Gladding doesn't like to dirty his hands. Even in his arms deals, he mostly acts as banker and facilitator. He leaves the heavy lifting to others."

"So Koon's our man for now," Russo said.

"I made some inquiries about the man," Teagarden said. "I thought his name rang a bell. He spent his twenties in Paris. At the time, a gallery owner on the Champs Élysées was on the fiddle, passing off forgeries as the work of high-priced artists. Koon was one of the people suspected of painting the forgeries, but he did a bunk when things got hot. Now that he's a success in his own right, his misspent youth would make him very susceptible to blackmail."

"And Moises Gladding's said to have an extensive private intelligence network," Towle noted. "Blackmail would be well within his capability."

Russo's young partner returned. "No luck. There's

no phone in Koon's name. No tax records in L.A. listing him as owner, either."

"A lot of celebrities in this town set up dummy corporations to keep the fans and paparazzi away," Russo said.

"That describes August Koon to a T," Hannah said. "A superstar in his own mind. It's not a problem, though. I don't know the address, but I'm pretty sure I could find the place again. Frankly, I wouldn't mind hearing myself what he has to say about that butt-ugly piece of canvas I risked my neck over."

Russo nodded reluctantly. "I guess. You can ride with me."

"No, I'll take my own car."

Detective Towle shook her head. "Forensics will need to examine your car."

"Excuse me?"

"I'm sure we all appreciate your help," Lindsay said, "but you're still a suspect here."

"Well, in that case, do you have a warrant to search my car?"

"You know it's just routine, Hannah," Russo said, ever the peacemaker. "We need to rule you out, that's all."

"What exactly do you think my car is going to tell you? That I broke Rebecca's neck by driving over her? Give me a break. I've already admitted I was here. I might even concede that I was the last person to see her alive—barring her killer."

"Look, you know how this works," Lindsay said. "You're a suspect until you're not."

"Guilty till proven innocent, is that it? Do you seriously think I snapped the neck of my sister's best friend?"

"Do you have martial arts training?"

"Yes. So?"

"Well, then…" Lindsay shrugged, as if it was self-evident.

"Look, if you intend to impound my car, you're going to have to get a warrant, and while you're doing that, I'm going to lawyer up. *That's* how this works, Detective. In the meantime, while you're standing around playing dimwit games, Rebecca's murderer is slipping further away."

"She was in business with a known arms dealer. So were you. You had opportunity and means."

"But not motive. How many times do I have to say this? I was working for Rebecca, not Gladding, and the only reason I took the job was as a favor to my sister. So I repeat, if you want my car, get yourself a bloody warrant."

"No. Not necessary," Russo said.

Lindsay started to protest, but he silenced her with a look. He turned back to Hannah. "Just come with me, show us where Koon lives, and I'll have someone bring you back for your car."

Hannah shook her head. "Not gonna happen. Unless you're planning to arrest me, I would like to go home sometime today. In fact, I'll need to drive down to Orange County to see my sister. She and Rebecca have been friends forever. She's going to be devastated when she finds out."

"She already knows," Russo said.

"What?"

"I found her number in Ms. Powell's cell phone."

"And you called her?"

"I told you, I was trying to track you down. I also wanted to know if she'd heard from her friend after you were here."

"Dammit, Russo." Hannah's heart sank, knowing Nora had found out like that—a phone call from a homicide detective. Nora didn't know Russo from Adam. Hannah hadn't even mentioned that she was kinda-sorta-maybe dating anyone, so it wasn't like it would have come easier because it was him relaying the news.

Her sister would be crushed. In addition to being college roommates, she and Rebecca had backpacked through Europe together, had been each other's maids of honor. Rebecca was Natalie's godmother. Given the difference in their ages, Hannah often felt Nora was closer to Rebecca than her own sister.

"Well, thanks so much," she told Russo. "All the more reason why I'll drive myself. I'm not wasting time coming all the way back here."

The tall Brit stepped forward. "In that case, would you mind awfully if I rode along with you, Ms. Nicks? I came over here with Agents Towle and Ito, but I'd love the chance to ask you some questions about that painting. That way, I won't ask you to delay getting to see your sister afterward."

Russo pulled his car keys out of his pocket and tossed them to his partner. "I'll come with you, too."

Oh, no, he wouldn't, Hannah thought. She was still ticked off that he'd discussed her business with Little Miss Bright-Eyed-And-Bushy-Tailed Lindsay Towle, who then proceeded to run tattling to her big brother the FBI Agent. And now, to find out Russo had dropped that bombshell on Nora, too?

"I don't think so," she said. "My little car is too small to take any more passengers. Mr. Teagarden, you're welcome to ride with me. I'm sure you'll have me well surrounded, Detectives. You'll want to be sure I don't kidnap our visiting friend and hold him hostage while I make my escape."

His face flushed, Russo took his car keys back.

Hannah held out an arm toward the highway. "I'm parked up the road a little way, Mr. Teagarden. Shall we?"

"By all means," he said. "Delighted, I'm sure."

It felt like a parade. Russo's unmarked car, the feds, and a Sheriff's Department cruiser followed Hannah's Prius down Pacific Coast Highway. Another black-and-white was ahead of her, and all of the other cars were flashing their lights and sounding sirens when necessary to plow ahead of traffic. The deputy driving the squad car ahead of her had been told Hannah was guiding them to Koon's studio in the Hollywood Hills, and he assured Hannah that if she signaled in advance where she wanted to turn, he'd spot it in his rearview mirror.

"Well, this is lovely, Ms. Nicks." Teagarden said, settled back in her passenger seat, enjoying the scenery. "I do love this city, and there's nothing like a police escort to move things along briskly."

Hannah smiled. The accent and deep, mellow voice were so appealing she could listen to the man read his grocery list and be fascinated. He was old enough to be her father, but William Teagarden could turn any red-blooded American woman into an Anglophile.

"By the way," she said, "feel free to call me Hannah."

"And I'm Will—or more often just Teagarden to my friends. Whatever you like. As my old mom used to say, 'Call me what you like, just don't call me late for dinner.'"

"So tell me, Will, do you really think that painting I took to Mexico was this—what was it called, the van Gogh?"

"*The Night Café.* I think it could have been. It'll be simple enough to find out using X-rays when we get it back. In fact, given how thickly van Gogh laid the pigment down on his canvases, we'll probably be able to see brushstrokes beneath Koon's overlayer. Although first, of course, we have to find Gladding and get the painting back."

She winced. "Actually, that's something I didn't

mention before. I never saw Gladding to deliver the painting."

"Excuse me?"

"You said you found a fax from Rebecca Powell at Gladding's villa?"

"That's right."

"So that means you were there after the bloodbath?" She glanced over in time to see him nod. "Well, me, too. I was delayed getting there, as I mentioned earlier. When I did, all I found were bodies and blood."

"Aha," he said. "Well, there's a mystery cleared up."

"What do you mean?"

"You turned off the oven in the kitchen."

She was dumbfounded. How the hell did he know that?

As if he'd read her mind, Teagarden said, "The foot-prints at the scene. They were all large, men's trainers, except for one pair of smaller boots. Those boots," he said, pointing to her feet. "You were very careful not to step into the tracks left by the invaders, so I couldn't be sure when your prints were laid down. But I did see one in the kitchen, so I wondered if it belonged to the same person who had turned off the oven. But I thought, that's something a woman would do, turning off the flame."

"It could have been the cook, or one of the killers."

"The cook would have taken the bread out of the oven before it burned, and the killers wouldn't have cared. In fact, I'm sure they couldn't have given a toss if the whole house went up in smoke. No, I was quite certain it was someone who'd come in after the killers, and after the bread was already burned. Otherwise she would have taken it out of the oven. Just something a woman would do."

"That's not very politically correct of you, Will."

He chuckled. "Oh, I know, but there it is. I'm just a foolish old fellow, stuck in my antediluvian ways."

"Not so foolish. So is it safe to presume you don't suspect me of being a mass murderer? Because I'm sure Detective Towle back there would think so."

"Quite the little bossy boots, isn't she? No, I didn't think that massacre looked like woman's work. Mind you, it's getting bloody hard to tell these days."

"So how did you end up at Gladding's villa?"

"I was in Puerto Vallarta following up on some intelligence I'd received. I was with a police captain, asking about Gladding, when a shots-fired call came into the station. He invited me along with them to investigate."

She nodded. "When you rounded that last curve just before the entrance to the villa, I thought you guys would hit me for sure."

"Aha! The gardener's truck. Big straw hat."

"Why, Mr. Teagarden," she said, grinning over at him, "you are a wonder. So tell me, are you sure the police didn't find Gladding's body?"

"No, but he'd been there, I think. One of the officers found a hidden tunnel in the office floor. Led to a vehicle parked on the far side of the property."

"Well, don't I feel stupid. Not only did I not notice the fax from Rebecca that you found, I didn't see any tunnel, either."

He patted her shoulder. "Don't fret, dear. I didn't see the tunnel, either. One of the young Mexican officers found it under a carpet. In any case, Gladding was long gone. There were fresh tracks, two men. They left in a hurry."

"So he could be anywhere by now. I guess you don't deal with the kind of people he does without having escape plans laid in at all times."

"All the more reason to see what August Koon has to say for himself."

Their little parade was speeding up Sunset Boulevard now, tourists on the strip craning to see who could be driving a Prius that warranted a major police escort. Hannah felt more than a little silly.

"So, how long has it been since you worked at Scotland Yard?" she asked Teagarden.

"Four years."

"And art recovery? Is that a good business?"

"I keep busy. Art theft is a five-billion-dollar-a-year industry. Not far behind the arms trade and drugs."

She whistled.

"Unfortunately," Teagarden added, "less than ten percent of what's stolen is ever recovered. Art is easily transported. Even if a customs officer sees a piece, a clever thief will convince them it's just a copy. Who's to say different, absent an expert—who, let's face it, is not exactly a common commodity. Once a piece leaves their jurisdiction, the police lose interest. That's why owners turn to someone like me."

"Maybe the van Gogh was just transported in plain sight, like you say."

"I'd be surprised," Teagarden said. "Van Gogh isn't just any old obscure artist. And the theft of *The Night Café* was recent. It got so much press that moving it undisguised would be risky. That's why the Koon overpaint theory makes the most sense."

Hannah nodded.

"How about you?" he asked. "Working private security is odd work for a woman—pardon my old, un-PC notions. It's not dangerous?"

"Not half as dangerous as my mother worries it is. She thinks I'm dodging bullets on a daily basis, but I get ten boring gigs for every death-defying job."

"Ah, well, moms—it's their job to worry, isn't it?"

"Mine thinks I'm doomed to an early death, like your buddy Vincent there. When I feel the urge to chop off my ear, I'll start to worry. Meantime, it's just a paycheck."

"Did you know that after that incident when van Gogh cut off his ear and presented it to a prostitute, the villagers in Arles, where he was living at the time, petitioned the mayor and the police to have him committed or driven out of town? They were terrified of him."

"Sounds like he was more of a danger to himself than anyone else." She flicked on her turn signal to let the cruiser ahead of them know to take the turn up Laurel Canyon.

Teagarden glanced behind to see if everyone else in the convoy made the turn, then turned back. "Actually, that's an interesting bit of trivia about van Gogh's ear incident. It happened in 1888, you see. That's the same year Jack the Ripper was cutting up prostitutes in London. The case was a worldwide sensation. Even in the south of France, people were reading the newspaper accounts of the Whitechapel murders. So when Vincent gave that bloody ear to a prostitute in Arles, it was just a little too familiar."

"So they rode him out of town on a rail."

"More or less. Actually, he had himself voluntarily committed to an asylum, poor fellow."

"Life's a bitch and then you die," Hannah said. "Okay, we're getting close now. Let's see…"

Teagarden held back further questions while she concentrated on following her mental map of the twisting route Rebecca had taken to reach Koon's studio. When she finally spotted the wooden sign at the bottom of his driveway, she felt quite proud of herself. She parked and helped Teagarden find the latch for his seat belt, but by the time they were out of the car, two of the sheriff's deputies had their guns drawn.

The door of Koon's studio was swinging open and shut, banging in the breeze. Each time it swung inward, they could see a foot in a paint-splattered Birkenstock lying still on the floor.

## Twenty-One

Russo unsnapped the holster under his jacket and withdrew his gun. Hannah watched as he slipped ahead of the uniformed deputies and approached the swinging studio door. Behind them, Detective Towle, her FBI agent brother and his partner Ito had all drawn their own weapons.

"August Koon?" Russo called out. "Los Angeles Sheriff's Department."

The door squeaked in the wind on its hinges.

"Police, Mr. Koon!"

But Hannah knew August Koon was in no position to invite them in. The foot in that grubby Birkenstock visible through the swinging door lay still as death. There was no telling if anyone else might still be in the studio, though. She wanted to push Russo away from the threshold. Why did he have to be the first to charge in?

"I wish I had my gun," she murmured.

"Don't care for the things myself," Teagarden whispered.

Russo waved the uniforms out of the line of sight of anyone who might be inside the studio and positioned himself by the hinges. Glancing back, he nodded at the others to stand ready, then slowly pushed the door inward. Koon lay in a crimson pool just inside the door.

Russo, Lindsay and the uniforms entered cautiously, spreading out to check for anyone else. After a moment, Hannah heard someone call, "Clear!"

She and the others approached, but Russo raised a hand. They stopped at the threshold.

"You guys," Russo ordered the uniforms, "check the house, see if there's anyone inside. Lindsay, get on the radio, give them the address, tell them we need the LAPD out here. We're in their jurisdiction. The rest of you stay outside. LAPD's not going to be happy if we mess up their forensics."

He crouched next to the downed man to check for signs of life, but it was obvious he was gone. His collar was soaked through with blood, the throat slit, possibly with the canvas knife that lay in the pool around him. It was the same curved blade Hannah had toyed with the morning she visited with Rebecca, the steel encrusted now with spots of blood. Koon's skin was pale, the eyes open and dull. His once cranky expression had settled into a vacant, vaguely surprised stare, as if something on the ceiling had transfixed him.

Russo glanced over. "Is this August Koon?"

She nodded. Pulling her gaze from the rumpled body, she took in the studio. Finished canvases that had been neatly propped against the walls were strewn about the room now. The easels were overturned, pools of paint mixed with blood spatter in a confused pattern of splotches not unlike Koon's own work.

She felt Teagarden close behind, peering over her head at the mess inside the studio. He smelled of something pleasantly spicy. "Please don't take this personally, Hannah, but trouble does seem to follow you."

"No, I seem to follow it. Jeez Louise, what a mess."

He took her by the elbow and led her away from the door. "Let's leave them do what needs must. You and I, meantime, can finish our chat."

Hannah sighed inwardly. *Here it comes.*

"There can be little doubt now what we're dealing with," Teagarden said. "Did it never occur to you that there might be something odd about the painting you were asked to courier?"

"After the mess at Gladding's villa—yeah, it did. I thought it might be about smuggled contraband. It never occurred to me that the prize could be that ugly picture, so I tore the frame apart. I thought it might be reconstituted drugs. I searched every square inch of the frame and the portfolio, looking for anything—money, documents, hell, even a microchip—but they were clean."

"And the canvas?"

"I could see from the back that it was old and grimy,

but Koon said he often painted over the same canvas several times before he was satisfied. I didn't think dirt signified much. I even checked the stretchers."

Teagarden blanched. "You took the canvas off the stretchers? Oh, please, Hannah, tell me you didn't roll it."

"Would it have mattered?"

"I told you, love, it was painted in 1888. The pigment will be unstable. Rolling the canvas could crack it and break bits off. It certainly would not be healthy for it."

"Assuming it is your missing van Gogh."

"True, although it's not a good way to handle any painting, old or new."

"Well, relax. I didn't take it off the stretchers, just examined them as best I could. I was already worried about having destroyed the frame. I didn't want Gladding on my case because I'd damaged his painting, too."

Teagarden looked visibly relieved. She knew what his next question would be, but he waited. He was a wily old fox, probably a master at interviewing in his days at Scotland Yard, letting the silence stretch awkwardly until the nervous suspect felt the need to volunteer something.

Well, Hannah could play that game, too. She turned away to watch as Detective Towle hung up the car radio mike and went back to talk to Russo.

"Well," Teagarden said finally. Score one for the kid. "You still haven't told me where the painting is, Hannah. I know you didn't leave it at the villa. Believe me, I searched everywhere. So I presume you brought it back to Los Angeles?"

She shook her head.

"Bloody hell! You left a priceless masterpiece behind in Mexico?"

"I was trying to get my butt out of there, Teagarden. I didn't know who might be looking for the thing."

"Please tell me you put it in a safe-deposit box."

"Yeah, right. I had no idea who I could trust. Who was to say Gladding didn't have every banker in Puerto Vallarta on his payroll?"

"An airport locker?"

"First of all, I wasn't going to walk into the airport carrying an art portfolio. And second, nobody has lockers anymore. You should know that."

"True," he conceded. "Not since the IRA decided they made good places to hide bombs. So—"

Russo chose that moment to come over, Agents Towle and Ito close behind.

"This is going to take a while," Russo said. "Hannah, you might as well go and be with your sister now. There's nothing more you can do here."

"Hannah tells me she left the van Gogh behind in Puerto Vallarta," Teagarden said.

"Correction. I hid a painting by August Koon. Until someone proves otherwise, that's what it is, far as I'm concerned."

Teagarden demurred, but Russo agreed. "I don't think there's any reason to suspect that Hannah knew she was carrying anything other than what it seemed to be."

She might have felt grateful for the vote of confidence, Hannah thought, if it weren't for the fact that she still felt like the world's biggest patsy.

"I believe we could cut through a lot of red tape if you were to tell me where you hid it," Teagarden said. "I can be on the next flight to Puerto Vallarta, recover the van Gogh and bring it back to the States to be returned to its rightful owners. I presume you could arrange for me to bring it through U.S. Customs?" he added to Towle.

The agent nodded.

Hannah weighed the offer. It might be a good idea, but how could she be sure? Once burned, twice shy—and at this point, she was feeling well and truly singed. Could she trust anyone? And what about Gladding? What were the odds he hadn't had Rebecca and Koon killed to cover his tracks? Could these guys protect her from him? For how long? The man was vindictive and he had a long memory, by all accounts.

If the painting *was* the van Gogh, then it should be returned to Yale, of course. But what if turned out to be just a Koon? Gladding had paid for the thing. No matter how lousy his taste, why he would want the thing, or how serious his other legal problems with the feds, he was the rightful owner until proven otherwise.

"I'd rather retrieve it myself. When I do," she said, cutting off Teagarden's protest, "you can examine it or have any expert you want look at it. But right now—and please don't take this the wrong way—I don't know you any better than I knew August Koon there."

"Then let me suggest something else," Towle said. "We have a contact in Puerto Vallarta, the man I told you about the other night, Hannah. We could send him to retrieve it."

Oh, right, she thought grimly. Donald Ackerman. Like she trusted him any more than the rest of these clowns. And like he was going to be thrilled to help her out after she'd left him locked in the trunk of his car.

"Look, guys, the painting is safe for now." *Please God, let that not be wishful thinking.* She turned to Teagarden. "I have a family emergency to take care of. My sister needs me. This can wait until tomorrow, right? Then, I promise, I will pull out all the stops to make sure the painting gets back here so you and your experts can examine it. Deal?"

It was obvious Teagarden wasn't at all happy about the idea, but he was off his turf here. And given the linked murders in Malibu and the Hollywood Hills and the probability they were related to a man wanted on a number of federal warrants, Yale University's missing painting was no one else's top priority today.

Hannah nodded to Towle and Ito. "Guys, you know where to find me."

"Tomorrow."

She glanced at Russo, then turned and started for her car. He caught up to her as she was opening the door. "Hannah."

"What?"

"Going back to Mexico is not on, you know that.

You're going to get yourself killed. You should let those guys take this over."

"I finish what I start, John."

"I respect that, but you don't know what you've gotten yourself into here. How many people have already been killed over this?"

Truthfully, she didn't really know. On the other hand, was she going to let John Russo start deciding what she should and shouldn't do? "So, you're worried about me? Is that why you had your trainee there sic her big brother on me? How could you do that, John?"

He sighed wearily. "I am really sorry about that. I swear to God, it wasn't deliberate and I've already read Lindsay the riot act about it. She was sitting at the next desk over when I was talking to you the other day and she heard me mention Gladding's name. She perked right up and asked me about it after I hung up. I knew she had a brother in the FBI, but it never occurred to me that she'd tell him."

Hannah rolled her eyes. "She's a pistol, that one."

"Extremely ambitious." Russo hesitated.

"What? Come on, spit it out."

"I know you've been worried about your finances. Are you sure it didn't cloud your judgment on this one? I mean, Moises Gladding?"

"Are you saying I sold my soul to pay a freakin' tax bill? Give me a break." She yanked open the car door. "I've gotta go."

It would have been gratifying to rev her engines and

roar off down the driveway, leaving the whole damn lot of them in the dust, but that was the problem of driving a little hybrid. It didn't really lend itself to the grand gesture.

Moises Gladding, aka the Argentine James Dunning, settled comfortably into the overstuffed armchair in his suite at the Beverly Hills Crowne Plaza. He selected a throwaway cell phone from his briefcase and dialed the associate scheduled to supply the radioactive explosive device that Liggett would use at San Onofre.

The Libyan had been a client for years, a frequent, well-financed customer for the goods and services Gladding offered. This was the first time the arms dealer had put himself on the receiving end of this relationship. There were few people with the skills and resources needed to prepare a weapon of this type, so it wasn't as if he'd had much choice in suppliers. But ever since the attack at his villa, he was beginning to wonder if he had made a wise decision.

The Libyan answered on the second ring. Gladding identified himself by the code name he always used with the man and asked for confirmation that his item was ready for pickup.

"It will be at the drop-off location on Sunday as agreed. And my payment? When can I expect it?"

"It'll be at the specified coordinates when your end of the bargain is fulfilled, not before."

The airwaves between them hummed for a moment, and then, "Of course. I would expect nothing less. After all, we are colleagues of long standing, are we not?"

"I thought so."

"And you doubt it now? But why?"

"There was a disturbing incident at one of my residences this week. I wonder if you know anything about it. The place was ransacked, as if the attackers were looking for something in particular—an objet d'art, perhaps."

"I am very sorry to hear of this, but you cannot think it had anything to do with our arrangement."

"I would hope not. And yet delivery of my purchase *was* delayed."

"Only because it is a delicate item and certain components can be difficult to acquire. It is nothing personal, I assure you."

"What happened at my villa was very personal."

"I am very sorry for your difficulty, but again, it can have nothing to do with our arrangement. Our business association is a sacred trust to me, a trust built up over years of excellent relations."

"Yes, years," Gladding said. All the more reason that he knew how to read the man, and knew he was lying. "I'll call you on Saturday to confirm the exchange."

"Excellent," the Libyan said. He sounded relieved.

He shouldn't be, Gladding thought, disconnecting. The Libyan would learn what happens to those who cross Moises Gladding—as would the courier who had disappeared with his painting. It was time to tie up that loose end as well.

## Twenty-Two

It was early afternoon by the time Hannah shook herself loose of the cops, the feds and the charming Brit she hadn't decided to trust. Squinting in the bright April sunshine, she was digging around in her messenger bag for her sunglasses case when her hand landed on her cell phone. She dropped it in the console, found her shades, and settled in for the fifty-something-mile trip down to her sister's place in Corona del Mar.

At the last stop before she merged onto the freeway, she glanced at her phone screen. The cell had been on vibrate while she'd been at the gallery and at Koon's studio, and she'd missed three calls, one from her mother's house and two from her brother-in-law's mobile phone. Multiple SOSs from Ma and Neal could only mean that Nora was incapacitated and that Hannah's presence was urgently required.

She barreled down the freeway on-ramp. She'd be

there soon enough. This business with Rebecca was too emotionally fraught to discuss over the phone. She was feeling pretty ragged herself and she'd lose it for sure if she heard Nora crying. Best not to risk it at seventy miles an hour.

As much as this circling of the family wagons was about Nora and her loss, Hannah had the uncomfortable feeling talk would inevitably come around to her own unconventional line of work. The family was pretty traditional, so every time the black sheep of the flock got caught up in some cockamamy incident, the weary sighs were bound to follow. *Oh, Hannah, what kind of trouble have you gotten into now?* This time, she feared there would be a new chorus: *What kind of trouble did you bring down on Rebecca?*

She smacked herself mentally upside the head. She had no time for self-pity. As for self-recrimination, the only blame she carried here was possibly leaving a masterpiece in a dank closet in a firetrap hotel. Brilliant. If *The Night Café* disappeared or was ruined, she'd go down in history as the moron who lost it—a dandy addition to her résumé.

Enough. She popped her iPod into the car adaptor, selected an upbeat playlist and cranked up the volume to drown out the squeak of the hamster wheel in her head.

An hour later, she pulled into the driveway of her sister's house on Shorecliff Road. The quiet little hybrid's silent arrival gave her a chance to steel herself before launching into the emotional Sturm und Drang to come. When she finally walked up to the entry, she'd barely touched the bell when the door flew open. Her mother and Nora were wedged in the space, arms wide, faces tearful but relieved.

Nora threw her arms around her. "Finally! We've been so worried."

"I'm so sorry I didn't get your messages earlier."

Her mother took Hannah's face in her hands. "Thank goodness you're safe."

Hannah kissed her warmly and put her arm around her, steering her inside. Nora's husband walked out from the den and gave her one of his bone-crusher hugs. Sixteen-year-old Natalie came bounding down the stairs, and then it was her turn, too, for hugs and tears and worried complaints about why Hannah hadn't called.

"Okay, give me a second here, guys," Hannah said. Her family allowed her a few inches of space, but that was all the invitation the golden retrievers required to move in and offer their own excited greetings, one nuzzling, the other slobbering, both tails wagging like frantic, furry metronomes.

"Come on. We were just going to have something to eat," her mother said.

Ah yes, food. The Demetrious family cure-all. Hannah ducked into the powder room to wash dog slobber off her hands, then followed the others into the kitchen. Her mother was shifting plates at the round table to make room for another setting.

"Here, Nana," Natalie said, "I'll do it."

But Nana couldn't be dissuaded. Hannah recognized her mother's need to bury her fears in busywork. As they settled down and said again how worried sick they'd been about her, she kicked herself for not having checked in as soon as she got home from Mexico. They didn't even *know* about the mess in Mexico. All they knew was that Rebecca had been murdered.

"I was pretty wiped when I got back yesterday, or I would have checked in with Rebecca sooner, too. That's why I only just found out."

"You push yourself too hard," her mother fretted. It always came down to Hannah's job, although today, it was probably better to think about that than the horror of Rebecca's death.

"I suppose it didn't really matter whether you heard about Becs yesterday or today," Nora said.

Hannah reached over and squeezed her hand. "I'm so sorry. Detective Russo told me he called you."

"It was awful. He really didn't have to notify me, but he said he found my number with Rebecca's things, and he seemed to know I was your sister. Did you work with him when you were in the department?"

"No, I only met him recently."

"He was anxious to know when you were getting back from Mexico."

"Is he someone special, dear?" their mother asked coyly.

Here it goes, Hannah thought. Her mother would never rest easy until Hannah had a "protector." Curiosity about her love life trumped all other considerations. Annoyed as she was with Russo at the moment, however, there was nothing to tell and at this rate, there probably never would be.

She reached for the lamb, Nana's never-fail remedy for grieving hearts. Maybe if she filled her mouth, they'd talk amongst themselves and drop the subject of the mysterious detective.

"Dad picked me up from school," Natalie said, "so I knew something bad must have happened."

He nodded. "I left the office and picked up Nana, too, as soon as Nora called."

"Poor Nora needed her family," Nana said. "She was sobbing and—"

"Ma, enough," Nora said. "It's not about me."

"Oh, I know, it's about poor Rebecca."

Nora glanced around. "She was here with us just a couple of days ago. I never imagined it would be the last time I'd see her."

"Who would do such a terrible thing?" Nana wondered.

Natalie, dark eyes moving from one adult to the other, looked like she thought she should add something but couldn't think what. Hannah empathized. What do you say about a nightmare?

"You said you talked to the detective," Neal said. "Do they have any idea who did it?"

Natalie leaned forward. "It's almost always a family member or someone who knew the victim well, right?" She was a big *Law and Order* fan.

"Detective Russo did ask about her divorce," Nora said. "He had a lot of questions about the kind of man Bill is and how he and Becs had been getting on."

"Must have been hard for you," Hannah said. "You guys were friends with him, too, for years and years."

Neal nodded, but Nora shook her head. "Not anymore. Not after what he put Becs through." She twisted her napkin in a tight knot. "I did say I didn't think he would ever hurt Becs physically. It had to have been someone else."

As tears welled in her sister's eyes, Hannah considered sharing what she knew about the possible connection between Rebecca, Koon and a missing van Gogh, but it would only raise more questions than she could answer. Nora didn't need added uncertainty, and their mother certainly didn't need to be worrying about whether her youngest child might be next on some killer's hit parade.

Neal squeezed Nora's hand, then turned to Hannah. "How was Mexico?"

"Hot." *In more ways than one.*

"Where were you?"

"Puerto Vallarta."

"Great spot. Remember, hon? We went there before Nolan was born."

Nora wiped her eyes and smiled wanly. "I remember. I was pregnant, and I'd just started showing. People were so sweet to us." A crease appeared between her eyebrows. "Detective Russo seemed really worried about you down there, Hannah. That's what had us thinking you could be in danger."

Well, at least he hadn't told Nora her sister was a murder suspect.

"Were you in danger, Aunt Hannah?"

"It was just a delivery job." *Gone horribly wrong.*

"That painting Rebecca wanted carried down?" Neal asked. Hannah nodded.

"Who'd you deliver it to?" Natalie asked.

*Ouch.* "A man with more money than taste."

"What do you mean?"

"Oh, the painting he bought was by an L.A. artist named Koon. I didn't think much of it. But hey, at least the client flew me down and back first-class. Wasn't for my benefit, mind you, only the picture's." And if it really was a van Gogh, she thought, that coddling made more sense.

Natalie rested her cheek on her fist, watching Hannah, her pretty face puzzled. Mystified, maybe, about the bizarre assortment of jobs her aunt seemed to land.

"Well, I'm glad you went first-class at least," Nana said. "You work such long hours."

Nora opened her mouth to say something, but before she could, Natalie smacked the table. "That's it!"

Nana jumped. "Natalie!" Nora chided.

"I remember where I heard that name! Aunt Hannah, I was watching TV before you came. There was a news break and they said that artist you were talking about was found dead in his studio. August Koon—it's the same guy, right?"

Every head swiveled toward Hannah. *Damn, damn, damn.* That was the problem with smart kids. They didn't miss a trick.

"Hannah, did you know about this?" her mother asked.

She sighed and nodded. "I went to Rebecca's gallery this morning. The police were still there, of course. After they heard about the job I'd been on for Rebecca, they wanted to talk to Koon, so I took them over to his studio. That's when they found him."

"Why did you have to go?"

"They couldn't find an address for him but I had gone there with Becs. I knew how to get to the place."

Nora's eyes widened. "You were at her gallery, too? Then you know how she died. Detective Russo wouldn't say."

Hannah shook her head. *Please don't ask me that.*

"Tell me."

Hannah glanced at Neal, looking for backup, but he said nothing. She sighed. "It was very quick."

"Was the gallery trashed?" Neal asked. "A robbery gone bad, maybe?"

"Not really. Things were disturbed, a couple of pots broken, but that's about all."

"How did she die?" Nora asked again.

"Oh, Nora, I don't think—"

"I need to know. I've had the most awful pictures in my mind ever since I heard, you can't imagine."

Hannah glanced at Neal and then, pointedly, at Natalie.

"Nat, go upstairs, please," Neal said.

"Dad, she was my godmother. I—"

"Natalie! Go!" Nora snapped.

Stunned by the unaccustomed outburst from her mother, the girl got up and left the table without another word. Nora turned back to her sister and waited.

"Her neck was broken," Hannah said quietly.

Nora sat back as if she'd been smacked. "Oh, Becs…" she breathed. No one said anything for a moment. Then Nora asked, "Maybe she fell?"

"No, honey, she didn't fall."

"Are you sure?"

Hannah nodded.

"But how—"

"Nora, look at me," Neal said softly. "There was an intruder. It happened quickly, Hannah said. Becs wouldn't have felt any pain."

Nora's eyes were huge, and Nana was crying softly. "You're sure she didn't suffer?" Nora asked. "Absolutely sure?"

"Sure," Hannah said. "She looked peaceful."

"You actually saw her?"

"Yes. And Neal's right. She didn't feel any pain."

I hope she didn't, Hannah thought. But she would have been terrified just the same.

It was after eight by the time she left the Quinns'. After Neal had gone up for a quiet talk with her, Natalie had rejoined the family. The evening had drifted along on small talk, memories of happier times with Rebecca and a few more tears. Each time a new wave of grief hit, they lost their footing for a while until the pain ebbed again.

It was dark when Hannah sailed back up the freeway on a river of red and white lights. At one point, she paged through her iPod until she found Randy Newman's "I Love L.A." Setting the song to repeat, she cranked down her windows and let the wind whip her hair, singing at the top of her lungs. It beat screaming.

And it certainly beat thinking.

After the double door locks were slammed into place against thieves, murderers and the grim reaper, Hannah leaned into a wall, teary eyed and exhausted. Her place was quiet and dark as a tomb, only the phone's blue message light casting eerie shadows on the walls.

Switching on lamps to dispel the gloom, she hung her messenger bag on a hook by the door, then dialed up her phone messages. The first two were hang-ups. A long silence opened the third. Then, a voice, a stranger. Male. A slight accent, maybe? Or not…

*"We will meet, Miss Nicks. You have something that belongs to me."*

Gladding. It had to be.

She checked the readout to see where the calls had originated. All three had come from the same number. Local. Terrific.

She rechecked the locks on the front door and then the patio, closing every curtain. Times like these, she wondered why she didn't own a dog, except how could she, with the amount of time she spent on the road? An attack cat, maybe? Cats were more independent. Not too intimidating, however.

Cats made her think of kittens, and she smiled in spite of herself, remembering Ruben's call, his voice disguised to sound like his sister Monica. She looked at the clock and considered calling, but the guys would be in the midst of the nightly battle to get Mellie to sleep, her poor little locked-up body often too achy to allow her to settle.

Ruben had to have been calling on Travis's behalf, anxious to warn her of something before she left for Mexico—except she'd gotten the warning too late. Would things have gone down differently if she'd received the message sooner? Would it have saved Rebecca?

She turned the television on low to cancel out the lonely silence, then headed for a long, hot shower. Afterward, dressed in her softest sweatpants and zip hoodie, she poured herself a glass of wine and settled in to watch the most mindless programs she could find on the tube. After a couple of hours, she was zoned out and almost relaxed.

But when the doorbell rang, she sat bolt upright, heart pounding. Sliding off the sofa, she tiptoed into her bedroom and opened the safe in her closet. She pulled out her gun, flicked off the safety and chambered a round. If Moises Gladding or some henchman on his payroll had come to call, she wasn't going down without a fight.

The doorbell rang again, and then she heard the rap of knuckles. She sidled up to the door and listened. Nothing.

One of the first things she'd done when she'd bought her condo was to replace the wooden exterior doors with solid steel ones. There was nothing like having a house blown up to make a person a tad paranoid about home security. Of course, the Achilles' heel of a solid steel door was the peephole. It might be urban myth, but it was hard to look through that little spyglass without imagining a thug on the other side with a .357 Magnum pointed at your retina.

She reached for a piece of junk mail on the hall table and held it over the peephole, just to see if its shadow invited a bullet.

"Hannah? Are you there?"

She nearly collapsed with relief. On the other hand, she could happily shoot him just for scaring the bejesus out of her. She flicked the Beretta's safety back on, unbolted the door and stood back to let Russo in.

He froze at the sight of the gun. "Are you okay?"

She waved him in, closing the door behind him and slamming home the dead bolts.

"What happened?" he asked.

She shook her head, still too shaken for coherent speech.

"I've been worrying about you all day," Russo said.

"I needed to make sure you were all right. And to apologize again for my partner and that business with her brother. I never meant—"

She put her fingers on his lips. "Shut up."

"I—"

"Russo, just shut up, will you?" She clamped her mouth onto his to make sure he did.

It knocked him off balance, back against the wall, but he recovered fast. As he pulled her to him, one of his arms wrapped around her, pinning her gun hand against her side. His other hand was buried in her hair, holding her close. She slid her free hand under his sport coat and around his back, welcoming the warmth of him under her palm. He tasted of mint and coffee, and smelled of something like musk and cloves. So damn good.

Turning, he pressed her into the wall, his own tension evident, his need as urgent as her own. Mouths and tongues explored. Then his lips moved down her neck, his hand cupping her breast, thumb circling, driving her crazy. When his mouth came back to hers, it was softer, slower, and then slower still. Finally, breathing hard, they stood forehead to forehead.

He closed his hand around hers, the one still clutching the gun—barely, she was that limp. "Do you think you could put this down now?" he asked.

"Not sure. I still haven't made up my mind whether to shoot you."

He chuckled softly and kissed her again. "Don't shoot me."

"Oh, yeah? What do I get if I don't?"

"This." He kissed her neck again. "And this." He kissed the lobe of her ear, then took it lightly in his teeth. A shiver ran through her and her fingers trembled, the gun slipping. He caught it, while the fingers of his other hand tugged the zipper of her hoodie and lowered it. "This, too," he said, his mouth moving to the bare hollow of her clavicle.

She put her head back against the wall, eyes closed, giving in to the sensations on her skin. "Hell of a good argument you make, Detective," she murmured.

He kissed her once more, lightly. When she opened her eyes, he was watching her, dark eyes smiling, smoldering. "I've got other arguments I wouldn't mind making."

She put her arms around his neck. "Oh, yeah?"

He kissed her lips. Eyes. Forehead. "Yup."

"Up for some really intense debate, are we?"

"I'm so up for it, you wouldn't believe."

She circled his hips and pulled him to her. "Oh, yes, I would."

# *Twenty-Three*

To Hannah's way of thinking, the perfect definition of hell was waking up with a stranger in your bed. By that measure, she was a long way from hell when the sun broke through her eastern windows. In fact, it was a pretty great morning, all things considered.

A short while later, Russo was dressed and sitting at her kitchen counter, drinking coffee, watching her and looking pretty contented himself, thank you very much.

"Do you always go into work this early?" she asked.

"No, but I need time to wipe this stupid grin off my face before I see my trainee or the jig will be up for sure. She's already as much as said my objectivity might be compromised where you're concerned."

"Is it?"

"No—although just because I know you're not responsible for those murders, don't think for a second I won't ask a judge to impound your passport or haul your ass in on a material witness warrant if you try to skip town."

"You know I have to get that painting back."

"Let somebody else do it. I mean it."

She poured herself a coffee. If it was Gladding who'd left that cryptic message on her machine last night, she was probably as safe or safer in Mexico than she was here in L.A. No need to tell Russo that, however, or he really would lock her up. She didn't have time for that.

"Okay, so work on your stone face, Detective. She's a tough one, that Lindsay. Gonna be your boss one day, so you'd better not tick her off."

"Not my boss. She's FBI-bound."

"Like her brother?"

"And their old man, too. She'd be there already, but the Bureau doesn't like to take people right out of school. They prefer their agents have military or police experience under their belts first. Lindsay's made it pretty clear we're just a way station on her way to the Hoover Building."

"Well, all the more reason for her to be holier than the Pope on procedure," Hannah said. "Can't argue with that."

He nodded. "This case could be her ticket into the Bureau, too. Now that the LAPD's involved because of the Koon murder, not to mention federal interest in

Moises Gladding and the stolen van Gogh, it's looking more and more like we're going to have a big inter-agency task force on this one. And that," he said, glancing at his watch and downing the dregs of his cup, "is why I've gotta run."

He came around, put his cup in the sink, then wrapped her up and kissed her. Moving away, he groaned. "Aw, now look what you've gone and done."

"What?"

"Put this stupid grin back on my face."

She smacked his butt. "Get outta here."

After he left, she headed for the shower, running through the game plan in her mind. The last thing she wanted to do was run down to the border today, but it was a matter of pride that she get the painting back and try to salvage what was left of her credibility. Not only that, but if Gladding was responsible for Rebecca's murder and he needed that painting as collateral for some big deal, then she would be delighted to throw a wrench into his plans and put the picture in Teagarden's and Yale's hands. Small enough payback for the havoc he'd wreaked.

She regretted sneaking around behind Russo's back, but what the man didn't know couldn't hurt him. He'd be so tied up with his interagency task force for the next couple of days that she'd be back before he realized she was gone. Meantime, she wasn't going to quiver in fear behind her locked steel door.

She'd considered flying out of LAX, but there was

no guarantee someone wouldn't be watching area airports for her passport. Driving down to the border and then catching a flight from Tijuana was her best bet. She wouldn't drive her car across the line, because it was a bottleneck, especially on Fridays, with weekend travelers heading for the white sand beaches of Baja California and legals of Mexican origin going home for weddings, birthdays or inexpensive medical care. Parking on the U.S. side and walking across was a cinch, however. As much as the border into the U.S. was becoming a new Berlin Wall, absolutely nobody looked twice at people walking in the other direction. There weren't even passport checks. Once across, she'd grab one of the infamous Tijuana taxis, hotfoot it to the airport, and grab a same-day return ticket to Puerto Vallarta, an hour each way. With any luck at all, she could be easily back before the late-night news.

Who knew? Maybe Russo would show up again. Now there was something worth hurrying for.

She rubbed a towel through her hair, then looked at herself in the mirror—a refugee from a revival of *Hair, the Musical.* On a domestic Mexican flight, she wouldn't have to go through Customs at Puerto Vallarta airport, but what if someone else was watching for her? A subtle disguise might be in order.

She dried and straightened her hair, then rolled it into a tight twist anchored with every hairpin she could find. Then, she sprayed the bejesus out of it. Hurricane Katrina wouldn't have budged this do. Makeup heavily applied felt unfamiliar, and with dark eyeliner and red lipstick, she worried she might be straying into street-walker territory. She found a hardly worn pearl-gray linen pantsuit at the back of her closet and put that on over a silk camisole and a single strand of pearls, with matching drop earrings for her lobes. An oversize Coach handbag, a Christmas gift from Nora, and matching black shoes finished the outfit—flats, however, just in case she had to run for it.

When she checked her reflection, she was stunned to see Nora peering back from the mirror, ready for one of her Newport Beach charity events. She'd be *so* proud, Hannah thought, grinning.

She was out the door and just locking the dead bolt when Russo called. "Hiya," she said.

"Hello."

Whoops. Very stiff. Lindsay Gonna-be-a-G-Man-like-My-Dad must be standing close by, she decided.

"I thought I should let you know that your prints were found on the murder weapon at August Koon's studio," Russo said.

"Well, I told you they would be."

"Yes, you did. They were also at the Sandpiper Gallery."

"Did you guys manage to track down Rebecca's ex-husband?"

"Yes, but it turns out he was attending a family funeral in Seattle. Flew up Saturday and just got back last night. His alibi looks solid. We're still checking out his financials for evidence that he might have hired someone to kill his ex-wife."

Hannah shook her head. "I'd be surprised. It's got to be connected to Moises Gladding and Teagarden's missing painting. It's the only thing that makes sense, with Koon dead, too."

"I think so. So we're going to need you to come in to give a formal statement."

"Why? I already told you everything I know."

"It's a multiagency investigation now," Russo said, curtly. No question there were other people in the room. "LAPD Robbery/Homicide has come late to the party, and since you're a prime witness—the *only* significant witness—they obviously want some time with you. I think the FBI may want to sit in again, too."

"Do I need to bring an attorney?"

"I can't advise you about that. You know the drill. I can send a car for you, or you can come in under your own steam, but this has got to be done."

He was in an awkward position, she knew, especially after last night. He knew she hadn't done anything wrong, but no one else knew that. If she lawyered up, the LAPD might see it as a sign of guilt. She didn't see how this could possibly go well then. "All right," she said. "When do you want me to come in?"

"As soon as possible. Come into the West Hollywood patrol station. We're basing the operation there— convenient for all the players."

And Sheriff's Department turf, Hannah thought.

Dollars to doughnuts the FBI guys had argued for running it out of their field office in West L.A., but neither Russo nor the LAPD detectives would have liked that option. Once the Bureau got control, they would edge everyone else out. Nobody had pointier elbows.

"Okay," Hannah said. "I'm on my way."

Moments later, Ruben flagged her down as she was backing out of the garage. He'd been out running. Sweat glistened on his muscular body as he pushed Mellie's stroller up alongside Hannah's car. Chucky jumped up on the Prius, panting dog breath in her face as his tongue stretched to give her a pooch-smooch.

"Chucky, down!" Ruben ordered. "Hey, neighbor! Welcome back."

"Hi, Rube. Hiya, Mellie!"

The tot responded with the happy smile she always had ready for family and friends, which meant everyone. Like Chucky, she didn't discriminate. She loved the whole world.

"You look hot today, girlfriend. Dressed to kill."

Yeah, right. "Going to a meeting."

"So no time for coffee?"

She shook her head regretfully, even though she'd much rather take refuge in his kitchen over one of his giant mugs of *café con leche* than face the Inquisition forces massing at the WeHo sheriff's substation.

He frowned. "You okay, sweetie?"

"Surviving." Which was saying something, Hannah

thought. "I got your message, by the way. Kittens?" She laughed. "You do have a flair for the dramatic, buddy."

"But of course. So, did you go? Because Travis really, really wanted to talk to you."

"I didn't get it in time, but I'm still interested to hear what he found out. Maybe later?"

"Mellie and I are meeting him at Tommy's burger at noon. Want to meet us there?"

"Sounds good. I'll try. If not, I'll call you guys later." *They have phones in jail, right?*

"Okay! See ya, doll!"

She waved, backed out the driveway and sped down the hill.

Teagarden had woken with a headache and a creeping sense of dread. The longer *The Night Café* was missing, the better the odds it would be damaged or lost forever.

He stood in the bathroom, feeling his years as he hooked his razor strop onto the towel hook. He was hunting in his kit for his razor when the hotel room phone rang.

"Señor Teagarden, it is Rolando Peña calling from Puerto Vallarta. Good morning."

"Captain Peña, good morning. How are you?"

"I am well. And how is Los Angeles? Are you having any luck in your search for the van Gogh painting?"

"Not really. I've met the courier and she confirms she

didn't leave it at the villa, so we know we didn't miss it in our search."

"What has she done with it?"

"Ah, well, that's the sixty-million-dollar question, I'm afraid. Any news at your end?"

"Some bad news, I'm afraid. There has been another body found."

"Gladding?"

"No, another American, however. A man by the name of Donald Ackerman. He owned a tourist café and bar here called The Blue Gecko. I have known him for many years. He has been found shot dead in the trunk of his car."

Teagarden's mind raced back to Hannah Nicks, and her account of commandeering an American barkeep to drive her to the airport and then leaving him in the trunk of his car while she made her escape. He would have to check with his colleague, Agent Towle, but this sounded like the same man. "Shot, you say?"

"*Sí.* I believe this may be connected to the shooting at Señor Gladding's villa."

"Why is that?"

"I have learned that this painting you were looking for was to have been delivered by a female courier."

"How do you know this?" Teagarden asked. He hadn't shown the fax he found to Peña.

"A confidential source," Peña said. "According to witnesses, a very attractive, dark-haired woman carrying a portfolio of the sort that might hold a painting was seen at The Blue Gecko earlier in the day. A waiter says the same woman showed up later that night, after the bar was closed, looking for Señor Ackerman. The waiter left them together. That was the last time Ackerman was seen alive."

"I see."

"I called you first, Señor Teagarden, because of the strong possibility these things are linked. If you have any further information about the whereabouts of this painting, it might tell us something about the Ackerman murder—and also, perhaps, those at the villa."

"Yes, I can see that it might. Well, leave it with me, Captain. Let me see if there is anything further to be learned here in Los Angeles that might help you."

"I would be most grateful, *señor*."

"Of course,"

Teagarden hung up and sat on the edge of the bed, rubbing the stubble on his chin. Hannah Nicks said she had left Ackerman alive in his trunk with his helper on the way to rescue him. Was she lying? And if not, who had murdered the man? And why were they so interested in seeing her take the blame?

Hannah parked in the parking lot of the West Hollywood substation on San Vicente Boulevard. She had worked patrol out of this station during her first year as a sheriff's deputy. It was great territory with plenty of nighttime action, between the gay bars of Santa Monica Boulevard and the hot clubs of Sunset frequented by young Hollywood royalty like Johnny Depp and Drew

Barrymore. *Vanity Fair* held their annual Oscars party at Morton's up the street, the rubbernecking matched only by Elton John's competing bash at The Factory. Eye-opening stuff for a girl from the Midwest.

At the reception desk inside, a uniformed deputy greeted her, all smiles. "Hey, stranger!" The woman had been a rookie the year Hannah's house got blown up and she had retired from the department. "You look great. Private sector must be treating you well."

"Oh, yeah. Easy street," Hannah said wryly.

The deputy got on the phone. "Detective Russo said you were coming. Let me call him out."

When Russo emerged from the squad room, he seemed taken aback. "Um…hello." He actually shook her hand.

Was it the interagency, this-is-a-formal-inquiry thing that had him off base? Or the Hannah-does-Nora look?

Russo led her back through the locked door and down the hall to the squad room. Lindsay Towle was there, perched on the edge of a desk, drinking coffee with three or four plainclothes detectives and a couple of uniforms, who seemed happy to put their work aside for a few minutes of shooting the breeze with her.

Lindsay's blond hair gleamed under the overhead lights. Her camel-colored slacks, ivory silk blouse and gold earrings completely outclassed the frayed cuffs and rumpled sport coats of the other detectives. There could be little doubt that this was a woman on her way up—and out, from what Russo had said about her hopes for an FBI career. But was even the Bureau big enough to contain the ambition of Lindsay Towle? Who knew? She was sharp, no doubt about it.

When she spotted Hannah, Lindsay got to her feet and followed her and Russo down the hall, the other detectives close behind. Russo led Hannah into an interview room and one of the older men joined them. The rest of the group continued on down the hall to what Hannah knew was a darkened observation room next door. So, they weren't going to jump her en masse. That was something, anyway.

FBI Agents Towle and Ito were nowhere to be seen, Hannah realized. But then, why would they bother wasting time while this bunch interviewed her? They knew where to find her, and obviously had no qualms about showing up uninvited at her door at any ungodly hour.

Russo indicated that she should take a chair on the side of the table facing the mirror.

"This is Detective Tim Walker of LAPD Robbery/ Homicide," Russo said. "Detective, Hannah Nicks. Formerly one of ours."

The LAPD detective shook her hand. How would he interpret that "formerly one of ours" business? Hannah wondered. One of us, so go easy? Or she's gone over to the dark side—do your worst?

# *Twenty-Four*

In his tenth-floor Beverly Hills hotel room, Gladding dialed a number on one of his many throwaway cell phones.

"Yes." The Israeli-accented voice at the other end gave no indication who he was or where he might be. Gladding didn't care. He had dialed a Zurich-based cell, but the satellites could be bouncing the signal halfway around the globe and back. As long as the former Mossad assassin was available when Gladding needed him, the rest was irrelevant.

"I have work for you," Gladding said. No need to identify himself. Not after all these years.

"You know my price. When?"

"Next week. Monday."

"Fine. Wire the advance, e-mail the details."

"Done." Gladding disconnected, then booted up his laptop. There was much about modern life he found aggravating, but the ability to communicate safely using encryption algorithms that not even the American National Security Agency could crack was very convenient.

He wrote a short e-mail and attached photos and other identifiers for Kyle Liggett, as well as a copy of the boy's Indiana driver's license. His instructions included the coordinates where Liggett expected to receive final payment for the San Onofre job. He told the contractor to leave Liggett in an open area with a facsimile of the license in a pocket. When the body was found, Gladding wanted there to be no doubt about its identity.

After sending the e-mail, he transferred twenty-five thousand dollars from one of his Cayman Island accounts into another account—also in the Caymans—belonging to the contractor. He could have hired someone cheaper, but reliability was paramount. Liggett could be crafty.

He shut down the system, then glanced at his watch. Time for his meds. He freshened his coffee at the breakfast cart a waiter had rolled in a while earlier and threw back a handful of pills. Then he dialed yet another number, this one local.

"G'day!" a cheerful voice answered.

"It's me." Another longtime associate with no need for names. "I need some information."

"Information's my middle name, mate."

The private investigator's Australian accent was still pronounced, although the man had been living in Los

Angeles for something like twenty years. "The sheilas dig it," he'd once told Gladding with a wink. The man could come across as a good-time Charlie, but it masked impressive efficiency. Like the man in Zurich, the Aussie gave good value for his steep fee.

Gladding gave him what he had on Hannah Nicks, which amounted to little more than an address and phone number. In the background, he heard a keypad tapping. "I want everything you can get on her by noon," he said.

The tapping stopped. "Today?"

"Yes, of course, today. Meet me at Musso & Frank."

"Can you give me an extra hour at least, mate?"

"One o'clock then. Sharp."

Gladding called down to the hotel concierge to have him book a table—a *quiet* table—at Musso & Frank Grill in Hollywood for one o'clock.

"You bet, Mr. Dunning. Number in your party?"

"Two."

Gladding rang off and settled in to read the *New York Times*. He had made it through world news and the business pages when a knock sounded at the door. He padded over the thick carpets, glanced through the peephole, then opened the door.

He shut the door behind Kyle Liggett. "Did anyone see you?"

Liggett pushed his sunglasses on top of his head. "Nope."

"You came in the side door?"

"Just like you said."

Gladding's instructions had been explicit. Within hours of the bombing, Liggett's picture would be splattered across the media. It had been risky allowing the boy to come to the hotel, but he wanted to see him and judge the steadiness of his resolve. This was Gladding's final hurrah, his goodbye message to a country that had answered his long service with betrayal. Liggett would be the instrument of his revenge.

"You look like you slept in the street," Gladding said. He'd ordered the boy to find a room in another part of L.A. No hookers, nothing to bring attention to himself.

"Stayed in a hotel by the Hollywood Walk of Fame. You know, that place is not as fancy as you might expect."

Gladding took an armchair and gestured to the sofa. Instead, Liggett walked over to the breakfast cart, poured himself a glass of orange juice, then proceeded to butter some toast and spread jam on it. Gladding swallowed his irritation. "I want you to drive down to San Onofre for a final survey of the target. Make sure nothing's changed."

Liggett slumped on the couch, legs sprawling, chewing noisily. "I been over it six ways to Sunday already."

"I'm not asking."

"You're the boss."

"Yes, I am. Call me before you start back here in case I have additional instructions. Now, go. Take the stairs down."

Kyle downed the last of his juice and set the glass on the cart, then pulled on his shades and left.

He steamed all the way to the ground floor and out the side door of the fancy Beverly Hills hotel. He wasn't the fool the old man seemed to think he was. And if the bugger didn't want Liggett to be seen, he should have stayed in a bigger place.

"Boutique hotel, my ass."

The hell with it. After this, he'd never have to deal with Gladding again—and never was too soon. But it pissed him off royally to have the man ordering him off on some wild-goose chase today. Wasn't necessary. Things were set. Gladding had never micromanaged him before, so why start now?

There could only be one reason. He wanted him out of the way.

Since the old man obviously still didn't have the painting, which was payment for the damn bomb, what was he even doing in L.A.? If he thought the courier had brought it back here, then why not send Liggett around to take it off the bitch?

He'd left his rental Ford in a parking lot across from the hotel entrance. Damned if he was driving to San Onofre, Liggett fumed. He was staying right here to keep an eye on Gladding.

Russo took the lead during the interview with Hannah, having her recount yet again how Rebecca

Powell had approached her about transporting an August Koon painting to a client in Puerto Vallarta, and how events had subsequently unfolded.

Walker, the LAPD Robbery/Homicide detective heading up their side of the joint investigation, injected the occasional question or request for clarification, but Russo was thorough—not least, Hannah suspected, to waylay the misgivings of his young partner in the next room about whether he could be objective where this witness was concerned.

Predictably, Walker was very interested in Hannah's visit to Koon's studio with Rebecca. He took her over that part of the story three times before he seemed satisfied. Yes, Hannah confirmed, she'd been in the studio. Yes, she'd handled the murder weapon. She saw no reason to hold anything back.

When it came to the FBI agents' visit the night before her departure, she was on shakier ground. She had no idea what Towle and Ito had told Russo about what they'd asked her to do, and she didn't see it as her place to volunteer, since it did seem to be a matter of some sensitivity. She was in enough hot water without getting caught up on some national security beef.

Russo, unfortunately, wasn't making this part easy for her. "Why, exactly, did the FBI want to talk to you that night?"

"Gee, Detective, I'm not sure. Seems they heard through the grapevine I was hand-delivering a painting to Moises Gladding."

At least he had the grace to look chagrined.

"But what was their interest in your trip?" Walker asked.

"It's no secret that Moises Gladding is an arms dealer. You guys know there are federal warrants out on him. Makes sense the feds would be keeping an eye on him, I suppose."

"Yeah. So what did they want you to do?"

"Well, this is where it gets dicey for me, guys. I think you need to ask them about that." She cocked a thumb at the two-way mirror and the invisible watchers on the other side. "Maybe Detective Russo's partner could tell you something more," she suggested. Well, all right, maybe she wasn't over being annoyed about that.

"Let's just get back to what happened when you tried to deliver Koon's painting," Russo said. "There were complications."

"Yeah, big-time," Hannah said. Since William Teagarden, a civilian and a foreigner, to boot, knew all about the shootings at Gladding's villa, she saw no reason to withhold details. She ran through sordid chapter and verse of her eighteen-hour Mexican misadventure, neglecting only to say what she'd done with the painting.

Walker sat back and crossed his arms, frowning. "Let me get this straight. You found five people shot to death at this estate Gladding had down there and you failed to call the police?"

"I think it was five bodies, yes."

"You wanna tell me why you didn't call the cops?"

"Because I had no idea what I'd walked into, who was responsible, or who was on the take. Call me paranoid, but I really didn't want to risk landing up in a Mexican jail—or dead—because I talked to the wrong people."

"I think we can agree that she had good reason to be afraid," Russo said, "especially knowing what happened to the other parties to this deal here in L.A."

"Maybe," Walker said, "but her story would be more credible if she could produce this alleged painting."

"I'm working to recover it," Hannah said. "I'm not sure how it's connected to your murder cases, but given that Rebecca Powell was an old friend of my family, I've got as much reason as anyone to find out if there's a link. Once I have it again, you guys, the feds, Yale University—hell, the Pope, for all I care—can examine it to see if it's a missing masterpiece. Otherwise, if it's not, it belongs to Moises Gladding."

"You'd give it to him?" Walker asked, incredulous.

"That's what I was hired to do. If he ends up in federal prison, it could be problematic but I'll cross that bridge when I come to it."

Walker and Russo exchanged looks. The LAPD detective sighed and shook his head. "Don't even *think* about leaving town, Ms. Nicks," Walker said sternly.

"My advice exactly," Russo added.

# Twenty-Five

Hannah sat in her car outside the Sheriff's Department West Hollywood station. The clock on the dash said eleven-forty. Obviously, driving down to the border, catching a flight out of Tijuana and getting back before anyone noticed she was gone was no longer looking doable—even assuming Russo or LAPD Detective Walker didn't haul her in the second she tried to cross the L.A. County line.

That left Plan B—take Teagarden up on his offer to have his policeman buddy in Puerto Vallarta pick up the painting. Did she trust Teagarden, charming accent notwithstanding? And what about the Puerto Vallarta police? How was she going to go about finding Teagarden, anyway? A call to Special Agent Towle was probably her best bet, but did she want to deal with him, either?

Her head hurt, and her empty stomach had apparently decided to hold her brain for ransom until she paid up with something other than the coffee she'd had that morning before Russo left her place. Ruben had said he was meeting Travis for lunch at Tommy's burger. Only a guy as fit as Rube could love a cholesterol camp like Tommy's, but she was just a hop, skip and a jump from there now. If Travis had anything useful to add to the mystery of Moises Gladding, a bustling place like Tommy's was the place to pick his brain.

She shot out of the parking lot and headed toward Beverly Boulevard. When she got to the drive-in burger shack, the place was packed with the lunchtime crowd. She lucked out when an SUV pulled out of a parking spot just as she pulled in. A pickup truck that had just rolled past the slot spotted the opening, too, and its backup light lit up, but the SUV was in its way and Hannah zipped into the spot.

"Sorry, bud. You snooze, you lose." The pickup driver grimaced and drove on.

Trav and Ruben were already in line for food, Mellie riding piggyback on Ruben in her sporty red carrier. Nobody in line complained when Hannah joined them. Tommy's was a laid-back kind of joint. She tickled Mellie and hugged the guys, and then they all studied the menu on the overhead placards.

Travis, she noticed, seemed nervous. Trouble between the two guys? Trouble at work? Or had Ruben blind-sided him by inviting Hannah along for lunch? Why would that be a problem?

They got their food, trays loaded with burgers and fries, then paid up, grabbed their sodas from the honor system cooler, and moved along until they found an open spot at one of the stand-up bars liberally supplied with much needed napkin dispensers. Consuming Tommy's grub seated wasn't advised unless a person wanted a lap full of chili, cheese and burger juice, but what it lacked in finesse, it made up for in flavor.

Ruben skinned a plain hot dog for Mellie, making it easier for her to chew. He reached over his shoulder and wrapped her fist around it. She proceeded to do a pretty good job of getting it to her mouth, only occasionally defeated by her uncooperative little body. The guys were always there to help her when she showed signs of frustration, but they encouraged her to manage what she could. She was a lucky little kid to have scored adoptive parents who would do their best to help her become as independent as possible. The guys, in fact, were in the process of trying for a brother or sister for Mellie.

"How's the new adoption coming along?" Hannah asked.

Travis nodded. "Good." He was far less verbal than his outgoing partner.

"We're going through the home visits now," Ruben said. "There's always a little hesitation with a gay couple, but I think we have a good shot."

Hannah smiled and rubbed Mellie's arm. "They only have to see how this little dolly's thriving to know what great parents you are."

She worked her way through the messy burger. Travis looked askance as Ruben piled more hot chili peppers onto his. "I swear to God, I don't know how you have any stomach lining left," he said.

"So I got Ruben's message from 'Monica.' Does that mean you found something interesting about our friend?" she asked.

Travis looked around nervously. If the earth had opened up right then and swallowed him, she suspected, he wouldn't have minded. Instead, he just shrugged and took a bite of his burger. Was that it? she wondered. The spook community was utterly ruthless about security breaches. Was Travis feeling heat?

"I don't want to get you in trouble," she said. Maybe that was all the anxious calls were about, a warning to back off and not mention his name if anyone asked what she was up to with Gladding. "I shouldn't have asked you to look into it for me, Trav. It was out of line. Probably not important now, anyway. Don't worry."

He finally looked directly at her. She wasn't sure if his expression was more grateful or relieved. "I'm just glad you're home safe and sound," he said.

She punched him lightly in the shoulder. "Hey, I'm a tough cookie."

He nodded at her outfit. "Looking pretty hot today."

She glanced down, then grimaced. "Yeah, right, especially with mustard on my lapel." She grabbed a napkin, poured a little of her water over it and went to work on the spot.

Travis finished his food, dumped his trash and kissed Mellie. He gave Hannah a quick hug. "Be careful," he said quietly. After a quick hand-squeeze from Ruben, he strode off to his Jeep.

"He was worried about you," Ruben said, as Travis pulled out of the lot. "We both were, when we didn't hear back from you."

"Thanks, Rube. It means a lot to me that you guys have my back."

He grinned and turned back to his daughter. "Well, of course we watch out for our Hannah, don't we, Mellie? 'Cause we love her."

Hannah crumpled up her trash. "Thanks. And right back at ya, too. I've got to go."

"Hot date?"

"Oh, please. All my hot dates are with you guys and a ten-year-old."

"Well, no wonder," Ruben said, flicking her pearls, "the way you overdress just for lunch at a burger joint."

The green neon sign overhead proclaimed Musso & Frank Grill the "oldest restaurant in Hollywood— *Since 1919.*"

Kyle Liggett hunched down in his rental car and watched Gladding emerge from the back of a black Rolls-Royce limo. The old man was wearing a silk ascot under an open-necked yellow shirt, a checked sport coat and, of all things, a tan Panama hat. So much for keeping a low profile. Who did the guy think he was,

Liggett fumed, friggin' Cecil B. DeMille? Meanwhile, he himself was staying in a fleabag hotel and driving a goddamn Ford Focus.

As the Rolls pulled away to wait up the block, the old man paused. He took a cell phone from his pocket, pushing up his sunglasses to read the screen. Then, he walked to a solitary spot in an alley a little way up the street and spoke briefly on the phone. After a glance around, he dropped the cell and ground it into the pavement with his heel. Picking up the pieces, he tossed them into a Dumpster, then walked back to the restaurant and went inside.

Smoke rose from back of the place, grill exhaust, by the mouthwatering smell of meat drifting across the road. Liggett was starving. The place looked pretty big, but not big enough that the boss's watchful eye wouldn't spot him inside. Probably wasn't dressed fancy enough for the joint, either. He watched the door a few minutes more to be sure there was no doubt Gladding was there for the duration. There was a taco stand up the block. He sprinted over, got himself some grub, then took the paper sack back to the Focus and settled in to wait.

Walking into Musso & Frank was like stepping back into a more elegant time, with its padded red leather booths, crisp white linens and ruby-jacketed waiters. The menu was traditional, the service curt but efficient—none of that vacuous "I'm Tiffany and I'll be your server" nonsense here. For a generous tip, the concierge had reserved a quiet corner table for "Mr. Dunning." For another generous tip, the maître d' had Gladding in his seat and a dry martini in front of him before he'd even tucked away his sunglasses.

He sipped his drink and studied the menu while he waited for the private investigator to arrive. Finally, ten minutes late, the long-legged Aussie slid into the banquette across from him and laid a manila envelope on the white tablecloth.

A waiter materialized to take his drink order. "I'll take a Foster's lager, thanks, mate," the P.I. said.

"No Foster's," the waiter said brusquely.

"Well, whatever, then. Just make it cold and wet."

Before he could get away, Gladding stopped the waiter with a peremptorily raised finger. "We'll order now, too. The roast of lamb and a salad for me. Roquefort dressing."

The Aussie tried to scan the long menu, then gave up and glanced around. "Smell's like steak. Works for me. Make it a rib eye, rare."

"No rib eye," the waiter said. He pointed at the steak section on the menu.

The P.I. exhaled heavily. "Fine. Porterhouse, then. Same salad as the gentleman, and don't forget that beer."

The waiter sniffed, took the menus and left.

Gladding got right down to business. "You have a tail on her?"

"Put someone on it as soon as you called. Matter of

fact, you'll get a kick out of this. She'd already left her place by the time my guy went around, but then we caught a break. Got information that she was at the West Hollywood Sheriff's station. Found her car in the lot there. I talked to a confidential source of mine. Turns out she's a material witness on a couple of murder beefs—maybe even a suspect."

Gladding raised an eyebrow. "Really? You're certain about this?"

"Absolutely. I'm plugged in. That's why I get the big bucks. After she left the cop shop, she had lunch at a burger joint with a couple of poofters, my guy said." He slid the manila file across the table. "It sounds like neighbors who live in the same condo complex as her. They've got an adopted daughter who's handicapped. My watcher said the poofters had a little kid who looked like something was wrong with her."

Gladding leafed through the pages, nodding. There was extensive biographical info on the Nicks woman— background, work history, even a few press clippings. "You might want to add a second tail on her," he said, scanning the clippings. "She seems wily, this one."

The P.I. nodded. "We put a GPS tag on her car, but I can add a second man, if you like."

"Do it."

She was divorced, Gladding read, her ex-husband remarried. She had a son who lived with the ex and the second wife. The file also contained information on an extended family who lived in Orange County—a mother and a sister and her family. There were also details on her neighbors at her Silver Lake condominium.

All good to know, Gladding thought, particularly the fact that she was friendly with the neighbors with the crippled child. He wouldn't use it unless he had to but he didn't have time to waste, so every bit of ammunition helped.

Gladding didn't like to exploit a target's family if it could be avoided. On the other hand, the American government had set the ground rules here when they'd roughed up his wife and son at his daughter's graduation, using his family for leverage after they turned against him.

Now, his own family was safely out of the country, and all bets were off.

## Twenty-Six

When her cell rang, Hannah glanced at the screen. She sighed. She knew Cal had phoned while she was in Puerto Vallarta, but she'd decided to put off calling him back to see if they could take Mrs. Jennings's advice to bury the hatchet for Gabe's sake. Well, she thought, no time like the present.

"Hi, Cal."

"So, Hannah, in yet another mess, are you?"

"Excuse me?"

"Two murders, and whose name pops up as a material witness—dare I say a suspect?"

"Now, wait a minute—"

"You'll have to keep away from Gabe until this is resolved."

"What?"

"You can resume visitation if and when you're cleared."

"Cal, you know damn well I didn't kill anyone."

"Maybe, but I have to insist, at least until this is cleared up. I'm just protecting my son."

"*Our* son." But she was talking to dead air.

She slammed her hand against the steering wheel. How the hell would he even know about this? But of course, he'd been a prosecutor in this city. He was still plugged in to sources in the D.A.'s office and on all the local police forces. Even if he now worked the other side of the aisle as a defense attorney, Calvin Nicks was very good at keeping the wheels greased.

What were the chances, she worried, that Gabe might one day start believing his father's version of things?

She'd made up her mind to track down Teagarden and take him up on his offer to have the painting picked up in Puerto Vallarta, but when she put in a call to Agent Towle at the FBI field office, he was in a meeting. She left her cell number for him to call back.

Once back home, she decided to go for a run to try to clear her head. After the call from Gladding, she wasn't going anywhere without her Beretta, even though it was a pain—literally—to carry the thing while she ran. But she had a concealed-carry permit and better to have it than be caught in the open with her ballistic pants down, so to speak.

Although, come to think of it, how exactly was the "concealed" part managed in a tank top and shorts?

Sweats and a brisk walk, then. She changed out of

her fancy duds and into sweats and a T-shirt, flopping onto the couch to pull on her socks and sneakers. She stopped by the mirror at the front door, trying to see if the holster under her shirt made her look like the Hunchback of Notre Dame. Not bad. Slipping her keys into her pocket, she pulled open the door to find a man standing there. She let out a startled gasp, dropping back into defensive position.

"You were expecting me, I see," Teagarden said wryly. Hands in his pockets, he leaned casually against the doorjamb, looking very Bond—James Bond, while she gathered her wits. At least he wasn't looking very Gladding—Moises Gladding.

She waved him in, double-locking the door behind him.

"Am I your prisoner, my dear? How delightful."

Was he flirting with her? The rascal. She smiled in spite of herself.

"Just feeling a little paranoid," she said. "Did you see anyone suspicious outside?"

"Other than myself?"

"Touché. Anyway, speak of the devil, I was just trying to reach Agent Towle to find out if you were still in town. Have a seat. Can I offer you something— coffee? Water? Soda? Oh, no, wait, is it tea time?"

"Not yet. Nothing, thanks. I take it you've heard from our friend Mr. Gladding?"

"How did you know?"

"Elementary, my dear Ms. Watson. You weren't

nervous yesterday despite having every reason to be. Today, you're as jumpy as a cricket on a hotplate."

"Well, I did spend the morning being grilled by L.A.'s finest. As for Gladding, I think so." She told him about the cryptic message on her machine the night before.

"You know this will never be put right until that painting is recovered, don't you?" Teagarden asked.

"I'm beginning to realize that."

"Well, I have that friend with the Puerto Vallarta police."

"So you said. But can you trust him?"

Teagarden exhaled heavily. "Actually, he called this morning. That American fellow you left in the boot of his car? The CIA chap?"

She nodded.

"He's been found dead. Tortured and shot."

"What? Where?"

"In the boot of his car. Captain Peña said he'd been last seen with a dark-haired American woman. He sent up some fingerprints they pulled off his car and the FBI has already run them."

"And of course they're mine. Oh, Lord…" She sank down into a chair. "Ackerman told me that Gladding would kill to get the painting. He also said he had a guy working for him who wasn't above torture."

"Did you tell Ackerman where the painting was?"

She shook her head.

"You didn't trust him?"

"Not really. I still don't know who I can trust. But if

he'd been able to hand it over, they might not have killed him."

"So you can see the painting needs to be recovered."

"How do you know your police captain friend isn't Gladding's creature?"

Teagarden shook his head. "Not Peña."

"How can you be sure?"

"Would your Detective Russo take a bribe?"

"*My* Detective Russo?"

He smiled. "Hannah, these eyes are old, but they don't miss much. So, Russo—would he?"

"No way."

"How do you know?"

"I just do." She slumped. "Okay, fine, I get it. As it was, I was trying to reach you anyway. I really can't leave town, it seems, thanks to *my* Detective Russo and the LAPD. And now, I suppose I'm a wanted felon in Mexico, too."

"You do seem to be well in it, love."

She got up and poured them cold water from the fridge. "When the van Gogh was stolen, people were killed at the museum, weren't they? To eliminate witnesses?" He nodded. "So Rebecca Powell and August Koon—same reason."

He took the glass from her. "Cheers. I should think so."

"So their murders come down to Gladding, too. But I don't see him shooting up his own villa, do you?"

"That *is* curious, isn't it?"

"And now Ackerman."

"It's worse than that, I'm afraid. Peña called again about an hour ago. A man and his family have been found dead, the fellow showing many of the same signs as Ackerman." He pulled a notebook out of his pocket and flipped it open. "Sergio Chavez was his name."

"Oh, my God. Gladding's driver. The one who tried to steal the Koon from me."

"The one you left tied to a tree? You must see it now, Hannah."

"Yeah. This much bloodshed—it has to be your van Gogh. Okay, I give up. Call your police captain and let him go get the damn thing."

"First thing tomorrow. Peña said he'd be unavailable for the rest of today. All hell has broken loose in Puerto Vallarta. Four murders in twenty-four hours in a town that lives on tourism—and one of the victims a well-known local American, to boot. Poor fellow will be lucky to keep his job. Meantime," Teagarden added, "I think we need to ensure your safety, my dear. I came over to suggest you pack a few things and come back to my hotel with me."

"Why William Teagarden, you devil."

"My intentions are completely honorable, I assure you. However, aside from the fact that you are a charming lady, I have rather a strong vested interest in keeping you alive."

"Well, thank you, I'm sure, but nobody's running me out of my home."

"Has anyone ever noted how obstinate you are?"

"All the time."

"Well, so am I, lass, so am I. I'll be spending the night here, then."

"I don't really have room for guests."

Teagarden glanced around. "Not a problem. That looks like a perfectly comfortable sofa."

# Twenty-Seven

She hadn't heard from Russo since she'd left the inter-view at the West Hollywood station, but Hannah wasn't all that surprised. No doubt he was insanely busy, co-ordinating the interagency case with the LAPD, the FBI and God only knows who else. There was also a good chance he was feeling the need to distance himself from her at the moment. She couldn't blame him, but it was a bummer just the same.

She showered, dressed and tiptoed out to the kitchen to switch on the coffeemaker she'd set up the night before. Teagarden was snoring rather loudly in the living room, but after she'd slipped out to pick up the paper from the driveway, she returned to find him peering at her over the back of the sofa.

"Good morning," she said. "Coffee?"

"Mind if I shower, first?" He rolled off the sofa, gathered the blanket around himself toga-style, picked up his shirt and pants, and shuffled off down the hall. She poured herself a cup of coffee and settled in to look at the paper. The *Los Angeles Times* had August Koon's murder on the front page and another piece inside the *Arts* section. Rebecca's death, on the other hand, merited scarcely a couple of paragraphs on page eleven.

The shower was running in the bathroom when her phone rang. Reading the puff piece on Koon, she answered distractedly. "Hello?"

"Hannah Nicks? You have something that belongs to me, Ms. Nicks."

"Mr. Gladding? Is that you?" She faked a note of relief. "I was so worried. I thought you'd been killed."

"I'm quite alive."

"I arrived at the villa and found—everything. Everyone…it was awful."

"Did you see who did it? See anyone leave?"

"No. Nobody was there. Nobody alive, at least. I was terrified. I just jumped on a plane and came back to Los Angeles. Have you heard what happened here? Rebecca Powell has been killed, too."

"I heard. I was shocked."

In a pig's eye, Hannah thought.

"But I'm a little confused, Ms. Nicks. You ran away, and yet I understand from sources of mine that you didn't take the painting back with you."

"I was afraid I wouldn't be able to get it back into the country. But I left it somewhere safe."

"I believe you were paid to deliver it. I would like my painting."

"You want it delivered in Puerto Vallarta?" She decided to go for broke, just to see how he'd react. "There's an American down there, Donald Ackerman. I think I could get him to pick it up."

Gladding said nothing for a moment. "Did you enjoy your lunch yesterday, Ms. Nicks?"

"Excuse me?"

"Those two friends of yours—and that sweet little child they have. Pity about her health problems, though. It would be a shame if anything were to happen to her caretakers."

"Wait a minute—"

"You have until nine p.m. tonight to deliver my painting. I'll call again later with instructions on where and how. Are we clear?" He didn't wait for a reply.

Staring at the phone in her hand, dial tone buzzing, she didn't notice that Teagarden's shower had long since ended. She turned as he stepped into the kitchen and took the receiver from her hand and hung it back up.

"Gladding?"

She nodded. "He wants the painting, he wants it yesterday, and he's made a threat against some close friends of mind."

"Tell me."

She recounted Gladding's message, including the

threat against Travis and Ruben. "How could he know I met them yesterday?"

"He must have you under surveillance. He might even have a bug on your car—and on your phone, for that matter."

"Well, if he wants to tap my phone, he's probably had to stand in line, given how many people want a piece of me at the moment."

She glanced around. What were the odds her house wasn't bugged, too? She grabbed the remote and turned on the TV, cranking the volume up loud. She moved in close to Teagarden.

"I need to go and warn my neighbors," she murmured. "I can get to their place through the garages without going outside. There's a connecting double door and we each have keys to the other's side."

Teagarden nodded. "Be careful. And take that gun of yours, will you? While you do that, I'll make some quiet phone calls."

Hannah grabbed her gun and keys, slipped through the kitchen entrance into her garage, and from there into Ruben and Travis's bay. Ruben's Mustang was there, but his partner's Jeep was gone. She tried the door to their kitchen. Unlocked. *Dammit, Ruben*. She tiptoed inside, dreading the silence.

Suddenly, Chucky-the-dog came padding out to greet her and she breathed a sigh of relief. Ruben was on the patio, reading the paper. He looked up and grinned.

"Well, hi, girlfriend! Mellie's—"

Hannah held a finger to her lips, then waved him into the kitchen, where she found a grocery pad and pen stuck on the side of the fridge. She pulled it down and wrote: *Danger + House may be bugged. Where's Trav?*

*Work,* Ruben mouthed.

She pointed at the radio on the counter, but he cocked a thumb upstairs toward Mellie's room and mimed sleeping.

*You have to get out of here,* she wrote. *I'm so sorry. My fault.*

He patted her shoulder, then took the pen. *You sure???*

She nodded fiercely.

*We can go to cabin.*

She shook her head and mouthed, *Not safe. Friends?*

He thought about it, then nodded.

She took the pen. *Go as fast as you can. Call Trav from the car and tell him what's going on. I'll call later to explain.*

The television was still blaring when she got back to her condo and Teagarden was on his cell phone, a finger in the opposite ear so he could hear the other end of the conversation. After he hung up, he came over to her.

"Did you talk to them?" he murmured.

She nodded. "They'll leave soon."

"Where will they go?"

"Don't know, don't want to know."

"I called Towle. He's doing some checking. Meantime, let's go someplace where we can talk more freely. Best we leave before your neighbor," he added. "That way, if you do have a tail, you'll draw them off."

"We hope."

"Indeed. I'll leave ahead, see if I can spot anyone who might be following you."

She nodded and wrote down a location not far from the FBI field office where they could meet. A few minutes later, the Brit left.

Hannah gave him a five-minute head start, then grabbed her messenger bag and headed out to the garage. Before she lifted the door, she crab-walked around her Prius, checking out the underside, feeling inside the wheel wells until she found what she was looking for. *Damn!* She pulled the GPS tracker off the right rear fender and stuck it in her pocket. Then, she jumped in the car, hit the garage-door opener and backed out onto the street.

She saw Teagarden in the rental he'd described, but they didn't make eye contact as she sailed past him down the hill. When she turned onto Sunset Boulevard, she wondered if he'd spotted the boxy black Volvo that had been parked at the corner. Watching in her rearview mirror, she saw the driver let a couple of cars get ahead of him, then pull out and follow. As she drove toward the freeway, she toyed with him just a little, slowing down slightly, speeding up a tad, changing lanes, but never erratically enough for him to think he'd been made. No matter what she did, he always remained a couple of car lengths back.

"All right then," she muttered. "Showtime."

She picked up speed, racing for the Santa Monica Freeway. He stayed with her. On the freeway, he settled into the standard two-car-length tail. She drove like a bat out of hell, changing lanes like a pinball, daring him to be coy with her now. Just when she thought she had him figured, though, he signaled right and took the next off-ramp.

She wasn't lulled yet. Sure enough, a hundred yards up, two cars came up the on-ramp and merged behind her. One of the two started executing the same crazy zigzags she had, but when the teenager passed her, car vibrating to the beat of the rap music blaring from his stereo, she wrote him off. That left the Honda holding a steady two- or three-car tail on her. After another mile or so, it was clear this was her guy.

She moved over to the fast lane, forcing him to work to keep up. Then, as they approached Robertson, she saw a semitrailer come up on her right and got ready to make her move. At the last possible second, she veered across the front of the semi, earning a blare from its air horn. The Honda was wedged between the semi and the carpool lane as she dodged across two more lanes and dropped down the Robertson off-ramp.

At the bottom of the ramp, she pulled over as soon as she could and rummaged around under the seats for the half-empty soda bottle she'd been hearing roll around under there for the past couple of days. Her hand wrapped around it and she pulled out one of

Gabe's half-drunk Dr Peppers. This was one of those times when it paid not to be too fastidious about cleaning her car.

Air escaped with a hiss when she opened the bottle. She took the GPS bug out of her pocket, dropped it in the soda, then closed the cap again and gave it a good shake. Talk about effective electronic countermeasures—nothing beat water and good old acidic soda pop. Spotting a trash can up ahead, she pulled up and lobbed the bottle in.

"Score!"

She drove away smiling.


Ruben packed clothes for the three of them to last a few days, plus Chucky's bowls and a supply of dog food. Taking the phone from the earthquake kit, he loaded everything up into the Mustang. It was a tight fit.

But the moment Mellie awoke, he knew they were in trouble. She screamed, tugging at her ear. She was prone to devastating ear infections and the pediatrician had warned them to be careful, lest she acquire hearing loss on top of her other problems. He put in a call to the urgent-care center covered by Travis's insurance, bundled her into the car and headed out. Terrorists and criminals would just have to wait.

Afraid he might be followed, he took surface streets, following a circuitous route.

"But let's face it, sweetie," he said, looking at

Mellie's unhappy face in his rearview mirror, "we wouldn't know a tail if it came with a matching pair of bunny ears, would we?"

He couldn't help but wonder what the social worker assessing their adoption application would think about all this. Well, what she didn't know wouldn't hurt them.

Hannah arrived at the rendezvous point with Teagarden before he did. The UCLA sculpture garden was both open enough for them to be able to talk without fear of eavesdropping, yet contained enough to spot watchers.

While she waited for him to show up, she dialed Travis's cell number.

"What the hell is going on?" he demanded as soon as she identified herself.

So she guessed he'd heard from Ruben.

"Ruben said we can't go home, we can't go to the cabin, and Mellie's got another ear infection, the third since Christmas."

"Are you at work?" she asked.

"Hell, no. I'm on my way to meet Rube and Mellie at the clinic."

"I'm sorry about her ear infection."

"Hannah, what is going on?"

She gave him an abbreviated version of events—which still didn't come out sounding very optimistic. "Is there anything you can tell me, Travis?"

He sighed. "Not really. There's been some increased

chatter lately, but the few specifics I do know, I can't share. They wouldn't help you anyway. Suffice it to say that things seem to be heating up."

Reading between the lines, she could only guess that Homeland Security had picked up intelligence about a possible domestic terrorist attack. "Is it possible that's why Gladding is so anxious to get that painting?"

But did that even make sense? Whatever other sins he might be guilty of, Hannah thought, Gladding was an American citizen. Why would he target his own country? Or was that even what Travis was talking about?

"I can't say. Truthfully," he told her. "Stuff heats up like this and then sometimes it just dissipates again. A false alarm. That's all I can tell you."

"Fair enough. But in the meantime, Travis, this threat I got from Gladding—it's not a false alarm. I am so sorry to have brought this down on you. Just lie low, okay, and I'll let you know as soon as the coast is clear. It shouldn't take more than a day or two, one way or the other."

And her own demise, Hannah thought as they signed off, would be one sure sign that the guys were safe to go home again.

Kyle Liggett ate yet another meal in his car as he sat outside Gladding's Beverly Hills Hotel, waiting to call in again.

The previous afternoon, he'd called to tell the old man he was ready to head back from San Onofre, only to have the bastard tell him to stay put down there for the night. Keep an eye on things, make absolutely certain no new security measures were being slipped into place under cover of darkness.

What a crock.

Instead, he'd spent the day tailing the old fart around Beverly Hills after he left Musso & Frank Grill, stopping in at a couple of Rodeo Drive boutiques. Shopping, for God's sake!

Liggett swallowed the last of his Coke, then dialed the number Gladding had given him.

"Where are you?"

"Near your hotel. Just got back to town."

"Where did you spend the night?"

"Camping on the beach at San Onofre, just like you said. Nothing much going on there. Same ol', same ol'."

"I told you to call before you started for L.A."

"Had some trouble with my phone."

"Well, get another one on your way over to Silver Lake."

"What's in Silver Lake?"

"The condo where the courier lives. She has some friends living next door, a gay couple. They have a child, handicapped, it seems."

Liggett narrowed his eyes. Fags? With kids? Please…

"I want you to get inside, secure them there. Then call me."

"Why don't I just take down the broad instead?"

Gladding sighed. "Because she, unfortunately, is in the wind at the moment. Until we have a fix on her, we have to make do with the next best thing, which at the moment is her friends."

"Fine."

"And Kyle? Don't be creative, all right? Don't use any more force than the minimum required to get the job done, and don't interfere with the care of the child. Do you hear me?"

Oh, he heard all right. He just didn't like it. Not one bit.

Hannah was beginning to seriously worry that Teagarden had gotten lost or worse when he finally showed up, toting a laptop shoulder bag. They found a corner table where they had a good three-sixty view of the area and Teagarden pulled out his machine and booted it up.

"Sorry to be so slow," he said. "I've been on the phone to Towle. He's been doing some digging on that fellow you said Ackerman mentioned. The one with the nasty torture fetish? He thinks they've got a line on him and he's trying to dig up a picture now to send over. He wants to know if it's the same man you spotted at the airport when you were leaving Puerto Vallarta."

"Who is he?"

"Young fellow by the name of Liggett. Kyle Liggett. Apparently Gladding talent-spotted him in Iraq where Liggett was working for a security contractor."

"Whoops. I think I resemble that remark."

Teagarden looked at her, bemused. "So I gather. My, my, but you are a busy girl. In any case, I'm sure you wouldn't have been keeping company with the likes of this fellow. Seems Liggett did a very brief stint in the U.S. military before being unceremoniously shown the door. Loose cannon, apparently. One of Liggett's little quirks is that he likes to blow things up. Then he got himself hired on with one of those private security contractors. Also not a happy experience. Seemed to be more interested in mowing down civilians than winning hearts and minds."

"A lot of that going around these days."

"Isn't that true, though? In any case, Gladding took him on as a bodyguard-cum-leg-breaker and, Bob's your uncle, Gladding's naughty driver and semiretired CIA handler go down for the count in Puerto Vallarta. Now, inquiring minds want to know if young Mr. Liggett did Gladding's dirty work there, since we know Gladding himself takes a 'clean hands' approach to these things. If so, I think our friends in Washington will be on the lookout for Liggett, too."

His laptop had come to life. Teagarden entered a password and signed onto an encrypted network.

Hannah was impressed. "A wireless modem?"

"Ah, yes, my dear. Not a complete Neanderthal, your Will Teagarden. All the mod-cons, don't you know?" He opened an e-mail that she saw came from *J_Towle@fbi.us.gov/lafo*, then clicked on the attachment. "Is this the man you saw at the Puerto Vallarta airport?"

"I only caught a glimpse," she said, studying the two

photos in the attachment. They showed the same whole-some-looking face, altogether unremarkable. He looked young in the first photo, dressed in an army uniform, the haircut high and tight. The second appeared to have been taken a few years on, not quite as young or as spit polished. He was not someone she would have looked at twice, had it not been for the fact that he was staring so intently at *her* when she saw him at the airport. That, and the shoulder-holster bulge under the jacket he wore over a white tee.

"That's him."

"All right, let me send a quick confirmation to Agent Towle. Then, I think we'd better get onto Captain Peña in Puerto Vallarta and see about picking up that painting if you're to have any hope at all of meeting Gladding's deadline tonight. Towle wants us to come over to the Federal Building. He's working with his contacts on ways to expedite things."

# *Twenty-Eight*

Travis Spielman arrived at the pediatrician's office just as Ruben was checking out.

"Same song, twentieth verse," Ruben said wearily. "Doc prescribed an antibiotic." He handed Travis the scrip. "Do you mind going downstairs to the pharmacy while we check out here?"

"No problem," Travis said. He rushed down the stairs, relieved to be doing something useful. Relieved, too, that at least they'd caught this now, before inflicting a sleepless night with a crying child on the friends in Studio City who were taking them in.

He was pacing by the pharmacist's counter when Ruben and Mellie arrived. "We have another problem," Ruben said. The look on his face said he dreaded delivering more bad news. "I left in such a hurry I forgot Saggy-Bag."

"Damn." Mellie loved the loose-skinned stuffed

elephant named after an ancient storybook that Travis had had since *he* was a toddler. Without her Saggy-Bag, she wouldn't sleep. "We can't go back," Travis said.

"We have to."

"Maybe the meds will make her sleepy."

"It's an antibiotic, not a sedative."

Travis was working up to an argument when the pharmacist called Melanie's name. He paid for the meds and met Ruben and Mellie by the door.

"I have a plan," Ruben said.

"Like pretending to be Monica and offering Hannah a kitten?"

"Okay, so that wasn't so great. Give it a rest already."

"What's your plan?"

"We go together. Leave the Mustang parked here. It's too full for a passenger anyway. We'll run by the condo, you stay in the Jeep with Mellie and Chucky and leave the motor running. I dash into the house—"

"I'll go inside."

Ruben snorted. "Sweetie, don't take this the wrong way, but I'm bigger and also in better shape."

He had a point. Together, they transferred their things and Chucky to the Jeep and got Mellie buckled into her car seat in back. Travis jumped behind the wheel. Ruben was just getting in the passenger side when he snapped his fingers.

"Oops! I forgot to lock the Mustang. Be right back." He slammed the door and dashed across the lot to his car.

Travis was trying to get Chucky to stop kissing Mellie when the Mustang roared out of the lot. As Travis cursed and turned the key in the Jeep's ignition, his phone rang.

"What the hell are you doing?" Travis bellowed. Mellie started to cry.

"I'm going alone. Do not follow me, Trav, I mean it. I'll meet you guys in Studio City."

"I'm coming."

"No. Look, it'll be fine. I love you and I love Mellie, but we can't risk taking her back to the house."

Travis could see the logic, but he didn't have to like it.

"Besides," Ruben added, "worst-case scenario, if anything were to happen, you're the breadwinner, cupcake. You have a better shot at getting Mellie the care she needs."

"Crap." Nobody could offer a child like Mellie—hell, any child—the care and attention she got from Ruben Hernandez.

"Hey, don't worry. I'll just run in and out," Ruben said. "Anyway, that Jeep of yours is such a rattletrap, me and my beautiful Mustang will be there hours ahead of you. Later, gator!"

There was a crowd milling around the sixteenth-floor boardroom of the FBI's Los Angeles field office. Several of the people there were wearing visitor badges clipped to their lapels, but it was a safe bet, Hannah thought, that she and Teagarden were the only civilians in the bunch. She couldn't begin to guess which agencies all of these people came from. From the sideways glances she and the Brit were getting, though, most of them had no idea what earthly reason might exist for the two of *them* to be included in what seemed to be some frenetic goings-on.

"Included," in fact, was a stretch. Agent Towle seemed to have convinced his superiors that there was a legitimate reason for them to be focusing on the recovery of the van Gogh, at the very least as a stalling tactic while they tried to work out what Gladding and Liggett might be up to. The quickest way to do that seemed to be to make use of Hannah, and of Teagarden's local contact in Puerto Vallarta—especially since the two of them didn't trust anyone else not to destroy the painting and possibly get Hannah killed in the bargain.

Hannah and Teagarden were in a small, bare office off to one side. "Make the call quick, before I change my mind," she told him.

It seemed to take an eternity for Teagarden to get an answer. "I'm sorry to disturb you at home on a Saturday, Captain Peña," he said at last. "Ah, working, too. Well, yes, of course. You've had a dreadful week. I have to ask you, though, for that favor you offered. But it's imperative that no one—and I mean no one—know what you're doing. I believe that Gladding has sources in your department."

He listened.

"I don't doubt you, but Gladding has a small fortune invested in this painting, and he'll pay well to get his hands on it now. And probably kill anyone who gets in his way. We believe it's going to be used to finance an imminent act of terrorism. The only way to prevent it might be to keep Gladding on tenterhooks as to the painting's whereabouts."

He listened again.

"No, my friend, I'm afraid it has to be today. Not only is there a severe time constraint, but if you try to travel via the usual means, word will leak out and both you and the painting may be lost.... Yes, that serious, I'm afraid."

With every objection the man at the other end seemed to make, Hannah felt time and her life slipping away.

But then, Teagarden sat up straighter. "Would your friend do it? Yes, yes. He can name his price—within reason."

Hannah smiled. A frugal man, William Teagarden.

"That would be excellent. Thank you, my friend. I'll be waiting to hear from you."

Teagarden disconnected and smiled at Hannah. "He has an acquaintance with a small plane. If he's able, he'll fly Peña to Tijuana. We can meet him at the border and bring the painting across."

"When will we know?"

"Soon, I hope."

Moises Gladding had cabin fever and a fever of the usual sort, as well. Used to well-orchestrated operations, everything about this one seemed sluggish. He wondered if his rage and declining health had conspired to cloud his judgment. Having to depend so heavily on

Liggett at this critical juncture was galling, especially since his instinct was to have left the little monster in the same car trunk in which Liggett had dispatched Donald Ackerman. But time was running out, and Gladding was determined to have his revenge on those who had humiliated him. Then, he would go home to his wife and live out whatever weeks or months were left to him.

He opened his pill dispenser and poured out the next dosage of the powerful meds keeping his symptoms at bay. As if she had sensed that something was wrong, his private phone rang, and his wife's voice was in his ear.

"What's the matter, Moises?"

"Nothing, Sylvia." How did she always know when he was troubled? It was uncanny.

"Nonsense," she said. "You sound dreadful. You said you were going to take some downtime when you were in Puerto Vallarta. I should have told my sister this wasn't a good time for a visit. If I'm not there to insist, you just will not relax, will you?"

Gladding massaged the knots in his neck. "You're right. But I'm coming home in a couple of days, and then I'll do nothing but put my feet up, read books, and enjoy your cooking." He hadn't told her about the last round of tests that showed a recurrence of the cancer, or about the abysmal prognosis.

"I'm going to insist," she said. "I'm going to hide your phones and that infernal computer. You're going to make yourself sick again. When are you getting back?"

"A couple of days. I'll call and let you know." A wave of intense nausea passed through him and he felt faint. "But I have to run now, dear. I'm right in the middle of something. I'll see you in a couple of days."

He disconnected. Poor Sylvia. She had accepted early on that his business would be a closed book to her, and that he would be gone for weeks and sometimes months at a time. She knew, too, the way women did, that he took companions when he was away. But he had never lied to her about anything really important. On most counts, he had been a good husband and father.

Now, he simply couldn't see what it served to have her worry about his health, especially since there was nothing to be done about it. She would only have wanted him to come home sooner, and that he couldn't do. Not until he had seen this last thing through. Then, he would go to her and she would know the truth. Sylvia would immediately perceive the change in him, even if it wasn't yet obvious to others.

He shuddered as another wave of pain passed through him. It had been getting worse with each passing day. Today, he'd been feeling especially low. If this logjam didn't break soon…

One of his infernal disposable phones rang—something else that needed his attention. But when he saw the number, his hopes began to rise at last. It was his contact in the Puerto Vallarta police.

"Captain Peña has been on the telephone a great deal today. His private cell phone, not the office line. He has been very secretive, too. He seems to be packing up his desk to leave, now, but he will not say where."

"Stick with him," Gladding said. "I want to know what he's up to."

Ruben was right about his sleek little Mustang. He made great time back to the condo. He circled the block a couple of times, looking for signs of trouble, but he had no idea what he was looking for. Their building seemed completely deserted.

He couldn't help wondering if this wasn't some great overreaction. It was so hard to believe they could really be in danger. Like something out of a novel.

On the other hand, much as he loved her, Hannah did have a knack for trouble. Sometimes, he had to shush the nagging voice in his head that whispered maybe her ex was right to have taken away their son. Ruben felt disloyal even to be thinking like that, but now that he had a child of his own, he knew he would do anything to keep her safe.

He pulled up in front of the garage, steeled himself and decided to make a run for it. In and out, easy peasy.

In the front entryway, however, he paused, listening. *Nothing.* Tiptoeing into the kitchen, he slid a razor-sharp boning blade out of the wooden knife rack. Holding it ahead of him, he crept up the stairs to Mellie's room and peeked inside. There was Saggy-Bag, right where they'd left him on the change table when he'd gotten Mellie up and dressed.

With the toy under one arm, Ruben looked around the pretty coral room for anything else he might have forgotten in his rush. He spotted his daughter's favorite blanket on the floor next to the crib. Folding the little pink afghan his mother had crocheted, he stuffed it, the elephant and a couple more toys into a carry-all from her closet. Then, breathing a sigh of relief, he padded down the stairs again.

His hand was on the front doorknob when he heard something, a soft snick from the kitchen. His imagination.

Had to be.

*Puerto Vallarta*

Tracking down a painting for that nice Señor Teagarden, Captain Peña had to admit, beat the paperwork he'd left on his desk. The politicians were screaming for his head and the newspapers clamoring for information on the murders—not to mention the chores his wife had waiting for him at home.

When Peña had called Teagarden back to say that his friend's plane would be available to fly him and the painting north this afternoon, Teagarden had put a woman on the phone to explain exactly where to find it. Peña knew the hotel she spoke of. Not an upscale place. Hiding Señor Gladding's picture there was either brilliant or very stupid. He would soon know which.

He had told Teagarden that it would cost one thousand dollars to have his friend drop everything and fly to Tijuana. It was spring planting season, after all, and the crop duster was very busy. Teagarden had been unfazed, however, so as soon as he left his office, Peña called his childhood friend to tell him the good news—he had negotiated a payment of five hundred dollars for the flight. The pilot had been thrilled.

Peña drove directly to the two-story hotel near the Malecón and went inside. Teagarden had told him to be very careful, but he was a captain of the police and not to be trifled with. He flashed his badge at the reception desk.

When he heard which room Peña wanted, the clerk shook his head. "Not available. Another, perhaps?"

Peña frowned and looked around the threadbare lobby. "I hear rumors that illegal drugs are being sold out of this hotel. Perhaps my people will have to close it down while we conduct a thorough search."

"The room is in use, *Capitán*," the clerk protested. "The poor woman must make a living."

"She will have to do it in a different room."

Head shaking, the clerk shuffled up the stairs. Peña stood aside in the hall while the man convinced the couple, not without some vague threats, to change love nests.

After they came out and scurried down the hall, Peña let himself into the room and shut the door. It was stuffy and a little rank-smelling. He threw open the window and took a deep breath, then dragged a rickety chair over to the closet and climbed up on it, balancing carefully so as not to step through the caning. He lifted aside one of the ceiling tiles.

Peña had seen everything and feared little, but he hated spiders. Bracing himself, he reached through the opening, patting lightly about in the dark with about as much enthusiasm as if he had exploring a pile of dog turds. *Nada.* He stretched further, with the same result.

Turning himself on the chair, he steadied himself as it wobbled, then extended his hand to explore the space on that side. Something sharp pricked his palm. He yanked back his hand, examining the palm in the dim light. Nothing he could see, but something had definitely bit him.

Was there a reward for the recovery of this wretched painting? If so, he certainly deserved to claim it.

He moved another tile aside and smacked his hand around, determined to kill whatever was up there before it bit him again. He moved as little as possible on the flimsy chair, trying to ignore visions of the chair collapsing beneath him. His probing fingers still found nothing. He was going to have to call Señor Teagarden back with the disappointing news that it had been a waste of time.

And then, his fingers connected with leather.

Not a tall man, Peña had to strain to grasp the edge of the case and inch it out from its hiding place. He did not bother to replace the tiles, but carried the tattered case gingerly to the stained and rumpled bed, where he unzipped it and peered inside. Pieces of a once-beautiful carving—a frame, it seemed—spilled out.

He withdrew a stretched canvas and stared at it in

amazement. It looked like something the cat had coughed up. This is what Teagarden was so desperate to find? What Gladding had been willing to kill for? Surely not.

On the other hand, he had found it where the woman said it would be, Peña thought. A deal is a deal. He would deliver this case and its contents as promised. He called his friend and told him to gas up the Cessna. Then, he called back William Teagarden, who sounded delighted.

"But be very careful, my friend. Now is not the time to let down your guard."

Outside, Peña slid the leather case across the front seat and climbed behind the wheel. He pulled a U-turn and headed for the main road. As he approached the corner, his eye caught a movement in the front of a familiar, battered old Ford Cortina. The driver ducked down, but not before Peña recognized Mario Sanchez—one of his own men. Peña himself had recruited and promoted him.

Peña let loose with a string of expletives. Teagarden had told him to expect a tail, that Gladding's deep pockets held men in his own department. But the last man he would have suspected as a traitor, Peña thought, was that little weasel Sanchez.

*Los Angeles*

"Why didn't you take it from him at the hotel?" Gladding demanded.

"Capitán Peña knows me, *señor.* I could not let him see me."

Pain roiled Gladding's body. This was what happened when you sent a fool to do a man's job. A year ago, it would never have happened. His strength was slipping, and his judgment along with it.

"Do you still have him in sight?" he demanded.

"*Sí.* I am behind him," Sanchez said. "What should I do?"

"Stay on him and do not, I repeat *not,* lose him. I'm going to send someone else after you. Keep your phone line open. He'll be calling to find out where Peña is."

"I think I know where he's going, *señor.*"

"Where?"

"A private airfield, about ten kilometers out of town. Capitán Peña has an old friend who flies a Cessna airplane from this field."

"How do you know?"

"He is my brother-in-law."

"Your brother-in-law? The man with the Cessna?"

"No, *señor.* Capitán Peña."

# *Twenty-Nine*

Once she had finished telling Captain Peña where to find the painting, Hannah felt like some useless drone in this busy little federal hive. They all had their well-groomed heads together, working out the logistics of collecting the painting, arranging for her to deliver it to Gladding by his deadline—making sure he didn't *actually* get his grubby hands on a masterpiece—and set the net and haul the man in before whatever he had planned could be carried out.

Since her going back to her condo seemed to be a nonstarter, she was left twiddling her thumbs in the dreary little side office in which Towle had parked her. Even Teagarden seemed to have been temporarily initiated into their fraternity—or had stormed the gates, maybe, since his primary concern in all this was the safe recovery of Yale's van Gogh.

She tried calling Ruben and Travis, but her calls kept

going to voice mail. Chances were they were still tied up at the doctor's office with Mellie. She hoped they weren't avoiding her calls—although who could blame them if they were? She asked them to call and let her know they were okay.

Somebody dropped by with a copy of the newspaper she hadn't finished that morning. She read that, drank some really bad coffee, leafed through a copy of *The Congressional Record* and memorized every gray hair and wrinkle on the presidential portrait on the wall. Finally, it occurred to her that there might be a way to check on Ruben and, as a bonus, hear a friendly voice— at least, she hoped it would still be friendly.

"Hey there, stranger," she said when Russo picked up his cell.

"Hi. I was just looking for you. Where are you?"

"Wilshire Boulevard, the Federal Building." She told him about the flurry of activity going on around her.

"Son of a bitch," he said. "What happened to interagency cooperation? Last I checked, we were supposed to have a joint task force between them, us and the LAPD. Suddenly the feds are nowhere to be found and we and the LAPD guys are wondering who moved the party. I'm only surprised it took them twenty-four hours to elbow us out. But hey, at least they're letting *you* play."

"Not hardly. All they've needed me for was to say where I hid the painting. Now they're just keeping me on ice until they can decide what to do about Gladding. I think I'm going to be the minnow on the hook when they're ready to reel him in. Is there anything new on Rebecca's murder?"

"Lindsay's just heading back from the crime lab now. We found some surfers who said they saw a car parked next to her red BMW on Monday night. Saw the driver toss a Coke can in the bushes. We recovered it and the lab is trying to pull prints and DNA."

"That'd be a break. Listen, I know you're probably swamped, but I wondered if you might be able to do me a favor."

"What's that?"

"Any chance you could swing by my place, check on my neighbors?"

"I just did, actually—drop by your place, I mean. Quiet as a tomb over there."

"That's because my neighbors had to go into hiding, thanks to me." She told him about the threats Gladding had made. "I left ahead of Ruben this morning, but I'd like to know he and the baby are okay."

"I'm just pulling into the office to meet Lindsay," Russo said. "We have some other calls to make. We'll swing back over to your place while we're out."

"There's an extra key to the guys' place hidden outside. Do you think you could go in, take a look around?"

"Sure. Where's the key?"

"Under the ficus pot on the patio."

"Under a flower pot? Are you kidding?"

"Ruben's a big guy. He worries less about intruders than he does about getting locked out with the baby."

"Good grief. Okay, we'll check it out." Russo chuckled. "You know, annoying as I find it that the Bureau has taken the ball and gone home, I know someone who's going to be really ticked off with her big brother. You're getting payback, kid."

"I don't need payback. She's okay. If things had gone differently, that might have been me. Anyway, I don't do catfights."

"That's my girl."

She hung up, smiling.

*Puerto Vallarta*

Unless he was mistaken, Peña thought, he was now being followed by two cars. Between him and Sanchez, his useless brother-in-law, was a white Corolla carrying three men. His wife's idiot brother he could handle, but who were these other men following him to the airfield?

Teagarden had warned him to be careful. Now, he began to regret that he had not brought backup. Of course, if a member of his own family could be bought, who could be trusted?

He pulled out his cell phone and tried not to swerve as he punched in the pilot's number. "Get the plane on the runway and keep the engine running. I'm almost there, but I'm being followed."

"What in the name of Jesus, Mary and Joseph are you getting me into?"

"I'll explain later. Just be ready to take off the second I'm on board."

"These people following you, they have guns?"

"Probably."

The pilot hesitated, and Peña feared his old friend might back out. Instead, he chuckled. "I haven't had a good fight in years. I am not without weapons myself, you know."

"You're armed?"

"Do you know how often I run into bandits and drug runners, my friend?"

"Tell me when we're airborne."

Peña almost took the last turn toward the airfield on two wheels, throwing up a spray of loose gravel. Sweat was running into his eyes, but he needed both hands to steer. He shot through a grove of trees and onto the taxiway. The Cessna was already revving its engines at the end of the runway. Peña was tempted to take a shortcut across the open field, but last night, an unexpected downpour had soaked the area. Good for the parched landscape, but bad luck for him. If he got bogged down, he'd have to run through mud with the bulky painting.

Instead, he roared to the end of the taxiway and careened into the unbanked curve, praying the car wouldn't flip. Behind him, the Corolla fishtailed wildly, then recovered. In his rearview mirror, Peña saw Sanchez's Cortina miss the curve and bog down in the mud.

"Good," he muttered. "Bastard!"

His back window shattered and he felt a buzz of air next to his ear. He zigzagged to the Cessna, hearing the rattle of metal on metal as bullets peppered the car. Slamming on the brakes, he grabbed the painting and jumped from the car, keeping low as he dashed toward the plane.

Suddenly, a loud boom sounded over his head. He glanced up to see his friend take aim for a second shot with a high-powered rifle. He fired again as Peña scrambled aboard. The plane was already taxiing down the runway as he pulled the door shut and rammed home the locking bar. By the time he dropped into his seat and buckled up, the plane was lifting off, the pop of gunfire behind them fading fast.

As the Cessna rose and circled, Peña waved to his grimacing brother-in-law, who stood ankle-deep in mud, a cell phone to his ear.

*Los Angeles*

Gladding ignored the call from the idiot policeman and took the one instead from the backup team in the Corolla that he'd been forced to gather at the last minute.

"The Cessna is gone," the team leader said. "The pilot filed a flight plan for Tijuana."

"You're sure?" Gladding said.

"Yes."

"All right. Stand down, then. No, wait," Gladding added. "One more thing."

"What?"

"Take care of that moron Sanchez. Then clean up and go to ground. Your payment will be wired within the hour."

Gladding hung up and drummed his fingers on the chair, ignoring the pain that racked his body. The game wasn't lost yet. The painting was heading for the border, which meant the courier had put wheels in motion, allowing it to be recovered from her hiding spot. This Nicks woman was obviously not without resources. He didn't fool himself that the government wasn't working in the background on the recovery effort, but with the right incentive, she could still be persuaded to pull an end run and get his painting to him. And convincing others to do his bidding was where he excelled.

The more Gladding thought about it, in fact, the more he realized that this might all work out. It was important for him to have the painting to hand over in trade to the Libyan. But after the bomb maker's double cross with the hit on his villa, Gladding had no intention of keeping his end of the bargain. He would take the bomb, kill the Libyan and keep the painting. He would arrange for it to be shipped back to Geneva and locked away— a posthumous bequest, perhaps, to his grandchildren, to be delivered a few decades from now. He would explore the legal ramifications and decide later. In the meantime, the Swiss could always be relied upon to keep secrets.

There remained only the matter of exploding the bomb, and Liggett, for his own twisted reasons, wanted this demonstration as much as he did.

Whether or not the dirty bomb did much actual damage to the San Onofre generating station was almost beside the point. The radioactive debris it contained would set off a wave of panic and hysteria that no amount of government reassurances would be able to counter. It would start a cascade of economic damage, from the cost of the cleanup effort, the inevitable population flight from Southern California, and a renewed opposition to nuclear power, which the public was only now, thirty years after Three Mile Island, beginning to accept as a possible solution to foreign oil. The demoralizing effect of this terrorist act would also be significant when it was learned it had come not from foreign enemies but from a homegrown one.

From such sparks are mighty conflagrations lit, Gladding thought. America was at a tipping point, and economic depressions had been triggered by less. The last superpower of the twentieth century was about to enter the spiral of its inevitable decline. The age of American domination was over, and the arrogance of the once powerful would be shattered with the realization of their own pathetic impotence.

And then, Gladding thought, he would die satisfied.

Russo's news could hardly have been worse.

"Blood?" Hannah gasped, when he told her what he'd found inside Ruben and Travis's condo.

"A fair amount," Russo said, "mostly in the kitchen, which was trashed. There's a bloody knife on the floor. We've sealed off the scene and we're just waiting for the LAPD."

"Are you sure the guys aren't in there?"

"We searched the whole house and the garage. No cars. What do they drive?"

Hannah described Ruben's Mustang and Travis's Jeep.

"We'll pull the DMV info and get an APB out right away."

Hannah nodded. There was a commotion outside the door of the room she was in, and she looked up to see Towle and Teagarden coming in. "Let me know as soon as you hear anything?" she asked Russo.

"You bet."

She hung up and told the others what he'd found back at her condo.

"I'm sorry, Hannah," Teagarden said. "But the fact that Detective Russo didn't find your friends is reason to hope."

She didn't feel very hopeful.

"In the meantime," Towle said, "we've come up with a plan of action. We need to take a drive."

"You want me to go?" Hannah said.

Teagarden smiled and held out an arm. "You, my dear, are the most important member of this little excursion."

The destination, it turned out, was August Koon's studio. There was no one around when they pulled up his driveway, but yellow tape was still strung around the scene and the LAPD *Crime scene—Do not enter* seal was on the door.

Agent Towle held up the tape for the others to pass under, then ripped the seal off the door and pushed his way in.

"Did you get clearance to do this?" she asked him.

He shrugged. "It's always easier to ask for forgiveness than permission. We'll make sure your name doesn't come into it, I promise."

"Gee, thanks."

The pool of blood where they'd found Koon had soaked into the wood floors and dried brown, and almost every surface in the place was coated with gray fingerprint powder. The paintings Hannah remembered as having been blood-spattered had been taken in evidence, as had the murder weapon, the curved blade on which she'd stupidly left her fingerprints.

"So, what are we looking for?" she asked.

Teagarden circled the room, measuring canvases with a tape measure he pulled from his pocket. After a while, he put the tape measure away and started lining paintings up along the workbench. He had about a half dozen when he waved her over.

"Take a look at these," he said. "They're the same size canvas as the van Gogh. Do any of these resemble the painting you carried to Puerto Vallarta?"

Hannah crouched down and studied them, one by one. She'd stared for hours at the one she and Rebecca had picked up on Monday, trying to see what was worth a quarter of a million dollars. She would have thought it was permanently imprinted on her brain, but as she looked at this bunch, they seemed to run together.

"Everything he does looks alike to me," she said, "but I think a couple of these might be close."

"You'll have to do better than think, lass," Teagarden said. "Your life might depend on it."

She looked at him, then at the federal agents, and their brilliant plan suddenly dawned on her. "You want me to deliver a fake to Gladding."

"A fake camouflaged van Gogh, maybe," Towle said, "but a genuine August Koon."

"We're going to give Mr. Gladding a taste of his own medicine," Teagarden added.

"Oh, joy. And I get to hold the spoon."

She turned back and studied the canvases more closely. As Teagarden said, her life could depend on it. She pulled four out of the line, compared them, eliminated two, then tried to decide between the other two.

"So I go in with the Koon," she said. "What's to keep Gladding from killing me?"

"Luck," Towle said. "And plenty of discreet backup, of course."

She grimaced. "Easy for you to say. Okay, fine. This one, I think."

It had too much blue in it, but if they were right and Koon's painting was just a disguise for a van Gogh, then Gladding had probably never even laid eyes on the overpainting job he'd blackmailed Koon into doing. He wouldn't care what it looked like, as long as he believed the van Gogh was beneath. She could throw paint on canvas herself and he'd probably be none the wiser. She handed it to Teagarden and he zipped it into a case.

"Of course, you realize that if we're wrong about this and Moises Gladding just had to have that one particular painting I was supposed to deliver, then I'm dead meat?"

Towle glanced around the studio and snorted. "Oh, hell, girl. Nobody could *want* to own this crap."

# *Thirty*

*Airborne, 18,000 feet*
*Sixty miles south of Tijuana*

After leaving Sanchez and the other three men in the mud at the Puerto Vallarta airstrip, Captain Peña and his old friend had settled in for an uneventful flight to the main airport at Tijuana to rendezvous with his new friend, William Teagarden. Peña was looking forward to introducing the two fine men. Perhaps a drink, exchanging some adventure stories.

But then, the Cessna began to buck, and Peña and the pilot shared a nervous glance. Suddenly, out the pilot-side window, an astonishing sight appeared. Peña nudged his friend and pointed. The pilot leapt, startled, at the sight of a fighter jet off his starboard side, dipping its wing in salute. The plane was gunmetal gray, the wings painted with the star-on-a-striped-flag insignia of the USAF.

Through their headsets, the two men heard the Cessna's call letters. "Good afternoon, gentlemen. The United States Air Force is here to provide you with an escort." They could see the fighter pilot's face almost as clearly as they saw one another's. He directed their attention to the Cessna's port-side wing, where a second fighter had appeared.

"F-16s," Peña's friend breathed.

"You are to proceed north-northwest," the fighter pilot added. Although English was the language of international aviation, he repeated the instructions in unaccented Spanish to be sure they were understood.

"Sir, this is Mexican airspace," the Cessna pilot radioed back.

"For the love of the Blessed Virgin," Peña hissed at him, "don't argue!"

"Your government has cleared our mission," the fighter pilot replied. "You will set down on an airstrip just south of Tijuana. The delay there will be brief. Then, you'll resume your current heading and flight plan."

His friend's panic-stricken face turned to Peña. "What shall I do? What shall I do?"

"Are you crazy? Do you see the bombs under their wings? Do what you're told!"

The Cessna pilot nodded. "Roger," he radioed.

The F-16s dropped back and rose up a few thousand feet, holding position there. The turbulence settled.

Peña's friend nodded at the leather portfolio. "What are you carrying?"

"An ugly painting, nothing more."

"Are you sure?"

"I examined it myself."

Five minutes later, the F-16s directed their attention to a well maintained oceanside landing strip. The Cessna pilot banked his craft, putting the small plane on the ground a few minutes later, where it rolled to the end of the strip and pulled off onto a taxiway. When they looked skyward, the F-16s were circling overhead, silver eagles soaring on the updraft.

The men on the ground waited. As the seconds ticked by, the pilot slid his rifle out of the scabbard in the door. "Just in case," he said.

Peña felt sure Teagarden would not have betrayed him, but he unbuckled his holster and rested his hand on the butt of his revolver just in case.

And then, they heard a low hum, soft at first, then louder. As they craned to see, a helicopter appeared out of the northern sky. The air force jets backed off, and the chopper set down a short way from the Cessna. Two men emerged, a young Asian-looking man and one with blond hair, both clean-cut and wearing suits.

As they approached, they withdrew leather folders and held them up to let the Mexicans to see their shields and identity cards. The younger man was also carrying a leather portfolio not unlike the one Peña had recovered from the ceiling of the hotel on the Malecón, except this one was intact.

"FBI agents?" Peña said, surprised.

"Are you sure this is a good idea?"

Peña opened his door. "Only one way to find out."

He stepped out and approached the men, who tucked their credentials away. "Captain Peña," the older of the two said, "William Teagarden, formerly of Scotland Yard, sends his regards. My name is Special Agent Joseph Towle, and this is Special Agent Ito."

"Where is Señor Teagarden?" Peña asked.

"You'll see him when you land in Tijuana."

"How do I know this is the truth?"

"Well, Teagarden said you play a mean Frank Sinatra. Apparently you know all the words to all the verses of 'My Way.'"

Peña smiled and shrugged modestly. "I am very fond of the music of Ol' Blue Eyes. So, what can I do for you gentlemen?"

"We need your help with a small ruse. You're familiar with a Moises Gladding, I think?"

Peña nodded.

"He's very anxious to have what you collected in Puerto Vallarta. We'd like to exchange your painting for a different piece. When you meet Teagarden and the lady with him, they'll know the paintings have been switched but they won't let on in case Gladding's agents are watching."

"Gladding has eyes everywhere," Peña muttered. "Yes, fine. If Teagarden wishes this, I am happy to comply. I will get the case."

He brought out the battered portfolio and made to

hand it over, but Ito opened his. "Actually, we think it's better if you hold on to that case and deliver our picture in it. It's a long story, but it will add to the ruse's credibility."

They pulled out their paintings and compared them side to side. "They look the same," Peña said.

"This one has more blue," Ito said, "but otherwise, they're pretty close."

"And both very ugly," Peña said. He zipped the new painting into the battered case.

Then, the FBI men stood aside as the Cessna resumed its scheduled course.

Hannah and Teagarden were waiting in the arrivals lounge at Tijuana's main airport. They'd flown down on a private Learjet owned by a government proprietary company that was fronted by a Marina del Rey man famous for the chain of seafood restaurants he owned up and down the California coast. Although he had served in the air force during the first Gulf War, nothing about the man's legend hinted that he was anything other than the silver-spoon playboy his friends, neighbors and business associates all believed him to be.

Hannah's eye kept scanning the lounge, but if Gladding had a watcher there, she couldn't spot him. Not surprising. The man's network was a little scary.

"The thing that niggles at the back of my mind," Teagarden said quietly, "is that the Koon you'll hand over isn't framed. He may know the other one was."

"Well, there was no time to frame the stupid thing. Anyway, I don't have any problem explaining what happened to the frame and why. He knows I was spooked by the mess at his villa. He'll buy it."

"I hope so."

Her hip vibrated with the buzz of her cell phone. She glanced at the screen—a text message from Russo. Your friends ok. Call them when you can. Me, too. She nudged Teagarden and showed him the screen.

"That's very good news. You should call once we're airborne again." He pulled himself to his feet. "Showtime." He stepped forward, smiling broadly. "Captain Peña! Good to see you again!"

"And you, my friend!" As they shook hands, Peña eyed Hannah curiously. Teagarden introduced them. "I think you have recently been in Puerto Vallarta, have you not?" Peña asked her.

"I've been a couple of times."

"Yet I would wager you had more adventures on your last visit than any previous time."

Teagarden touched his arm. "My friend, no one knows better than I the kind of terrible week it's been in your town."

"More than you know."

"I know about the other cases, too," Teagarden said quietly. "I give you my word, Captain, Ms. Nicks is not your suspect. When this is over, I promise that you will know everything I know. In the meantime, the person responsible for those deaths is about to be brought to justice as the direct result of the help you're giving us here today."

"You swear this, Señor Teagarden?"

"On my honor."

"It is good enough for me, then. I look forward to our next meeting." He handed over the battered portfolio.

Hannah unzipped it, glanced inside and saw the too-blue canvas she'd selected at Koon's studio a few hours earlier. With a look of dismay, Teagarden picked out a couple of pieces of the frame she'd destroyed and turned them over in his hand.

"Museum quality," he said with a sigh.

She winced. "Sorry."

"Are you sure you wouldn't prefer the limo again, Mr. Dunning?" the concierge asked.

"Not this evening," Gladding said. "I'm in the mood to drive. Something not too small, with all this traffic. An SUV, I think."

"I can get you a Toyota Highlander."

"That'll do nicely."

"Very good, sir. We'll have it waiting downstairs whenever you're ready."

Perfect, Gladding thought. Los Angeles was a car-loving city, and nothing was more anonymous here than a Toyota or an SUV. Plenty of cargo space for everything they would have to carry, including the painting and the dirty bomb. By the end of the night, he would have possession of both. When dawn broke on Liggett's and the Libyan bomb maker's bodies tomorrow, identifying them would be the least of the region's worries. Southern Californians would be too busy trying to get out of the way of the lethal radiation carried on the wind. Eventually, of course, the pieces of the puzzle would start to come together, but Gladding himself would be long gone, sitting halfway around the world, enjoying the chaos and fear he had unleashed.

Hannah spoke to her neighbor as the Learjet flew from Tijuana back to Los Angeles. She caught Travis as he was leaving Glendale Memorial Hospital to take Mellie back to their friends' house in Studio City. "Are you sure Ruben's all right?" she asked after he recounted how his partner had tried to sneak back home to collect the toddler's favorite stuffed elephant.

"He was almost out the door when he heard a noise in the kitchen. The minute he went in, this guy jumped him. I don't know who was more surprised, Ruben or the other guy. I really don't think he expected a gay man to put up the kind of fight he got."

"Detective Russo said the kitchen was trashed."

"Yeah, it was quite the battle royal, from the sounds of it."

"Poor Ruben! He could have been killed."

"He went in there with a knife. In fact, he feels a little sheepish about it, but that's actually how he got hurt. Our spice rack went down in the mayhem, and he thinks he tripped on the oregano or something. He landed on the knife. He lost quite a bit of blood—barely made it to the gas station up the street before he passed out. They're keeping him in the hospital overnight for observation, but he should be fine."

"What about the other guy?" Hannah asked.

"Oh, well, Rube's feeling pretty pumped about that. Scary dude, he said, but he managed to clock the guy with our wooden knife rack. Thought he might have killed him, but when he saw him move, he beat it out of there. That's when he tripped and fell on the knife."

"Russo said the intruder was long gone by the time he got there."

"Yeah, but he told me they've got an idea who it was. Hopefully they'll find the bastard."

Dollars to doughnuts it was Kyle Liggett, Hannah thought. "I'm just glad Ruben's okay. You give him a big smooch for me, okay. And one for you and Mellie, too. And Trav? I'm so sorry."

"Not your fault. You just take care of yourself."

Shadows were long by the time they got back to the FBI field office. Somebody sent out for food and most of the team ate when it arrived. There was no telling when the next communication from Gladding would come in, giving Hannah details for the drop. When it did, everyone would be in scramble mode to get surveillance and backup laid in. Cases like this, people ate when they could, not when they were hungry.

But the sun went down, the supper hour stretched

into evening, and the evening began to get late. Hannah was beginning to wonder if Gladding had decided things were too hot to try for a handover. How could he possibly think he would walk away from this?

And then, a little after ten, her cell phone rang. They'd hooked up a recording device to the cell, so while Hannah talked to him, Towle and others listened in on headsets.

"I understand you have my painting."

"Hello, Mr. Gladding."

"The man from Marina del Rey whose Lear you took to Tijuana—a friend of yours?"

"We have mutual friends."

"How fortunate for you. And the tall older man who went with you?"

"A private investigator. I thought I could use some help on this. So, now that I've got the painting back, where would you like it delivered?"

He described an all-night diner in San Juan Capistrano. "One-thirty a.m. Come alone." As usual, he didn't repeat himself, and he didn't wait for confirmation.

"It can't be this easy," Agent Ito said afterward. "He's gotta know we'll have it covered."

"I don't think it would be advisable to underestimate Gladding," Teagarden said. Although Towle had hinted that the Brit's part was over now that the painting had been recovered, Teagarden had no intention of leaving the piece unattended or—apparently—of standing back while Hannah walked into the lion's den on her own.

"He told me to come alone," she pointed out.

Towle agreed. "It's not going to happen at the diner. I think it's a safe bet that once she's there, she'll get additional instructions."

"All the more reason why I should stick with her," Teagarden said. "I can conceal myself in the back of her car."

They all looked at him skeptically. The idea of the older gent folding his six-foot-four frame into the back seat of her puddle jumper hardly bore thinking about.

"You're welcome to ride down there with me," Towle said. "In any event, we've already put a tracking device under the dash of your Prius."

What was it with people bugging her car today? Hannah wondered.

# *Thirty-One*

*San Juan Capistrano*
*Sunday, April 23*

When the witching hour arrived, she found a parking spot easily enough near the old Spanish mission in San Juan Capistrano. At this hour, about the only people around besides the night owls in the diner up the road were homeless people and the drunks beginning to spill out of the Swallows Inn.

The battered portfolio bumped awkwardly against her leg as she crossed the road toward the diner. Looking through its plate-glass window, she did a double take when she recognized one of the prepositioned watchers inside—none other than L.A. Sheriff's Detective Lindsay Towle. So had Russo convinced the feds to play nice again? Or was it true what they said, that hell hath no fury like a kid sister scorned?

The tiny two-way radio she wore was well hidden by her hair, she knew, but it still felt conspicuous and awkward.

"You reading me?" Agent Towle's voice murmured in her earpiece.

"Yeah," she said, lips hardly moving. The mike embedded in the radio unit was so sensitive that Towle could probably hear her heartbeat.

Just as she arrived at the threshold of the all-night diner, a rambunctious group of giggling girls spilled out the door. Hannah held the door as they flounced past, oblivious. "You're welcome, I'm sure," she said.

Her cell rang the second she stepped inside. A voice— not Gladding's—instructed, "Fourth booth on the right."

Liggett? she wondered.

About half a dozen tables were occupied by people who looked like students or night owls, plus at least one sleepy homeless guy nursing the world's slowest cup of coffee. Aside from Lindsay, Hannah recognized a couple of other faces, but she had no idea how many might be cops or FBI agents—and how many might be working for Moises Gladding.

She pushed the leather portfolio across the bench of the fourth booth. Sliding in after it, she spotted a manila folder tucked behind the condiments, her name scrawled on the outside.

"Coffee?" the waitress called from behind the counter.

"Not sure. Let me check the menu. By the way," Hannah added, "who sat here last?"

The waitress grimaced at the door. "The ditzes who just left. Why?"

Hannah shrugged, picked up the sugar dispenser and feigned tightening its top. "I just noticed that the lid's loose."

"Great. Comedians."

In her ear Hannah heard Towle's voice. "Okay, thanks for the heads-up. We'll haul them in, see what they know."

She opened the envelope so Lindsay and the other watchers would see that she'd received further instructions. When she tipped it, a throwaway cell phone and a note spilled out. Blood drained from her face as she read the note.

*You did not come alone. If you so much as move your lips, your mother, your sister Nora and the entire Quinn family will die—including Nolan up at Stanford. Then we will move on to your son, Gabriel. Not today, not tomorrow, but soon.*

After what had happened at Travis and Ruben's place, Agent Towle had put watchers on her entire family, including Gabe, plus the house in Studio City where her neighbors were staying until it was safe to go home. It didn't matter worth a damn, Hannah realized. Gladding could circle back at any time and take them out at his leisure.

*Leave your own cell phone in the envelope, along
with the wire I'm sure you're wearing. Order coffee and leave payment on the table. Be ready to
walk out with the painting as soon as you get the
signal. It will be unmistakable. Head south on the
5 Freeway. There is no doubt a tracking device on
your car. If you want your family to survive, you
will get rid of it.*

"What does it say?" Towle murmured in her ear.

She picked up the menu, glanced at it briefly, then
called to the waitress. "You know, I can't say what I
want. Just a coffee, I guess."

"Okay, can't talk, right?" Towle said.

The waitress brought over a coffee and set it down.
Hannah blew across the top and took a sip. "Uh-huh,"
she hummed softly.

Fishing her cell phone out of her bag, she dropped
it and the note in the envelope. Removing the earpiece,
she added that, then reclosed the envelope and laid it on
the bench. After that, she put a couple of dollars on the
table to cover the coffee.

Then she waited.

William Teagarden and Agent Towle were in a black
Ford Explorer up the road, both men watching Hannah
through high-powered binoculars. Towle cursed when
they saw her take the receiver out of her ear.

"Something is afoot," Teagarden said.

"Ya think?" Towle growled, switching the radio over

to the frequency his watchers were on. "Keep an eye on that envelope. If she leaves it behind, see if anyone retrieves it. Otherwise, grab the damn thing. I want to know what it says."

The Bureau Explorer was parked deep in shadow on a side street where they could observe without being easily observed themselves. Towle scanned the area, looking for Gladding or Liggett. He flicked the radio talk button again. "Lindsay, you there?"

His sister radioed back an affirmative.

Towle pressed the talk button again. "See if—"

The blinding flash was the first sign of trouble. They heard the explosion, felt its concussive force a split second later. If the watchers had been undercover until then, the jig was up now. Half a dozen night owls in the diner and drunks by the Swallows Inn cried with pain, yanking out earpieces. Across the road, a car in flames rolled and careened through the window of a souvenir shop.

Towle grabbed the shotgun racked behind him and leapt out of the SUV. "Stay here!" he shouted at Teagarden.

The souvenir store was burning now and two other cars had also caught fire. As Towle approached, the gas tank on one exploded, liquid flame spewing in every direction.

Teagarden, meantime, saw Hannah fly out the door of the diner, racing for her car. Agent Towle had left the keys in the SUV's ignition. By the time Teagarden had scrambled behind the wheel, Hannah's Prius had already made a U-turn on a shriek of rubber and was barreling away from the commotion. Teagarden threw the Explorer into gear and tore out after her. As the Prius approached the freeway, he saw her fist emerge from the driver's side window. She opened her hand, palm up, and held it there for a moment before tossing something away. Teagarden saw a flash of metal bounce on the pavement before coming to land in front of an oncoming car. Teagarden peered at the crushed device as he passed it in the road—the GPS tracker the FBI had planted on her car. Gladding's instructions had obviously been specific and thorough.

Towle had dropped the portable radio on the floor, and now the Brit heard the agent's voice bellowing, "Teagarden! Get your ass back here!"

He couldn't reach the radio to respond. With both hands gripping the wheel, it was all he could do to remember to stay on the right-hand side of the road. The FBI had vehicles aplenty. His best bet was to keep going and hope Hannah realized that at least one set of headlights behind her was friendly.

Liggett beamed. Nothing like a nice explosion to lift a guy's spirits. He'd been furious when Gladding had ordered him to create a diversion in the midst of a street crawling with feds and undercover cops. If he got his ass arrested here, who was going to set off the device at San Onofre? What about the mission then?

But then he'd found a car parked nearby in a lot by

the Swallows Inn, where surrounding cars afforded him some cover, and he'd rigged it to blow. Unfortunately, the car's driver had come out before Gladding gave the go-ahead, so by the time Liggett hit the detonator, the car had pulled out of the lot. He saw the blast in his rearview mirror. A couple of seconds later he watched the collateral damage as a store and a couple of other cars caught fire. A moment later one of those cars, too, blew up.

Liggett threw his head back and laughed. "Kaboom!"

But the sudden movement shot a spear of pain through his head. He winced and fingered the lump on the back of his skull. It hurt like a bitch. That damn faggot had been surprisingly quick, and the next thing Liggett knew, the bastard had brought a knife block down on him. By the time Liggett had stumbled out of the condo, the guy had been gone. When this was all over, he was going to track the bugger down and cut his throat.

As he took the freeway on-ramp, he saw emergency vehicles streaming in the opposite direction, heading toward the center of town, flashers spinning and sirens wailing. Any other time, Liggett would have loved to stick around and watch the party, but tonight he had bigger fish to fry.

Every time Gladding disconnected after one of his terse calls to the throwaway phone, Hannah was tempted to use it to dial 9-1-1 for help. But then what? Stand by while he took out the people she loved, one by one? Gladding had even anticipated the GPS tracker the feds had put on her car. Who would risk defying a guy that obsessive?

Traffic at the southern edge of Orange County was light at two in the morning. When she glanced in the rearview mirror, the only vehicle that seemed to have been there since the diner was a dark SUV, but it could be the feds, Gladding, Liggett, or nobody.

Gladding's latest call had directed her toward a service road on the southern edge of San Clemente State Beach park, about twenty minutes south of San Juan Capistrano. When she found the road, deep in the park's interior, it was dark and utterly deserted.

"There's a barrier across the access road, but the chain has been cut," Gladding said. "Push through and drive to the clearing where the road dead-ends."

When her headlights picked out the service road, she turned in and nudged the gate gently with her bumper. She unsnapped her holster, thankful that Gladding hadn't thought to order her to come unarmed. Perhaps it was an oversight, but Hannah doubted it. A more likely explanation was Gladding's confidence in the superior force of whatever awaited her at the end of that dark road. The Kevlar vest Towle had insisted she wear was bulkier than her own custom-fitted one and its bulk limited her maneuverability, but it was the most protection she was going to get out here.

She followed the twisting, narrow, tree-lined road to

the end. "When you get there," Gladding had said, "kill your lights, get out of the car and wait next to it."

Would he already be there—him or Liggett? Someone else? If she got there first, did she dare risk deviating from his instructions to give herself some small measure of advantage?

Behind her, the SUV sailed past the turnoff.

Teagarden saw her turn, but he deliberately overshot the service road, not wanting to risk being seen following her in. As dark as it was, he could see enough to suspect there wasn't much depth to the track she'd taken. A couple of hundred yards farther up the road, he pulled the Explorer deep into brush, then killed the lights and got out. He waited for a moment, listening and trying to acclimatize to the darkness of the nearly moonless night. Before setting out, he searched the vehicle for a weapon, but Towle had taken the shotgun, and he apparently didn't stock spares.

Pity, Teagarden thought.

There was no sound more mournful than the call and response of a coyote pack, Hannah thought. A desolate wail sounded from somewhere across the hills, and then a bleak response that built to a ghostly chorus. Standing in the darkness, the leather portfolio propped against her car, she felt as lonely as ever she had. Had Gladding planned for a night when the moon would be scarcely a sliver in the sky? There was something surreal about being in one of the most densely populated parts of North America and yet feeling lost in utter wilderness.

Minutes passed—five? Ten? Suspended in solitary darkness, she felt herself losing track of time. Suddenly a twig snapped and she started. An animal? Or—

The blow came out of nowhere, vicious. Senses reeling, she felt her knees buckle. As her body slammed into the ground, her consciousness slipped over to the dark side of the moon.

"Hannah?"

She flinched.

"Shhh…it's Will Teagarden. Wake up, lass. Come on, let me help you."

She was facedown in the gravel, hard steel digging into her ribs—her Beretta, still clutched beneath her. He pulled her to a sitting position, but she swayed, disoriented, head pounding, brain refusing to function. Finally she remembered where she was and she scrambled to her knees. Tried to, anyway. "The painting…"

"It's gone," he whispered. "They took it. There were two of them standing over you when I got here. They were arguing about whether to finish you or revive you. Gladding, I think, wanted to hold off. Before they could work it out, I heard another vehicle coming down the track. It stopped up a way and that's when they took the painting. I haven't heard anyone leave, so we need to be quiet."

"But what are they up to? We should follow…"

He steadied her weaving body. "I'll see if I can spot them," he murmured. "You wait here."

She pressed her gun into his hand. "Take it, Will. And be careful."

He touched her cheek and she thought she saw him smile. Then, dizzy and sore, she watched him disappear back down the track. She grabbed the car and pulled herself to her feet, waiting for a moment until the world stopped careening around her. Then, step by agonizing step, she started after Teagarden.

Teagarden had never understood the American love affair with guns, but it didn't mean he didn't know how to handle them. He was, in fact, a splendid shot.

He'd heard nothing much since Hannah's attackers had walked away from her. It could be that he had missed hearing them leave. If they were gone, he would retrieve the FBI vehicle and bring it back for Hannah. He suspected she was concussed, at the very least, and the sooner he got her out of this bloody place and to a hospital, the better.

He backtracked the way he'd come in, keeping well to the edge of the dirt road. He could smell the ocean, and though he couldn't hear surf, he knew they were very close to water. He was almost at the downed chain barrier again when he spotted the glow of lights up a side track he'd missed seeing on his way in. He ducked into a grove of fragrant eucalyptus trees and followed the lights toward another small clearing, where three vehicles were visible—two cars and a white panel van. The back doors of the van were open, casting a bright rectangle onto the gravel roadway, silhouetting two men. Blinded by the lights, they would be unlikely to spot him in the darkness, he calculated.

Teagarden was a mite vain about his own night vision. For a man his age, it was remarkably good. His hearing, however, was another matter. Although he could make out the murmur of conversation, he was unable to understand the gist of it. He checked to see that the Beretta's safety was off, then edged forward, staying well under the dappled cover of the trees. Two men stood in the light spilling from the open van, the tattered portfolio propped against one of the bumpers. Inside the van, a mounded mass was staked down under canvas and secured with bungee cords.

From where Teagarden came to a stop, the light was angled enough to finally make out the faces of the men. One was Gladding. The other, dark haired and dark complexioned, was definitely not Liggett. Teagarden scanned the perimeter. So where was that young scoundrel? It was he, Teagarden was fairly certain, who had attacked Hannah. It made sense that he was still in the vicinity. Gladding would not have come out here alone—and neither, come right down to it, would the other man have been likely to.

The men's conversation was pitched low, muffled by wind in the branches, by the chirping of crickets and frogs, and by the occasional coyote howl. It should have made for good auditory cover for his own movements, but night sounds were eerie and unpredictable. Tempted as he was to crouch low to reduce his mass, he daren't risk his creaky knees, Teagarden thought. In any event, there were rattlesnakes in this part of the country. He could only hope they were napping or hibernating.

Suddenly the conversation by the van rose to the pitch of argument. He caught only snatches of phrases, but the words *double-cross* and *villa* came through loud and clear. Bloody hell, Teagarden thought—a falling-out of rogues. He predicted there was about to be big trouble here, and he and Hannah had the very bad luck to be caught in the middle of it.

He could only guess that the reason Gladding and Liggett hadn't finished her off as soon as they had the painting was that the other party to this transaction had chosen that precise moment to arrive. Should all hell break loose and they emerge triumphant, however, they would no doubt circle back and finish what they had started.

Which still begged the question, where was Liggett? Had he already gone back for Hannah?

Teagarden was just turning to go back for her when a muffled shot sounded—more flash than crash—and the man with Gladding slumped to the ground. Then feet were running in every direction and Teagarden heard the eerie, muted pops of silenced weapons. Those reports hardly seemed decent, given their deadly effect.

It lasted ten, fifteen seconds, no more, and when it was over, the slight form of Kyle Liggett emerged from the trees. He walked toward the van, stopping occasionally to kick the lifeless forms of the other men who'd materialized in the clearing when the shouting started.

"Is that the bomb?" Liggett asked.

Gladding nodded and cocked a thumb at the tarp, utterly indifferent to the dead man lying at his feet.

Liggett pulled the canvas aside and peered at the mass beneath, his fingers lightly surveying the components. "Looks good. Detonator, timer. Better than I'd even hoped."

"It *should* be good, for the price," Gladding muttered.

The portfolio with the painting was still propped against the van's bumper. This, Teagarden thought, was a debt the man had never intended to pay.

As she made her slow progress up the track, Hannah forced herself to tread lightly, her head reverberating painfully with each agonized step. She still had Gladding's throwaway cell phone. She'd tried to see if she could make a quiet 9-1-1 call, but the icon on the screen told the tale, the "no service" signal flickering uncertainly.

She ducked instinctively when she heard the first *whap* echo through the trees. Almost before her brain could register the meaning of a sound that was all too familiar to her, it came again, and then was repeated over and over—the quiet staccato of an efficient massacre. Her hand reached to steady herself on the trunk of a eucalyptus, her mind willing the pounding of her head and heart to stop, certain that the whole park had to be hearing the din she was.

Suddenly, as abruptly as the fusillade had started, it stopped. In its place came male voices, a few short sentences. There was silence for a moment, only the wind in the trees, before a single, deep, outraged shout. Another *whap!* sounded, and then two more shots.

*Tap, tap.* An execution.

She started to run, knowing Will Teagarden was up ahead somewhere, praying he was well hidden and that none of this had anything to do with him. No such luck. There came a distinctive bang, one she'd heard many times before, both on the firing range and out in the field. It was the sound of her own Beretta.

He got off one shot, and only one.

It was answered by two retorts, fast and loud from a weapon without noise suppression. Clearly, someone had changed guns, and the time for stealth had passed. Her heart sank.

A few seconds later she heard one final shot, and she felt the sickening realization that it hadn't come from her gun.

William Teagarden, former Detective Superintendent, Scotland Yard, had gone down.

When she got to the clearing, she spotted Kyle Liggett. He was silhouetted in the light of an open van as he wrestled with bungee cords to tie down a tarp, grappling the hooks into rings in the floor. Whatever was underneath there was bulky, about the size of an ottoman.

Hannah crouched low in the shadows, still as the death all around her, while he finished the tie-down. He stepped over a body to retrieve the battered leather art portfolio she'd carried into the park. Another body lay faceup a short way away, this one larger, the belly mounded, the interior lights catching silver-white hair. Moises Gladding.

Liggett slammed the rear doors of the panel van and walked around to the driver's side, where he put the painting inside and climbed in behind it. She heard him curse. Climbing back out, he moved from body to body on the ground, rifling pockets until he found the keys.

When it finally roared to life and the back-up lights came on, Hannah shrank deeper, praying he wouldn't spot her in the rearview mirror. The tires spun on gravel as he careened back in a tight circle, one of the wheels bumping over a man's leg. As the headlights panned over the clearing, Hannah saw the rumpled tweed coat of Liggett's last victim and tears sprang to her eyes. Then Liggett shifted gears and the van roared back toward the main road.

Eyes readjusting to the dark, she got to her feet and hurried over to Teagarden. She crouched next to him and reached out to his still form, feeling for a pulse, knowing she wouldn't find one.

"Oh, Will—I'm so sorry."

Sorry he was gone. Sorry to be patting down his pockets for the cell phone she hoped he was carrying. Sorry he'd ever followed her out here.

She found a cell phone as well as the Beretta that had fallen from his hand. After one last, regretful squeeze of his arm, she got to her feet and ran to check the other car in the clearing, a big white Toyota Highlander. The keys were in the ignition. She jumped in and fired it up, heading back toward the main road and turning in the direction she'd seen the taillights of the panel van disappear.

As she drove, she dialed 9-1-1 and called in the scene on the service access road. "You need to let Special Agent Joe Towle of the FBI's Los Angeles field office know about this, too," she added.

"Officers are on their way," the dispatcher said. "I want you to stay—"

"Call Towle. He'll bring the cops up to speed."

"Ma'am, you need to remain—"

But Hannah had already disconnected. Then she dialed another number from memory.

Russo bellowed as soon as he heard her voice. "The GPS on your bloody car isn't working!"

"I know. I chucked it. Were you there at the diner? I spotted Lindsay."

"Yeah, but we got caught up in that damn diversion. Why did you throw the GPS away?"

"Did they find the instructions Gladding left me?"

"Yes."

"Well, then you know why. He knew there'd be a bug on the car. I was worried he'd have eyes on me the whole time. The instructions were specific."

"Teagarden took off after you in a Bureau SUV."

She was silent for a moment. "He's dead, John. Liggett killed him." She told him about the ambush in the park.

"Liggett killed Gladding, too?"

"I think so. Or one of the other guys, I'm not sure. There was a falling-out, by the look of things. Now Liggett's on the move and he's in a hurry. I'm trying to catch up to him and figure out where he's going."

"No! Dammit, Hannah, just pull over and let us take it from here. We'll find Liggett. Tell me what he's driving."

"You don't get it, Russo. He's got a bomb. You know what they said about the guy—he likes to blow things up. Well, he sure as hell looks like a man on a mission now. He didn't even bother to go back and finish me off, on the off chance some campers or something heard that massacre back there and called it in. He was hurrying to make tracks when I last saw him. To me, that says he's determined to see this thing through."

"Okay, try to see if you can spot him," Russo agreed reluctantly, "but stay well back and keep the damn phone on. I'm going to call it in to Towle and then I'll get right back to you."

"He's in a white panel van. Towle will probably want to lay in roadblocks north and south. And by the way, I'm in a white Toyota Highlander at the moment. The keys to my car disappeared, so I had to commandeer this boat. Tell Towle what I'm in so his guys don't decide to get trigger-happy."

"Roger," Russo said.

Hannah frowned. "John? He's gonna go south."

"What?"

"Liggett. Think about it. What's down here that would make a good target for a nut job like that?"

Russo hesitated only a split second—it was that obvious. "The San Onofre nuclear power plant."

"Bingo."

"Okay, let me call it in to Towle. I'm on the 5 South now, so I'm not too far from your position. And Hannah? Try to spot him, but do not put yourself in harm's way. Got it?"

"Yes, boss."

"You got anybody on base with experience disarming bombs?" Agent Towle shouted over the noise of the rotors. He and Ito had been picked up by an FBI chopper.

"We're the United States Marine Corps, sir," the major from Camp Pendleton said dryly. "We do it all. What kind of bomb you got?"

"Not sure. Conventional? Nuke? Dirty, maybe?"

"How soon you want the team, and where?"

"In your backyard and *now*. We think the target might be San Onofre, so one way or another, it could go hot fast."

"Roger that. *Semper fi.*"

"*Semper fi.*"

As Towle signed off, Ito, sitting behind the chopper pilot, tapped his boss on the shoulder. "You're an ex-Marine?"

"*Former* Marine," Towle corrected, "never ex. How much longer?" he asked the pilot.

"Not long. You know where you want to set down?"

"Stand by."

By the time Hannah caught up to the white van, it was back on the freeway and almost at the San Diego County line. Russo had called her back after speaking to Towle.

"He's a couple of car lengths ahead of me," she said.

"I'm about five miles back. Stay on him. Towle's on his way in a chopper and he's got a crisis response team mobilizing out of Camp Pendleton."

"Good."

The nuclear plant was cheek by jowl with the Marine base. At this point, Hannah thought, she'd take her breaks where she got them.

"Hold it…" she said, and then, "he's exiting the freeway. Picking up the old coast highway."

"Okay, so that pretty much clinches it. Try to keep him in sight as long as there's other traffic, but if it comes down to just you and him, back off. I'll call it in to Towle now and get right back to you."

But Liggett was moving like a bat out of hell now. What she hadn't told Russo was that there'd been next to no traffic from almost the moment they'd turned onto the back road, so Hannah had zero hope she hadn't been made.

A couple of minutes later the van's red taillights disappeared.

When Russo called back, she tried to describe exactly where they'd been when Liggett had killed his lights. "He turned up a sand track about a quarter mile later. I wouldn't have known if I hadn't seen his brake lights flash. He obviously knows exactly where he's going."

As Hannah had followed Liggett around the turn, she'd wrestled out of her jacket and tossed it out the window. "I left you a bread crumb, Hansel," she told Russo now, describing what she'd done. "I love that jacket. Pick it up when you see it, okay?"

"Forget it. I'll buy you a new one."

"Big spender. I've gotta hang up now, John. I need both hands to drive."

"Hannah—"

Two could play this game, she thought, killing the Highlander's headlights. She took the bumpy trail at a snail's pace to avoid hitting her brakes and giving him a red glow to more easily spot her in the rearview mirror as he moved toward the power plant. Distances were tough to judge in the dark, but the white panel van picked up and reflected what little light there was, so she spotted him periodically a few hundred yards up ahead. She rolled down the windows to listen for his engine, but all she heard was the Highlander. Another argument for driving a hybrid.

Over the next half mile, the road turned more and more hilly. She had backed off the accelerator, afraid the heavy SUV was getting too close to the van, but as a long hill rose ahead of her, her speed dropped so precipitously that she feared bogging down in the sand. She gunned it a little going up the incline, but just as she topped the crest, a spectral gleam appeared in front of her.

"Dammit!"

She slammed on the breaks—too late. The Highlander plowed into the van, the airbag exploding in her face, knocking the wind out of her and pounding her aching head into the headrest.

It took a few seconds before she could breathe. Scrabbling for the seat belt, she hit the release just as her car door flew open. Hands grabbed her and yanked her out. Liggett slammed her against the side of the Highlander, his rage all too visible in the glow of the SUV's interior lights.

He grabbed her once more, by the T-shirt this time, and threw her down in the dirt. He was strong and she was hurt and disoriented—but not helpless, she told herself. She came up in a fast crouch, watching his eyes and the blade that had somehow materialized in his hand.

"You're that goddamn Nicks woman."

"And you're Kyle Liggett."

"I knew I should have killed you back at the service road."

"Why didn't you?"

"Because the other guys showed up, and Gladding wanted to deal with them first."

"Well, I guess you've dealt with them all now, haven't you?"

"Damn straight."

He came in fast and low, but Hannah feinted to his off-hand, dodging the knife. As she spun, the side of her fist came down at the base of his neck.

His grin was creepy. "Like it rough, huh, babe?" He followed as she circled away from the knife.

"So you killed Gladding and took the painting, too," she said.

He nodded. "My retirement."

"Ha! You wish." Her laugh obviously startled him and she took advantage of the opportunity to try to land a kick to his groin.

At the last second he grabbed her ankle and pushed her backward, but she went with it, rolling. He didn't let go in time, giving her the time she needed to latch on to his hair and leverage her feet against his gut so that she could fling him over her head. The knife flew from his hand and she heard it clatter against one of the vehicles.

She sprang to her feet, but he recovered fast. His eyes were darting, trying to locate the knife, when the sky erupted with a rumble. Off in the distance behind him, she saw a chopper approach, searchlight panning the ground.

She was reaching for her gun at the small of her back when the heel of Liggett's hand smashed into her nose. She felt the sickening crack of bone and cartilage, and she fell back, her face hot and wet, her balance momentarily lost. She went down on one knee, but not before she had the Beretta out of her holster.

Liggett, however, had gone back to the van and opened the driver's side door.

"Liggett," she yelled. "It's over."

"No! You can't stop this."

Her hand was shaking and her first shot only took out the mirror of his closing door. The van roared to life and he gunned the motor, but the van's bumpers were locked with the SUV's. He gunned it again, but the two vehicles only rocked a little, then rolled back as his spinning tires kicked up a dust storm.

Hannah staggered to her feet. Liggett climbed out of the van and walked toward her, cursing, a gun in his hand now. When he fired at her, nearly point-blank, the blow to her sternum knocked her back, but not before she fired again, and then once more. This time he went down, but so did she, her head spinning, choking on her own blood.

She was flat on her back, the roar of the chopper deafening now, its searchlight blinding and threatening to set the dry grass afire. Maybe this was hell. The earth certainly seemed to be opening up, pulling her down.

Her final thought was that if she wasn't already dead and Liggett came after her again, it was over. She had nothing left.

# *Thirty-Two*

*Saddleback Memorial Medical Center*
*San Clemente, California*

The pain in her side was the first thing Hannah noticed when she came to—in a hospital, she realized, opening her eyes to a yellow striped curtain pulled around the gurney on which she lay, head elevated. Wincing, she reached up to touch her ribs under the thin cotton of a short gown. Her fingers gingerly probed the lump she felt there. It hurt like the dickens, but it didn't seem as if any bones were broken. She splayed her hand across the swelling, offering up fervent mental thanks to the inventor of the Kevlar-lined bulletproof vest. That had to be a whopper of a bruise, but black and blue beat dead, which is what she would have been had Kyle Liggett's point-blank shot had the intended effect.

A light snore sounded nearby and she looked over

to find Russo dozing in a chair. His cheeks and chin shadowed by stubble, he looked as exhausted as she felt.

Her head ached something wicked and her nose was stuffed up like the worst cold ever. The skin on her face also felt stretched and taut over cheekbones that seemed to have grown larger overnight. She must look god-awful. When she reached up with her other hand to explore her face, something pinched her skin.

Russo's hand shot out. "Careful," he said, laying her hand back on the mattress. "You're hooked up to an IV line."

"Hey there, Sleeping Beauty."

"Sorry, I guess I nodded off. Have you been awake long?"

"Not long. Where are we?"

He got to his feet, stretched wearily, then moved in close and brushed a lock of hair off her forehead. "San Clemente. You've been here about four hours. It was the closest E.R."

"Oh, right, I remember—sort of." There'd been sirens and flashing lights. Running feet and loud voices. "You were there in the ambulance."

He nodded. "They tried to keep me out, but I pulled rank, told them you were in my custody. You're still in the E.R., but they're moving you up to a room pretty soon."

She glanced around, but although she could hear voices beyond the curtain, they were alone for the moment. "So everyone here thinks I'm a criminal?"

"Nah, I fessed up. Told them you're actually the hero of the day. How do you feel?"

"Like I was hit by a Mack truck. My head hurts like a son of a gun."

"You've got a nasty concussion, among other things."

"Other things?"

Russo hunted around until he found a stainless steel spit pan, then held it so she could see her reflection. Hannah grimaced. Her nose was swollen to twice its size, the cotton-packed nostrils explaining the stuffed-up feeling. Her face was puffy, and both eyes were ringed with what she knew would turn into whopping shiners.

"I'm going to start calling you 'Rocky Raccoon,'" Russo said.

It all came back to her now—the to-the-death battle with Liggett in the sandy field next to the San Onofre nuclear station. Seeing stars when his fist smashed into her nose. The pain when his bullet slammed into her rib cage.

"What about Kyle Liggett?" she asked.

"Dead."

"Did I shoot him? I remember fighting with him, but I can't remember if I got off a shot or not."

Russo nodded. "I think you did—you, the FBI agents in the helicopter, the Marines who landed on the beach. Me, too, for that matter. We all showed up just as you went down, and at that point all hell broke loose. I guess we won't know until the autopsy how many bullets he finally took."

"What about the bomb he was transporting?"

"Defused. The Camp Pendleton disposal team said it was a highly explosive conventional weapon heavily packed with radioactive materials. The feds are saying the nuclear power plant was never in any real danger—"

"Well, they would say that, wouldn't they?"

He nodded. "Yeah, but the onshore winds would have carried fallout from the bomb nevertheless. Maybe not enough to pose a serious risk, but who knows? There are a couple of million homes in the dispersion zone and they would have had to order at least a temporary evacuation while they assessed the danger. And after that, no matter how many reassurances they got, how many people would want to go back and worry about whether they or their kids were going to get cancer five or ten years down the road?"

"That was probably the point," Hannah said. "To create panic and uncertainty. It's the purest kind of psychological terrorism. Do we know—"

Just then the yellow curtain swung open and her mother and sister burst in. One look at Hannah and her mother burst into tears.

"Ma! It's okay," Hannah said. "Don't cry. I'm all right." She winced as her mother threw herself on her, weeping, but she gritted her teeth rather than cry out.

Nora came around to the other side of the gurney and took her hand. "Oh, Hannah, you look awful." Then she glanced over at Russo. "What did the doctors say?"

He repeated what he'd told Hannah about the concussion, then turned back to the stretcher. "I phoned your sister to let her know you were here."

"I called Cal's house to tell them, too," Nora said. "I hope you don't mind, Hannah, but it's all over the morning news. Your name hasn't been mentioned so far, but it's bound to come out and I didn't want Gabe to be frightened."

"No, that was a good idea," Hannah said, dreading what would happen if this misadventure of hers, too, became a schoolyard story. It would be more grist for the mill of Cal's complaints. "So, this is my sister, Nora," she told Russo, "and my mom, Ida Demetrious."

"I see the resemblance, all around," he said, his gaze traveling from sister to sister to mother.

"I'm surprised you're still here, Detective," Nora said. "Surely your questions can wait until Hannah's feeling better."

Russo opened his mouth to explain, but Hannah's mother beat him to the punch. "I don't think the detective is here on official business," she said, looking just a tad mischievous.

Hannah raised an eyebrow—or tried to, but even that hurt. Not much got past Ida Demetrious, she thought, bemused. And naturally, since her mother knew her baby wasn't a terrorist, she would assume it would be obvious to everyone else, including this dogged detective.

Nora looked confused for a moment, but finally the penny dropped. "Oh! Really?"

Inwardly Hannah groaned. *Oh, lord. And so it begins.* "John's a friend." Glancing at him, she added, "A good friend." Might as well head them off at the pass.

The arrival of a nurse and an orderly forestalled any more questions, subtle or otherwise. The nurse shooed the visitors off, suggesting they go to the cafeteria for coffee. "It's going to take a while. The E.R. resident wants to look her over again and then we're taking her for X-rays. After that, we'll be moving her upstairs to her room. She's going to be on Three West. You can meet her there. For now, though, you need to scoot. You, too, Detective," she added firmly. Clearly the *she's-my-prisoner* line wasn't going to cut it anymore.

It took over an hour before Hannah was finally settled in a sunny room on the third floor, by which time her roster of visitors had grown to include her neighbors. Everyone seemed to have introduced themselves, and Russo had brought them all up to speed on how Hannah was and how she'd landed in the hospital. At that point it was just a matter of filling in the blanks. Apparently the near-disaster at the San Onofre nuclear power station was the lead news story on every TV and radio station.

"Travis pulled out all the stops to find out where they'd taken you," Ruben said. "Of course, there is *nothing* that Mr. Information can't uncover. I went over to your place to get some things I thought you might need. Found some really cute Garfield jammies."

Hannah groaned. "Tell me you didn't bring those."

"No, I wouldn't be that cruel. I'm sure the press is going to be all over you and we want to be sure you're ready for your close-up. But that face…" Ruben crossed his arms and rested his chin on his hand, looking dismayed. "Honey, there is not enough makeup in the world to camouflage that."

Just then, from down the hall came the squeak of rubber on tile announcing the arrival of Gabe, who burst around the door. His very pregnant stepmother showed up a few weary steps behind. Hannah waited, dreading the appearance of her ex as well, but Christie, it seemed, had brought Gabe down alone.

Gabe was stopped in his tracks by the sight of his mother. "Mom? Holy cow, are you okay?"

"I'm fine, sweetie. It looks worse than it is. Come on up here and give your old mom a smooch."

"But carefully, Gabriel," Nana said. "Mama's got a sore side and a bad bump on the head."

"I will." He climbed very gently onto the bed.

Hannah hugged him, then shifted over so he could nestle in under the crook of her arm. She kissed the top of his head. "See? Just bruises, that's all."

"Christie says you're a hero. You stopped a terrorist who wanted to bomb California."

"Not just me. Lots of people stopped him, including Detective Russo here and the FBI and the U.S. Marine Corps. Even a nice policeman from England," Hannah added, feeling a twinge at the memory of poor old Will Teagarden.

"Wait till I tell the guys at school."

"Oh, maybe that's not such a good idea, honey."

"Gabriel's proud of his mom," Christie said. "And so he should be."

Hannah looked up, surprised.

Russo pulled up a chair for Cal's wife. Christie settled in gratefully, then turned to Hannah. "I hope you don't mind me barging in, but Gabe was anxious to see you."

"No, I'm really glad you came."

"Hannah, Cal told me about the meeting with Gabe's assistant headmaster. I agree with her. It's high time things changed, and if I have anything to say about it, they will. You have my word."

"Thanks, Christie. I appreciate it." Hannah hugged Gabe again. "We're all going to do better, aren't we?"

He nodded, then peered down at something on the floor next to the bed. "What's in the box?"

"Box?"

"Oh, I forgot." Travis lifted onto the end of the bed a large, flat cardboard box covered with FedEx stickers. "This came for you yesterday. Ruben signed for it. We weren't sure if it was important, so we brought it along."

"Who's it from?"

Nora peered over Travis's shoulder to look at the return address. "Oh, Hannah," she breathed, "it's from Rebecca's gallery."

Hannah's heart sank. "I guess you'd better open it."

Travis handed it to Nora and Russo pulled out a penknife to help her slit the packing tape. As they tipped the box sideways, an envelope slipped out, then a bubble-wrapped painting in a frame. Russo cut the tape around the bubble wrap and they peeled it off.

"Oh, my gosh," Hannah said when he held up the painting for her to see. It was the Southern California beach scene with the little boy. "He reminded me of you," she told Gabe. Then she looked up at Russo. "It's the piece I thought was missing after the attack at the gallery. I'd told Rebecca I liked it and she offered to throw it in along with my fee for couriering Koon's painting down to Puerto Vallarta."

"Open the note, dear," her mother said.

When Hannah ripped open the envelope, a check made out to her fell out first—her fee for carrying the painting—and then a handwritten note on a pretty card.

*Dear Hannah,*
*I'm so grateful to you for taking this job. Who knows? Maybe this will be the beginning of a whole new career for me as an art buyer. Don't fight me on this gift. I know you loved the painting. It's small thanks in light of your help.*
*Enjoy!*
*Rebecca*

With a lump in her throat, Hannah handed the note to her sister. As Nora read it, tears spilled down her cheeks, and she looked at Russo. "Why?" she asked. "Why was she killed?"

"Probably for the same reason August Koon was," he said wearily. "According to what the feds have been able to piece together about Liggett's and Gladding's final days, this operation had all the hallmarks of a grand final gesture—particularly on Gladding's part. They found meds among his personal effects suggesting he had advanced cancer—probably terminal, from the amount of morphine he was on. He felt aggrieved that Washington had turned its back on him after years of using his contacts, and he wanted his career to go out with a bang—literally. Liggett, meantime, was just a sociopath with a messianic complex. In the end, he even killed Gladding for not giving him enough respect. Before that, though, neither wanted to risk leaving loose ends that could trip them up before they were finished what they'd set out to do."

"And the painting I carried?" Hannah asked. "Was it the stolen van Gogh?"

Russo nodded. "The restoration experts have taken a preliminary look and it seems Teagarden called it exactly right."

"Why did he follow me last night?" Hannah asked, frustrated and heartbroken. "There was no need for him to get mixed up in any of this once he'd recovered the painting. He could have returned it to Yale University and gone back to doing what he did best. He was no match for that monster Liggett. Why didn't he just leave well enough alone?"

"I think you know why," Russo said quietly. "He'd

grown very fond of you, Hannah, and he was an old-school kind of gentleman. Not the kind to let a girl walk into trouble alone."

Hannah took Russo's hand in hers. "Old-school gentlemen—a lot of that going around, it seems. Best back-up I could have asked for."

There were murmurs of agreement all around.

# #1 *NEW YORK TIMES*
## BESTSELLING AUTHOR
# DEBBIE MACOMBER

What do you want most in the world?

Anne Marie Roche wants to find happiness again. At 38,
she's childless, a recent widow and alone. On Valentine's
Day, Anne Marie and several other widows get together to
celebrate…what? Hope, possibility, the future. They each
begin a list of twenty wishes.

Anne Marie's list includes learning to knit, doing good for
someone else and falling in love again. She begins to act on
her wishes, and when she volunteers at a school, little Ellen
enters her life. It's a relationship that becomes far more
important than she ever imagined, one in which they both
learn that wishes can come true.

# Twenty Wishes

"These involving stories…continue the Blossom Street
themes of friendship and personal growth that readers
find so moving."—*Booklist* on *Back on Blossom Street*

*Available the first week of May 2008 wherever books are sold!*

**MIRA®**

NEW YORK TIMES BESTSELLING AUTHOR

# KAT MARTIN

Neither sister can explain her "lost day." Julie worries that
Laura's hypochondria is spreading to her, given the stress
she's been under since the Donovan Real Estate takeover.

Patrick Donovan would be a catch if not for his playboy
lifestyle. But when a cocaine-fueled heart attack nearly
kills him, Patrick makes an astonishing recovery. Julie
barely recognizes Patrick as the same man she once
struggled to resist. Maybe it's her strange experience at
the beach that has her feeling off-kilter....

As Julie's feelings for Patrick intensify, her sister's health
declines. Now she's about to discover what the day on the
beach really meant....

# SEASON OF STRANGERS

"An edgy and intense example of romantic suspense with
plenty of twists and turns."
—*Paranormal Romance Writers* on *The Summit*

*Available the first week of June 2008
wherever books are sold!*

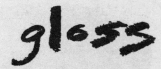

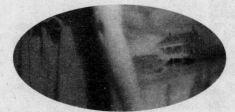